CUSTOMER TRAGO

MIGNON WARNER

A CIP catalogue record for this title
is available from the British Library.

ISBN 978-0-9547484-4-9

FOREWORD

The Old Wainhouse Inn, which dates back to the sixteenth century, stands to this day on the corner of the crossroads mentioned in this novel. An earlier 'wynehouse' stood a short distance farther along the Atlantic Highway (now known generally as the A39) and it is this inn which I have recreated from my imagination and then transported to the corner of the crossroads. The smithy which did, in fact, stand on the opposite corner of these crossroads was only recently converted into living accommodation, while the Holy Well of St James referred to in my novel still remains along the pilgrims' route from Wales through the ancient highways of the North Cornwall coast to Compostela in Spain.

The Author

Visit my website at
https://www.mignonwarner.com/

CUSTOMER TRAGO

PROLOGUE

The assassin's eyes were blacker than a moonless Cornish night, primed with hatred and ready for the kill. His right knee pressed down hard on the dying man's chest, expelling what little life-supporting air remained in his lungs. The curved blade of his engraved, silver-handled dagger hovered briefly several inches above the dying man's fluttering eyelids and was then passed before them in a slow sweep. It was a curious, somehow purposeful action which an onlooker, had there been one close at hand, might well have read as a sadistic desire on the assassin's part to ensure that the dying man was given an opportunity to admire the splendid instrument that no one could have been in any doubt was intended to be used to slice open his throat from ear to ear and finish him off.

The dying man's right arm came up instinctively, his hand clutching defensively but feebly at the assassin's leather jerkin and fine linen undershirt, drawing on them to expose a peculiar arrangement of motley scars ringing his neck. Scars not to be proud of – like those, for instance, won honourably in hard fought battle. These were unmistakable scars; scars left by the remorseless tightening of a hangman's rope.

This then had to be the final ignominy for any man of high birth, to die, body deep in clinging, foul-smelling mud at the hands of a man no better than a common villain. The dying man would have thanked God it was their secret, and that this shame would remain so to be taken by him to his grave, had it not been for the fact that the last moments of his life were fast ebbing from his savagely wounded body, plunging him even more deeply into a blissful, uncaring nothingness.

In the same instant that a warning shout went up, the hand on the assassin's jerkin was swept aside contemptuously.

There was a rush of hoofbeats. The savage roar of men's voices. The dying man was sucked even deeper into the stinking mud. Merciful silence.

It was over.

Chapter One

They set upon him on Launceston land, on hallowed ground, within sight of the priory manor itself.   A small band of robbers, murderous vagabonds, or that treacherous monk, Sir William Gennys and his wretched supporters; the dying man knew not which. It mattered little, if at all now, which of those companies of villains represented the greater evil to him. Suffice it to say that given the choice, he would have as soon diced with the Devil any day!

The letter to the new prior's clerk of his coming was his undoing; that accursed affliction that drove him to attend with such immaculate devotion to every pettifogging little detail. His old tutor, Brother Emanuel, had solemnly avowed that it would be the making of him: in truth, it was the finishing of him. Should there be any doubt about this, he would humbly offer up in his own solemn defence, the mortal sword wound in his left side.

He lay solidly wedged in one of the deep, muddied ruts made by the heavy wheels of the oxen-drawn hay carts from the rectory farm.   The last, oozing droplets of his precious life's blood steadfastly mingled with the ice-cold streamlet that trickled remorselessly onto him from the rain-sodden, rolling green meadow bordering the narrow track.

What had become of his horse, he knew not. His vile murderers had left him for dead, and this being no night for any living man or beast to be abroad, the sensible animal had prudently thrown in its lot with them, abandoning him to endure, alone and friendless, this pitiful end.

Emanuel had told him – this was when he was but a mere boy – that to die was no easy thing; it took quite a bit of effort, far more than would be required of his young pupil to come to grips with the Latin grammar that had provoked his heartfelt plea for a merciful early death.

So there was nothing else for it, a bit of effort was called for to hurry things along; some form of physical exertion to encourage a fast weakening heart to pump, a little more purposefully, the last drop of blood from this poor, mud-caked flesh of his.

His murderers had robbed him of his purse, his sword, dagger and signets, but had left him clothed and shod. He had no idea why this should be so, why those evil men should trouble themselves to leave his poor corpse decently clad. The answer, he decided, had to lie within the four walls of the priory itself where surely there must remain one or two saintly souls – maybe as many as three, if Emanuel still lived – any one of whom might have come upon these callous, black-hearted villains and interrupted them at their murderous business.

His thoughts drifted back to Gennys and his supporters. Would they risk such an attack so near to the priory? They might, but surely not while Emanuel lived. Emanuel had powerful friends, both in the Church and at Court, and Launceston Priory had troubles enough without the Vicar-General, Thomas Cromwell himself, being obliged to send someone down to investigate the possibility of further mischief by its unruly brethren.

The dying man let out a small sigh. For Emanuel's sake, he must not die here on Launceston Priory-land.

Cautiously, he tried to move his stiffening body in the thick, cloying mud that wrapped itself about him like a shroud and then, with the mud sucking and squelching beneath him, he began to ease himself carefully onto his right side. Water from the streamlet trickled down his forehead and into his eyes and nostrils, ridding them of some of the mud caking them.

Spitting mud from his mouth, he lay perfectly still for almost a full two minutes while he caught his breath and made ready to steel himself against the searing flash of pain he knew awaited him once he attempted to get up onto his feet.

'Prove it to me, Emanuel,' he hissed through gritted teeth. 'Prove it to this poor, miserable sinner that death comes not for the asking; that I shall not die of my death wound until this worthless body of mine falls in its final death throes on unhallowed ground.'

His murderers had pursued him north of the priory, past the parish Church of St Stephen on the brow of the hill, all the while with the savage north-easterly wind raging at his back. For once with him, if he continued northwards, away from the valley of the Upper Tamar and the priory and deeper into the heart of the Hundred of Stratton. He had never before travelled this far north of the priory. South-west once, many years ago, across the black, forbidding moor to the Augustinian priory at Bodmin where, again, Emanuel had friends and influence and, in equal measure, as he had often cautioned him, not a few enemies. More frequently, though, far west, riding on horseback – as ever, those deferential few yards behind Emanuel – to the rich and powerful monastery at St Michael's Mount, seat of the Cult of St Michael. East? Yes – again some years ago now – when he had travelled to Exeter with Emanuel and then, with the Bishop's blessing, had bade farewell to Emanuel and ridden on alone to Oxford.

The dying man swiftly brought down a shutter in his mind on that time of his life, Oxford and the studies he had abandoned there in the mid-summer madness of his twentieth year when he had played at Dick the Fool and taken complete leave of his senses, and England, to sue for the hand of the beautiful Anna-Lucrezia. A small cry of despair nevertheless escaped his lips as an image of her sweet face floated tantalizing across his line of vision and then, all too quickly, faded into a bleak, black emptiness.

He closed his eyes and murmured her name. *'Anna-Lucrezia.'*

They had met at the home of the Provost of Penryn where she and her father, the Venetian Ambassador, had lodged while their ship had been detained at Falmouth in foul weather, outward bound for Spain.

Brought sharply back into the present by the gnawing pain in his side, the dying man braced himself, momentarily squeezing his eyes tightly shut and then cautiously inching himself up and onto one elbow. He looked about him. He had no idea how long he had lain on the track. The mortal chill of his flesh, the merciless stiffening and aching of his bones, seemed to point to it having been some hours since his murderers had ridden off with their ill-gotten gains and left him in those last few moments at dusk when, in the blinking of an eyelid, day becomes black, pitiless night. A dirty night. As dirty a night as he would ever wish to recall from the sheltered, untroubled years of his childhood and early manhood spent at Launceston Priory under the tutelage of the even then – or so it had seemed to him at the time – creakingly ancient, former Bodmin civil lawyer, Emanuel.

His eyes misted over and for a fleeting instant he saw a vision of Emanuel hovering anxiously at his side in the white habit and black scapular of the Holy Order governed by the Rule of St Augustine. As a boy, there had been little doubt in the dying man's mind that the softly-spoken, wise old civil lawyer had entered his Order when it had been founded in the twelfth century nigh on three hundred years ago.

He thought he heard Emanuel softly calling his name, but it was only the wind whispering in the hedgerow.

He squeezed his eyes tightly shut and concentrated his mind. The further north he travelled – and with the luck that had thus far ridden with him back into the West Country – the wilder and dirtier the night would become. Northwards to that part of Cornwall of which Emanuel had written – as it happened, in Emanuel's last communication with him – following Emanuel's visit to the Norman Church of St James of Penalym at Jacobstow in the sparsely populated Hundred of Stratton. According to Emanuel, it was a rule of thumb that if it wasn't raining in that northernmost Hundred, then one could have every confidence that it soon would be. Moreover, so fierce was the wind there – whether it be from the north-east, or from the rugged west coast and the great ocean beyond – that the rains, when they came, would sweep horizontally across the lush, perennially green fields and meadows, and with even greater mathematical precision and relentless force and fury, between the forbiddingly high banks and black hedges bordering the sides of the muddy tracks and roadways.

Why had Emanuel travelled to such a wild, uncivilized place? To mediate on some dispute over Church land? It was going on all over Cornwall now. At Bodmin, Launceston, at all of the monastic houses liberally scattered about Church and Duchy land to the westernmost Hundred of Penwith. Since the Vicar-General's reforming injunctions, the holy priors and their near and distant relatives were having a fine old time of carving up Church land and making a gluttonous feast of it among themselves. Quarrels and disputes were the order of the day and enough to put any man off the idea of troubling himself to die elsewhere. Emanuel would surely think *this* dying man every kind of fool for making the effort.

This then would suffice; the final resting place of Customer Trago. Not for him the Tower of London where the Plantagenet Pretender to the Throne of England, Perkin Warbeck, to whom Customer believed himself to be related – if only distantly on the distaff side of Warbeck's family – had first been imprisoned by Henry Tudor and thence been removed to attend at his own execution on the hangman's scaffold.

Customer paused for a moment and cast his mind back, picturing himself as a small boy standing, as always, that respectful step back from Emanuel while watching and listening to, but never quite understanding, the whispered conversations and covert looks that some of the other monks would cast in their direction.

Had all of that meant nothing? Was it not hope he had seen in their eyes, hope that come the next Cornish rebellion – and come it would – another Plantagenet would rise up and lay claim to the Throne of England and this time lay the Tudors by the heels?

Emanuel had smiled at his solemn vow that until his dying day, he would never give up his belief that he was of Royal Plantagenet blood, and that he had been placed in the care of the good holy prior at Launceston by his forebears' supporters – wealthy, titled Cornish gentlemen – to protect him from Perkin Warbeck's enemies at the Court of Henry Tudor's successor.

Well, here it was, Customer Trago's dying day, and he scarce past his twenty-sixth summer!

So much for sucking up to the Scots and rallying the strong, brave Cornishmen – yeomen, tinners, men of the sea – and seeing Henry Tudor's son and heir off the Throne of England! So much for Customer Trago's having entered Oxford; for his pathetically sincere intentions of practising civil law at Bodmin; of following faithfully in Emanuel's footsteps!

So much for marrying his beloved Anna-Lucrezia and pursuing the courtier's life of rich and splendid idleness at the Courts of Europe's sovereigns!

So much for Emanuel's promises that on his, Emanuel's, deathbed he would reveal all, the identities of Customer Trago's financially generous benefactors and his true lineage.

This was Customer Trago's deathbed, and there was not a living soul in sight, man or beast, friend or foe. He was going to die alone, here in this body-mould of merciless, sucking, squelching Cornish marsh mud, never knowing the truth about himself.

If, as the prior's clerk had guardedly led him to believe, Emanuel was likewise on his deathbed *(a warmer, much dryer one than his own, Customer sincerely trusted)*, they might possibly meet up along the road to the Hereafter and he could prevail upon Emanuel there to confess to him his true origins.

In all honesty, though, what would be the point? Customer Trago was a dead man. It was too late, all over for him. He wasn't so sure, anyway, that he had ever aspired to sit on the Throne of England. Nor had he ever been all that keen on the idea of spending all of his time fighting the French and the Spanish. He simply wished to be recognized and accepted at Court as a member of the Plantagenet dynasty – or, if Henry insisted, as a minor European Royal. Perhaps dished out a nice little manor house and farm to keep him in the manner to which he had grown accustomed. That would have done handsomely!

As much as it was a mortal sin for any true, red-blooded Cornishman to think it let alone admit to it, the truth was that Customer Trago had no quarrel with Henry Tudor's successor, Henry VIII.

Long live the King!

Chapter Two

It was time for the truth from Customer Trago, now that he was, as near as didn't matter, a dead man. He couldn't raise himself out of this stinking marsh mud, let alone raise an army against the King. Maybe this was because he wasn't who he thought he was. That, in truth, he was nothing more than the illegitimate offspring of some wanton peasant girl, a serving wench at one of the manor houses owned by the prior: a poor, bastard boy-child the kind-hearted holy brothers had taken pity on.

No!

From the wrong side of the bed linen, without a doubt, but Customer Trago had that same cowardly streak running strong and pure in his blood that drove Perkin Warbeck to desert his loyal Cornish troops in the dead of night only hours before the brave Cornishmen's final and inevitably hopeless battle against Henry Tudor nigh on forty years ago outside the walls of the town of Exeter.

Well, there was at least one good thing about this pitiful state of affairs for Customer Trago regarding his perceived kinship with the Plantagenet Pretender to the Throne of England, who claimed to be Richard, Duke of York, one of the Princes of the Tower. Customer Trago had no loyal troops to desert, only one tired, infinitely kind and patient old Augustinian monk who, as God would bear witness, had done his best by him. No matter what the cost in pain and suffering and personal humiliation, he refused to desert Emanuel now by dying there on Launceston land and thereby bringing shame and trouble upon his head, principally in the form of the ruthlessly ambitious Gennys whom Emanuel had long suspected of harbouring hopes (false hopes, as it turned out) of election as prior of Launceston, the largest of the Cornish monastic houses.

Customer thought again about the Church of St James of Penalym, the mention Emanuel had made of his visit there.

The Vicar of St James...

Friend or foe?

In these troubled, highly dangerous times, God alone would

10

know the answer to that question, but the way Customer Trago's luck was running, thought Customer morosely, the latter, almost certainly. Nevertheless, he would make the Church of St James of Penalym his destination. Not that he would ever reach it, but one had to have a purpose, some definite goal to aim for in life, even if what was left of it could be counted in hours, possibly minutes. Furthermore, his plan must be clearly defined.

First he must get out of this stinking bog; next, well clear of Launceston Priory-land, the priory itself and Gennys and his black-bearded henchmen. *(The more Customer considered his present sorry plight, the more likely it seemed to him, rightly or wrongly, that it was the monk he knew to be Emanuel's sworn enemy, Gennys, and his treacherous lot whom he had to thank for it.)* Then he, Customer Trago of Royal Plantagenet blood, could pass from this life to the next. Regrettably, not with a clear conscience, but then one couldn't have everything.

It was a good three, maybe four days' walk from Launceston Priory to the Church of St James of Penalym. Longer, depending on the state of the oxen-tracks which, in close company with the capricious natural waterways, meandered through the hills and valleys, twisting first this way and then that, north-west to the coastal highway and then true north, up through the old town of Stratton along the ancient Roman street which had given the town its name.

Longer again for a dying man with less than a wine glassful of blood to sustain his strength!

Taking a deep breath, and with one determined thrust, Customer broke free of the equally determined grip of the mud, lurched wildly forward and then staggered drunkenly up and onto his feet.

His side burned, there was little else that could honestly be said of his death wound. Hardly any pain. But then death was almost upon him; would be for certain if he didn't distance himself as quickly as possible from these dangerous parts and Gennys and his wild bunch set upon him again, armed to the back teeth with swords and daggers, and finished off their job on him properly.

He wrapped his mud-soaked cloak around his shivering flesh.

Fever, of course. Delirium was waiting for him round the next bend in the track. And the bend after that–?

An inglorious death. Covered from the roots of the long, thick, jet-black hair of his head to the fashionably pointed toes of his best riding boots in sticky, stinking Launceston Priory-land mud which, from its odour, had little in common with sanctity and much with the beasts of the field. *(A blessing, perhaps, that no one, not even Emanuel, would recognize him by sight or sense of smell!)*

He paused for a moment and got his bearings, waited while the steadily rising north-easterly wind momentarily cleared the skies of their thick, black cloud, and then walked with a huge, ivory full moon, trudging northwards through the night, driven by the wind and then by stinging, icy rain; beneath his feet, always, the heavy, wearying, never-ending, thick, cloying, squelching mud.

At some point – he had no idea in which night or during what day – he lost consciousness and fell down in a dead faint. He awoke to a clear, bitterly cold, frosty morning and the throaty sighing of a toothless old woman leading a solemn funeral procession that had all but passed directly over his prostrate, half-buried body. The corpse of the old man on the crude wooden handcart being drawn behind her by two, strong young men was that of her husband.

Customer heard the old woman's cry – *'Kemeres tregereth war!'*; thought, for one feverish moment, that in his delirium, he had long overshot his mark and had walked countless miles farther northwards than he had intended and into Wales. Then his brain cleared of its fog and he realized that he was mistaken, the woman was not speaking to him in Welsh, but in the increasingly little-used Cornish tongue, two Celtic languages that are not dissimilar. He knew some Cornish and a little Welsh, was more or less able to answer her questions with a degree of intelligence. He was a traveller *(a holy pilgrim, he thought it best to describe himself)*, bound for the Church of St James of Penalym at Jacobstow in the Hundred of Stratton, and set upon by thieves and murderers who had left him for dead. It was a risk, of course, describing himself thus, as a holy pilgrim. Set forth in the Vicar-General Cromwell's reforming injunctions was the new dispensation that there was to be no gadding about on pilgrimages. Customer, however, considered it perfectly reasonable for him to expect that his short life expectancy would afford him more than a full measure of safety from the wrath of John Tregonwell, the Vicar-General's enforcer engaged in that particular suppression.

The woman appeared to understand Customer's attempts at her mother tongue, obviously saw that he was a dead man, and with the help of the two young men in her company, her sons, room was made on the cart and he was lifted up onto it alongside the corpse of her husband.

The funeral procession continued with due solemnity. Customer was giving consideration as to whether or not he should be thankful that he was not having to walk to his death when he slipped into unconsciousness again, waking many hours later (a whole twenty-four or more of them for all he knew) in total darkness, not with the hard wooden boards of the bier beneath his tired and bruised body, but neatly laid out on a bed of relatively dry bracken and black heather. Of the funeral procession there was not a trace.

Wind tore savagely at the stunted trees he could vaguely discern growing about him, chilling the bones in his aching face and making his eyes water and his nose run copiously.

He was lost. Somewhere on Bodmin Moor, as likely as not. If he had understood the kindly widow-woman correctly, that – moorland somewhere or other – had been the funeral procession's ultimate destination and her late husband's final resting place.

The pity of it was that she and her two brawny sons hadn't decided to inter Customer Trago alongside the corpse they had been transporting.

Perhaps they had; perhaps he had died sometime during the day and he was now resting along the road to Purgatory. There was no pain from his wound. *Well, maybe just a twinge, a rather unpleasant burning sensation if he dwelt upon it for too long!* And it had to be said: this, being dead, was an interesting experience for him. He hadn't thought much about it before, but was a little disappointed that he was to carry his mortal aches and pains with him all the way to the Gates of Heaven. And sorrows and remorse, his genuine regret that he had disappointed Emanuel so cruelly. Not that Emanuel had ever chastised him for his weaknesses; his sloth and vanity and fond attachment to the carefree, easy life. Quite the contrary. To his confession that he had abandoned his studies at Oxford for the inevitably futile love of a feckless woman, Emanuel had gently replied that it was God's Will. That he, Customer Trago, was merely fulfilling his destiny as was God's Purpose for him, and that Customer should never forget that whatever happened to him in this earthly life, God never made mistakes.

So typical of Emanuel to make excuses for him. A good, forgiving man. A saint.

Something stirred in Customer's memory.

Didn't Emanuel make some mention once of a pilgrim's route from Wales down through Cornwall to Compostela in Spain, a long succession of churches and chapels, all dedicated to St James, Patron Saint of Spain, and standing along ancient highways of the North Cornwall coast, through Kilkhamton to Boscastle, with the Church of St James of Penalym at Jacobstow in the Hundred of Stratton located somewhere 'twixt the two? Is this why Emanuel had travelled to the Church of St James at Jacobstow – as a holy pilgrim? Had he known then, all those many long months ago, that he was suffering from some disease of the body only a blessed miracle procured for him by St James, could cure?

A terrible coldness came over Customer, a coldness that went through to his very soul and turned it to ice. Even as he had ridden to the priory, as if with the Devil himself at his heels, and been set upon by those murderous villains in saints' clothing, it had been too late.

Emanuel was dead.

Grief overcame Customer.

He struggled to his feet, his mournful cry of despair mingling with the howling of the wind as it swept like a raging, incoming tide across the undulating meadow at his back.

With no thought of what he was doing, or where he was going, he threw back his wet cloak and stumbled blindly forward.

His right foot connected unexpectedly with something granite hard *(a step?)* that sent a cruel judder right up through his body and propelled him headfirst forward into a deep, black, eddying well of unconsciousness.

Chapter Three

Customer awoke in a place that was completely alien to him and with the rising sun shining directly into his eyes.

His sluggish gaze took in his surroundings, searching for a clue to his whereabouts. This was not the Bodmin Moor he recalled from his boyhood. He was hopelessly lost; could answer positively only one of the questions troubling his mind.

Last night, in his pain and despair, he had unwittingly risen to his feet on the edge of a shallow ridge, below which there was a wide area of marshy ground and the small hollow or basin in which he now found himself lying. The ridge, which rose to about three or four feet above his head, followed the perimeter of the marshland to a point where it flattened out into a rolling expanse of meadow on which, in the far distance, he thought he could distinguish, against the sparkling, dewy green of the grass, a few ragged Cornish sheep idly grazing.

Not one of the trees growing in the marshland basin in which he lay, stood tall and straight and for one feverish moment, he saw them as holy brothers of the church, bent forwards over him in their woollen habits of heavy browns and blacks, their arms and hands reaching out to him in benediction. He was not a religious man in the sense that Emanuel was (although, like all good Cornishmen, Customer would admit to a true fondness for their Celtic saints), but he was deeply moved. This, wherever it was that he found himself at that moment, was a mystical, magical place; all of his senses told him so. Paradise itself, he shouldn't wonder; the Gateway to Heaven. His earthly remains had been left on the ridge by the widow-woman and her sons to be collected by the Gatekeeper. Who obviously had other business abroad, but who would doubtless get round to him sooner or later.

With a soft sigh of resignation, Customer settled down to await collection, drawing his cloak close about him and then falling almost immediately into a deep, but restless sleep.

Anna-Lucrezia's voice woke him, a gentle, musical sound that sent a surge of warmth and longing throughout his tired, spent body. He opened his eyes quickly and there she was, kneeling at his feet. He was saddened to know that she, too, was dead, but he was nevertheless selfishly pleased that if not in life, then in death – that is if present indications were anything to go by – they would be together forevermore.

Her face was averted from him, as if frozen in time, but it made little difference. The pale blush of her cheek and its gentle softness were even more beautiful than he remembered. He wanted desperately to reach out and touch her face; yearned to hold her once again in his loving arms.

The girl kneeling at his feet, who was making ready to prise off his boots, felt his slight stirring on the ground and stayed her hands on the heel and toe of the boot on his right foot, turning her face full on to him.

His heart turned to stone. The other side of the girl's face was a grotesque contortion of misshapen sunken bones and pale skin gathered in over them in taut, bluish-grey tucks.

She – this cruel parody of womanhood, this witch-child – was not his beloved. He had been tricked by the same lust and longing that had bewitched him while a guest at the house of the Provost of Penryn. This was Purgatory still, and she, this wretch of a girl stealing his precious boots, was the Devil's handmaiden.

She rose awkwardly, with his boots in her hands, and then disappeared behind the fallen, moss and lichen-covered trunk of a dead oak tree. He tried to raise himself up on one elbow to see where she went, but he was too weak to move.

The girl returned empty-handed a few minutes later, knelt at his side and then gazed deeply into his eyes.

Customer returned her gaze boldly and steadily, masking, as any true believer would, his revulsion at her fantastically deformed facial features, and casting aside all personal feelings and thoughts of her and the evil she represented. He was quite proud of himself (*a lesser man,* he assured himself, *would have cringed in fear and trembling before her*), but before he could congratulate himself on his remarkable self-control, a face, huge to the point of being twice the size of any normal human being's, full-bearded, with eyes the colour of the petrified ponds of Hades itself, was suddenly thrust close to his.

He cried out in mortal terror as hands larger than meat plates

16

drew aside the cloak covering him.

Glimpses of yellow teeth as timeworn and strangely shaped as the ancient Cornish Celtic crosses that Emanuel had told him had once guided the traveller safely across the moors, showed between thin, hairy lips as the beast spoke.

''Tis but a mere scratch, he'll not die this day;' and if it were possible *(and Customer would have solemnly sworn on sacred oath that it was)*, the crumpled and creased half of the girl's cruelly malformed face softened.

She made no sound; rose to her feet and then stepped back so that the bearded, evil-looking one could examine more closely the wound in Customer's side.

Clearly, the bearded beast was dissatisfied with the size and quality of his death wound; disappointed that Hades' new recruit was not in greater pain. Customer felt a moan or two would not have gone amiss, for his side had indeed begun to hurt agonizingly, but he restrained himself. At least he would have the satisfaction of denying the beast that pleasure. He, Customer Trago of Royal Plantagenet blood, would proceed with the beast and his handmaiden into the very depths of Hades' fiercely burning fires and be damned for all eternity if any sound should ever escape his lips!

'Can you stand, young sir?' asked the beast.

Customer paid close attention. The beast's voice was that of a Cornishman born and bred, and yet soft, gentle as a woman's. Too soft and gentle. Customer was not fooled and held his tongue. The beast would get no quarter from him by thinking to trick him into believing he was among friends, his own kind.

The beast fingered Customer's cloak. 'This cloth is not of these parts. I have seen such as this before on travellers, one such from Padua only this autumn just gone. He is not Tregonwell. An ambassador from some far off foreign land, more like. Travelling alone and set upon along the highway by robbers.'

Tregonwell? *Dr John Tregonwell, the eminent Cornish civil lawyer?* The beast, or rather his minion, the girl, thought they'd netted Tregonwell?

A pretty morning's catch indeed!

Tregonwell was rumoured to be in the South West – Devon, Somerset and Cornwall – on the Vicar-General Thomas

Cromwell's orders, allegedly removing valuable holy artefacts from its monasteries and churches. Emanuel had made mention of these whisperings which, so far as Cornwall was concerned, he had dismissed as being without foundation. He could not see Henry risking another rising by the deeply religious and superstitious Cornish by sanctioning such plunder.

Grudgingly, Customer had to give credit to the beast. He had a sharp eye for a fine piece of woollen cloth, which Customer had indeed purchased while travelling in a far off foreign land, from a merchant in Padua.

The beast was eyeing him contemplatively. ''Tis possible he is a German master miner, travelling from Wales on tinners' business.'

There was doubt in his voice, and doubt now in Customer's mind. The beast could surely do better than this, make such a wildly inaccurate guess concerning his presence thereabouts?

A German master miner indeed! Customer was not flattered. And what, pray tell, would a German master miner be doing in Wales when, unless there had been some major rearrangement of the geography of Britain since Customer Trago's last visit to her shores, her tin mines were in the south-west of Cornwall and quickest and best reached from Cornish seaports?

The beast obviously read his mind for he answered his unspoken question.

'Timber to shore up Cornwall's tin mines must nowadays be sought in Wales. Cornish timber was used up for shipping vessels and housing long before your time, young sir – mine, too, for that matter.'

The beast certainly took an active interest in current local affairs, Customer would grant him that!

The beast, who had been crouching down close to him, rose slowly to his feet and as he did so, a large iron key secured on long fob of braided leather attached to the wide, buckled belt encircling his broad waist, swung high and wide.

Customer looked up at him, his attention caught momentarily by the fascinating swinging and swaying of the key, and then he trembled in awe.

Was there no end to the beast?

Higher and higher he rose, an absolute giant of a man. Seven feet of him, give or take an inch or two.

Customer had heard it said that the rebel Cornish archers who had fought alongside Michael Joseph, the blacksmith, at the battle of Blackheath in London against Henry Tudor, had used shafts a good yard in length. No more would he doubt that story. The longbow that would draw such a shaft would be a mere twig in the great hairy fists of this Cornish giant!

''Tis doubtful he understands what I say,' said the beast to his handmaiden, who responded by putting out a pale, slender hand and lightly touching the sleeve of Customer's once dark green, but now even darker, mud-stained velvet jerkin, and then looking up into the beast's face with eyes that Customer could only describe as bordering on the saintly.

She uttered not a sound, but the beast knew, or read, her mind.

He nodded his great head. 'Yes, little one: I, too, think he could be a holy pilgrim.'

Little one? Holy pilgrim? These gentle words were not the normal language of the Beast, the Evil One himself, surely?

'Where am I?' asked Customer.

The beast looked at him in some surprise. 'He speaks! Why, young sir, 'tis the Holy Well of St James that you find yourself lying before.'

The beast pointed at the ridge to the left of Customer's shoulder.

Customer twisted his aching head round and was astounded, truly humbled; understood now the benediction of the old trees in the marshland basin, their attitude of holy supplication. Never, in all his travels, had he seen a place of such sweet, gentle beauty. A holy well, built into the ridge of natural Cornish stone in warm browns and soft greys, down over which, through a misty veil of lacy ferns and strong, rich green ivy and wild blackberry, trickled the crystal clear spring water which he had mistaken for the voice of his precious lost love.

'The little one comes here to the Holy Well of St James seeking a blessed miracle. 'Tis she who came upon you and fetched me to your side to do what best I could for you,' explained the beast.

He did not elaborate on the girl's miracle. It was pitifully obvious what she sought at the holy well.

'The Church of St James of Penalym stands near this place?' Customer's tone was feeble, his senses muddled by all that he heard and saw about him.

The beast waved a huge, hairy paw to the north-east. ''Tis but a mere cock's stride farther down Witchypool Lane yonder; sheltered in a gully with a sweet, swift-flowing stream at its side. You cannot see it from here. Nor will you hear its bells. 'Tis the north-east wind that once carried the soul-lifting sound of the bells of St James's to us. For now they are silent.'

There was no need for the beast to elaborate on the silence of the church bells. With a small nod of his head, Customer indicated that he was aware that the King had ordered the confiscation of clappers from Cornish church bells in order to replenish his seriously depleted coffers. Wars cost money.

The two men shared a moment or two's reflective pause and then, in a mildly inquiring voice, the beast asked, 'You are a friend of the Vicar of the Church of St James, young sir?'

Having made careful note of that pause, the lawyer that Customer Trago might have been had things gone differently for him, strongly advised him to be prudent with his reply. Another like Sir William Gennys skulking about down there in the gully in priest's clothing would not be impossible, and if so, there would be no love lost for any fledgling of Emanuel's in this Cure.

Customer shook his head. 'I have heard talk of the church, that is all.' He searched his memory. 'I was told it has, or had, three bells.'

The beast threw back his head and laughed with such heartiness that Customer all but felt the ground beneath them shudder. 'That is untrue – about the bells?' he inquired, abashed.

''Tis true enough,' said the beast, nodding his great bear's head. 'Three bells in a tower built of good ashlar granite and finished with battlements and crocketed pinnacles.'

All three of which bells no doubt carried up into the aforesaid handsome tower, stacked one atop the other, on the great beast's broad back! thought Customer wryly. 'You are a stonemason?' he hazarded. *The keeper, perhaps, of some dark, foul place of confinement reserved specially for the likes of one Customer Trago, enemy and spy of this parish?* he wondered, more than ever conscious now of the key that dangled from the beast's waist, and unaccountably certain that should he ever have the misfortune to chance upon the door whose lock it fitted, his name would be writ large and bold upon it.

Again the beast threw back his head and laughed and the earth beneath them shook. 'And what of you, young sir?' he asked Customer. 'How come you by the fine cloth of your gentleman's apparel?'

So this was how it was to be between them? Cornish cat and mouse games, neither giving as much as an inch to the other?

'So far as I am concerned, I am a dead man,' said Customer in an arch voice.

'*Dead?* Of that piddling nettle-sting? *Tety-valy!* A poultice of Lady's dung will soon set that to rights... My milking cow,' the beast explained in response to the bemused look on Customer's face. 'Isn't that so, little one?'

The girl made no response to the beast's roar of laughter. *Out of fear?*

Customer looked deep into her eyes, but they, like the beast's, were true, Cornish slate-grey eyes and kept their counsel well to themselves.

There was something strange here, odd, but he couldn't lay a finger on it. And then the beast read his mind again.

'The girl's name is Rebecca, but I call her "little one". She tends my cow and when the fancy takes her, serves alongside old Agnes at my inn. The rest of her time she spends here at the Holy Well of St James. She has little hearing and speaks not a word, ever, of anything she sees, which is everything.'

'And you, kind sir? Your name?' inquired Customer.

'Eber Pendragon at your service, young sir.'

Aware that he was under close scrutiny, but unable to help himself, Customer's gaze was drawn back to the key dangling at the beast's waist. He considered it for a moment and then hazarded a guess at its purpose. It secured the door of a wine cellar. Eber Pendragon's business was that of innkeeper. Hadn't he said as much himself?

Eber Pendragon's ability to read minds was truly astonishing. His great head began to shake from side to side, the grizzled, shoulder-length locks adorning it flying wide with his earthquaking mirth. 'No, young sir. Eber Pendragon is the blacksmith of Wynehouse Corner.'

Chapter Four

The shame of it!

Customer Trago of Royal Plantagenet blood – and welcomed as such in the Royal Courts of Europe – too weak to stand and walk on his own two feet and hoisted up onto the beast's back, legs astraddle, like some small child at play! The worst of it? That the beast made no attempt to restrain his amusement at this dishonour to him, and that he, Customer Trago, was also further required to endure the intermittent quivering of the beast's broad shoulders as he let loose his merriment at his back-passenger's undignified exit from the sanctified precincts of the Holy Well of St James.

In one mighty stride, Eber used the holy pilgrim's granite step to ascend the ridge. He walked for a short distance across a gentle, grassy slope to a ragged breach in a thick, black hedge which gave onto the narrow overgrown track known thereabouts as Witchypool Lane. Here he turned left, walking at a steady pace on level ground for a few minutes, untroubled by the thick, cloying mud that squelched beneath his enormous feet, and then abruptly, he stepped through another ragged, half-concealed gap in the high hedge that bordered the coastal highway.

Turning left again, and walking in company with the rugged north Cornish coastline in a south-westerly direction, they proceeded, again on reasonably level ground, for about a quarter of a mile along the brow of a hill known locally as Highway Hill. Glancing round Eber's head, Customer saw, in the middle distance where the highway swept downwards and the roadway, gently curving and flat, stretched away from them as far as the eye could see, two fairly substantial dwellings standing directly opposite one another along another roadway on the left-hand side of a crossroads.

This then was their destination, Wynehouse Corner, and Customer Trago, for one, would not be sorry to reach it.

Eber had commented on the fact that Customer was neither armed nor shod, assuming that this specific loss of his personal belongings had been his robbers' gain, and Customer had not bothered to correct him. Customer did not feel particularly well-disposed towards the servant girl, Rebecca, who followed quietly in their wake, but somehow he didn't have the heart to name her as the thief of his precious boots. It seemed to him that she had trouble enough.

At some point in their silent trek to the south-west, she disappeared, possibly, thought Customer, to the left along the wide, straight track they had just passed, spread out across one corner of which, twinkling in the crisp morning sunlight, there was a pond.

Walking sedately towards them from the direction of the two dwellings on the crossroads at Wynehouse Corner, in single file, were a drake, a duck and their fluffy young brood. It might have been a fancy of Customer's imagination, but as he and Eber drew level with them, their leader glanced at them with a wary eye and bobbed its head at Eber.

Always, on their far right, three miles distant and yet clearly visible, there was the sea – just a fleeting glimpse of it every now and again with the gentle rise and fall of the low, emerald green hills that flanked the north Cornwall coastline. The small, barren, principally bird-populated island of Lundy stood out proudly in the dark blue sea like a large, smooth round pebble.

It took them twenty minutes to reach the smithy, the first of the only two dwellings within Customer's range of sight. Built of local stone, slate and cob, the smithy faced the highway, with the blacksmith's cottage attached at the rear of it. Standing to the left of this cottage and directly across a narrow roadway from it – and like the smithy, facing the highway but set back farther from it – there was the inn which, although it bore no sign to designate it so, was commonly known as the Wynehouse Inn.

Of such a disorderly jumble was the stone, cob, timber and slate construction of the inn that it seemed decidedly probable to Customer that it had been built by a half-blind, apprentice master stonemason working in the dead of night! One really determined gust, either from a strong westerly wind, or the even more vicious, bitterly cold north-easterly, and the lot would surely give up the ghost and tumble, roof and walls, inwards and then collapse in a great dusty heap of rubble!

The squally, bitterly cold westerly wind, which had been with them all the while, seemed to be gathering force the nearer they

23

came to the crossroads and the inn.

'Windy Wynehouse us calls this place,' said Eber, which settled the matter for Customer once and for all; explained the stonemason's haste to be done with his work and away from those exposed, wind-wracked crossroads as quickly as possible.

Customer was carried across a forecourt and into the inn, through a heavy, crookedly hung, weather-stained oak door, and thence into a large public room niggardly furnished with the barest minimum of crude wooden tables and chairs, on one side of which there was an open hearth. He coughed as the heavy smoke given off from the peat fire burning dispiritedly there, filled his lungs. The fire, which burned day and night throughout most of the year, appeared to be more efficient at giving off smoke than heat, for the room was damp, smelt strongly of decaying timber and rampant mould, and was so gloomily grey and cold that Customer's teeth began to chatter uncontrollably. Having spent, so far as he was aware, at least two days and nights entirely out of doors at the mercy of the elements, he felt well qualified to defy anyone to attempt to assure him that it was colder outside!

Structurally, matters did not improve within the inn. The narrow, creaking timber staircase up which Customer was borne by Eber was so riddled with the worm that Customer could all but see and hear them at their mischievous work. The heavy wooden beams which crisscrossed the crudely plastered walls and supported the upper floor, fared no better.

He was taken to a room at the end of a narrow passage, above the door of which, through a hole in the roof, Customer caught sight of clear blue sky. Eber claimed it was the best room at the inn. Customer pondered on this for a moment; wondered what the worst would be like, bearing in mind that the best one had an interesting feature on its south-western wall of thick, black mould which covered it completely from bare flooring boards to sinking, beamed and plastered ceiling.

In one corner of the room there was a ragged hole in the floor where the timber boards had rotted away. The single shuttered window in the room was another interesting architectural feature, its plastered reveals being smoothly rounded on one side and sharply right-angled on the other. The room also had five walls, four roughly the same length and height, the fifth about four feet long and angled across one corner, quite purposelessly so far as Customer could determine from the casual observation that he had made of the outer fabric of the inn which had appeared to him to be uniformly square on all four of its corners.

A madman had built this place. And not impossibly, its present owner who probably found this architectural disaster over which he undoubtedly presided as high king (as his Cornish surname, Pendragon, insinuated), vastly amusing.

Customer was deposited, with little ceremony or consideration for the death wound in his side, on bedding that was even damper than the clothing he was wearing.

'Saint Agnes is at her work in the kitchen; I'll fetch her to you,' said Eber. His big, bearded face with its slate-grey eyes regarded Customer in silence for a moment or two, and then he added, 'I call her *Saint* Agnes for it is she who keeps my public house in order.'

From what little Customer had thus far seen of the place, the type of trade it would attract, order would need to be kept, and with an exceedingly firm hand. Particularly if the people who lived thereabouts and who used the Wynehouse Inn frequently were as wild and untamed-looking as its host!

Eber left him to ponder his fate. The innkeeper thought him a spy, a sympathizer with Cromwell, of this Customer was sure; would probably contrive with the saintly woman of whom he had spoken, to do away with him at the first opportunity that came their way. Some kind of poison in his food or with his wine, or he would contract some serious infection from this cow-dung poultice he had been promised and doubtless die in mortal agony of that!

He heard a noise at the door, what little there was of it. Rats, he supposed, had gnawed the great chunk that was missing from it at floor level.

A woman entered carrying a bowl of water and some clean linen for bandages.

''Tis only old Agnes come to clean and dress your wound, young sir,' she said. 'Us'll not harm 'e.'

Agnes was not what he had expected, and while she was not young, he would certainly not have thought her old; perhaps somewhere in her mid to late forties.

Her hair was grizzled, wind-blown, every bit as wild as Eber's; her face was wise, kind, somehow sad and yet barely lined by the troubles Customer was sure had plagued her life; her eyes the colour of the dazzlingly bright, north Cornish summer sky that reflects the blue of the great ocean out to the west. She was neither tall nor short, neither thin nor stout, and yet the touch of her hands as she began to remove his clothing, conveyed an inner strength and capability that Customer knew would match Eber's in every particular.

Customer assumed that she shared Eber's bed, but with the same talent for reading his mind that Eber had displayed, she explained that Eber came to the inn only of a Saturday night to play at games of chance with local men; at other times, only when there was trouble. Eber kept himself to himself; lived quietly and apparently contentedly alone in his cottage behind the smithy, cooked and kept house for himself and left Agnes to take care of the inn and those who had a mind to use it, as she thought fit.

Customer winced as she carefully peeled back the folds of his heavily stained cambric shirt which had stuck fast to his flesh as the blood from his sword wound had congealed and dried.

'Is there often trouble at the inn?' he asked through gritted teeth, quite sure there would be.

'Only for them as come looking for it,' she replied. She gazed directly at him as she spoke and he read the look in her eyes. She, too, thought he was a spy, and was warning him to have a care.

'I'm not what you think, mistress,' he assured her with a petulant frown. 'You see lying before you a penitent on holy pilgrimage, cruelly struck down by heathen vagabonds and left for dead by them, and if you have a mind to ask, your master will swiftly confirm as much.'

'Us minds our own business,' she said with a sniff, shifting her gaze to peer myopically at his wound, which now lay bare before her.

He waited with breathless anticipation for the pendulous droplet of moisture he could see collecting on the tip of her nose, to drip directly into it. 'Us'll soon have you healed and back on the road to your journey's end,' she added while, at the very last moment, deftly wiping her nose dry on the back of her hand.

Her touch, though gentle, sent wave after wave of pain surging savagely upwards from the pit of his stomach and into his chest and throat until at length, when he could bear it no longer, he slipped

26

thankfully into unconsciousness.

Agnes gazed at him with a mixture of curiosity and longing. There had been many men in her life, but none such as this. He was quite the most beautiful man she had ever laid eyes upon. Almost *too* beautiful. She could find no other way to describe him.

He would have had many lovers, she was sure. Fine young ladies whose milky-white hands were softer and smoother than the rich silks and satins they wore on their elegant backs. He might even be married; have a pretty young wife waiting for him somewhere.

She touched the back of one of her red, work-roughened hands to his hot forehead, left if there for a second or two and then gently brought it down over his right cheek and across his chin. With a forefinger, she traced the outline of his lips. She could really love this young man, she thought wistfully; would do anything he asked of her and humbly kiss his hand for the honour.

She could not tear her eyes from his face; felt almost as if someone had cast a spell on her.

'Don't you fret, my lovely: just let old Agnes take care of 'e and all the nasty pain'll soon be gone,' she murmured; and then, sighing softly to herself, she began to clean his wound.

Chapter Five

Customer most certainly was not returned to the road to good health nor, for that matter, to the road to anywhere else.

All went well for the first day and night. Finally regaining consciousness, he even swallowed, like a man and without complaint, the nettle broth that Eber apparently insisted he should be spoon-fed. *(No doubt roaring with laughter over this deliberate joke at his expense!)* And then, without warning, the fever came; fever and pain such as Customer had never before experienced. At times he had his full senses and was conscious and alert, if only for a moment or two, and then Agnes would be there, pressing a cool, damp cloth against his burning forehead. Sometimes it would be Eber's great hairy face and head that would appear before him as the mists of delirium and pain rolled momentarily back from his feverish gaze. *Never* the girl, Rebecca. But she must have come at sometime or other. His boots suddenly appeared one morning in a corner of his room, dried and cleaned of their mud; almost good as new. Boots Customer Trago would never again wear, of that he was quite certain. He was done for this time, and no mistake about it.

Late one night – though this was probably the fever again and none of it was real – he thought he heard horses and riders milling about on the muddied forecourt of the inn. Voices were raised in anger and Rebecca's name was spoken, followed by a roar of such beastly ferocity that it could only have been Eber out there with the nightriders, for soon afterwards there was a thundering of hoofbeats as the horsemen rode off furiously into the night.

Then late another night, with the wind tearing savagely at the shutters on his window and gusting pitilessly through the hole in the roof, Anna-Lucrezia visited him. Word had somehow reached her that his life was fast ebbing away and that he would not last another night.

Her visit, in itself, was astonishing enough, as was the fact that, as if by some sixth sense, he opened his bleary, bloodshot eyes at the precise moment that she appeared in the open doorway of his room, naked as the day she was born and as eager for him as he was for her. Somewhat plumper than he remembered, a condition he attributed to the solace she had obviously sought at their enforced parting, in comfort eating.

He spoke her name hoarsely, groaning in ecstasy as she drew back the bedcovers and tugged up his nightshirt and then lowered herself onto him, pressing her wet mons veneris urgently against the hot swelling of his loins.

She let out a moist, breathy sigh and almost as if he couldn't get enough of her, he drew it into him hungrily, filling his lungs with every last droplet of it and then coughing once sharply when a biting tang of brandy caught suddenly at the back of his throat.

Was it the fever raging in his brain playing cruel tricks on him? A base falsehood, surely, that his beloved was heavily intoxicated and, indeed, drunk as a monk on holy wine!

Customer's shock was instantly supplanted by a rush of humility and he cursed himself roundly for his lack of charity. Unquestionably, his beloved had been so overcome with grief at the thought of his imminent passing from this life to the next, that a strong medicinal dose of brandy had been the only prescription that would fill the need in her to keep up her spirits until he slipped forever from her loving embrace.

His face became lost in her full, soft breasts; she offered one of her hardened nipples to his mouth and he sucked on it eagerly and noisily. The moment, however, was too great for him. The sacrifice of his beloved's pure, sweet body to him on his ignominious deathbed, the proof of her true love for him – and not for her wretchedly controlling father – overcame him, and although he struggled determinedly against it with every ounce of strength left in his pathetically weak, fever-wracked body, he slipped with a soft sigh of regret into the old familiar blackness.

Then suddenly, equally without warning, the fever broke and he opened his eyes to a room filled with cheerful, warming sunlight that somehow made the wall mould look more like a luxuriously rich, blue-black velvet wall-hanging – quite soft and friendly, in fact – and the rats' ravenous night-time gnawings at the woodwork, merely quaint and adding character to it. He even enjoyed the nettle broth and thick chunk of unleavened bread that Agnes eagerly fetched up from the kitchen for him, asking her for a second helping.

A subtle change in Agnes's manner puzzled him. She was as solicitous as ever, but had suddenly acquired a curiously tentative look in her eye, as if she wished to raise some important issue between them and was reluctant to be the one to broach it. He pondered on this for most of that day, finally concluding that she feared his miracle recovery was not going to last and that at any moment, possibly even as she had watched him sup up the broth she had brought him, he would slip back into that old familiar, deep well of unconsciousness from which, finally, there would be no hope of recovery.

The following day, with Agnes's help, he managed to get out of bed. He sat for a while at his open window, looking out over the stable to the rolling meadows and distant low hills, cut neatly like a deep frown into the brow of one of which – as pointed out to him by Agnes – was the holy pilgrims' roadway to Boscastle. He was sticking firmly to his pilgrim story and assumed that Agnes had been testing him with this piece of local geographical information. He gave her what he hoped was a satisfactory response, that he hoped to be fit enough soon to continue along that roadway to Boscastle on his holy pilgrimage to the Church of St James in that ancient coastal settlement.

He was puzzled that Agnes continued to cast tentative glances in his direction, usually when he wasn't looking directly at her, and he wondered if she sought some verbal assurance from him of a determined and permanent return to full health, or whether – and this seemed increasingly likely to him – she was waiting for him to make some mention of Anna-Lucrezia's night-time visit to his room. Indeed, when he could stand the suspense for not a moment longer, he asked Agnes outright if she expected him to speak of it.

'Us knows of no young maiden's visit to the Wynehouse, at night or by day, young sir,' was as much as she would say in reply; and his heart swelled warmly in his breast at her discretion and loyalty. Agnes had obviously been sworn to secrecy by Anna-Lucrezia, and Agnes, good Christian soul that she was, would not break her word to her. Like all women, though, Agnes was insatiably curious and doubtless hoped to be taken into the confidence of the other party to the forbidden lovers' tryst who had shared those unbridled, if short-lived stolen moments of passion.

A few more days and Customer was able, aided by the uneven walls on either side of the narrow passage outside his room, to reach the room at the other end of it. In better condition than the one he was occupying, but without benefit of sun. For most of the day, when the weather was fine, his room was bathed in cheering sunlight.

Standing close to the door of the room at the end of the passage there was a crude wooden chair, and drawing it towards him, he shuffled it ahead of him across the floor, leaning heavily on its back rest for support. Then, exhausted by these physical exertions after so many long weeks in bed, he paused, panting a little, at the window and looked out across the roadway at the blacksmith's cottage.

He could hear Eber working in the smithy, but he could neither see him nor anyone in need of a smith's services. Recalling the nightriders who on that one occasion had disturbed his rest, Customer wondered if horses were left at night in the stabling at the inn to be shod by Eber the next day and then collected the following night after their owners had finished their toil in the fields or shippens, or were done for the day with whatever else gainfully employed the men of those parts. Master Blacksmith, Customer decided, ran a strange business and an even stranger inn, all of which pointed in one rather worrisome direction. The trade upon which Eber Pendragon relied for his living would be no less strange.

Chapter Six

Once or twice during the period of Customer's walking convalescence, he heard men's voices downstairs in conversation with Agnes, none of them Eber's. The business of selling and consuming brandy, wines and ale and the cider brewed by a local farmer twice a year was confined more or less exclusively to a Saturday night. This was the night, as Agnes had told him while tending his wound for the first time, that Eber would put in an appearance, in his case, not to imbibe a little liquid refreshment and relax for an hour or two in the company of friends after a week spent slaving over his hot forge in the smithy, but to sit down to the serious business of playing at cards and dice. According to Agnes, Eber did not drink anything stronger than the crystal clear spring water from the well sunk into his kitchen floor and had not touched a drop of brandy, wine, ale or cider, since the night he lost his wife in childbirth.

These were not the only creature comforts Eber denied himself. Sleep, apparently, was something else to be done without. Night after night, as Customer grew steadily stronger, he went to the room at the other end of the passage and watched the yellow lantern-light which showed fleetingly on the small panes of glass in first one window and then the next of the blacksmith's cottage on the other side of the roadway. Agnes said it was a penance. Eber blamed himself for his wife's death in childbirth and he punished himself by keeping a night-watch. Occasionally less than quietly, which prompted Customer to wonder if self-flagellation were another of Eber's night-watch occupations.

'Is Rebecca Eber's daughter?' Customer asked Agnes following one long night of watching the lantern-light flit across the windows of the cottage opposite. It seemed a reasonable enough assumption to him. A difficult birth resulting in the girl's terrible facial deformity and the mother's death would be enough to make the strongest of men succumb occasionally to melancholy and, in the depths of despair, move a man to curse God in His Heaven for His lack of mercy and compassion.

'No,' replied Agnes. 'Eber's child did not live a minute beyond its birth. Rebecca is like you and me and Lady out the back there in the shippen, and the ducks that parade every morning from the Wynehouse to the pond; snatched from the jaws of death itself by Eber. Us knows how you came to the Wynehouse, young sir, but as for Lady, she was for the slaughterhouse, and old Agnes here was to be sold off to the highest bidder in payment of her dead husband's debts.'

'Eber paid off your debts for you?'

'No,' she said, and her remarkable blue eyes looked at him levelly. 'That night Eber won at the dice.'

Customer stared at her. 'Eber gambled with your debtor, with you and your debts as the stakes?'

'Debtors: there was more than one of them,' she corrected him, her tone mild but tempered, he thought, with sadness at the memory of past desperate circumstances.

'And Rebecca? How was that game won? With the dice again, or by a turn of the cards?'

'There are times when there is no chance in the game Eber chooses to play,' said Agnes.

Customer frowned at her. 'Are you saying that Eber cheated at the game of chance he played that night?'

Agnes's blue eyes regarded him thoughtfully. 'Would you call it cheating for one man alone to hold off and then grab up Rebecca's brothers, one after the other – there are six of them, each bigger, uglier and meaner-hearted than the one born before him – and then her father, who is the biggest, ugliest and meanest of the entire Trelawney tribe, and hurl them through the side wall of the Trelawneys' shippen where Rebecca was kept tied up like a wretched animal, day and night, for their cruel, vile amusement?'

Customer pictured the scene, Eber's demonic fury, the mayhem that must have ensued, but he made no comment.

Agnes continued, 'Then when Eber had put down the rebellion and granted the Trelawneys their pleas for mercy, he untied Rebecca from her stall and led her away from them forever. They come on horseback at the end of each and every week, made brave and reckless by the rough farm cider they have swilled, and hurl threats and abuse at Eber, swearing that they are going to take the girl back to where she belongs.'

'Pose and posture and nought else,' said Customer with a knowing nod.

'And you would act differently?' Agnes asked him simply.

Truthfully? He most certainly would not! He had sat upon those rippling muscles of Eber's; experienced their enormous strength, even in good humour. Time, he decided with a faint shudder, for this holy pilgrim to be moving on. Fortunately, with so few travellers on the roadways during the long, harsh Cornish winter months, there had been very little likelihood that Eber would discover much of any consequence about him. But it was spring now, milder and drier than usual, and who knows who might ride up to the crooked front door of the Wynehouse Inn seeking refreshment, or one of its perennially damp beds for the night, or have a horse in need of shoeing, and pause and pass the time of day with the smith across the road. Perish the thought, but should that traveller happen to be someone from Launceston Priory who recognized him, and Eber was less than pleased with what he learnt of the poor, sword-wounded stray pilgrim whom he had restored to health and vigour...well, not to put too fine a point on it, Customer did not relish the thought of finding himself picked up like some hurling stone and chucked through the side of Eber's own shippen!

Chapter Seven

Customer found it impossible to keep track of time during his recovery from what he still thought of as being his death wound, but if asked, would have said it was somewhere in the early part of the fourth week of his convalescence at the inn on the crossroads of Wynehouse Corner that, as he sat at the window in the far room, a stranger arrived, leading a lame horse.

Customer watched as Agnes came out and spoke to the stranger, a man near his own age, Customer would have thought. Agnes and the stranger were joined moments later by Eber, who spoke with the stranger and then crouched down and examined the right foreleg of the man's horse. Eber then led the horse away to the stable and the stranger followed Agnes into the inn.

It was a scene that left Customer feeling unnerved and anxious, the more so when later on in the day, he learnt from Agnes that Eber had granted the stranger's request for bed and board, both for himself and his horse, while the animal recovered from its injury. There had been something familiar about the stranger, a hunch to his shoulders, which were nevertheless broad and strong, and something of a lack of co-ordination, from his hips and then down his legs to his feet, which affected his gait. He walked quickly, without any obvious need for haste and with his hunched shoulders riding up and into his neck. It was of little comfort to Customer, when told by Agnes that the stranger's name was Pawley, that he could think of no one of that name sharing the years he had spent at Launceston Priory, nor remember having met anyone by the name of Pawley while travelling abroad. Neither could Customer remember Emanuel ever having mentioned someone of that name in any of his correspondences with him during those years.

That night as Customer and Agnes sat in companionable silence before the hearth in the public room downstairs, he looked across at her suddenly and said, inquiringly, 'The stranger, Pawley, is not to join us this evening?'

Something guarded came into Agnes's eyes. Turning her head from him, she busied herself stoking the fire. 'Master Pawley takes his meals in his room while he recovers his strength from his long forced walk this day with his injured horse and makes ready for more of the same should the animal not recover from its injury and need to be put down.'

'Another like Eber, then,' commented Customer. 'I mean,' he added quickly when she shot him a fleeting glance, 'who chooses his own company to eat and sup.'

Agnes stayed her hand on the poker she was using, shifting her gaze from the fire and then letting it linger on Customer. 'No, another such as yourself, young sir, making a holy pilgrimage to Boscastle and yonder.'

Her words sent such a chill through Customer that his bones began to ache. *So what, or who, was Master Pawley running from?* They were brothers under the skin, Customer was sure of it. Both consummate liars if and when it came to saving their necks.

There could be no mistaking the look in Agnes's eyes. She doubted the stranger Pawley's story about being a holy pilgrim as much as she did Customer Trago's!

Customer could not help but feel a little irked. He considered it a great kindness on his part that the less Agnes and Eber knew about him and the events leading up to the death wound in his side, the better it would be for them. Eber was a brave, strong man, but no match for Gennys and his wild bunch should they learn of Customer Trago's whereabouts and determine to finish the job they had started on him.

Customer spoke in an arch voice. 'I think that in a day or two, I shall be strong enough to continue on the next leg of my pilgrimage to the Churches of St James and make a start for Boscastle.'

'It is for Eber to say when you are fit and able to leave us, young sir,' said Agnes pleasantly.

He decided to be bold: he would have to face the truth sooner or later. 'Am I a prisoner here?'

'Am I?' she replied. 'Or Rebecca, or poor, half-blind old Lady, or the ducks that sit and quack uselessly on the pond all day?'

Customer scowled at her. He wanted to rebuke her for the ambiguity of her reply and demand a proper one, but he checked himself. Agnes was well in with the beast across the way, and Customer was anxious not to give him any excuse to flex his muscles in anger on his account.

He suddenly realized that he hadn't seen Rebecca since the day he came to the Wynehouse and he pointed this out to Agnes.

'She comes, she goes; sleeps where she wills, does what she wills,' said Agnes with a small shrug.

'I would like to thank her,' he said.

'She knows you thank her.'

'For fetching and cleaning my riding boots,' he explained. 'I was careless and left them at the holy well,' he added.

'She knows you thank her for that, too.'

'I would still like to thank her in person before I leave.'

'If she so wishes.' Agnes regarded him for a moment and then she nodded her head once. 'Us'll see.'

He hesitated, frowning. Then he asked, 'Why did she give my boots back to me?' He hesitated again; gambled that he had little to lose by speaking out. They had seen his wearing apparel, its fine quality; hadn't needed to be told that he was a gentleman who had travelled much in foreign lands. They would know he had friends who were well placed and that in all probability, he had access somewhere to funds. 'I could have replaced them with another pair – in time, that is... When I am fully recovered and able to go on about my business,' he added cautiously. 'Rebecca could have kept them; sold them for her trouble, and welcome.'

Agnes fixed him with a mildly rebuking look. 'Rebecca is no thief. 'Tis pity she took on you, young sir. She thought only to save your life by taking your boots from you and hiding them in the marshland.'

He looked at her uncomprehendingly.

'The one they say as rides in these parts in search of church treasure would have worn such fine boots,' explained Agnes. 'The pitiful poor of this parish, who are not feared or wished ill by any living soul hereabouts, are not properly shod and as often as not, go barefoot.'

He thought he understood and nodded. If, while Rebecca had gone to fetch Eber, someone else had stumbled upon him in his gentleman's riding boots, things might not have gone so well for him.

And then he suddenly remembered.

Rebecca had taken his boots from him in those few minutes following her return to the holy well after going to fetch Eber and while she was waiting for Eber to join them.

Customer did not dwell on the matter. Quite obviously, given time to think, Rebecca had feared that Eber would see the gentleman's riding boots and jump to all the wrong conclusions, refusing him succour.

'And if I had been the lawyer Tregonwell it would seem I could have been mistaken for?' Customer inquired boldly.

'Rebecca prayed to St James that you weren't, and the blessed saint heard her prayers.'

No proper answer. Did anyone here ever answer straight and true?

Agnes looked at him for a moment and a great sadness came into her eyes, dulling them perceptibly. Would that James, blessed saint of this sinful parish, see likewise fit to hear a prayer or two of old Agnes's while he was about it. Had the young sir no idea at all of how pleasing he was to her eye? The more so since that faint trace of weakness in his chin had been masked by the short, black beard that had grown over it during the weeks of his fever.

She resisted a sudden urge to touch her fingertips to his face and explore it even though she knew each line and curve of it better than her own, and instead gave her head a wistful shake and vowed solemnly to herself to think no more of her own personal wants and desires. There was only one true tragedy here, and that was the girl, Rebecca. She loved the young sir, too. She came to the inn at the dead of night and gazed at him by flickering candlelight through the gaps in the planks in the door of his room, and he had not the faintest notion of it, nor that he was the answer to that poor wretched maiden's prayers and dreams. And one day soon, with Eber's permission, he would go from the Wynehouse, taking with him, in the palm of his hand, the aching, bleeding heart of that tragically star-crossed girl who loved him in vain.

Agnes sighed and placed a hand over the heaviness in her breast and said, 'Yes, 'tis best you should go, young sir, and soon. Best all round. Us'll speak with Eber.'

'I thank you, mistress, but I am well able now to cross to the other side of the roadway and plead my own case.'

Agnes was shaking her tousled head. She pursed her mouth. 'You must be patient and wait for Eber to come to you, young sir. No one but Master Allsopp, the wine merchant, is welcome over

Eber's threshold.'

Customer stared at her.

She went on, barely pausing,''Tis how it has always been, near as us can tell, since Eber's wife passed on. Master Allsopp is an old friend; he and Eber have known one another for many years. Us is not sure, but us thinks since the time when Mistress Pendragon was alive. Master Allsopp comes to Wynehouse Corner twice a year, in the spring and at the end of summer. He stays a night with Eber and then in the morning, he goes on his way.'

'And how, I wonder, do innkeeper and wine merchant spend their time together? At dice to see who shall pay for the wines and brandy Eber orders from Master Allsopp?' Customer suggested in a wry voice, and was surprised to see, very briefly, a spark of amusement in Agnes's eyes.

'As like as not,' she said. ''Twould be a lie to say that Eber is as free with his purse as he is with the generous charity of his good nature to those in desperate need. Eber will house you, feed you, care for you, protect you from your enemies, expect not a thing in return save an equal measure of charitable goodwill, but us should not like to say what would be the outcome of a request to him to lift aside his leather smith's apron and open the purse he keeps secure at his waist.'

'I shall bear that in mind in my dealings with him,' Customer promised her in a dry voice.

He smiled to himself. There was a new game of chance that he had been taught to play while tarrying awhile in Pisa this past summer, a game known as *Tarocchi* and played with tarot cards. A game, as it so happened, he played rather well (even if he said as much himself), and he wondered if Master Blacksmith would care to sit a hand or two with him one Saturday night.

He thought for a moment of the wine merchant, Allsopp; how much of his night spent at the cottage of the blacksmith of Wynehouse Corner would be passed in the discussion of the cost of wine, and how much on discussing the political issues of the moment. Trouble was brewing. It was touching on forty years since the Cornish Rising of 1497 when Perkin Warbeck had marched into Bodmin with his army and proclaimed himself Richard IV, and the Cornish – conquered then as they had been destined throughout their entire history – were again becoming restive. Master Wine Merchant would doubtless have a good ear and plenty to tell those who had a mind to listen. Was probably a rebel spy. Perhaps this was why Eber's cottage door was held wide open for him and him alone. Only a fool would think that Eber Pendragon would go down on bended knee and kiss the ring on Henry's hand... And it would be a strange state of affairs indeed if no treason was ever talked at the Wynehouse Inn's gaming tables of a Saturday night!

'When exactly is the wine merchant expected to call on Eber again?' asked Customer.

'Soon. A week, maybe two, from now,' replied Agnes. 'You will know when Master Allsopp is come.'

'What if he arrives at night while I am asleep and he leaves before I rise in the morning?'

She smiled and gave her head a small shake. 'You should know old Agnes will not be tricked as easily as that, Master Pilgrim. You will know when the wine merchant is here. Only the very young are foolish and impatient and want everything made simple and easy for them.'

'I seek news of some friends,' said Customer, his tone truculent as a child's. 'Would ask him to convey news of me to them.'

She looked at him for a long moment in silence. Then she said, ''Twould be best then, young sir, that you should leave your bed made up for a time and keep a long night-watch yourself at the other end of the passage.'

He gave her a petulant look, to which she rejoined, 'The comings and goings of the wine merchant, young sir, are Eber's affair–'

Customer cut in sharply. 'No need for you to say it, mistress! I know... Us minds our own business!'

40

Chapter Eight

Customer was unable to sleep that night. His conversation with Agnes about the wine merchant, Nicholas Allsopp, and her remark that he, Customer, had best stay awake all night if he wished to make absolutely sure of not missing him, had left him feeling badly unsettled. He hoped she had been speaking in jest, but he couldn't rid himself of the notion that he had detected a sinister undercurrent in her words, a warning that the wine merchant, like Eber, was not a man to be trifled with.

Customer freely admitted that it was equally possible that his restlessness had something to do with what Agnes had told him of Rebecca, some hidden anxiety there which, try as he may, he could neither bring to the forefront of his mind, nor quite put a name to.

The minutes and hours of the night dragged on interminably and then suddenly he heard someone moving stealthily in the passage beyond his room. His heart began to race. They – *Gennys* – had found him. *Customer Trago was a dead man!*

Trembling with fear, Customer slid quietly out of bed and crept to the door. Opening it cautiously, he saw Rebecca in the pale moonlight that lit the passage, fluttering away from him like a startled nestling towards the stairs and then down them.

He gave chase, following her out of the inn across the forecourt to the stable door where he finally managed to grab hold of her and pull her up short. Her fragile body strained away from him as she struggled to keep the crushed side of her face averted from his gaze.

'Be still,' he commanded. 'I'll not harm you.'

She wrested herself free of his grasp and in the split second before she ran from him and was swallowed up in the black shadows of the night, she looked up into his eyes. A shaft of moonlight lay across her pale face and he saw in her upturned gaze what he had prayed endlessly to the Good Lord, on bended knee, to see shine out for him for all eternity from his precious lost love's eyes and been so cruelly denied.

It could not be. He prayed he was wrong. But there was no denying the evidence of his eyes. Rebecca loved him as he had loved Anna-Lucrezia and shamed as he was to confess it, with no hope ever of his returning her love. Affection, yes. Admiration for the sweet purity of her gentle nature. Sadness for her wretched affliction and the misery she had endured at the hands of her beastly family. But love; alas, no. The memory of Anna-Lucrezia was carved too deeply in both his heart and his soul. He would never love another.

He wished he had stayed true to his nature and remained shivering and shaking like a craven coward in his bed. He would far rather have faced an assassin's dagger than this. Death, even a painful one, would be more bearable.

He turned aside and gazed out across the highway, trying to decide what he was going to do about this catastrophic turn of events when, out of the corner of an eye, he glimpsed something moving in the distance, due west of the inn, near the treacherously muddy, narrow bridle pathway known as Butterfly Lane.

A horse and rider stood momentarily motionless, outlined in black against the horizon.

Customer's heart kicked out hard against his breast. Didn't Agnes make some mention once of the Trelawney manor and farm, that they were quickest reached by Butterfly Lane?

There was mischief in the air and here he was standing alone and unprotected on the forecourt of the Trelawney family's mortal enemy, Eber Pendragon, with neither sword nor dagger at his side to speak for him.

Customer continued to stare fearfully into the night. His eyes were not deceiving him, it was useless to wish it otherwise. Unless he was very much mistaken, the rider was approaching the inn and would soon be upon him. Would see him and cut him down like a blade of grass if he tried to flee back to the safety of the inn.

The stable!

Customer flung himself at the stable door, which had been left slightly ajar, and squeezed through it. Dropping to his knees in the stall occupied by Will, Eber's gelding, he contrived to cover himself with the fresh hay he had glimpsed Eber forking in there after finishing his work at the smithy late in the afternoon of the previous day.

Customer's teeth began to chatter violently, and not entirely with the cold. He had no doubt that he would be killed if he were found.

Kidnapped and held to ransom and then run through mercilessly with the kidnapper's sword. An eye for an eye, that was how the Trelawneys would see it. Eber had snatched their kin from them and they would balance the books by snatching from him the wounded stranger to whom he had granted shelter and protection.

There was perhaps a slim chance that the lone rider had found some fresh epithets to fling at Eber and had merely come to try them out.

Customer thought he heard the stable door creak; felt his flesh crawl as a pale, ivory light bobbed along the far wall.

Will moved restlessly and Customer froze, fearful that with the next breath he took, he would be discovered. Then he thought he heard the door creak again. He brushed the hay from his eyes and mouth and peered through Will's forelegs, but could see nothing in the pitch dark. Then a second or two later, he heard the sound of a horse being led quietly away across the forecourt by someone on foot.

He didn't move, waited; was on the point of congratulating himself on his latest narrow escape from the snapping jaws of death when Will suddenly moved again, rearing up on hind legs and whinnying in fear.

Smoke!

As he scrambled desperately to his feet, Customer's nostrils flared almost as wide as Will's. The stable was well alight. He grabbed a handful of Will's mane, trying to restrain him. And then suddenly someone had him by his own mane of hair and was dragging him, howling with terror, from Will's stall and out into the night.

Eber!

Customer recognized Eber's roar of fury – once heard never forgotten! – but this wasn't the worst of it. Eber clearly thought he was the perpetrator of the mischief in his stable.

Eber's huge hands closed round Customer's throat, but somehow Customer managed, in the instant before his windpipe would have been crushed and made useless forever, to gasp out the name *Trelawney!* It worked as if by magic. Eber released him and Customer fell from him onto his knees, gasping for air, his own hands clasped to his burning throat.

Still gasping and coughing as if his lungs would burst, he

crawled like an infant to safety as Eber abruptly abandoned him for Will and the two horses stabled with him in separate stalls, and then led them to safety.

Still on all fours, Customer looked up, suddenly aware that he was not alone on the forecourt.

The stranger Pawley, dressed all in black like some fearsome night creature, paused momentarily with his horse, looking back at him momentarily over his right, hunched shoulder and gazing at him. Turning away, he tethered his horse to one of the badly rusted iron rings embedded in the front wall of the inn.

Eber likewise tethered the horses he had rescued, to rings in the wall of the inn. He spoke briefly with Pawley, who immediately afterwards returned indoors, and then Eber walked back to Customer.

'Master Pawley spotted smoke coming from the stable a few minutes before I did,' Eber explained. 'He hastened down from his room to investigate and is quite mortified that you were in there and that he had thought only to rescue, first his horse, and then if I hadn't come to the rescue, as many of the other horses as he could before being driven back by the fire.'

So Master Pawley was another who kept a night-watch from the window of his room overlooking the stable? The question is, what else did he see?

Customer Trago with Rebecca, for sure, thought Customer with a shudder. *Pawley couldn't have failed to see the two of us together on the forecourt. What if he misinterpreted what had passed between us?*

There was no doubt in Customer's mind that Eber would kill him if he thought, or had been told, that he had harmed a hair of Rebecca's head.

Something else to worry about, thought Customer gloomily. *Whether or not he should seek out Pawley in the morning and make it clear to him that no harm had come to Rebecca at the hands of Customer Trago. Agnes would surely bear witness for him...*

Eber and Customer, each immersed in his own thoughts, their faces illuminated by the bright glow of the fire that had now taken a firm hold of the stable, stood side by side. They watched in silence as the stable burnt to the ground, for the first time united as one by the common bond between them, their direct descent from the

44

Celtic saints and kings and chieftains and their tribes who had settled and colonized their county.

'Which of the Trelawney vermin did this thing?' growled Eber when all that remained of the stabling at the inn at Wynehouse Corner was a smoking shell.

'I don't know, Eber,' said Customer, his voice low and hoarse from the smoke and the brutal pressure that had been placed upon his throat by Eber's hands. Then, quickly rearranging the facts to exclude any mention of Rebecca, which he felt would be best all round, he quickly continued, 'I was restless: my side was sore and aching and I couldn't sleep, so I left my bed and opened the shutters on my window and looked out, thinking to pass a little time while waiting for daybreak. A lone horse and rider were approaching the stable and inn at a walk from Butterfly Lane, and knowing something of the Trelawneys from Agnes – that they are mischief-makers of the worst type – I thought I should come downstairs and make sure that all was in order with your property.'

There was a troubled look on Eber's face as he gazed in the direction of Butterfly Lane. 'One rider, you say? That would have to be Lowarn Trelawney, the one they named after the fox. The eldest of the vermin brood.'

Customer recalled to mind the horse and rider he had seen outlined against the skyline, the stealth and cunning in their movements and the manner in which the rider had then, or so he firmly believed, gone about his dirty business inside Eber's stable. The Trelawneys had named their son well, and Customer prayed to God that he and this particular member of their tribe should never have occasion to meet in person.

'I am in your debt, young sir,' said Eber. 'You will forgive the haste of my actions and beyond all doubt, but for your crying out as you did, I would have choked the breath of life from you for sure.'

Customer ruefully massaged his bruised and aching Adam's apple. 'A mistake anyone could have made,' he croaked. He frowned to himself. The strange look on Eber's face made him uneasy. There was something on Eber's mind. He was worried. With good cause, so far as Customer was concerned. The next time the Trelawney fox called in the night, it might be the inn or the cottage at the rear of the smithy that went up in flames. Lives, including Customer Trago's, could be lost!

For his part, Eber was nowhere near as sure of the Trelawney fox's hand in the fire that had destroyed his stable. He thought back. Agnes did not trust the stranger who called himself Malachy Pawley and who claimed to be on holy pilgrimage from Ireland to Compostela in Spain. Nor did she believe his story of how his horse came to be lame.

'And for what reason, mistress,' Eber had inquired of her after listening to her express these doubts about their visitor, 'would Master Pawley have need to fabricate a story about the deep cut to its foreleg and how his horse came by it?'

'Us'll tell you when us finds out,' Agnes had retorted.

Customer broke in on these thoughts of Eber's.

'Let me borrow Will and I will ride to Bodmin at first light and fetch the deputy bailiff.'

The deputy bailiff of Launceston would have been quicker fetched to the scene of that night's mischief, but that would be too personally risky for Customer Trago. For all he knew, that serpent in sackcloth, Sir William Gennys, had the deputy bailiff of Launceston in his pocket. In any event, the state of the narrow, little-used roadways and tracks from Wynehouse Corner to the town of Launceston some fourteen miles distant, as he knew from his own recent experience of them, would remain treacherously muddy and virtually impassable for several weeks to come yet. Bodmin it must be, if Customer Trago were to be called as a witness to this night's trouble! The highway to Bodmin, which followed the coastline, was in reasonable condition. Weather permitting, and with a good, strong Cornish nag beneath one's seat, the town could be reached in a day.

'Us takes care of our own problems,' said Eber, his face grey and grim.

How? thought Customer. There would be no traditional "sitting" on the Trelawneys' front door-step and fasting against them until they were shamed into making just retribution for what had taken place at the Wynehouse Inn this dark night. What had worked for the Celtic saints and their tribesmen would not work with the Trelawneys! The Trelawneys were clearly barbarians; passed over by the good saints when they brought Christianity and civil law and order to the region. They would as soon slice off your ears and feed them to their pigs as you sat there, starving yourself

46

to a pitiful heap of bones outside their door, as take pity on your condition! Furthermore, this reference to *"us taking care of our own problems"* in relation to *"them"*... Hopefully, a colloquialism and not to be taken literally! Far be it from Customer Trago to be mean-spirited in this affair of the Trelawneys, but they were Eber Pendragon's enemies not his and, by all accounts, made by his own two hands. It may have escaped Eber's attention, but Customer Trago was a gentleman, born and bred, with sword, dagger and signets as proof of it (though, admittedly, not currently in his possession, through no fault of his own!). As such, Customer Trago neither would nor should countenance being drawn into any form of vulgar public alehouse bellowing and brawling, as it would seem was commonly indulged in by Eber Pendragon and the Trelawneys and their ilk. It was the duty of a man of Customer Trago's breeding and position to use his best offices as a mediator. *But only if he must!*

Customer frowned. 'It is none of my business,' he said (and meant it most sincerely), 'but if you will be advised by one who, in all honesty, is naught but an impartial observer of these unfortunate proceedings, you will dispatch me forthwith to summon the deputy bailiff of Bodmin to see for himself the wanton destruction of your property this night and then let him deal with the Trelawneys in accordance with the letter of the law. There is trouble here, Eber, and more of it to come. Do this thing, for pity's sake, before blood is shed.'

Eber didn't reply. He had no intention of being rushed into raising the ire of the Trelawney tribe until he was sure of his facts and had discounted the possibility of a second party being the perpetrator of that night's destruction of his property.

It would be wise, he thought as he turned with Customer from the smoking ruins of the stable, to wait on Agnes's findings on the stranger Pawley. Customer Trago had crossed the threshold of the Wynehouse Inn entirely through unfortunate mischance, but not so Malachy Pawley, according to Agnes, who would not be shaken in her belief that Pawley was a wolf in sheep's clothing. She seemed less sure about his business, so dressed, at the Wynehouse. *"Us'll see,"* she had said when pressed. And maybe, thought Eber, they had. This very night.

Chapter Nine

'Man is born unto trouble, as the sparks fly upward!'

So said Job. Brother Emanuel, too. Frequently.

Emanuel had been generalizing; in such matters he was seldom specific. Customer had no such reservations. To paraphrase both Job and Emanuel, man was indeed born unto trouble: this man, Customer Trago, in particular.

He was dreaming. A strange dream. Muddled. Part Emanuel, part the stranger Pawley.

In his dream, Customer was but an observer, a mist shrouded bystander to a conversation taking place between Emanuel and Pawley. Emanuel was charging Pawley to account for himself and with a small, deferential bow to the old monk, Pawley responded that he was a holy pilgrim from Glendalough, an Irish monastery. Emanuel, in Customer's dream, had been delighted to hear it.

Which was puzzling, bearing in mind that English troops had destroyed that particular monastery in 1398, well over a hundred years ago!

Customer surfaced momentarily from him dream to recall that Emanuel had spoken to him of the desecration he had witnessed while making a personal pilgrimage to the ruins. As a highly respected civil lawyer, Emanuel had been in Ireland at the time on church business for the Holy Father, the Pope.

Customer dreamed on. Time stood perfectly still. Neither Emanuel nor Pawley spoke and then, in that somehow familiar way, as if suddenly conscious that they were being observed, Pawley looked back at Customer over his right, hunched shoulder.

With a sharp gasp, Customer sat up suddenly in bed, his torso supported on one elbow, and watched his troubles multiply before his eyes as he gazed up at Agnes's face which hovered anxiously over him and which, overnight, had acquired a line for each of her forty-nine years and a weariness stretching far beyond them.

'Agnes?' His voice was thick with the deep sleep from which he had been aroused, his mind befuddled by his curious dream about Emanuel and Pawley and an uneasy feeling that had he not been awakened so abruptly, he would have remembered something. Something he had been foolish to forget. Or worse still, did remember but failed to see its significance.

The room was bathed in bright sunlight. The morning was well advanced; he had overslept which he felt went a long way to explaining why he had been dreaming.

'What is the trouble, mistress?' he asked.

It went against the grain, but he had to know. He could not bear to see Agnes looking so tired and time-worn.

His thoughts raced ahead of him. *The stable… Agnes has seen there has been a fire out there during the night and fears that Eber knows nothing of it and will lose all self-control when the news is broken to him and set out with black murder in his heart to avenge the vile deed!*

Agnes replied before Customer had a chance to tell her that Eber was already privy to this latest piece of Trelawney mischief which Customer was still determinedly placing on the head of one particular member of that family.

'Rebecca has not come to the kitchen to wash at the well and sit at table and eat this morning,' she explained.

Agnes was looking hard at him, accusingly, with eyes that said they had seen it all; what had passed between Rebecca and Customer out on the forecourt during the night, the torching of the stable, more than likely by one of Rebecca's kinsmen, and Customer's close brush with death, his windpipe being crushed mercilessly in Eber's huge hands.

Customer chided himself for not realizing that Rebecca's love for him was no secret from Agnes. Agnes had seen where the girl's heart lay; she knew how things stood with Customer Trago, that it was a lost cause.

'She is not with Lady?' he suggested lamely.

Agnes shook her head. 'Nor gone back to her evil tribe, nor been forcibly taken by them, 'tis certain of that.' The unspoken accusation Customer could see in Agnes's eyes was now in her voice. 'You must look further afield than Rebecca's natural home if you genuinely think to find her there, young sir.'

An unkind thrust at him, thought Customer, deeply wounded by the suggestion that he should think that without the love of Customer Trago, Rebecca would sooner face a miserable life with her kinsfolk than a life standing in the protective shadow of Eber Pendragon.

Customer threw back the bedcovers with a sigh. 'She will be at the holy well. I shall go and fetch her to you.'

''Tis best you should, and quickly; before Eber returns and asks why her bowl of *yos kergh* is untouched.'

Customer looked at her despairingly. 'How am I to handle this, Agnes? What am I to say to Rebecca that will not make the hurt worse?'

'You are the one with all the learning and fine manners, young sir: you tell old Agnes how best to mend a poor girl's broken heart.'

'I did not wish for this to happen, mistress,' said Customer with a faint scowl. 'I would sooner die than bring grief and misery to Rebecca.'

Agnes sighed and her face softened a little. 'Us knows it, young sir. It was not a purposeful thing you've done, but Eber might not see it so charitably. Go quickly and bring her to us. Old Agnes cannot heal the pain, but she'll do what she can for the child to ease her suffering.'

'Where is Eber this morning?' Customer asked, puzzled. 'You said, *"when he returns"*. Why isn't he working at his forge?'

'He rode out on Will at first light, south-west along the highway towards the town of Bodmin, to speak with Master Trenwith. There is some business that needs settling between them.'

Customer was pulling on his breeches over one of Eber's long, white cotton nightshirts. He looked at her with a mildly teasing smile. 'What were the stakes this time?'

'Master Trenwith's best pastureland, though old Agnes will thank you, young sir, to keep this between ourselves,' she said, fixing him with a warning eye. 'Eber wants to put it under the plough this spring.'

Customer had been jesting to ease the tension between them: he had not, for one moment, truly thought that Eber's business with this man, Trenwith, had its origins at the gaming tables downstairs one Saturday evening.

'Eber won this land from Trenwith?' he asked in some surprise.

'Can you say how else he would have come by it? Us surely knows how things stand between Eber and his purse.'

Customer considered her for a moment. 'How much of the land

50

hereabouts does Eber own?'

'Everything as far as the eye can see to the south-west: two fields to the west left of the crossroads and right of the crossroads; to the north, as far as the eye can see and beyond, almost to the Celtic cross that marks the holy pilgrims' path to the Holy Well of St James.'

'And the land standing at our backs beyond the Wynehouse Inn and smithy and stretching away due south to meet with land belonging to Launceston Priory? How much there is owned by Eber?'

'None that old Agnes knows of.'

'An oversight, surely!' said Customer in a dry voice.

'No,' said Agnes. 'Samuel Trelawney did not include any land in his wager, though there's plenty of it there for the wagering that he claims as his own. The smithy and blacksmith's cottage and the inn were all that were put up by Samuel Trelawney downstairs that night.'

Customer stared at her, dumbfounded. His ears were playing him tricks. *Trelawney, did Agnes say? Pray God, some offshoot of the Butterfly Lane Trelawneys. Perhaps not even of their tribe...*

She saw his dismay and gave a slow nod. 'Aye, those Trelawneys. Samuel Trelawney is Rebecca's father.'

The blood drained from Customer's face. 'I am surprised they haven't murdered Eber as he sleeps in his bed. Us as well.'

'It was an honest wager: honestly lost, honestly won. Samuel Trelawney has no quarrel with Eber there.'

'Ah, but what of those six sons of whom you spoke? What do they say and feel in this matter?'

'The Trelawneys have land and property enough, some of the best in north Cornwall, most of it along the coastal cliffs both to the north and south-west of Wynehouse Corner. The loss would not have been felt too deeply in their purses.'

How little Agnes knew of rich men and their purses! Though on second thoughts, the Cornish were a shrewd and crafty people and with – so far as Customer had been able to ascertain – the inn and smithy showing little or no sign thus far of being profitable enterprises, it might have suited the Trelawneys to be rid of them and their attendant problems. Eber showed not the slightest interest in the inn and its moneymaking possibilities beyond the convenience it afforded him of providing him with gamesters of a Saturday evening. Travellers along the highway likewise showed little interest in making a night's stopover at the inn, thought the reason there might well be seasonal and have nothing to do with the quality of comfort and good cheer on offer.

Customer sighed heavily.

'Aye,' she said with another slow nod of her head. 'And well you might sigh. Though us'd be a little more sparing with our breath were us you, young sir. If old Agnes knows anything, you'll be needing a deal more of it to fuel your sighs before this sorry day is out.'

His heart sank. Rebecca was not the worst of it. There was more trouble to come, something that had his name, Customer Trago, writ even more largely on it; he could see it in Agnes's eyes.

A stab of annoyance went through him. They didn't trust him, they never would. Why, then, not be done with the irksome matter of the young sir, Customer Trago, once and for all and either finish him off or turn him loose to become a thorn in someone else's side? Or if it better suited their purposes, use that key at Eber's waist and throw him into whatever mysterious hellhole it secured and leave him to rot?

'Speak out, mistress,' he said in a cold voice. 'Say your piece and be done with it.'

'Us has had visitors,' she said bluntly.

He relaxed a little. So that was it! She knew of the visit of a Trelawney in the night – as he had more or less expected she would – and she was berating him for not having mentioned anything of it to her.

'I know, I am sorry, Agnes. I did not wish to trouble you while you slept…'

'The trouble is not mine, young sir. Asleep or awake. 'Tis yours and yours alone, I seek no part of it. They arrived soon after Eber left, Will's hoofbeats had scarce had time to fade into the mists of dawn's early light. And it would be as well that they should leave before he returns. Be quick and fetch Rebecca to us to soothe and pacify as best us can, but first do your business with this odd pair who would speak with you. I'll not betray you to Eber, you have my word on that, young sir, but they must be gone from the Wynehouse before nightfall. You with them. I will make things right with Eber when he returns and finds you gone. 'Tis for the best, young sir.'

He could not agree more with her. Now that he had been found, he must quit this place with all speed. Agnes had not offered any names for the pair who awaited him downstairs, which seemed to suggest that they had not seen fit to introduce themselves. *Too many strangers,* he thought. *First Pawley... And now two more?* That was truly worrying. He should forget about Rebecca, Eber, Agnes, the inn and take flight immediately. From the window of this room, if he had any sense!

Customer called Agnes back as she turned to leave. 'Has the stranger Pawley made any mention either to you or Eber of where he is from?'

'Only of what he is,' Agnes replied. 'A holy pilgrim and where he is bound. The vow of silence he said he has taken forbids him to speak more than is absolutely necessary.'

Very convenient, thought Customer.

'He has never mentioned the monastery at Glendalough in Ireland in what little conversation he has had with you?'

'He is not a Gael, if that is what you wish to hear.' Agnes hesitated, eyeing Customer thoughtfully. 'He speaks much as you speak, young sir. He has had learning, and us would say is of some fine place not so very far distant from wherever it was that you first saw the light of day.'

Launceston Priory?

The possibility made Customer's blood run cold. It was what he feared most of a multiplication of strangers seeking him out.

Agnes eyed him curiously. 'Your visitors, young sir? The woman awaits your pleasure with some impatience. As does old Agnes her swift departure,' she added after a small pause.

Chapter Ten

Customer stared at Agnes. *A woman? Here? Seeking Customer Trago? And in the company of whom?*

'I urge you to speak quickly, Agnes. Who are these people...this odd pair? The look in your eye and tone of voice hint at further trouble afoot.'

She gazed at him for a moment in silence. Then, in a wry voice, she said, 'They, too, call themselves pilgrims; come by way of Launceston Priory. Seems we have a wealth of them of late. One can scarce turn round for risk of falling over them, young sir. The woman seeks news of her old Italian wet nurse, who has since taken holy vows at St Lawrence's in Bodmin, and information concerning the present whereabouts of a very dear friend. They – the woman asking for you by name and the man with her – travel onwards this day to Bodmin after they have taken some rest and a little light refreshment.'

Since when did holy pilgrims come by way of Launceston Priory? This was the Devil's business. Some fresh mischief of Gennys'. Agnes had knowingly given hospitality to spies of the King; had as good as put a fresh sword in Customer Trago's side. *But why?* Agnes was fond of him, of this he was sure, and while she might not trust him, he could never believe that she would deliberately place him in harm's way.

'Their names, Agnes! I fear I do you no injustice when I say you believe me to be this mysterious very dear friend the woman pilgrim seeks.'

'She calls herself the Countess Ballini.'

Wife of Count Ballini? That creaking, old Italian coxcomb? *That* painted fop?

'There is some mistake, Agnes. You have misheard the lady. I know Count Ballini well, though I make no boast of it. A rich man – in fact, a very rich and influential man. A man who should have a wife, but who, alas, is a confirmed bachelor and, at my last hearing of news of him, was as near to his deathbed as to have one foot already firmly rooted in it.' *In company with the young, honey-*

skinned, Ottoman servant boy who will share the aforesaid deathbed and who is undoubtedly already between the bed-sheets warming them for him!

Agnes did not argue with him. 'The man – the woman's servant, us would think – spoke her given birth name once. Anna-Lucrezia, us believes us heard him say. They wait upon you in the public room.'

Agnes did not bat an eyelid as she gave the given name of Customer's beloved. She was patently holding true still to the vow of silence she had made at the time of Anna-Lucrezia's previous visit to see him. And small wonder, if indeed the woman, this Countess Ballini who awaited his attention below, *was* his beloved!

His senses were reeling. Anna-Lucrezia, *a married woman?* Married to a man old enough to be her father; nay, her grandfather? And a sodomite, to boot!

There was something not quite right here. In fact, something very wrong, his every instinct for self-preservation told him so.

'I commend your loyalty, Agnes,' he said with a small frown, 'but I must ask you to break your sworn vow of silence and confirm to me that this lady and the one who visited and comforted me on my sickbed in the dead of night a week or two ago, are one and the same.'

Agnes looked at him levelly for some moments, but she made no reply.

'Your reticence does you credit, Agnes. But please, I beg of you, speak out. Tell me the truth, I beseech you.'

'Us must be strong and see for ourselves,' she said, and turned and left the room without another word.

So it *was* his beloved Anna-Lucrezia. There could be no mistake; the answer he feared was there, cleverly concealed, and without betraying any confidences, in Agnes's reluctance to commit herself either way to answering his entreaty. Something else, as well. He would be the first to admit that he was a vain man, but of this he was certain and with vanity playing no part in it: Agnes was jealous.

He followed her downstairs with a heavy heart.

The Countess Anna-Lucrezia Ballini rose as he entered the public room. She had been sitting, pale-cheeked, by the heavily smoking open fire, every bit as beautiful and graceful as he remembered. She approached him unhurriedly, with her right hand outstretched limply for him to take it in his and raise it to his lips.

The man with her – tall and slim, every bit as beautiful and graceful as his female companion, dark-haired, and somewhere in his late twenties, Customer noted – rose from his seat near the window, and bowing graciously to them both in turn, left the room silently.

Customer opened his mouth to speak, but Anna-Lucrezia placed a forefinger gently across his lips and said, 'Hush, my love. Let us not spoil this precious moment with words.'

A reference, he was sure, to their last passion-filled meeting when conversation of any description had been the last thing on their minds. He wondered for a moment if he were expected to sweep her up into his arms and carry her aloft to his room for more of the same; if this accounted for the discreet departure of her male travelling companion.

He continued to ponder over these uncertainties as they gazed into one another's eyes. 'Shall we, my beloved?' he said at length, lifting his eyes meaningfully to the ceiling.

She delicately withdrew her hand from his. 'There is so little time, my beloved,' she said. She went not to the doorway, preparatory to climbing the stairs to his room, as he expected and fervently desired, but to one of the windows which overlooked the forecourt. 'I must make haste and seek sanctuary at the old lazar house of St Lawrence in Bodmin before my father catches up with me and forces my return with him to the Palazzo Ballini in Italy where I have been kept a virtual prisoner these past six months.'

Customer swallowed hard over the sudden seizure that had gripped his throat. Make no mistake about it, this was a small army of bounty hunters his beloved was referring to, not just her father. Heavily armed men sworn – for an agreed price – to return an errant wife to her lawfully-wedded husband.

'I do not understand,' he said. 'How did this unfortunate marriage between you and Ballini come about?' There was no point in mincing words. How else could such a hellish union be described?

She sighed deeply. 'My poor father fell upon difficult times. His enemies accused him of treachery and he – we,' she murmured, lowering her gaze unhappily, 'lost everything in his fight to clear

56

his name. An arranged marriage of convenience between us – Ballini and me – was our only, our last hope.' She looked pained. 'Please, I beseech you; take that look from your face, my beloved. My poor father and I were desperate; we needed money, to be restored to our rightful place in society. Ballini's needs were simpler. He had all these things...' She lowered her long, pale eyelashes coquettishly and flushed a little. 'Except an heir. And time, as well you know, is no longer on my husband's side. I confess I could have been happy enough if there had been a child, someone on whom I could lavish all my love and affection, the love and affection I have for you...' Her voice tailed off wistfully.

'And what has gone awry here in your desire for a child who would bask in all this love and affection that should be mine and is being denied me?' asked Customer with a small scowl.

'Your voice grows cold, my beloved,' she reproached him. 'Hear me out and then be my judge. The answer is simple enough where my marriage to Ballini is concerned.' She lowered her gaze demurely. 'Our union has yet to be consummated. I am yours to have and to hold, my beloved; body and soul, now and forevermore. No other man shall have me. We will be one: I made this solemn vow to myself when first our eyes met that afternoon as I walked in the beautiful gardens of the home of the Provost of Penryn.'

Indeed? Their heaving, burning flesh having already melded into one not so very long ago – the more intimate particulars of which, unfortunately, he now had only the sketchiest of recollection due to his wretchedly high fever at the time – made her passionate wantonness (what he could recollect of it) all the more remarkable. The woman who had made love to him that night was fully experienced, and – dare he say it? – had rape foremost on her mind!

A tiny doubt niggled at him. He had been as close to death that night as he had ever come and quite possibly, his fevered imagination had merely been kind to him and provided him with those brief moments of sublime ecstasy with his beloved that, in reality, were far more restrained and more in keeping with her nature which was, beyond question, that of a true gentlewoman.

He spoke his thoughts out loud. 'Forgive me, my beloved. Seeing you again after all this time has scattered my senses. Ask what you will of me; I am your slave to do your sweet bidding. I will ride with you to St Lawrence's and ensure your safety in that holy place.'

'I place a greater burden on your brave, strong shoulders, my beloved, should you truly wish to ensure my safety. My loyal servant, Alfonso, has been charged by those who wish only for my happiness, with seeing me delivered safely into old Sophia's hands…'

Alfonso? The libertine with all the pretty manners lurking bat-eared in the passage beyond yonder closed doorway, as like as not missing never a single word?

'I ask only this one thing of you–' she continued. 'So that we might be forever together, my beloved. As one,' she added. 'Body and soul.'

Customer's heart stood still. She was going to ask him to mediate with her arrogant, bull-headed father and his mercenaries, to be her advocate and plead her case with His Holiness the Pope for an annulment of her grotesque marriage to Ballini; he could see it in her eyes.

She casually took from the folds of the skirt of her royal blue velvet gown, a soft, suede leather drawstring purse and held it out to him. 'My husband, Ballini, has always been much taken with your gentlemanly ways and exceptionally fine good looks, my beloved. He has spoken kindly to me of you often, how much he admires you and laments your loss of Royal privilege and position here in your homeland. There will be no lack of welcome for you in his private chambers. He presently visits with an old friend, Lord Molton, at Molton Hall near Glastonbury where you can be assured of receiving a warm reception, not only from my husband, but from Lord Molton himself, with whom I believe you are acquainted. It was there that word reached us of your present whereabouts. We have all been most distressed to learn of your recent misfortune while travelling to Launceston Priory seeking news of your old tutor, Brother Emanuel. The new prior has himself spoken of you in the warmest of terms.'

Customer felt the blood draining from his face. So all was known. Customer Trago could be picked off at any time convenient to Gennys and his wild bunch. But that was the least of his worries. Could it really be true that his beloved was actually asking him to sacrifice himself, *his body*, to that vile debaucher of noble but impoverished young manhood, Ballini, on her account? Was he to be the price that must be paid for her freedom from her wretched marriage?

As for Molton, Customer had met him, but only casually and with no thought or desire to further the acquaintanceship. Molton was by far the superior sodomite. Ask any young man of good breeding and fine physique!

The countess had hesitated. 'You grow pale, my beloved. But listen carefully to me: you are young and strong, full of vigour, an accomplished swordsman; Ballini is old and feeble and can barely hold his knife and fork at table let alone a dagger or a sword. It is no lie that he is not long for this world, but I grow impatient and anxious and – you will forgive my boldness! – can wait but a short time longer for the consummation of our love for one another, with no shame attached. This purse will cover all of your expenses and more. Alfonso and I will await you at Bodmin. Go quickly...'

The door opened unexpectedly and with some force, startling them. Agnes stood on the threshold with Rebecca's bowl of untouched porridge in one hand and with an unmistakable look of displeasure on her face.

As Customer turned to face Agnes, Anna-Lucrezia pressed the purse quickly into one of his hands and then squeezed his fingers so that they closed tightly around it.

Agnes did not speak.

'I – I was just leaving, Agnes,' he stammered guiltily. 'I'll take the chestnut mare and be back with Rebecca within the half-hour.'

He looked hesitant. Then, with a quick glance at Anna-Lucrezia, he said, 'Try not to worry.' He wondered bemusedly to whom he was really speaking. Was it to the woman who, unless he had completely mistaken her intentions, had just hired him to prostitute himself to her husband as a prelude to his assassinating him? Was it to Agnes that he was doling out this advice? Or was it to that perennial coward, Customer Trago himself?

'Rebecca will be at the holy well, I know it,' he added, smiling weakly at Agnes. 'Leave everything to me. I will find her and bring her to you.'

Chapter Eleven

The promise was broken before it was made.

Rebecca was already found. Welsh pilgrims to the Holy Well of St James came upon her sprawled out in front of the well, head face down in it, and with her long hair streaming out across the surface of the crystal clear spring water like tangled black pondweed.

They thought at first that there was some special reason for this strange position she had taken up before the well; that this was some form of religious obeisance unfamiliar to them, and then finally, that she was bathing her face in the holy spring water in a symbolic gesture of washing away the sins of her body and soul.

Minutes passed as they waited in polite pious silence, and with folded hands and heads bowed, for her to complete her devotions and rise and acknowledge their arrival, which had been far from silent for they had been arguing heatedly among themselves over their exact whereabouts a mere second or two before discovering the granite pilgrim's step set into the ridge.

At length, one of their number became suspicious, anxious, and stepped forward and touched Rebecca lightly on the back of her neck where her hair had parted and floated away from the sides of her head.

The morbid chill of her flesh told its own story. She was dead.

'Drowned…poor, sweet child,' sighed Genefer, one of the three women in the pilgrimage, as the two men with them carefully raised Rebecca from the well and laid her gently on her back on the bracken and black heather where, weeks earlier, she had found Customer Trago.

Without exception, the sight of the crushed side of Rebecca's face made the holy pilgrims recoil from her and momentarily suck in their breaths in shock.

'She thought to wash the Devil's mark from her face and was overcome by the freezing chill of the spring water in the holy well and fell into a faint,' said Bridget, another of the female pilgrims.

'She might have been on a fast and at the peak of her emotion, became dizzy with weakness,' said the third female pilgrim,

Gwyneth, nodding her abnormally large head so hard that her plump, dark red cheeks wobbled.

'Those strange marks showing on the fragile flesh covering her neck and throat…' said one of the male pilgrims, frowning down at the girl. 'How came the child by those?'

Everybody considered for a moment, and then Gwyneth of the plump cheeks nodded her head and said, 'Her neck scraped against some large pebbles in the well as she fell forward into it.'

'I see no pebbles in the well,' said the male pilgrim, peering into its shallow depths, 'large or small, to cause such cruel black bruising to her pale flesh.'

'Nor I,' said the other male pilgrim, looking up with the rest of his company as one of their horses, which grazed on the ridge, lifted its head and snorted a warning that someone, a rider, approached from the south-west across the rolling grassland.

Before dismounting, Customer paused on top of the ridge to gaze into the upturned, questioning faces of the holy pilgrims.

They drew back silently from the well, widening their semicircle around Rebecca's body so that the new arrival could see it clearly.

'Do you know this poor child, sir?' asked Genefer as Customer stepped down from the ridge and joined them.

Ashen-faced, Customer knelt at Rebecca's side and then gently picked the strands of wet hair from her deathly grey cheeks and blue-tinged lips. 'This is Rebecca,' he said in a strained voice. 'From the inn at Wynehouse Corner. She comes here each morning to pray at the holy well.'

'We know of the Wynehouse,' said Gwyneth, 'and have heard speak of the innkeeper, Master Pendragon.' She looked down pityingly at Rebecca. 'She must have been overcome with emotion and in an excitement of religious passion, fell into the well and drowned, poor child.'

But not by accident, thought Customer, gazing at Rebecca wretchedly. The well was too shallow for that. No, this was suicide. Plain and simple. Rather than face life without having her love for that worthless popinjay, Customer Trago, returned in kind, Rebecca had taken her life, ended it here at the Holy Well of St James where she had found him. He would confess all to Eber; tell him how things had stood between Customer Trago and Rebecca Trelawney, with no tampering of the true facts and no contriving to

61

make this pitiful tragedy anything other than what it was. He, Customer Trago, had the blood of this poor young maiden on his hands, and he would face the consequences, fearful as they may be. Eber could choke the life out of him for this terrible thing he had brought to pass this morning, and welcome. In truth, it would be a blessing to one with half his troubles, Customer thought morosely. There was the black-hearted Gennys and his murderous lot at his back, ahead of him, his beloved, the desirably lovely Countess Ballini and her handsome servant, Alfonso (both of whom – or so Customer imagined – were, at this very moment, making their way to Bodmin with all speed to await impatiently news of the tragically sudden, but not so unexpected death of the head of the House of Ballini). On his right flank, Anna-Lucrezia's implacable father and his paid army of cutthroats, as like as not closing in on him by the second. Anna-Lucrezia had found him easily enough, hadn't she? And so would her father. (Courtesy, no doubt, of the prior's clerk whom it would be reasonable to expect was in league with Gennys, and who would therefore have had no hesitation in planting the feet of either one of them, daughter and father, squarely on the trail that would lead them straight from Launceston Priory to Customer Trago!)

His unconditional love for Anna-Lucrezia hadn't quite clouded his vision of how things were going to stand between her father and himself. A blind man could see that he was going to be cast as the villain of the piece in this little imbroglio, and that he would be dealt with accordingly, swiftly and severely. He trusted his dear beloved with his life, not for one moment would he suspect her intentions: it was the one with the stylish manners and the dark, shifty eye who accompanied her whose motives he would call into question. Customer would even go so far as to say that the shifty-eyed one had some evil hold over her and her family which she had been unable to confess to him, and that this terrible deed which he, Customer Trago, had been charged with of murdering her husband in cold blood had therefore been made under extreme duress.

As yet, nobody loomed large on Customer's left flank – at least, not so far as he was aware – but he had every confidence that the fates would conspire against him once again and all in good time, conjure up something of suitable fearsomeness there to keep him awake at night. Then again, a space should be reserved somewhere in all of this ghastly tangle for his kind, but quick-tempered benefactor, Eber Pendragon, who, sometime later in the day, would return from his visit with Trenwith – one would imagine in a reasonably congenial frame of mind – only to be greeted by Agnes with as sorry a tale of woe as Eber was ever likely to hear. Eber was not going to bow his head meekly and offer up a prayer for the dead. Eber would let out a mighty roar and immediately set to and seek vengeance for Rebecca's death, and woe betide the man or woman who advocated temperance and stood in his way.

Customer heaved a sigh, quickly gathering his troubled thoughts when one of the male pilgrims broke the long silence of the small company gathered beside Rebecca' s body, to ask, 'Can you think, sir, how this poor, disfigured child came by those cruel marks on her throat?'

Customer gazed at them and his heart was seized by a fresh spasm of pain. All too clearly he saw strong hands clasped mercilessly around Rebecca's throat, crushing her delicate windpipe as she struggled with her murderer and then fell, or was cast aside, into the well.

'Eber Pendragon did this evil thing,' said a thin, sharp voice. 'Show me the man who says otherwise and let there be no surprise on the face of any one of you here present when I call him a barefaced liar!'

Chapter Twelve

Customer looked up quickly at the speaker, a man somewhere near his own age, who was standing on the ridge, hands on hips and with legs spread wide apart. The fierce scowl on his face, his swaggering stance and the manner of his speaking were somehow triumphant. His yellow eyes glittered with unconcealed malice.

There was little doubt in Customer's mind that this was Lowarn Trelawney. The man's long, narrow face was that of a fox, and standing downwind of him, as was Customer now, he had the strong odour of one about him. His hair was dark like Rebecca's, but auburn, not black. He wore a wispy, pointed beard on his chin and a thin, drooping moustache. His body was lean and lithe like that of the fox; the hand that had moved from his right hip and now rested menacingly on the dagger at his side, was long and sinewy.

Lowarn Trelawney stepped down from the ridge, pushed the silent holy pilgrims roughly aside and then looked down at his sister. He reached down as if to raise her skirts, and automatically – and with, uncharacteristically, no thought of the consequences to himself – Customer stayed Lowarn's hand and held it fast.

Lowarn scowled at him.

'This be my little sister, sir: I have the right to know if Eber Pendragon has violated this sweet, innocent young girl's body in addition to crushing the life from it with his bare hands as those bruisings to her throat surely attest.'

'This is deputy bailiff's business, sir,' said Customer in a firm voice.

'Us has our own means of settling things,' snarled Lowarn, wresting his hand free of Customer's grip. 'Outlanders like you had best beware of meddling in affairs that are of no concern to them. Unless, of course, I have completely misread the signs here, my fine feathered young sir, and your interest in this sorry affair concerns you and you alone and I do Eber Pendragon a terrible injustice.'

Customer's mind worked quickly. He was caught between a rock and a hard place. Launceston and Bodmin. Less than an hour ago, he would have had no hesitation in naming the former as the less attractive proposition: the Countess Ballini's visit, however, had changed everything. Each of those towns could now boast a share of real danger attached to them for Customer Trago.

It was a terrible gamble for one such as he who normally recognized trouble and walked round it in an ever-widening circle, but he had to take a chance that Lowarn Trelawney's mental agility was neither that of the fox nor that of Customer Trago.

He looked at Lowarn boldly, praying inwardly for the strength to carry through the artifice he was about to practice. 'What matters first and foremost, must be this, sir. Rebecca's body must be borne forthwith to the inn at Wynehouse Corner. Someone – an independent party showing no bias one way or another – must be instructed to ride thence to Launceston to fetch the deputy bailiff to look into this matter.'

'Who are you, sir, to dare to speak so bluntly to a Trelawney?' demanded Lowarn, a dangerous look in his eye.

'I, sir, am Customer Trago, a traveller from foreign lands who has taken lodging with old Agnes at the Wynehouse Inn up yonder. And I warn you, sir, that I know something of the King's Law with which you would seek to tamper. You say Eber Pendragon has done this wicked thing; I say he has not: you suggest that the blame for this heinous crime lies with me, and I say it does not. I therefore hereby advise you, sir, that I shall defend both Eber Pendragon's and my own right to a fair hearing – to the death if needs be.'

Lowarn's yellow eyes had narrowed with suspicion. 'You have friends in Launceston, sir?'

'It has been some years since I last passed through that town and was made welcome at Launceston Priory, but yes,' Customer admitted coolly, 'I am on close friendly terms with several of the town's prominent citizens, including the good holy prior of Launceston Priory and his clerk. Perhaps, should you have a mind to ask that I name several of these worthy souls in support of my bona fides, they will not be unfamiliar to you.' It was true enough that the old prior, Prior Baker, and Customer – through Customer's close association with Emanuel – were no strangers to one another, but a barefaced lie that John Shere, the new prior, and Customer were acquainted. Furthermore, his acquaintanceship with the new prior's clerk could not be measured beyond a briefly formal exchange of correspondence.

Customer acknowledged to himself that it was a huge gamble to bandy words such as these with Lowarn Trelawney, but bearing in mind his determination to keep as much distance between Launceston Priory and Launceston town's citizenry and himself as possible, he considered it a risk worth taking. For the present, anyway.

Lowarn's eyes narrowed further as he contemplated the endless possibilities of a corruption of the law by this self-composed young stranger standing before him and his allegedly well-placed friends in Launceston, and whether or not it was naught but bluff, and then he said, 'If a deputy bailiff is to be summoned, then let it be the one from the town of Bodmin where there can be no suggestion of any taint of collusion between the officers of the law and one of the witnesses at the scene of this heinous crime, if not its perpetrator.'

'I shall take no offence at your remarks, sir, for I know the shock of this terrible sight has placed you under some considerable emotional strain and scattered your senses, but am I not right in thinking that Wynehouse Corner would come under the jurisdiction of the deputy bailiff of Launceston?' Customer inquired ingenuously. He knew he was pushing his luck to a dangerous degree here, but it was imperative that Lowarn Trelawney's suspicions about him were not aroused by his being won over too easily on this Launceston versus Bodmin issue.

'My foully murdered sister's true home lies with her loving family on the other side of the highway, to the far south-west of this place, and stands well within the jurisdiction of the deputy bailiff of Bodmin. I agree to your demand that a deputy bailiff should be fetched to look into this sordid affair, but it is the Trelawney family's duty, by reason of domicile, to send for the deputy bailiff of Bodmin whenever the need arises.'

Lowarn's right hand was on the hilt of the dagger at his side, but he left it sheathed. *But for how long?* wondered Customer, relieved that Lowarn lacked the wit to see that he was being led by his sharp nose in the direction of Bodmin, but nevertheless conscious of the fact that their contretemps could suddenly take a turn for the worse and end in bloodshed. Customer had met his like often enough and was not deceived. Lowarn Trelawney's gentlemanly posturing and speechification were thinly veneered onto the coarse flesh of an uncouth, ill-mannered ruffian!

'You say you are this poor girl's brother…' Customer began. 'If this be so, sir – and having heard gossip at the Wynehouse Inn of the bad blood that flows thick and fast between this girl and her kinsfolk – you would perhaps be kind enough to tell this honest company gathered here before you, what business brings you to the Holy Well of St James this bitterly cold March morning.'

'My sole business at the holy well this day is my sister, Rebecca, who lies foully murdered at my feet,' replied Lowarn. 'I came to fetch her home to her poor, dear mother who lies dying on her bed of pain and cries out mournfully for her.'

'You admit, sir,' said Customer, 'that you know your sister comes each morning to the Holy Well of St James to pray?'

'I know nothing of what my sister does, whose company she keeps, or where and how she spends her free time since she was abducted from the bosom of her loving home by Eber Pendragon and then brutally forced into employment at his inn as a common serving wench. 'Tis old Agnes at the Wynehouse who sent me forth to fetch my sister back home to comfort her poor mother on her deathbed.'

'I know Agnes, sir,' said Customer indignantly. 'She would do no such thing, not while her master is away from the inn all day on business!'

'Agnes told me of you, Customer Trago; that she had sent you to fetch Rebecca back to the inn for her morning meal,' confessed Lowarn with a sneer. 'Agnes was confident that you would mediate between us – Rebecca and me – and decide what should be done about her returning home with me to kiss her poor, dying mother a last fond farewell. I came here with all good intentions, sir, and would have abided by your decision in this matter.'

'Do not dig yourself into a deeper pit with more lies, sir!' snapped Customer. 'The one in which you stand is quite deep enough.'

There was a small smile on Lowarn's cruel mouth. 'Then let us, one and all, go and ask old Agnes of the Wynehouse Inn for the truth of the matter from her own lips.'

The holy pilgrims were nodding their heads and agreeing among themselves in subdued mutterings that this was a reasonable enough suggestion. As one, they looked at Customer and waited to hear what he would say to it.

'I cannot argue with that, sir,' said Customer.

Lowarn nodded. 'Then, as you have already suggested, sir, we will take Rebecca with us to the inn, to await the arrival of the deputy bailiff of Bodmin.'

Customer hesitated. He would really have preferred to leave Rebecca's body where it lay for the deputy bailiff and his men to see, but he could not bring himself to trust the Trelawneys not to meddle with the scene of the crime to Eber's – not to mention his own – certain disadvantage once his, Customer's, and the holy pilgrims' backs were turned.

He looked questioningly at the pilgrims. 'How was it exactly that you found this poor girl?'

Genefer replied. 'She was lying forward with her face submerged in the holy spring water, sir. Thomas and Feock here–' she indicated to the men standing on either side of her '–took pity on her condition and raised her up and laid her on the heather. It was then that we observed those cruel marks on her throat.'

Customer cast an eye about him. The slippery mud beneath their feet had all the appearances of having recently been passed over by a herd of stampeding bullocks. He could see nothing there, nor anything about the bare trees and dead stumps in the marshy hollow, that he could bring to the deputy bailiff's attention in the furtherance of clearing Eber and himself of all blame for this brutal crime.

There being no argument forthcoming from Customer, Lowarn stepped astride his sister's body and stooped to scoop her up in his arms. He took both of her upper arms in his hands, raising them up out of the heather in which they had lain half-concealed. He hesitated, frowning. 'What is it that my sister holds there in her pale hand?' he asked abruptly. He dropped her arms and prised open her right hand which was clenched in a tight fist.

Everybody craned forward to see what he took from it.

He looked at Customer with flashing eyes and then triumphantly held aloft a long, narrow strip of brown, burnished leather for all to see.

'What say you to this, sir?' he asked Customer. 'Is this not the proof I hold here of the fiend who choked the life out of my poor, dear, dead sister? Does this not point directly to the one whose cruel hands viciously inflicted those pitiful bruises all but a very few could but fail to see marking her throat? Do I not hear you say this is one of the ties from a leather apron such as that worn by the master blacksmith, Eber Pendragon, who works at his blazing hot forge at Wynehouse Corner each and every day?'

Customer remained silent. There was no denying that the strip of leather in Lowarn's hand came, in all probability, from the type of apron to which he referred.

Lowarn swept a challenging gaze over the assembled company. 'You are my witnesses to this terrible thing I hold in my hand which my sweet, loving little sister, as the last breath was squeezed from her gentle body, tore from about the waist of her vile murderer.'

Customer saw in the defiant gleam in Lowarn's eyes, the whole terrible truth. The strip of leather Lowarn had taken from Rebecca's hand, the tie that would later be discovered to be missing from Eber Pendragon's brown leather smith's apron, had been deliberately placed there by someone – Lowarn Trelawney, or one of his wretched tribe – prior to the holy pilgrims having discovered her body.

Customer maintained a steady, blank countenance despite the turmoil of his mind. If Lowarn Trelawney guessed for one moment what was going through his head – that he, Customer Trago, knew him to be a liar and almost certainly, a murderer – he and the holy pilgrims would more than likely never leave that place alive.

Customer nodded. He spoke soberly. 'I'll not argue with you there, sir. It is as you have said: you hold the proof of this terrible deed in your own hand.'

Chapter Thirteen

A posse comitatus, not of deputy bailiff's men, but made up of black-bearded Trelawneys and their hatchet-faced servants awaited them on the forecourt of the Wynehouse Inn.

Customer's heart lurched sickeningly in his breast when he caught sight of their longbows and swords. He and the holy pilgrims would either be cut down from their mounts and not live to see the sun set on this dark and unhappy day, or they would be kidnapped, held prisoner by the Trelawneys until Eber Pendragon's body was swinging aloft from a hangman's rope. The Trelawneys would then seize Eber's lands and property and declare them their own.

Who was to stop them? Who was to say they had no legal right to anything of Eber's? There were no deeds of title held for safekeeping by the respective holy priors of either Launceston or Bodmin relating to land hereabouts. A man's unalienable right to his land was by word of mouth, *his* word, *his* verbal delineation of the boundaries of his property, without benefit of support of any legal document. If a man held a piece of official-looking parchment to back up his claim to a parcel of land, it was in all probability drawn up in his own hand and likewise in his own hand, smoked over candle-flame to give it an aged and therefore genuine appearance. Kidnapping to settle such disputes, was not uncommon. The disputants might hold a man's wife and his sons and daughters and servants until he saw reason and gave up all right to the disputed territory (or the territory the kidnappers had decided to annexe to their own). Murder was not uncommon...

The thought struck fresh terror into Customer's heart. *Agnes!* If they had harmed a hair of her head, by all that was holy he would–

She came hurrying out of the inn as she heard their approach, clasping her hands to her bosom and letting out a thin wail of distress when she saw Rebecca's lifeless body cradled in Lowarn Trelawney's arms.

The riders dismounted and the waiting Trelawney posse followed suit. The beating wings of a flock of starlings sighed in sorrowing concert as they flew across the forecourt to the meadows beyond the inn where they would spend the day feeding before rising, at four o'clock in the afternoon, like a black cloud across the sun, and then returning to the forests to the south of Wynehouse Corner where they roosted for the night. No other sound disturbed the chill morning air. Everybody stood in silence and waited. Lowarn held Rebecca's body aloft like a signal (a call, Customer fully expected, for his kin to take up arms and mount the attack); and then, wordlessly, Lowarn turned aside and carried her into the inn. The Trelawneys, and the men who rode with them, followed him. After them came the holy pilgrims and then Agnes and Customer. Rebecca's body was laid out on one of the tables in the public room.

The biggest of the Trelawneys, a man of similar breadth to Eber Pendragon but standing some six inches shorter than he – Samuel Trelawney, Customer guessed from the strands of grey streaking the man's heavy black beard – stepped up to the table and gazed down at Rebecca.

He was silent for a moment and then he pointed to the marks on her throat. 'I see the thumbprints of the beast's hand that made those cruel stains on my sweet, innocent child's throat,' he growled. 'This is the work of Eber Pendragon, blacksmith of Wynehouse Corner.'

There was no shock or horror in his voice; it was a bald statement of the facts as he wished to present them and, if Customer might be permitted to say so, delivered by a very poor stage actor who had rehearsed his lines thoroughly beforehand, never faltering once, but lacking the true professional actor's ability to put them across with any real conviction. Customer had never seen such a pathetic attempt at fastening an accusation of murder on an innocent individual.

'I have seen all that I need to see: we will settle this here and now,' said Samuel Trelawney, and one of his sons turned, unbidden, and went upstairs. To keep watch for Eber Pendragon and give the shout when he rode into view along the highway, Customer guessed with a pounding heart. If, in the next few minutes, he didn't think and act quickly, there would be a hanging on the forecourt of the Wynehouse Inn this coming night.

The holy pilgrim Feock suddenly spoke out (and Customer

blessed his brave soul). 'It has been agreed among us, sir, that despite the damning evidence that points the finger unwaveringly at the perpetrator of this evil deed, the deputy bailiff of Bodmin should be entreated to look into this tragic affair and give his opinion of it.'

Samuel Trelawney looked at Lowarn. 'Is this the truth?' he barked. 'Have you given your word in this matter?'

'I gave them my word,' said Lowarn, and a look Customer saw but couldn't read passed between father and eldest son.

'So be it,' said Samuel Trelawney, his dark eyes passing menacingly over the assembled company. 'We will cool the heat of our emotions at this outrage against us and put away our hanging rope, and when the blacksmith, Eber Pendragon, returns – *if* he returns – we will ride with him to Bodmin bearing my sweet, innocent child's body as proof of his crime for all of its townspeople and the deputy bailiff to see.'

Bodmin where, thought Customer grimly, *the Trelawneys would find no less than two thousand good and upright souls to bear witness to Samuel Trelawney's claim that the lands of Eber Pendragron, and all that stands upon them, are forfeit to the Trelawneys in retribution for this evil deed of murder committed on one of their tribe.*

This consideration aside, Customer agreed with the decision, but kept a silent counsel. Eber stood a far better chance of justice being served properly if he went willingly and quietly with the Trelawneys to the town of Bodmin to face the charges laid against him. Provided, of course, it was the Trelawneys' intention to permit him to reach his journey's end, which Customer had to admit was far from certain.

Samuel Trelawney turned to Agnes. 'When do you expect your master to return, mistress?'

'Not until dusk this evening, sir,' said Agnes with a small, deferential bob of her head.

'And what is so important abroad that it keeps Eber Pendragon from his hot forge this day?' asked Samuel Trelawney.

'Us does not know, sir,' said Agnes, avoiding eye contact with Customer lest the glance that passed between them should betray the lie. 'He did not state his business, nor where that business would take him: he said only when old Agnes should expect his return.'

'We will wait,' said Samuel Trelawney.

'*All* of us, sir?' asked the holy pilgrim Bridget with a protest in her voice. 'My companions and I are expected in Boscastle this noon by friends of the Church of St James in that ancient settlement who will surely fret and send out riders in search of us should we fail to arrive before nightfall.'

'Be thankful, mistress pilgrim,' said Samuel Trelawney, scowling at her darkly, 'to have something far more worthy to distract your bony knees and keep them in a straightened position for a change!'

Agnes quickly intervened. 'Please take your rest here at the inn, good holy pilgrims. I shall fetch food and wine to help bide the time until my master returns.'

Customer followed Agnes quickly out to the kitchen. 'The countess–' he hissed. 'What has become of her and her travelling companion?'

'Very little, us would think, that you need concern yourself with, young sir. She left word for you to join her in Bodmin with the joyful tidings that she knows you will soon have for her.'

Agnes began ladling mutton stew into pewter bowls from the large black pot that simmered on an open fire. 'Have a care, young sir,' she went on, avoiding his gaze as she placed the bowls of steaming hot food and spoons to sup it with on a tray on the table. 'They play you for the fool. No good will come of this. None that can be attached to the name of Customer Trago.'

'They, Agnes? The Trelawneys?'

'Us thinks you know who us means, young sir. Us'll thank you not to play old Agnes for a fool.' She picked up the tray, ready to carry it through to the pilgrims. 'Shame on you, young sir, for if it is your wish to be the cuckold, old Agnes fears you are too late.'

Customer's eyes blazed with anger. 'Silence! I'll hear no more of this. Shame on *you*, Agnes!'

She swept angrily from the room with the food for the pilgrims, returning a few moments later to fill a large pewter urn with wine.

'It is a puzzle to old Agnes,' she said, looking up at Customer with a scowl, 'how a fine young sir such as yourself, who keeps a constant watchful eye at every turn and who sees treachery and wrongdoing where none lies, cannot recognize the one real threat to his life when it is thrust stinking under his nose.'

'You go too far, Agnes,' he said, glaring at her angrily as she walked to the door with the wine. 'You know nothing of me and my enemies.'

'Us knows everything us ever needs to know, young sir; *and* about you and that pretty pair who would use you for their own sinful ends.' She stood in the doorway, cradling the urn in her arms. 'You will not find your enemies in the past, as you choose to believe, Customer Trago; you have the intelligence and the word of Eber Pendragon on that. Trust old Agnes when she says that you must look much farther to the south-west than Launceston Priory and into the future for treachery and wrongdoing that are as newborn as this day once was. Heed old Agnes's words and turn aside from the wife-whore who beguiles and bewitches you with her silver tongue and fancy, ladylike ways before it is too late.'

'I can only think it is jealousy and envy that prompts these unkind words from your lips, mistress,' Customer growled. 'And on those grounds, I excuse you for them. But I will hear no more from you on this matter. Go about your business and be silent. And I would caution you, mistress,' he added, pointing a warning finger at her, 'to watch that inquisitive ear of yours or the day will come when the words you take such pains to overhear are solely in relation to you yourself and are not to your liking.'

She looked at him. God forgive her for the wickedness of her body, its sinful yearnings that make her think and sometimes lose her senses and do wantonly depraved things of which later she had little recollection, but could the young sir not see why she had spoken out as she had? Could he not guess that she loved him desperately, that the temptation to save him from himself and arrange for that evil woman, with all her sweet-talk and bag of fool's gold, to be dispatched forthwith, along with her simpering lapdog, back to their Maker, had all but torn her asunder? It need not be like this, not now, with Rebecca gone. Dear God in Heaven, could the young sir not find it in his heart to love old Agnes just a little bit?

Finished with the Welsh pilgrims, Agnes went upstairs to Pawley's room and knocked lightly on the door. When there was no response, she opened it cautiously, no more than was sufficient for her to see if the room were occupied. Pawley was on his knees, with his back turned to her, for once rigidly square and straight, and with his gaze fixed on the wooden crucifix standing on the window ledge. She had intended to suggest to him that it would be wise if he were to remain in his room until the company presently occupying the public room downstairs had quit the premises, but as he made no move to acknowledge her presence, she suspected that he was in the grips of a religious fervour that more than likely entailed a certain sexual element and she left him to it.

Agnes did not see the hand that, at her knock, had moved swiftly to the sheathed dagger at his waist. Nor that as she quietly closed the door and then, a few moments later, clomped heavily back down the stairs, Pawley rose swiftly to his feet and then stepped up to the window and looked out across the forecourt.

Waiting, as was everyone else, for Eber Pendragon's return to the inn.

Chapter Fourteen

It was a long day, a wake held not so much for the dead girl lying on a table in the middle of the public room of the Wynehouse Inn, but for the man who would ride with his back to the setting sun and, at its close, be seized by the Trelawneys and hanged for a crime that Customer firmly believed he had not committed.

Customer had attended only one true wake in his lifetime, at Launceston Priory when one of the canons choked to death on his tongue after having been stung repeatedly on his lips, tongue and at the back of his throat by a swarm of bees, and but for Emanuel's sharp elbow in his ribs, Customer would have dozed throughout it. There was, however, no problem with drowsiness this day. Customer had never felt so keenly alert to every sound, every movement, in his entire life. Nor had he ever felt so utterly helpless. He deeply mistrusted Samuel Trelawney's given word. As dusk had approached, one of the Trelawneys' servants had stationed himself behind the door of the inn with a thick rope in his hands. For certain, a noose would be slipped over Eber's head as he crossed the threshold and that would be the end of him.

There was no doubt in Customer's mind that Eber would pause at the inn after stabling Will in the shippen. He would recognize the horses standing out on the forecourt and know that the Trelawneys waited within; and Eber, being Eber, would throw caution to the wind, act without thinking, and come charging through the front door like an enraged bullock.

Customer closed his eyes and prayed that when he opened them in a moment or two, he would be upstairs in his room, gripped with fever still and with Agnes bending anxiously over him, mopping his brow, and Eber waiting on one side with a bowl of steaming hot nettle broth.

Surely this terrible day was a fever-induced nightmare and nothing more!

Chapter Fifteen

It began to drizzle in a hazy, depressing mist that matched the mood of the day when, shortly before five o'clock, the shout went up. Eber Pendragon was riding towards the inn in the fast gathering shadows of evening.

The atmosphere in the public room was tense. Everybody – the Trelawneys and their servants, Agnes, Customer and the holy pilgrims alike – became alert, straining their ears for the sound of hoofbeats close at hand.

Customer glanced anxiously at the man standing guard at the door and then, turning to Samuel Trelawney, he said, 'I do not much care for the look of this, sir. If harm comes to Eber Pendragon, I swear I shall see to it that it goes against you and your kin with the deputy bailiff to whom I shall have no hesitation in giving a full and honest account of this day's dark happenings.'

'Then will you, sir,' replied Samuel Trelawney, 'kindly step forward and volunteer to subdue the savage beast as he comes charging through yonder door? I leave this matter entirely in your hands.'

Well put, sir! thought Customer. Samuel Trelawney had brain and wit where his thick-headed eldest son had none. If Eber's temper were up, it would take a lot more courage and strength than Customer Trago could muster to check him.

'On reflection, sir,' said Customer, 'it would seem to me to be the wisest course of action if I, or some other person of your nomination agreeable to us both, were to speak quietly with Eber and acquaint him of this day's proceedings before he dismounts and wreaks havoc upon all and sundry.'

Samuel Trelawney looked at him for a moment and then he nodded his head in agreement. 'You have not much brawn about you, young sir, but I think you speak well enough. You have gained my attention. Now, let us see how well your silken tongue works for you with Eber Pendragon. Only be quick about it before the molten lava of his temper overflows the pot!'

Customer needed no further bidding. As he hastened to the

door, he glimpsed, out of the corner of his eye, the Trelawneys and their minions swiftly taking up defensive positions at the windows of the inn that overlooked the forecourt and then making ready with bows and arrows.

So this was how it was to be all along, he thought with a shudder. A shaft in the back for Customer Trago and one in the chest for Eber Pendragon. And as for Agnes and the holy pilgrims, well, there were daggers aplenty to silence their tongues forever!

Customer waited out on the forecourt, making sure he kept in full view of Trelawney eyes, with the goose bumps on the base of his spine dancing a merry jig and his teeth chattering with nerves. His eyes locked fearfully with Eber's as Eber rode up to him.

The huge hairy head cocked a little on one side questioningly.

'Stay seated a moment on Will and hear me out...' Customer began in a nervous gabble, his hands raised in a halting gesture. 'There is trouble at the inn, Eber – a shaft for each of us should you make one wrong move.'

Eber's gaze hardened. 'What mischief is this? Those horses yonder...' He indicated his head at them. 'Trelawney nags, or I know nothing of horseflesh. Are you saying the Trelawneys have taken over the inn in my absence and are holding Agnes and Rebecca against their will?'

Customer grimaced. 'Were that all that has gone awry this black day, Eber, my heart would beat more comfortably in its socket.'

The light of battle began to show in Eber's eyes: they glinted like freshly-honed steel. 'Can anything be worse than that? Speak quickly, young sir. The shadow of my patience with you and the Trelawneys diminishes with the fading light of day!'

'It is Rebecca, Eber. She is dead; murdered, I fear.'

'By whose hand?' bawled Eber, lurching forward in his saddle, as if to dismount.

Customer cried out in fear. 'Stay awhile... For God's sake, listen to me, Eber! Trouble awaits you; a hangman's rope. It is you, Eber Pendragon, the Trelawneys accuse of Rebecca's murder; you they would take to Bodmin to face the questions of the deputy bailiff and his officers of the law; you they would have answer for this crime in a magistrate's court.'

Eber let out a ferocious roar. Customer reared back from him, away from Will's skipping legs.

'One false move from either one of us, Eber,' Customer cried out, 'and we are dead men! If you will not think of yourself and me, then think of Agnes, her fate if Trelawney archers bring us down in the next two or three seconds. There are the lives of other hostages to consider also: Welsh pilgrims to the Holy Well of St James who came upon Rebecca's body there this morning. Do you want the blood of these innocent bystanders on your hands? Listen to me, Eber: hear what I have to say and believe every word of it. I will do all that I can for you; stand beside you and bear witness to your upright character and true Christian goodness. I will swear out an affidavit that sings the praises of your kindness and gentleness to the utmost in the highest; seek out and instruct the finest legal brain in Bodmin to take on your defence and reclaim your good name and honour from the deep abyss of this foul charge that is being brought against you.'

Eber was silent. His eyes bore like ice picks into Customer's. 'No, young sir,' he said at length. 'I cannot agree to those terms. You mean well and I do not doubt your word, but you are an innocent and know nothing of our ways, how things are settled here. The Trelawneys have too many friends in Bodmin; my fate is already sealed. If I am to die, then it shall be this day and as a true Cornishman, one who has fought to the death!'

'No, Eber, you are entirely wrong about me! I, too, have friends in Bodmin; many friends of long-standing. I will match my influence there with that of the Trelawneys any day.' *Not entirely true, but Customer was desperate and regarded any half-truth that would calm the savage beast within Eber Pendragon's breast and save the day as justified.*

'But what of your wits, young sir?' asked Eber, eyeing him shrewdly. 'Does the same thing stand for your wits against theirs?'

Customer looked at him.

'I have listened long and hard to your feverish babblings, young sir,' Eber continued. 'I know who you are, where you are from, the names of your friends and those of your enemies, and that the Bishop of Exeter himself gave his blessing to your furthering your education at the great seat of learning at Oxford.'

Customer spoke quickly and urgently. 'I studied at Oxford, that is no lie – and with the Bishop of Exeter's blessing, I admit that, too; but my true education has been in the fleshpots of Europe where vainglorious young men such as myself swank and swagger and have little genuine education, only an intrinsic knowledge of how best to use their wits to live without conscience off the honest earnings of others. I am worthless, Eber. Selfish, idle; unworthy of the trust decent, honest men such as yourself place in me.'

Eber looked at him stubbornly. 'Your wits against the Trelawneys', young sir, or I go in there now and settle this matter with my fists while you stand out here alone and worry about how things will go for you if things go badly for me.'

Customer watched in horror as Eber dismounted; waited to feel a shaft pierce his back between his shoulder blades. 'Very well,' he said. He swallowed nervously and glanced quickly behind him at the inn. Then, looking back at Eber: 'Make no move: stand true and tall beside Will so there can be no mistaking your intentions. I give you my word: I will do what I can for you.'

'That is not enough for Eber Pendragon, young sir,' said Eber. 'You must swear to me on the memory of your Royal Plantagenet antecedent that you will use all your wits and those handed on to you by your old tutor, Emanuel – of whom I have heard much said other than from your own feverish lips, that is good – to prove me innocent of this crime of which you say I stand accused, and I will give you my word that my life is placed willingly in your hands to do with as you see fit.'

Customer winced. So he had told all, left nothing unsaid whilst in the grips of that wretched fever. A pity that Eber had accepted without question his claim to be a Plantagenet. This was still to be proven; and indeed, if Eber, in one of his fabulous tempers, let this piece of information slip from his tongue while he was incarcerated in Bodmin Gaol (or worse, in the dungeons beneath Launceston Castle, which was the more likely), there could be some unpleasant repercussions for his not so quick-thinking and learned counsel, Customer Trago. Much, admittedly, would depend on the recollection of the kith and kin of the Bodmin men whom the Plantagenet Pretender to the English throne, Perkin Warbeck, had deserted on the eve of their last battle with Henry Tudor outside the walls of the town of Exeter, and whether or not they were of the type who bear grudges!

'Is there no safe way of our getting word to Emanuel of your plight and seeking his intercession on your behalf?' asked

Customer.

'Which of us would you have seek the Trelawneys' indulgence while we humbly kneel and, casting our eyes Heavenwards, implore Emanuel to offer a petitionary prayer on my behalf?' asked Eber in a dry voice. 'I fear there is little else Brother Emanuel can do for either one of us now, young sir, no matter how much you might wish it otherwise. Emanuel is dead, as you have long feared and cried out in your feverish night-time ramblings...'

Chapter Sixteen

Eber looked at Customer pityingly; his voice softened. 'I see the distress in your heart and beg your forgiveness for the callous directness of my words which, I assure you, only a dilemma such as the one facing me at this moment could have wrung from me.'

Customer had clasped his hand to his wounded side to still the terrible gut-wrenching pain that had suddenly flared up there. It was a moment before he could catch his breath, such was his shock at hearing confirmation of Emanuel's death. 'How?' he gasped. 'When?'

'It is best that we discuss this later,' said Eber with a slow shake of his head. 'Now is not the time.'

'No, *now*, Eber! I beg you to tell me that Emanuel died peacefully in his sleep, his saintly old heart tired and worn out.'

Eber gave his head another small shake and shifted his gaze from the young man looking up at him imploringly.

'It was Gennys, wasn't it?' said Customer in a bitter voice. 'I see it in the way you avert your eyes from mine. Emanuel was murdered; struck down in cold blood.'

'Your obsession with Sir William Gennys does you no credit, Customer Trago,' said Eber with a scowl, looking back at him. 'The wrong-doing you suspect of Gennys is a figment of your imagination. Enemies Gennys and Emanuel might well have been, as seems to give you so much childish pleasure in thinking, but Gennys had no hand in Emanuel's death. Nor, I would willingly wager, in the attempt that was made on your life.'

'Answer me this, then, Eber,' Customer demanded. 'Whose hand was it?'

'Hot-headed and impatient as you are, I know it will be difficult for you to accept that this has yet to be established. As for Emanuel, all that is known for certain there is that he was called upon to settle a domestic dispute. The rest is speculation, but on the surface of things, it would appear that he was set upon by a band of robbers much as you were while making your way back to Launceston Priory.'

Customer was shaking his head. 'You are wrong, Eber. Whoever gave you this information has been seriously misinformed. Emanuel did not involve himself in domestic matters. No such dispute would have enticed him away from the precincts of the priory.'

'You must listen to me.' Eber frowned; he spoke urgently. 'My source is unimpeachable. I spoke with Trenwith this day on your behalf concerning Brother Emanuel. The Mistress Trenwith has connections at the priory, a close friend of her late father to whom she has always referred as "uncle". It was to the home of her older married sister, Elise, in the neighbouring county of Devon that Emanuel was summoned.'

'But why?' Customer looked up at Eber with a perplexed frown. 'Why would Emanuel, a civil lawyer, involve himself in a domestic affair? I was at his side, his student and constant companion for many years, no one knew him and his involvement in day-to-day happenings involving the church and its holy brethren better than I. He would not, I say, be called upon to intercede or mediate as you have implied.'

'I cannot argue with you on that score. I know nothing personally of Brother Emanuel's obligations under the strictures of his holy order. I am merely repeating as much as Trenwith felt able to tell me without further distressing his wife who is currently suffering from some form of nervous malady as a result of her sister's problems. Mistress Trenwith hovered about us too close at hand for Trenwith to divulge more than I have told you. Be satisfied. Emanuel and the fate that befell him while journeying back to the priory, which I would think will prove to have had no bearing on the family matter he was called upon to settle, is all you need concern yourself with. For now, you must put all thought of Emanuel from your mind and be strong and decide for as both, quickly, how this present affair with the Trelawneys will go. We will look further into seeking a full and satisfactory explanation of the circumstances surrounding Brother Emanuel's death from Trenwith, and at the priory, at a later date. This I promise you.'

Although far from satisfied with what he had been told, and more than ever convinced that Emanuel's murderer, and not impossibly, murderers, could be found within the priory itself and not with some conveniently conceived band of highway robbers,

Customer nevertheless nodded his acceptance of Eber's terms.

'You will go to Bodmin with the Trelawneys willingly, without fuss?' he asked Eber in a wary tone.

Eber gave a nod. 'Docile as a lamb.'

'Do everything I say, with no argument?'

'No word shall pass my lips that you do not wish to hear me utter and which has not first been sanctioned by you.'

Customer considered for a moment and then nodded his head again. 'Very well, I agree: I shall return indoors swiftly now and acquaint the Trelawneys of your decision. My feeling is that they will wish to make a start for Bodmin as soon as possible.'

A cloud crossed Eber's face. 'Stay a moment longer; there is something I would know. How did the little one meet with her end? I pray with a measure of kindness and that death came swiftly to her.'

'I do not know how she died, Eber: this is something we must ascertain once we reach Bodmin. I shall request that Rebecca is taken immediately to one of the old lazar houses and insist that despite the evidence that is plain for all eyes to see, a physician is instructed to examine her body and give his opinion of how and when she died. The answers to these two questions are crucial to your defence, Eber. The Trelawneys are claiming that bruisings to her throat and neck are plain evidence that she was throttled, and by none other than you, the blacksmith of Wynehouse Corner. I myself am not so sure that the answer is quite as simple as this and would wish to hear what an expert in these matters would have to say about it.'

Eber frowned. 'I ask only one thing before we leave for Bodmin, that I may be permitted to see the little one.'

Customer was shaking his head. 'You must do nothing that will bring flame to the twisted flax of the Trelawneys' torches and set them ablaze, Eber. Their passions are running high and swift, but due to the good offices of Samuel Trelawney, are largely being held in check. How long he will hold sway with the young hot bloods among them, I would not care to say.'

Eber was nodding his head thoughtfully. 'Samuel Trelawney is no fool. There is much at stake here if all goes well for him in Bodmin. He would want to see this thing done properly so that no accusing finger can be pointed in his direction after the hangman's noose has been fixed tightly round my neck and the ladder kicked out from beneath my feet.'

'They will not be putting a rope round your neck if I have any say in things,' vowed Customer.

'I place my life in your safekeeping, young sir,' said Eber. He bowed his head, momentarily bringing his hands together as if in prayer. 'Guard it well. And this, also.'

He removed the key dangling at his waist and then handed it to Customer, who took it from him with a puzzled look.

'This key,' said Eber, 'unlocks the door of the wine cellar. Trust its safekeeping to no one but yourself.'

The key burned hotly in Customer's hand. He was instantly suspicious. There was more to this; something of far greater consequence to Eber than any of the alcoholic beverages that were served up to visitors to the inn. 'If I am to be entrusted with this key's safekeeping, I must be made privy to what it secures that is of such importance to you that you will entrust it to no one but me.'

'The importance of that key is attached firmly to Agnes, young sir; not to me.'

Customer stood momentarily stock-still, shocked into stunned silence. Eber had dismounted and was preparing to lead Will across the forecourt and, staying him with a hand on his arm, Customer asked, hurriedly, 'Are you saying that you do not trust Agnes, she is a thief and would steal your goods and sell them for her own profit?'

'Agnes is no thief; pray God that thievery was all the blacksmith and innkeeper of Wynehouse Corner need concern himself with here. Never more so than when Agnes is in her cups and out here on the forecourt mewing shrilly at the moon, either stark naked, all sense of decency and decorum cast into the savage winds that plague us, and her sexual passions raging, or indoors as she stealthily prowls the inn's dark passages late at night. It is no lie that Agnes has acquired for herself the dubious reputation of being one who preys with wilful determination on any traveller who has had the misfortune to seek lodging at the Wynehouse overnight, oftentimes forcing herself upon him in her feral need to satisfy her lustful bodily desires. Brandy fuels the fire in Agnes's belly: be advised and hold it, and the key to the lock that secures it, safe in your keeping at all times.'

'I do not believe a word of this,' Customer declared hotly. 'I have never seen Agnes the worse for drink!'

''Tis glad I am to hear it,' Eber rejoined dryly. 'Pray God you never do!'

Chapter Seventeen

A-a-a-tishoo!

'Bless you, my sweet, dearest heart,' murmured Alfonso Graviano, cousin (many times removed) of Count Maurizio Ballini and determined aspirant to his title. Quite needlessly, as it happens, as Alfonso was first in a very short line of hopefuls to inherit both Ballini's title and all of the land and property that went with it should some regrettable mischance befall the count before he could beget himself a male heir. Having prudently taken the necessary steps to remove the one and only, albeit slim possibility of this unfortunate state of affairs coming to pass, the future was looking particularly bright and promising for cousin Alfonso. But only if he could find it in himself to be patient and wait, and did nothing to jeopardize the warmly intimate relationship he was presently enjoying with the count's beautiful young wife, Anna-Lucrezia, before her foolishly besotted former lover, Customer Trago, had disposed of the old lecher for them.

Anna-Lucrezia sat up weakly in her sick bed, a victim of the virulent chest infection that was currently sweeping through Bodmin. Alfonso was standing at the window of their room at a hostelry in the centre of the town, blatantly ogling the flirty-eyed young maidens who milled about the noisy thoroughfare below. A very pretty, dark-haired young girl, glancing up at the window at which he stood, caught his eye, and he inclined his head in a little bow of acknowledgment. She blushed scarlet and hurried on about her business.

'I fear you do not love me any more,' said Anna-Lucrezia through her streaming nose in a thick, self-pitying voice, 'and that the moment word reaches us that the beast, Ballini, is dead and gone, and that you can now rightfully step into his shoes and call all that was his your own, you will find some means of disposing of me.'

Alfonso turned his head from the window with a well-practised smile – the one the countess claimed melted her heavy heart into tiny rivulets of pure, unalloyed joy – and gazed at her for a moment. She was right, of course; she was nothing more to him than she had ever been to her poor, cuckolded husband; a means to an end. A pleasant enough diversion these past weeks while they had been occupied in a dogged search for the feeble-minded dupe who would hopefully rid them of Ballini for all time, but no more than this. Alfonso had seen a portrait painting of her mother, what a great beauty she had once been and what a raddled old mare she was now. Only a fool would expect time to treat the daughter more kindly. His interest in the Countess Ballini would extend not a second beyond that moment when matters were finally brought to a head with dear cousin Maurizio. In no circumstances would the *Widow* Ballini figure in the life and times of the new Count Alfonso Graviano-Ballini; Alfonso gave himself his solemn word on that.

'I fear,' he said in a teasing voice, 'that if the apothecary does not arrive soon with your physic, my sweetest of loves, I will have no need to dispose of you, the job will be done for me.' A not altogether disagreeable prospect: in fact, from Alfonso's point of view, there was much to commend it.

'You are a cruel man, Alfonso,' said Anna-Lucrezia, pouting but not displeased by what she accepted was nothing more than a little light-hearted banter between two lovers as close as she had been given to believe they were. 'You break my heart.'

'Then we are a good pair.'

'It is not fair that you should speak so to me when I am in such low spirits,' she said, this time genuinely pouting. She glared at him, her watery eyes narrowed under red and puffy lids. 'I know you speak of Customer Trago and his love for me, and the heartbreak that lies in store for him once I am a free woman again, but you do not understand him as I do. It is a kindness I have done him in sending him on this errand for me. And when the deed is done and I tell him, sadly, that my conscience weighs heavily upon me, and that I know there can be no future for us, we could never live happily ever after in each other's company with such a terrible burden of guilt upon our shoulders, he will enjoy all the more the role he will then be required to play of martyr. It is a role he knows well, if not by heart, and enjoys playing, anyway,' she finished to the accompaniment of another bout of violent sneezing.

'Having seen him, I rather fancy I view him in an entirely dif-ferent role, that of a lily-livered coward,' said Alfonso, speaking through the large, lace-edged fine linen handkerchief he was now delicately holding over his nostrils and mouth to ward off an invasion of the infection he could all but see being sprayed all over him by the sneezing woman in the bed. 'But then I have nothing like your intuitiveness in such matters, my sweetest of dear hearts. If you say Customer Trago is the man for the job, then I defer to your better judgment. Though I confess it concerns me not a little that you felt the need to concoct that fanciful tale of your father's alleged wrath over your flight from your marriage bed, and that you have used it as a spur on Trago's rump. I am seriously beginning to think that it has had the exact opposite effect on that handsome young fellow and set his heels galloping in a quite different direction to that which we would have him take.'

As he spoke, Alfonso had paused in reaching out to close the wooden window shutters, his vaguely bemused gaze following a familiar, lithe young male figure who, from his hesitant manner, had all the appearances of attempting to seek information from those who brushed shoulders with him, most of whom ignored him and walked swiftly on.

Dabbing thoughtfully at his nose with his handkerchief, Alfonso continued:

'We must not rely too heavily on Maurizio's drooling, lip-smacking pleasure at seeing that fine specimen of young manhood again lest it clouds his mind to such an extent that he neglects to mention that it is with his blessing that you are absent from his protection – and that of Lord Molton of Glastonbury with whom Maurizio presently visits – while you are safely escorted to the holy house of St Lawrence by his trusted cousin Alfonso.'

Narrowing his eyes as the young man he was watching approached a crippled beggar boy leaning heavily on a crudely-hewn wooden crutch, and the boy, with a wave of his free hand, made some reply to whatever it was that he had been asked, Alfonso added, 'I would, however, be interested to hear your views on Customer Trago's presence here this day in the town of Bodmin – with sword and dagger at his side, I might add – seeking, I suspect, intelligence of the Countess Ballini and her travelling companion and not, as we would have hoped and expected, of her lord and master, the Count Maurizio Ballini at Molton Hall near Glastonbury, a hundred miles to the north-east of here.'

Seized with a coughing fit, it was several moments before Anna-Lucrezia was able to respond.

'Customer is here, in Bodmin?'

'In the street below, my dearest sweetness, seeking directions, it would seem, from a crippled beggar boy.' Alfronso was frowning as he spoke. It bothered him that Trago kept looking back over his shoulder, as if expecting to see someone creeping up on him. *An uncontrollable nervous tic?* The man was a cretin, Alfonso had no doubt of that, and perhaps this explained why Trago repeatedly jerked his head back over his shoulder. He couldn't help himself; probably had no idea he was doing it.

Alfonso's eyes searched the street below. He saw nothing sinister, nothing that Trago should fear, anyway. Just townspeople going about their daily business. He wondered if he shouldn't go down into the street and give Trago a hand in his search for the countess.

Alfonso decided against it. Best to let things take their natural course. The bumbling idiot would find his way to her eventually. Always assuming, of course, that it was the Countess Ballini he sought.

Chapter Eighteen

Piers Heard...

Customer gazed hesitantly at the nameplate.

That was the physician's name, wasn't it?

Piers Heard... Emanuel's boyhood friend?

Customer would not have believed Wynehouse Corner's windswept desolation could have had such a marked effect on him in so short a time, but Bodmin, with its stinking, crowded streets and lanes, was oppressive to him, suffocating. He was relieved to have found the physician's residence, which was also his place of business, so quickly and be away from all the hustle and bustle that the town, with its burgeoning population of two thousand souls, had on offer.

An unpleasant tingling sensation at the top of Customer's spine made him glance behind him for what he knew to be the umpteenth time that day. He'd had the feeling ever since riding out from the Wynehouse Inn yesterday with Eber and the Trelawneys.

Pawley.

There was the problem.

He had the man on the brain. First Sir William Gennys and now the stranger Pawley. Customer still couldn't remember where or when in the past his and Pawley's paths had crossed, but Customer was sure they had and would again, sooner or later.

Was Pawley simply waiting patiently for some sign of recognition before making himself known and renewing their acquaintanceship?

Somehow Customer didn't think so. There was something sinister about Pawley. *Or – with Gennys having been declared innocent by Eber of any wrong-doing – was this as Eber had implied; Customer Trago's fevered imagination playing tricks on him?*

Why was it so difficult to accept that Pawley was an innocent holy pilgrim, with nothing but God's business on his mind?

Customer pulled thoughtfully on the rusty bell-chain dangling at the side of Piers Heard's front door. He seemed to recall standing in more or less that precise spot as a small boy and watching

Emanuel ringing the same bell and then gazing in fascination at the pink-painted walls of the physician's residence. It had reminded him of icing on a cake. It still did.

It all seemed so long ago, part of another life and, at times, not even his life. It was a thought that had been with him constantly during these past twenty-four hours. His whole life seemed to have taken on an air of unreality, the more so since his bizarre conversation with Anna-Lucrezia in the public room of the inn at Wynehouse Corner two mornings ago. Pride forbore that he should admit of nothing to Agnes, but everything she had said to him later concerning the Countess Ballini and her foppish travelling companion, had hit painfully home.

To help pass the tedium of the previous day's long ride to Bodmin with Eber and the Trelawneys and their men, Customer had given much thought to the whole distasteful business, at length mentally resolving to find some means of returning, with all speed, the countess's tainted purse of gold to her at her place of sanctuary somewhere there in Bodmin. Pre-ferably, he had added as an afterthought, through the good offices of some discreet third party. This done, he would make sure that he took swift steps to distance himself from her and the unthinkable demand she had made of him. He could then wipe the whole unfortunate episode from his memory so that if questioned at some future date (he had no doubt that one way or another, the Count Maurizio Ballini's days were definitely numbered), he could claim no knowledge of the affair. It was a bitter lesson he had learnt, one he vowed never to forget. Women, especially those of great beauty like the Countess Ballini, were dangerous, unworthy of an honest man's trust, and henceforth best avoided.

Customer had had no fear of encountering the countess while seeking directions to Piers Heard's house. He was confident that she would not dare take the risk of arousing the interest and curiosity of the Bodmin townspeople who would naturally be only too eager to relay the information of her exact whereabouts to her father if and when he and his men finally caught up with her. Customer reminded himself of this as he waited outside the physician's front door, assuring himself that if he kept strictly to within the precincts of the town while this dispute between Eber and the Trelawneys was being settled, there would be absolutely no danger of his weakening and falling prey to the Countess Ballini's beguiling charms, or of being enticed to do her devious bidding by the rattle of gold against gold in that temptingly bulging leather purse of hers.

The physician's door opened and a girl of about seventeen or eighteen stepped out, clutching a large bottle of a pale pink liquid mixture to her dainty bosom. Closing the door behind her, she glanced at him once shyly, her soft, creamy pink cheeks reddening under her long, dark eyelashes, before hastening past him into the busy street beyond.

He turned his head idly and watched her for a moment. She was not unwell, her vibrant colour, glossy chestnut hair and quick, sure step discounted any possibility of that. She was probably the physician's servant girl sent on an errand to deliver a nostrum to one of his patients. One half of Customer hoped for her return before he was finished with the physician so that he might have the pleasure of gazing upon that sweet, innocent face of hers again, his other half called him every kind of fool for not heeding the wisdom of the vow he had made where beautiful women were concerned, and for being so eager to rush in blindly and break it before the sun had so much as set upon it for the first time.

He breathed in deeply to rid his nostrils of Bodmin's all-pervading stench of unwashed human flesh, but it was still there, strong as ever, and he could only wonder at what the town must be like during the dry, dusty months of high summer when its many fairs and a natural seasonal movement of people from one place to the next brought a heavy influx of visitors to it. Emanuel had hated this evil-smelling town only a fraction less, he claimed, than he hated Venice and its sewer-stinking waterways. Hated the torrents of disease-carrying filth that swept down through Bodmin's streets and into the houses when it rained, and having no great affection for cholera and other life-threatening infections, he would not drink of its water, nor permit a drop of it to pass young Customer's lips. The town's water supply was contaminated by the graveyard through which it flowed.

An old woman finally answered the door, so slatternly in her appearance that Customer looked again at the nameplate to be sure that he was at the correct address. She had been drinking. Quite heavily. And not alone. If Customer were asked afterwards to choose between the two and say who had been the more heavily intoxicated, the master or his woman servant, he would have been at a loss to respond.

Standing in the hallway to the left of the door there was a small table on which stood an identical bottle of the same pinkish liquid he had seen moments earlier clutched in the girl's hand. Some special physic much favoured by the local populace as a general restorative, Customer imagined. And in all probability of about as much use as a bottle of honeyed water!

The hollow-cheeked man sitting at a table in the gloomy, dusty room into which Customer was shown was not the Piers Heard of his youth. Piers Heard's son, most probably; a man of about thirty-five, taller than Customer, with fine, shoulder-length fair hair that was showing signs of thinning on top, a dangerously high colour and if his habit of squinting were not an affectation, then as short-sighted as a mole poking about in broad daylight on the earth's surface in search of familiar surroundings. There was no sign of the lanky, grinning skeleton that Customer vaguely recalled used to hang from a hook in a corner of that particular room. The sight of a skeleton hadn't particularly alarmed him as a child, but perhaps other children, patients of the physician consulting him here at his home, had not been quite so indifferent to it and it had since been consigned to a less prominent place of display.

The physician gripped the edge of the table at which he was sitting, intending to rise from his chair, and then, as if on second thoughts, he slumped back onto it lethargically. 'Piers Heard, physician and apothecary, at your service, sir,' he said.

'I apologize for this intrusion, sir,' Customer began with a bemused frown, 'but I fear there has been some mistake on my part. I regret that you are not the man I thought to see.'

The physician nodded his head; made as if to rest an elbow on the table and missed it completely, toppling from his chair onto the floor. 'Think nothing of it,' he said, rising unconcernedly, and with surprising agility, to his feet. He waved Customer into a chair and then he sat down again. 'Everybody says the same thing... Where is the white-haired old fossil who dishes out the bottles of pretty pink cure-all?'

Piers Heard gazed fixedly at Customer, as if waiting to be asked to confess to his having had a hand in the disappearance of the man it seemed his new patient had expected to find sitting in his place at the physician's table.   Then his face relaxed into an easy grin. 'It is my father you were expecting to see, sir. Passed on, I am sorry to say. Gone back to his Maker. Worn to a frazzle by all the toing and froing between this table and the inner sanctum of medicinal compounds yonder.' He waved a hand in the general direction of a heavy oak door to the left of him. 'But enough of this: one must not allow one's thoughts to linger on these morbid matters. What can I do for you, sir?' He peered myopically at Customer. 'Not a lot, by the look of things.   You have all the appearances of enjoying vulgarly rude good health. But then again, one mustn't be too hasty about these things. We all live in hope of one thing or another and I am no exception. Your tongue, sir. Poke it out.'

'You are quite correct in your diagnosis, sir,' said Customer quickly.   'It pleases me to be able to report that I am in near splendid health. I come seeking the advice of a physician on a delicate medical matter.'

'Say no more,' said Piers Heard, attempting to tap one side of his nose with a forefinger and coming perilously close to poking himself in an eye. 'I get your meaning... A rich, fat, ugly wife, many years your senior, with too tight a hold on the purse strings and little or no understanding of the needs and wants of a handsome young fellow such as yourself.'

Customer stared at him. Was he suggesting what he thought he was suggesting? *What manner of madman was this?*

Chapter Nineteen

The physician misinterpreted Customer's hesitation. 'I am wrong? Your kind pardon, sir. Your problem lies with your father. No? Then it is your parsimonious old mother who holds the purse strings in too tight a grasp. May I suggest wasp poison, sir? Cunningly concealed in a bottle of my good, late father's pretty pink cure-all, swift and to the point. As luck would have it, I have some to hand at this precise moment awaiting collection by sweet Lucy Trenwith on behalf of her father whose dwelling house is persistently invaded by these tiresome pests each summer. Or so I have been given to understand. Far be it from me to think that a man of Jacob Trenwith's high moral character and good standing in the community might have other, more sinister notions in mind of adding a measure or two of wasp curative to the wine cups of his enemies. Take a bottle and welcome, sir. I shall mix more for Lucy in next to no time. A pleasure, I am sure.'

Jacob Trenwith? The same Jacob Trenwith with whom Eber had dealings on the day of Rebecca's murder? Customer wondered uneasily, rising swiftly to his feet.

'I came about murder, sir, I admit that, but not concerning one I wish to arrange, but about one that has been committed.'

'You want me to swear that your wife – mother, father? – died of natural causes... That should present me with little problem. I doubt that I would recognize the cause of the deceased's death, anyway. I confess to not a little trickery at the time of the sitting of my final examinations: in fact, sir, I like your face, it strikes me as showing charity and genuine understanding and I shall therefore be frank and honest with you. My final examinations were taken for me by another, by one of my fellow students of remarkably similar physical appearance who was in sore need of funds.'

'You are corrupt, sir!' Customer exclaimed.

'It is my heartfelt desire to become so, though whether I have actually already achieved my ambition is open to debate.'

'Not one word of what you have said to me could possibly be true. I shall therefore be frank and honest with you, sir, and call you a liar! You are also drunk.'

'True.'

'Completely lacking in professionalism.'

'As a physician and apothecary, yes, I must agree with you there. As a drunkard? No, sir. In every respect, there I am a true professional. I have made it my life's work.'

'It is clear that you cannot help me, sir. I bid you good-day. Your late father has my deepest sympathies.'

The physician's eyes pricked up. 'You knew him, sir?'

'I met him once many years ago when I accompanied my tutor, Emanuel, from Launceston Priory on a visit to your town.'

'Ah, yes,' said the physician in a slow voice. His eyes searched Customer's face. 'I recall you now... The tongue-tied foundling boy with the anxious grey eyes. Now...what was his name?' He tapped a forefinger on the tip of his nose in what seemed to Customer to be little more than a rather obvious gesture of pretence at searching his memory. 'Yes, I remember... Customer – Customer Trago. Such a strange name, I recall thinking when I was a lad and I heard it spoken for the first time.'

'I do not recall meeting you, sir.'

Piers Heard pointed at the door of the room that was obviously his dispensary. 'I saw you through the keyhole of that door over there. I wanted to see you for myself.'

Customer eyed him suspiciously. 'And why, sir, was that?'

Piers Heard thought for a moment. 'Why, bless my soul, I do believe I have forgotten! There was something interesting about you, something I seem to recall overhearing my father discussing with Emanuel, but it has gone now. My fondness for fine old French brandy, I regret to say, has greatly diminished my powers of recall; and alas, some things are vanished from my memory forever. But one mustn't complain: one muddles through somehow.'

As if by the flick of his fingers, the physician was no longer quite so drunk and Customer thought he could guess the reason for this. Piers Heard remembered only too well what it was about Customer Trago that was so interesting to a young boy standing with one inquiring eye pressed up hard against a keyhole!

Customer's heart drooped heavily in his breast. The slattern who had answered the door to him... Now that he'd had time to reflect upon it, she was the pretty young slip of a thing who had fetched Emanuel and him refreshments that long ago day. He had watched her comings and goings with all the interest of a naturally inquisitive young boy brought up in a male dominated environment, and had found her ease and grace of movement, the soft contours of her body, utterly fascinating. To see what had become of her in the intervening years was a sad jolt and something of a warning to be borne in mind should he ever weaken in his resolve and at some future date contemplate any further dalliance with the opposite sex.

'Well, Customer Trago,' said Piers Heard, 'whose murder brings you to Bodmin after all these many years? I have heard talk of the troubles at Launceston Priory.' He paused, eyeing Customer contemplatively. 'None that concerns you personally, I trust.'

'What occurs there no longer interests me. Not now that my old friend and mentor, Emanuel, is dead. I left the priory many years ago...'

The physician nodded. 'Yes, it all comes back to me now. To study the King's law.'

Customer made no comment. 'A good friend of mine stands wrongfully accused of the brutal murder of a young girl at Wynehouse Corner in the Hundred of Stratton.'

'You have undertaken his defence? Commendable. Yes, highly commendable. This would bring tears of pride to Emanuel's eyes. He was very proud of you, Customer Trago. Had high hopes of splendid things to come from you.' Piers Heard paused, squinted at Customer thoughtfully and then waved a hand in the air. 'But I dare say you were aware of that?'

Customer ignored the question that underscored the physician's remark. He had not come here to discuss Emanuel, Customer Trago or the priory; *anything* connected with the past and that included his failure to complete his studies at Oxford. 'I have undertaken to clear my friend's name, no more should be required of me than this one simple task. My friend is so palpably innocent of the crime of which he stands accused that it is most unlikely that he will ever be required to answer the charges laid against him in any court of law.'

'I admire your confidence in yourself, sir,' said Piers Heard dryly. 'Where is the accused at this moment? On the run for his life? In safe hiding from our good deputy bailiff and his hearty men?'

'No, sir. He agreed to surrender himself willingly into the hands of Bodmin's law officers while I pursue my inquiries into his innocence and, in the meanwhile, he is being held securely under lock and key in the town. The deputy bailiff has graciously granted me time to present my case. He can, of course, afford to be magnanimous and humour me in this with the Spring Assizes still some weeks off.'

The physician was eyeing him shrewdly. 'You have something against the deputy bailiff of Launceston?'

'It was at the insistence of the murdered girl's family that Bodmin's deputy bailiff should be in charge of proceedings, although in memory of your late father, for whom Emanuel had the highest regard, I shall be frank, sir, and admit that there are reasons why it would be best for Customer Trago to distance himself from the town of Launceston, and its priory, for the time being.'

'You really are a most interesting fellow, Customer Trago. You intrigue me. Emanuel, if my memory serves me correctly, was dry as old sticks, a civil lawyer to his backbone. You must tell me more about yourself. So little happens these days that is interesting and exciting. Indeed, I feel stirred to insist that you tell me more of the murder at this curious place you have mentioned, and that you are precise in regard to how I could be of service to you and your innocent friend.'

'I require a fully qualified physician to examine the body of the murdered girl and tell me how she died?'

The physician inclined his head a little on one side and regarded Customer thoughtfully. 'You do not know how she died?'

'She might have been strangled; she might have drowned. Both are equally possible, and I would have a physician tell me beyond a shadow of doubt which it was. The deputy bailiff and the murdered girl's family have raised no objection to my request, and I am anxious that I should have my answer before I cease to be an amuse-ment to them and they tire of humouring me.'

Piers Heard's eyes began to widen, but instantly, as if fearing a sudden exposure to light would be too much for them, he screwed them back up into a tight squint again.

'Fascinating,' he said. He thought for a moment. 'I would have thought the answer there should be arrived at soon enough.'

'Then I ask that you should hasten this very minute to the old lazar house of St Lawrence where the good holy sisters, acting upon the instructions of the deputy bailiff, have prepared the murdered girl's body for your examination. Pray then tell me which it was, sir... Was Rebecca Trelawney strangled, or did she drown in the blessed consecrated water of the Holy Well of St James?'

The physician, with his head inclined a little still on one side, scratched the side of his nose thoughtfully. It was a moment or two before he spoke. 'You choose not to accompany me and witness my examination of the murder victim for yourself?'

Customer gave a quick shake of his head. 'There are reasons, sir – none of which I am at liberty to discuss with you, or with anyone else, for that matter – which make it imperative that I should not set foot outside this town. I beg your indulgence in this affair and ask that you take no offence at my inability to take you as fully into my confidence as I would otherwise wish.'

Piers Heard considered Customer meditatively. He wondered if he were correct in thinking that there was a beautiful woman at the heart of this matter Customer Trago was not at liberty to discuss with him. A certain kind of beautiful woman... The beautiful married kind uncommonly handsome young men like Customer Trago seemed to have as little difficulty in attracting to them as the sugar bowl does to the fly.

Chapter Twenty

'Mingles, sir. I mingles. Mingles and watches.'

Having cleared up this little matter to his satisfaction, the speaker lapsed into a thoughtful silence while contemplating how best to tackle the large chunk of thick white bread, with its even thicker wedge of hard yellow cheese which, as he spoke, one of the least slatternly-looking of the two alehouse serving wenches had placed before him on the crude oak table at which he was seated.

He looked up suddenly at the stranger dressed all in black who shared the table with him and added, 'Not in any official capacity, you understand, sir. But I mingles. Mingles and watches.'

That said, the speaker – who claimed his mother had named him after St Petroc for whom, he said, she had a great fondness – bit greedily intro the wedge of cheese and then down through the bread it sat upon. He chomped noisily on the bread and cheese for several moments and then, wiping away the saliva that had collected in the corners of his mouth with the back of his free hand, he said, 'The deputy bailiff is always more than happy to hear of anything amiss in his town. Pays me handsome if what I see while I mingles and watches puts a stop to any mischief upsetting the even tempo of his day.'

Petroc paused at this point and squinted meaningfully through his right eye at his listener. Which wasn't necessary. Malachy Pawley was well aware that the mingler and watcher, Petroc, had thought him worthy not only of his interest, but of possibly that of Bodmin's deputy bailiff.

Having been kept under close scrutiny by the deputy bailiff's hired man for some while, Pawley had deliberately drawn him into the alehouse. Pawley had seated himself at a table near the one window which looked out directly across the street at the physician, Piers Heard's front door, and had raised no objection to company when asked by Petroc if he might join him. Pawley doubted that the mingler and watcher's sharp nose, which Petroc certainly had, for winkling out mischief-making, root-and-branch, before it took hold, was sniffing in his direction with any degree of certainty, but it was better to play it safe and perhaps, by extending a little goodwill to the deputy bailiff's man, find out for sure.

Petroc had slid almost furtively – which, not impossibly, had much to do with his occupation of mingling and watching – into the chair opposite Pawley's. The long earflaps on the grubby, bleached linen skullcap Petroc was wearing put Pawley in mind of a dog he had once owned. He hadn't cared much for the company of the animal and had every expectation of feeling the same about the man sharing his table whom he knew to have been keeping equally doggedly close on heels.

Pawley, who was actually passing time while waiting for Customer Trago to leave the physician's house, was paying little attention to Petroc's discourse. A man Pawley adjudged to be of limited intelligence, Petroc had thus far had little of interest to say to him. He was a man, Pawley decided, who kept talking until he found something *to* say. So far mostly about the weather which, as often proved to be the case in Cornwall, showed every promise of offering up samples of all four seasons in one day.

Pawley continued to concentrate his thoughts on Customer Trago who was proving himself to be an interesting man. A surprising one. Having survived one attempt on his life, did that make him kin of the cat and with another eight left? Pawley wondered whimsically. Hopefully, not. But moving as Trago did in such very curious and currently dangerous circles, Pawley considered it all the more important that he should risk staying his hand in that quarter for a while longer. Trago was going to learn of Emanuel's death sooner or later, it was no use thinking he wouldn't. Maybe he already knew the senile old fool was dead. Trago had gone nowhere near the priory since riding into Cornwall some weeks ago, of that Pawley was sure, and the Wynehouse Inn had so few travellers pausing there, it was doubtful that any of them had brought news of the monk's death.

Pawley realized that Petroc was finally proving his expectation that, in time, he would eventually find something to say worthy of interest.

'You keep an eye on the physician's place of business so that you do not miss the moment when he becomes free,' Petroc observed in a matter-of-fact voice. He wiped more saliva from his mouth. 'You look well enough to me, sir, well enough that as a thank you for your genial company, I would suggest that you give serious consideration to any thought you might be entertaining of entering the aforementioned premises. I'll wager you'll be a lot worse off than you are now – aye, a thousand times worse off – if you do not heed my advice. The man's a drunkard, sir. Place not your trust in him. Many's the poor person I've seen while mingling and watching who has come out of that place across the street, a sight worse off than when they went in. All clutching the same thing. A bottle of the physician's precious pink liquid. Poison, sir. *Poison*, I tell you! One swig and all your troubles will be left far behind you. You'll be beyond caring, if you follow my meaning. Dead. Gone. Finished. Knocking on St Peter's front door, clutching your belly in agony and gasping for mercy!'

Petroc paused while he took a long swig from a jug of ale. 'I think your spirits might be a little down, sir,' he said after a reasonably discreet burp into the back of one of his hands and a polite "pardon". 'The Trelawneys, as wild a bunch of villains as you or I are ever likely to encounter in our entire lifetime, are in town with a murderer they are intent on hanging. There is sure to be some lively action before this day it out. Why not pass a little time in the meanwhile, wandering the streets to cheer yourself up?'

Pawley shifted his gaze from the window and looked directly at Petroc. 'You think so...that with luck there will be a hanging today?' he asked in a pleasant voice. 'I've heard it said it is far from certain that the man the Trelawneys have brought to town to face justice, is guilty of the deed with which he stands charged... The foul murder of a young, innocent girl, I believe it is being said in the town.'

Petroc nodded and said, 'Aye, a young girl, scarce in her teens; kin of the Trelawneys.' He paused to take another swig of ale and then, using the back of one his hands to wipe away the froth he rightly imagined formed a frill along his top lip, he added, 'The Trelawneys are not to be messed with, sir. No, not to be messed with. Not for an instant. They will have their way. Trust me on that,' he assured Pawley with a firm nod of his head.

A pity, if this was actually the case, thought Pawley. The one with the swagger and all the talk – Lowarn, wasn't it? – wouldn't take too much pushing in Trago's direction when it came to looking to lay the guilt at his feet for killing the girl. It was a temptation

103

almost too good to resist, but resist it Pawley would. Though watching Trago hang for the girl's murder would be a joy beyond measure. What really mattered now, and should never be lost sight of, was how much Trago knew of other things. Other far more important things than the murder of a hideously deformed servant girl whose right to life was not worth giving a moment's consideration.

The girl had known things that she would have done well not to have known. One would have to be blind not to have seen that. Night was as day to her, and she was everywhere, seeing everything. That was the first thing Pawley had established after arriving at the Wynehouse. But how much had she spoken of what she knew to others...to Trago? She was fearless – except in her feelings for him. She had betrayed herself badly there, Pawley recalled, mentally picturing the scene he had witnessed from his room, of Rebecca Trelawney with Customer Trago on the forecourt of the inn shortly before the stable burnt down. And die she had because of it. Not one word had been forced past her lips, neither concerning the secret she held close to her – and Pawley knew there was one, he had seen it in her eyes – nor of her love for Trago. There was no pleading, no cry for mercy. The Trelawneys would have been proud of her, thought Pawley, smirking inwardly. That is, if they had been there and had witnessed her dying moments...

Pawley realized that the mingler and watcher was squinting thoughtfully at him again, trying to size him up. He was a fool. Clumsy with his talk of the dangers of consulting the physician across the road. It was a blind, an attempt to get him to open up and tell him what business he had there in Bodmin that day. Petroc had been watching him long enough to know, or guess, that it was another stranger to the town, one Customer Trago, and neither the physician nor his dubious pink medicinal compound that was of interest to the man whose table he, Petroc, was sharing.

And that was a pity, too. For the mingler and watcher, that is.

Petroc finally abandoned hope of getting anything out of Pawley and made ready, ostensibly, to pursue his occupation of mingling and watching in a more fruitful direction. Pawley knew better. The man had a natural curiosity that he would do his level best to satisfy. He would not give up the scent which Pawley knew Petroc had been following diligently for most of the morning. Petroc was never going to wander so far distant from his present surroundings as to lose sight of who came and went from the physician's and of who was following whom, undoubtedly (Petroc lived in hope) with mischief in mind.

Petroc bade Pawley a good afternoon, courteously doffing his cloth cap and bowing and thanking him for his hospitality, and then he departed. Pawley followed him after a moment or two, but at a discreet distance. Pawley found it amusing that a mingler and watcher, who was busy doing what he did best, mingling and watching, had no idea that he was being treated in kind.

Petroc darted abruptly down a narrow, rubbish-strewn deserted lane to relieve himself of the ale that had uncomfortably filled his bladder to bursting. (At first, Pawley thought it was because Petroc had spotted him.) Totally unaware of Pawley, that he had come up stealthily behind him, Petroc sighed contentedly as the pressure in his loins eased and he rearranged his breeches to his satisfaction. He didn't see Pawley unsheathe his curiously shaped dagger, nor feel it thrust upwards, deep between his shoulder blades before being swiftly withdrawn.

In a fluid, sylph-like movement, Pawley drew back and vanished from sight in the darkened entryway to a cobbler's shop, hanging crookedly on a rusty nail hammered equally crookedly into the door of which was a yellowing, fly-specked hand-printed notice giving an alternative address for business, due, it said, to the rats.

Unaware that he was dying, and that he would soon be dead, Petroc walked blithely on up the lane past the cobbler's towards the busy main thoroughfare through the town. He felt no pain; had no idea that he had been stabbed to death.

Pawley stood over Petroc when finally, after no more than a dozen steps, Petroc fell lifeless to the ground. Looking down on him, Pawley thought again of the dog he had once owned. And had never liked.

Chapter Twenty-one

This was intolerable…

Alfonso Graviano flung open the shutters and gazed angrily out of the window, searching the crowded street below for a man whom he might properly describe as being an apothecary and who was, hopefully, bearing the appropriate physic for the treatment of an acute chest infection. A boy had been sent to fetch the physic hours ago, only to return a short time later empty-handed due, the boy had explained breathlessly, to an unusually heavy demand that morning for the apothecary's special pink cough and cold remedy. The apothecary was struggling to keep pace with the infection which, the boy cheerfully informed Alfonso, was spreading like wildfire and beginning to kill off the townspeople like flies. One of the apothecary's customers had apparently expired while the boy had been waiting in an anteroom to be attended. The apothecary had promised that the moment he had finished mixing up a fresh batch of the remedy later on in the morning, he would either deliver a bottle of it to the hostelry himself, or send his servant over with it.

Alfonso was as much concerned for himself now as for the countess. He had developed quite a sore throat in the past half-hour. Always an ominous sign.

He closed the shutters, scowling irritably. 'I shall wait but a short while longer and then I shall go to the apothecary's place of business and fetch the physic myself,' he informed the feverish woman sleeping fitfully in the bed.

The countess opened her eyes drowsily, but hadn't heard a word he had said and was far too ill to be bothered to ask him to repeat himself.

Piers Heard had meanwhile advised Customer Trago that as time was of the essence – certainly from the physician's point of view, with the town's chest infection claiming more victims by the hour and showing every sign of turning into an epidemic – Customer should await his return with a report of his findings on the exact cause of Rebecca Trelawney's death. The physician did not labour the point, but in the circumstances, his already heavily committed

106

workload could not be stretched an inch farther to include his having to do the rounds of the local taverns searching for Customer should he prefer to pass the time in the interim sating his thirst. Bearing in mind the attraction these places held for a habitual drinker such as himself, Piers Heard knew this might well run into some hours of his time.

Customer had accepted the suggestion gladly. He felt safe at the physician's house, safer than he had felt in days.

It had thus far been a lovely, sunny, early spring day, unseasonably warm, and he opened the shutters wide to let in some fresh air before making himself comfortable on a carved settle near the window where, by a simple turn of the head, he would be able to look out at the street and keep watch for Piers Heard's return. He was extremely tired after the long hours he had spent in the saddle the previous day, followed by a night with little proper rest due to a cot infested with insatiably thirsty, blood-sucking bedbugs, but there was no question of his falling asleep while he waited. Sleep, he told himself, was a luxury he could ill afford.

He nevertheless slipped almost immediately into a deep slumber and would have continued to sleep heavily throughout what little remained of the morning and well into the afternoon had it not been for the sudden change in the weather shortly before noon, which was not uncommon at this time of year. The skies rapidly darkened with steel grey clouds and an accompanying stiff breeze chilled him to the bone where he rested before finally succeeding in awakening him.

His heart gave a sickening jolt as he reached out quickly to close the shutters against the storm that threatened. The Countess Ballini's travelling companion, walking not too quickly because he was in the company of the crippled beggar boy who had given Customer directions to the physician's house, was heading straight for him. The boy had obviously been questioned by the fop, Alfonso, and for all Customer knew, the boy was the countess's paid spy and had been keeping an eye out for him around the town. The boy had also apparently taken it upon himself to ensure that Alfonso made no wrong turns along the way and actually reached his objective.

Customer dived breathlessly into a tall cupboard standing near the door to Piers Heard's dispensary, only to discover that it was already occupied. The skeleton that used to hang from a hook on the wall next to it was hanging on the back of the cupboard door. There was no time for second thoughts. Customer drew the door tightly shut, quickly steadying the swaying skeleton with one of his trembling hands.

He waited with a painfully thudding heart, scarcely daring to breathe.

Out in the street, Alfonso gave the beggar boy a coin for his trouble and then he pulled heartily on the chain outside Piers Heard's front door. When there was no response he knocked loudly and then impatiently opened the door and looked inside.

An old woman was lying in a drunken stupor on the stairs; he could smell the rough cider on her from where he stood. He studied her for a moment; thought it more than likely that she had been on her way down the stairs to answer the door to him and was so drunk, she had missed her footing, tumbled down them and then passed out. Either way she was clearly of no use to him in her present state.

Stepping into the hallway, a bottle of pink mixture standing on a table near the door immediately caught his eye. He snatched it up with a satisfied grunt and then turned and strode outside, slamming the door shut behind him. The apothecary had kept the countess waiting for the physic and now it was his turn. Let's see how he liked being kept waiting for his money!

Chapter Twenty-two

Customer heard the front door slam, but was too scared to budge from his hiding place in the cupboard. He didn't move until he heard Piers Heard's voice remonstrating with his womanservant out in the hallway.

Customer stepped gingerly out of the cupboard, closing the door quietly behind him before diving back onto the settle, and with only seconds to spare before Piers Heard entered the room.

It was at this point that the skeleton in the cupboard collapsed in a rattling heap of bones. Customer gave a slight start, but there was no reaction at all from the physician. There was something on his mind far more pressing than what may or may not be going on inside a cupboard that he rarely bothered to open. What really concerned him at that moment was Lucy Trenwith whom he knew for a fact had collected only one of the two bottles of wasp poison her father had requested him to make up. Piers Heard had definitely seen the second bottle standing on the hall table when he had left the house earlier, and it was gone on his return a few moments ago.

The obvious answer to its mysterious disappearance was that the girl had realized her mistake and had returned for it while he was out, taking it from the hall table without reference to Gertrude, his woman-servant, who could be counted on to be drunk and incapable by mid-morning, every morning. Hydrocyanic acid, the principal constituent of the wasp poison he had made up for Jacob Trenwith, was deadly, and not only to wasps. He could only hope that Gertrude would have collected her senses by the time he had finished with Customer Trago in order to tell him why Lucy Trenwith had taken only the one bottle of the poison when she had called earlier, and then more importantly, confirm what he expected and sincerely hoped had happened in regard to the second one.

With a small sigh, he turned to Customer and said, 'The place is a madhouse, sir. A madhouse. I consider myself lucky to have es-caped with my wits intact.'

The lazar house was a refuge for lunatics?

Piers Heard saw Customer's confusion and correctly interpreted what lay behind it. 'The town, sir. I speak of the town. Everyone has gone mad. Those who do not run in fear and trembling from a bunch of black-bearded ruffians who presently strut their stuff throughout the town, walk in mortal fear of a tall, dark, vaguely hunchbacked stranger dressed all in black, dagger in hand, whom they believe to be ready to snuff out their lights. Added to which the deputy bailiff and the unruly mob who make up his henchmen search under every stone and in every nook and cranny for the fellow... The one who would snuff out everybody's lights, you understand. A homicidal maniac, for sure.'

Customer's heart gave another sickening jolt. *A tall, dark stranger dressed all in black and with a mild curvature of the spine? Pawley? Surely not! What would Pawley be doing in Bodmin? Was he in some way connected with the Trelawneys, their spy at the Wynehouse?*

'I sense I have hit a nerve here,' observed the physician, eyeing Customer shrewdly.

'No, no,' Customer assured him quickly. 'I know of no such stranger. What exactly has he done to warrant all this fear and trembling by everyone?'

'Murdered one of the deputy bailiff's men. One of his spies. A simple fellow named Petroc, wily after his fashion, but like I have said, something of a simpleton. A girl meeting her lover on the sly stumbled upon Petroc's body in a deserted lane shortly after he and the tall, dark stranger had left a nearby alehouse where she is employed. My understanding is that the act of murder itself had no witnesses as such. Judgment on the stranger in black was reached and passed by the simple expedient of adding two and two together – more appropriately, one and one in the case in point – and coming up with what appears to be accepted by the general populace as being the correct answer and with no need for anyone to wrack his or her brains further. Petroc, poor fellow, was stabbed in the back. I dare say something of the sort was bound to happen sooner or later. The man did have a long nose. Petroc, that is. I am pleased to say that I have not had the pleasure of making the acquaintance of the tall, dark stranger, and I would advise you to be on your guard when you leave these premises. Just in case, you understand.'

'In case of what?' asked Customer uneasily.

'In case I am right and this mysterious tall, dark stranger is a homicidal maniac who chooses his victims at random. Or should that be those with a long nose who poke it where it is best not poked?' Piers Heard went on, without pausing: 'As to the other matter, I fear you have been sadly misinformed, sir; led so completely astray as to be hopelessly wide of the mark. Neither strangulation nor drowning was the cause of the girl, Rebecca's death. She was struck on the back of the head with some heavy object and I believe it was that which killed her. Perhaps not immediately, but soon after the blow was struck. I doubt that the poor girl saw what was coming to her.'

'I commend you on your thoroughness, sir,' said Customer, frowning. 'And beg your pardon for my unkind words to you earlier. You are indeed most professional. I had no inkling of any wound to her head.'

'Nor I,' confessed the physician with another small sigh. 'It was Sister Eunice who drew my attention to a faint stain on the white collar attached to the back of the girl's smock. Sister Eunice noticed it as she prepared to wash the girl's body and was removing her clothing. She thought it might be blood. The stain had been submerged in cold water and was much washed out, but there could be no doubt in either of our minds – Sister Eunice's and mine – that at one time, it was a very deep, ruby red bloodstain. I then began my search for the source of the blood and ultimately found what I was looking for at the base of the girl's skull, buried deep in her thick, black hair. I would wager that the bruising to her throat came at some other time – though what purpose this served I cannot begin to imagine, for as I have said, the wound to her head tells me that she must have been as good as dead when her murderer's hands were clasped about her neck. Clearly, as an attempt was also made, you say, to drown the poor girl, I would think you should seek someone who leaves nothing to chance.'

'This fits well with my idea of the evil person who committed this terrible crime,' said Customer, his tone grim. 'There is much at stake here; her kin would not dare risk leaving anything to chance.'

Customer fell momentarily silent while he digested the information he had been given. Something he couldn't quite give a name to, puzzled him. He looked at the physician inquiringly. 'It does not seem at all likely to you that the bruising to her throat came first, before she was struck on the head?'

The physician shrugged. 'Before or after, it makes little difference. It was the blow to her head that killed her, as I have already said.'

'I beg your pardon, sir, if I have offended you by my remark,' said Customer, thinking he detected a faint trace of hostility in Piers Heard's tone of voice. 'You misunderstand my motive in putting this question to you, which in no way challenges your findings. I seek merely to form a clear picture in my head of this crime and frankly, I can find no place in it for the bruising to her throat by her killer *after* he had struck her on the head and her life began to ebb away from her. Would it not seem more logical to you that her killer tried first to throttle her with his bare hands and that for some reason, he felt unsure of this method of murder – there might have been some doubt in his mind as to when death by this means would actually occur – and so he decided to act in a more positive fashion and selected some heavy object to carry out the deed to his complete satisfaction?'

'You are a deep thinker, sir; I see that now,' said Piers Heard in a wry voice. 'It is my turn to congratulate you on your professionalism.'

'Do not patronize me, sir!' said Customer in a cold voice. 'There is the life of an innocent man at stake here. It is absolutely imperative that I should know everything there is to know about this savage crime, and the manner in which it was committed, so that when I present the hard, indisputable evidence of my imprisoned friend's innocence to the deputy bailiff for him to lay before a Justice of the Peace, an order for the immediate release of the prisoner will be given unhesitatingly. Let there be no doubt in your mind, sir, that I have made it my solemnly sworn duty to ensure that the girl's kin, the Trelawneys, are made to acknowledge publicly that the wrong man has been accused of this vile crime.'

'That name – Trelawney – is not familiar to me,' said Piers Heard with a faint frown.

Customer's face hardened. 'It is Rebecca's eldest brother, Lowarn the fox – no doubt with the connivance of other male members of the Trelawney family – whom I believe to be guilty of this crime.'

112

'I have heard it said that the fox is not an easy creature to run down to earth and that the same creature is artful, sly and cunning and will best his hunters every time.'

'Lowarn Trelawney will lead me a merry dance, I am prepared for that, but I shall snare him in the end, have no fear of that.'

'I would hear more of this,' said Piers Heard. 'Let us adjourn to the nearest tavern and I will listen to your plan of campaign and give you my honest opinion of it...see if there are not some improvements that can be made to it. You should also be advised by one such as myself, cognisant as I am of which way the wind blows in Bodmin and where one is most likely to find enemies lying in wait to trip up the unwary.'

'That is kind of you, sir, but thank you, no. You have helped me enough. Bodmin town crawls with Trelawney vermin; the leader of the pack – the girl's father, Samuel – his six sons and the rabble they call their servants.' *Not to mention the unresolved issue of one faithless Countess Ballini whom, if truth were to be told, Customer feared far more than the Trelawneys, singly or in force!* 'The Trelawneys,' he added, 'return at first light tomorrow to Wynehouse Corner with the body of the girl, Rebecca, to arrange her burial.'

'And you, sir? What are your plans?'

'I, too, shall return to Wynehouse Corner, but alone. The answers I seek are there, not here.'

'There seems to be no doubt in your mind that these people will allow you to pursue your vendetta against them.'

'This affair has become too public; they would not risk harming a hair of my head. It is in their best interests that the due process of law is observed in every particular, with my friend tried at the Launceston Assizes this spring. That said, they seek to see him found guilty of murder and then be hanged by the neck for his crime in Launceston's town square in full view of its citizenry.'

Piers Heard considered Customer for a moment. 'Well, Customer Trago, should you be mistaken in this and come to grief, you know where to come to have your broken bones mended.'

'There is just one question I would ask before I take my leave of you, sir,' said Customer.

With an abrupt nod of his head, Piers Heard said, 'I shall save you the bother. The answer is no. The girl was not a virgin, of that there can be no question. But by the same token, neither had she lain with a man in the hours or minutes immediately preceding the moment of her death.'

'You would swear to it, that she was not taken against her will and raped?'

'I am sorry if you thought to find something of that nature here, Customer Trago. You must seek elsewhere for the motive for this crime.'

'You misunderstand me, sir. I was merely covering all possibilities, as indeed I am sure the Trelawneys will. As for the other, the motive for this crime… That is already known to me.'

'Is it indeed, sir?' said Piers Heard, his tone dry. 'Then let me be the first to congratulate you; the battle is as good as won. Provided, of course, that you can win over our good deputy bailiff to your way of thinking!'

Customer regarded the physician thoughtfully. 'Are you suggesting, sir, that the officers of law and order in this town are open to corruption?'

'These are rapidly changing times, Customer Trago; you know as much yourself by your admitted avoidance of Launceston Priory at the moment. In the pushing and shoving that is going on everywhere among the Cornish noblemen and yeomanry for church land – and Bodmin Priory land is as prime an example of the current trend in church affairs in Cornwall as you will find anywhere – friends have become mortal enemies, wrong has overnight not only become right, but perfectly acceptable, and greed has become the natural circumstance of man, with corruption and lawlessness the means of fuelling that sorry condition within him.'

'Should I scent the faintest whiff of any perversion of justice, I have friends in London and elsewhere – powerful friends – from whom I can seek a swift redress of the balance,' Customer warned him in an arch voice.

'Something tells me you are going to need your powerful friends and more before this thing is through, Customer Trago. But I wish you well. You will not find Piers Heard blocking your path in your endeavours to free an innocent man of this terrible crime.'

'Your fee for your services, sir?' asked Customer, raising his eyebrows inquiringly.

Piers Heard squinted at him for a moment or two in silence. 'Suffice unto me your word that when you return to Bodmin next, Customer Trago, you will tell me of your adventures and how goes your case against the Trelawneys.'

Customer thought for a moment. 'Can I trust you, sir?'

'It has been some little while since I last saw any virtue in trust and honesty, but perhaps, if there were some specific favour you had a mind to ask of me, I might – for old time's sake – make an exception in your case.'

'Only that you might be kind enough to keep an ear to the ground for me here in Bodmin while I am engaged elsewhere in the business of clearing my friend's name.'

'I was going to do that anyway, for my own interest.'

'You will get word to me of anything that you think might be of importance to my friend's case, even if your information goes badly for him?'

Piers Heard nodded. 'You have my word on it.'

'Then we have a bargain, sir. I shall ride out from Bodmin in the morning safe in the knowledge that someone is watching my back for the assassin's knife.'

Piers Heard smiled. 'What a fanciful imagination you have, Customer Trago.' The physician's eyes narrowed fractionally. 'Who would think to harm a well-intentioned, strapping young fellow such as yourself?'

'Who indeed?' rejoined Customer, his tone wry.

Chapter Twenty-three

Piers Heard hastened through the town with the bottle of cough remedy he had promised the crippled errand boy that at the very first opportunity available to him, he would deliver personally to the high-born woman in her sick room at the hostelry where she was currently in residence. A countess from a far off foreign land, the boy had said, eyes wide, voice respectfully hushed. Piers Heard doubted it. The quick glimpse of a corner of Spanish lace and a flash of fine silk and that particular boy would elevate a rich Devon or Dorset landowner's wife to the nobility. He was surprised the boy hadn't said the sick woman was the King of Spain's daughter!

The owner of the hostelry greeted him anxiously, wringing his hands and urging him to make haste. 'I was about to send the boy for you. I fear my news is grim, sir. Your special remedy was of no use; they were both too far gone when they sent out for it and should have taken more positive steps to turn the sickness on its head much sooner than they did.'

Drawing in his breath in a shudder, the hosteller then went on, 'My good wife took a tray of chicken broth up to the gentleman and his lady and when she returned a short while later to collect it, they were both gone; fatally expired. Succumbed to this terrible affliction that plagues our town. Gone blue round the lips in their agony. And her such a fine, beautiful young lady, too. A countess, she said.'

Piers Heard's heart almost stopped dead. *Blue? Was that what the man said? Blue... As in cyanosis?*

The physician surreptitiously pushed the bottle of cough remedy farther down into his jacket pocket and thanked his lucky stars that he was not carrying it in his hand where the hosteller could see it. There was a God in Heaven after all! The man was unmistakably under the impression that the luckless pair had taken delivery of a bottle of his perfectly harmless cough and cold physic earlier in the day. So far so good. For the physician and apothecary, Piers Heard, if for no one else!

He hastened after the man upstairs and into the countess's room.

They had scarcely crossed the threshold when the proprietor's wife called to him on some matter she claimed needed his urgent attention below stairs and Piers Heard was left alone.

One quick look at the bluish-purple discolouration of the countess's skin, and in particular, the nasal mucous membranes of both the dead woman and the man and the flesh around their lips – the man appeared to have collapsed in his death throes onto the foot of the countess's bed and died there, she had died beneath the covers – told the physician all he needed to know. He quickly grabbed up the ominously, half full bottle of pink mixture that he could see standing on a side table, pouring into it the equivalent of two hearty doses from the full bottle of physic he had brought with him, and then exchanged one for the other, burying what was beyond all question Lucy Trenwith's second bottle of hydrocyanic acid wasp poison deep in his jacket pocket.

He didn't bother to ponder the whys and wherefores of the shocking double tragedy that lay before him, it was enough that he had been in time to save his own skin. But he would definitely have to call upon his better nature to prevent himself from taking a riding crop to that raddled baggage, Gertrude, and then throwing her out into the street for what had come to pass in this room today.

Merciful Heaven, this was a day Piers Heard wasn't going to forget in a hurry! And maybe it was time he gave serious thought to weaning his patients off this curious fixation of his late father's with the colour pink. It was, of course, a shade too late to say it now, but it could prove fatal!

Chapter Twenty-four

Eber was giving up the fight; Customer could see it in the blacksmith's heavily clouded eyes as Eber looked up from the wooden pallet on which he was sitting, and watched the gaoler unlock the door of his cell.

It was a pitiful sight to see in the murky grey light of the fading day... The beast of Wynehouse Corner – protector of outcasts, the weak and unfortunate – beaten and cowed and made a weary old man in less than forty-eight hours, his heart filled with remorse and undoubtedly in danger of breaking as a result of Rebecca's savage murder while his back was turned and his mind occupied with matters concerning the enlargement of his purse.

'Come now,' said Customer heartily, and with what he hoped was a confident smile, as he walked up to Eber. 'All is not quite lost.'

'You think not?' said Eber. 'No, I fear I am a dead man. The deputy bailiff and those loutish curs he calls his men will see me swing for this; I see it in their eyes as they measure me up for size.'

'The eyes you should inquire into are mine, Eber, not theirs.'

'I have, young sir. What I see there is a handsome young fellow, stout of heart, loyal and true to his friends; but what I cannot help but also see is that he is riding a fine white steed like some heroic holy crusader of old, and with his head held so high in the clouds he cannot see the savage realities that surround him down here on the cold, hard, pitiless earth beneath his feet. The Trelawneys have too many rich and powerful friends here in Bodmin. I fear the critical mistake you have made in permitting yourself to be talked into agreeing to my being brought here, is going to find me in my grave – and should you not tread with great caution, your own alongside it for good measure. You have been tricked, young sir: you have walked right into Lowarn Trelawney's trap, leading me with the hangman's rope already about my neck.'

Eber sat hunched forward, head bowed dejectedly over his huge paws which were clasped in front of him on his thick, strong knees.

Customer watched him for a moment and then he said, 'If you

118

wish to punish yourself for having allowed this terrible thing to happen to Rebecca in your absence, then I ask you to say so now and thereby save me a deal of time, trouble and effort on your part, and for my own, save my skin to which I am greatly attached and which the Trelawneys would seek to peel from my flesh layer by layer!'

Eber looked up at him with great, sorrowing eyes. 'Would my going to the hangman's scaffold to appease my guilt for having abandoned all of you to the greedy, grasping wiles of the Trelawneys' bring the little one back to us?' He shook his head. 'Eber Pendragon has no wish to play the martyr in this affair, young sir. Be assured of that, if of nothing else.'

'Very well, then; let us get down to business. Tell me of your movements from the moment you left the inn to ride out in this direction to visit with your gambling acquaintance, Trenwith. I need to know everything.'

Eber looked puzzled. 'There is nothing to tell; I swear it on the sweet memory of my dearest beloved wife, Katharine! I was looking over my property with Trenwith during the latter half of the morning and into the early part of the afternoon. I cannot claim that Trenwith is my friend, but neither is he my enemy. He is an honest, God-fearing man and he will vouchsafe that I was with him until a little after an hour gone noon when I set out for home.'

'We will come to that presently. Tell me of your movements before you started out from Wynehouse Corner for the Trenwith place.'

Eber looked even more puzzled. Then he sighed resignedly and said, 'I arose at five o'clock, an hour earlier than usual and shortly before the morning began to grow light. I then packed some bread and cheese and a flask of water for my journey before crossing to the Wynehouse – the shippen – to saddle Will. I was on my way well within an hour of my rising from my bed, and I did not pause to break bread until I was in sight of Trenwith's farmhouse, something like five hours later. It is a four and a half hour ride from Wynehouse Corner to Trenwith's farm. He will confirm that I presented myself at the front door of his home shortly before the hour of eleven that morning, as arranged with him last Saturday evening when he played with me at cards and wagered and lost some pastureland of his, which is now my rightful property and which Trenwith has agreed with me is to be put under the plough this spring.'

Customer nodded. 'What of Rebecca before you left Wynehouse Corner? Did you speak with her before you rode off on Will?'

Eber frowned and briefly there was a spark of the old fire in his eyes. 'What is this you say? Has someone said I was with her? This is Lowarn Trelawney's doing: he is the one making this false allegation about the little one and me.'

'You stand accused of Rebecca Trelawney's murder, Eber,' Customer reminded him in a grave voice. 'Of course the Trelawneys are saying you were with Rebecca in the minutes and seconds before she met with her end.'

The spark died. 'As God is my witness, young sir, I swear that as many as three or four days had passed since I last saw the little one.' Eber looked worried. 'I won't lie to you, young sir. The little one was angry with me and I think she had run off from the Wynehouse. Where, I do not know, but it would not have been back to her evil tribe, and it is certain that she would have come back to us at the Wynehouse sooner or later. It was not the first time she had left us – Agnes and me – and disappeared for days on end.'

Customer was both surprised and uneasy at this unexpected admission of bad feeling between Rebecca and Eber. Lowarn Trelawney had known something of this and had made capital of it; of that Customer was sure. 'What happened between you and Rebecca?'

'I drowned the kittens – the ones infesting the old shippen where I shelter Lady.' Eber frowned at him. 'It broke my heart into a million tiny pieces to do it, young sir, but I had no choice, they were overrunning the place; worse than the mice and the rats. Fifteen of them at last count, wilder than mountain lions, and more due any day. I lied to the little one when she searched for them. I deliberately spoke of some crippling disease, which was not entirely untrue, and that in their weakened condition, the long tail must have carried them off in the night to his lair and made a hearty meal of them. But she knew the truth of it, she knew they had seen the bottom of my old wooden bucket, and she was much distressed.'

'You have no idea at all where she might have gone?'

Eber shook his great head. 'Where does the wind go when it tires of playing merry hell with us at Wynehouse Corner? Never so far that it cannot return to us when the mood takes it, like Rebecca, young sir. Agnes will tell you that.'

'Did Rebecca have any friends, someone aside from Agnes and you to whom she could turn for comfort in her distress over the drowned kittens?'

'No one. Rebecca was an outcast from the moment she was born. Shunned by all except us – old Agnes, who loves the girl as if she were her own, me, and now you who have shown her much kindness since your first day with us at the Wynehouse.'

Customer was puzzled. 'And yet I am told that her mother is calling for her to be at her bedside as she exhales her final lungful of air.'

Eber frowned. 'Mistress Trelawney has been asking for Rebecca?'

'You seem doubtful,' observed Customer. 'Is there some special reason why a mother who waits at death's door would not wish to see her daughter before passing on through it to the other side?'

'Mistress Trelawney is the toughest and strongest of the tribe, with the constitution of an ox. She will live to dance on the graves of all her brood. All our graves!'

'You doubt Lowarn's insistence that his mother lies on her deathbed?'

The blacksmith's shaggy eyebrows shot up. 'The same bed in which she lay while giving birth to Lowarn, and as his slimy head slithered out from betwixt her legs, named him the fox for his fine, handsome, trustworthy features?' Eber's eyebrows rose even higher. 'The same bed from which she kicked the pathetic bundle of swaddling clothes that was Rebecca, her one and only daughter, moments after the little one's birth?'

'I must say you paint a charming picture of the Mistress Trelawney,' remarked Customer in a dry voice.

'I would not deny her that small charity,' said Eber, a glint in his eye.

'I shall remember to carry my crucifix with me when and if I decide to call upon her.'

'I would be inclined to place more faith in the powers of my sword and right arm, young sir. Keep that one always before you, face-to-face, make no allowance for the assumed gentleness of her sex, and at all times expect the worst, and more to come. Watch closely for the rusty dagger she keeps concealed within the folds of her skirts and at all costs, avoid any bite from her teeth which it is said she paints with the undiluted venom she milks from the adder that infests their scabby, wind-ravaged moorland. Agnes will bear witness to all that I have said and tell you of the servant girl who was slow in doing the Mistress Trelawney's bidding and who was bitten on an ear by her mistress and died in agony of her foully poisoned wound three weeks later.'

Customer visibly shivered with revulsion. A visit to see and speak with the Mistress Trelawney was definitely something to which grave consideration should be given before being undertaken.

Both men fell silent and then Customer gave a small nod. He made as if to leave, but after hesitating for a moment, he turned back to Eber.

'The stranger, Pawley,' he began. 'What do you know of him, Eber? I mean, really know of him?'

Chapter Twenty-five

Eber gave Customer a curious look. 'This man, Pawley, bothers you?'

Customer frowned. 'There is something about him–'

'I fear you have been listening to Agnes and now share her doubts about the fellow and his motives for calling in at the Wynehouse,' Eber remarked in a dry voice.

'No, it is more than that, Eber. I know him, I am sure I know him, but I cannot recall from where or when. I have never seen him up close,' Customer confessed after a moment's hesitation, 'so I have had no clear look at his facial features...'

'But?' said Eber when Customer hesitated again.

'But I am sure we have met at sometime in the past.'

Eber gave his great bear's head a slow shake. 'I fear this feeling you have about Pawley can be traced directly back to the weeks of fever you suffered from your sword wound and has not the slightest basis in reality. Perfectly understandable. A fever such as you have suffered would heighten the imagination of any man to the point where he finds himself seeing danger lurking in every nook and cranny he looks into and in the face of any stranger whose path crosses his. You have suffered a terrible ordeal: I know I made light of it, but the truth of it is that I truly feared you would die.'

'I recall nothing of it,' Customer admitted in a slow, thoughtful voice. 'Not of the attack that was made upon me, nor of the men who lay in wait for me. Only the sound of hoofbeats as they rode off. I still hear that sound, in my sleep and sometimes even when I am wide awake. It haunts me.' He paused. Then, in a hesitant voice, he went on, 'That is why I have always felt so sure that Sir William Gennys of Lauceston Priory was behind the attack.'

Eber was shaking his head. 'He would not trouble himself. Not Gennys. What gain would there be in it for him in harming you? Forgive my bluntness, but what great seat of power do you sit upon that might feasibly pose a threat to him in his ambitions?'

'The attack on me has something to do with Emanuel. If not something to do with his life at the priory and with his problematic relationship with Gennys, then with Emanuel's death and the manner in which he died. I am sure of it.'

The two fell silent. Eber was the first to speak again. 'To return to Pawley and this uneasy feeling you have about him... You would be well advised to keep all thought of renewing any acquaintance with the fellow at a long distance, like your sight of him. I know I risk fanning the fire of your mistrust of him when I admit to you that after having had time to reflect on a number of issues over the past twenty-four hours concerning all of us at the inn, it strikes me that Pawley was a little too quick on the scene to rescue his horse from the fire in my stable that night.'

Customer looked hard at Eber. 'You think it might not have been one of the Trelawneys who is responsible for the fire?'

Eber gave a small shrug.

'But why, Eber, *why*? Why would Pawley want to burn down the stable of the man who has shown nothing but charitable goodwill towards him?'

'Agnes who, much as you are, is prey to wild, fanciful imaginings, seems to think this fellow might be keeping a close watch on you.' Eber let his voice tail off. His eyes searched Customer's, waiting for his reaction.

'What are you suggesting?' A shocked look crossed Customer's face. 'That he saw me go into the stable, and–?'

Customer paused, struggling to collect his thoughts which were scattering in all directions. 'He tried to kill me, hoped to burn me alive – is that what you're saying?' he asked at length.

Eber was silent for a moment. Then he said, 'I think you must ask yourself why Pawley would wish to see you dead. Where and when you met in the past pales into insignificance alongside the answer you will find to this question if you search hard enough for it. Always assuming, of course, that there is an answer to it to be found. If Pawley was the guilty party and he is the one who set fire to the stable, knowing full well that you were in there, then this is a man with a passion – a passion to destroy all trace of Customer Trago from the face of this earth. But I caution you not to act or speak in haste. It is by no means certain that it was this particular stranger's hand that held a lighted torch to my property. I'll not pretend with you, young sir: I waver much more in favour of the Trelawneys when it comes to pointing a finger in the direction of the fire lighter.'

Customer gave a slight nod and turned away. The cell door clanged shut behind him and Eber listened pensively to the sharp sound his footsteps made on the slate floor as he walked away.

Eber reflected for some moments on his conversation with Customer concerning the stranger who, several days earlier, had called at his inn with a lame horse. He had discreetly inquired about Pawley, but only of those requiring the services of a blacksmith since Pawley had arrived at the inn. None knew the man, but interestingly, the one person who had apparently set eyes upon him, albeit briefly, shared Agnes's mistrust of him.

And mine, thought Eber. But he had to admit, so far without foundation. Pawley might or might not have set fire to stable. Then again, so might Customer Trago. Not intentionally, but by some careless action to which he was loath to confess for fear of the wrath of his kind benefactor whom he knew to have a fierce temper, Eber allowed with a fleeting smile.

Tucking a stray strand of his long, grizzled hair behind an ear, Eber lay back on his pallet to think some more.

There was one person who might well be able to clear up the mystery of Pawley's true objectives, whether they were as straightforward and honourable as claimed or not, but would that person arrive in time to forestall the possibility of any further mischief befalling Customer Trago?

Eber touched a hand to his neck. He could already feel the hangman's noose fitting snugly around it, courtesy of the Trelawneys. Nicholas Allsopp's piercing black eyes peering at him through those iron bars of his cage would, for once, thought Eber, never be more welcome.

'Make haste, Nicholas,' Eber murmured. 'Unfortunately for Eber Pendragon, the boy, Trago, is all good intentions, but little else, I fear.'

He was suddenly aware that Customer had paused somewhere along the passage beyond his cell. Eber listened intently, expecting to hear Customer engaged in conversation with someone. But in the absolute silence that followed, Eber decided that he had been mistaken and closing his eyes, he drifted off to sleep.

Customer, however, was but a short distance from Eber's cell and deep in thought. Something Eber had said to him had reawakened his memory of a conversation that Emanuel had had with him as a child. Customer wasn't sure how old he was at the time, no more than five or six years old, he would have said. He had suffered a severe chest infection and fever after almost drowning in a deep pond on common land near the priory. He had told Emanuel that one of the other orphaned priory boys who had gone with him to the pond, had deliberately tried to drown him, pushing him into the pond and then, instead of helping him out, forcing his head down under the icy water. Emanuel had told him it was the fever speaking, all in his imagination, and that his near-drowning was the price to be paid for his having left the priory unescorted by one of the holy brethren and without first seeking the prior's permission to leave.

But soon afterwards, the boy who had tried to drown him – Customer could not remember his name – disappeared from the priory. He never saw him again.

Customer had an overwhelming feeling of having seen that boy since. The boy who was now a man, like himself.

Pawley?

Customer gave himself a little shake and walked on. *Imagination!*

Chapter Twenty-six

Eber's dour advice concerning the Mistress Trelawney came uncomfortably back to Customer while he was riding back to the inn at Wynehouse Corner late the following day.

Customer anticipated catching his first glimpses of the inn and the smithy from the brow of one of the high hills that loomed before him. Pale lamp and candlelight would soon show on the windows of the inn in the gathering dusk of early evening. None on those of the smithy. Not tonight, nor for many more nights to come and perhaps never again if the Trelawneys' version of events held sway in Bodmin and Eber Pendragon went summarily to the gallows for Rebecca's murder.

The narrow track to the small town of Launceston swung away enticingly to the right of the highway along which Customer was presently riding, and reaching it, he abruptly reined in his horse and paused. It wasn't a crossroads, and yet this was where he felt he had halted, at a crossroads in his life, with his old, safe world of easy, wantonly carefree living beckoning to him on one side, and with the Mistress Trelawney lying in wait for him with rusty dagger drawn and viper's teeth bared – as fearsome a spectacle as he had ever visualized! – on the other.

A little voice inside his head urged him to turn onto that narrow, murky track on his right and take his chances that the band of villains who had attempted to cut him down all those weeks ago had no connection whatsoever with Launceston Priory and would have forgotten all about him. It was no coincidence that both he and Emanuel had been similarly attacked – the two incidents were somehow inexorably linked, of this Customer had little doubt – but for the moment, he would defer to Eber Pendragon's assertion that he should look other than to the priory for his answers.

Customer continued to hesitate. Common sense should prevail, he told himself. Eber Pendragon, old Agnes, poor Rebecca, and the crumbling, mould-blighted inn at Wynehouse Corner ought to be put far from his mind. If the Bodmin officers of law and order were as readily corruptible as his conversation with the physician Piers

Heard had led him to think, then Eber's purse was deep enough to take care of things in a far more satisfactory manner to all parties concerned than Customer Trago ever could by his wits alone. There was very little that money could not buy, particularly now in these deeply troubled times for Cornwall.

Customer fingered his beard and then ran his hand slowly across his forehead, smoothing the heavy fringe that Agnes had cut in his hair one afternoon while he was slumbering in his chair at the sunny window of his room, and which she claimed strengthened his features.

What was it that he really feared? That someone in Launceston would recognize him? Surely that was not likely after all these years. The new prior and he had never met, nor, so far as Customer was aware, was he acquainted with the prior's clerk, and the monks that Customer could still put a name and a face to had been very old and doddery, or had seemed so to him at the time. They would have long since passed on. He could take some other name; make inquiries at the priory of the circumstances of Emanuel's death and then seek out the place where he had been laid to rest to pay his respects. Having done all of this, he could then close the book on that chapter of his life forever, take his leave of the priory once and for all and then ride out from Launceston with a clear conscience, never to return to this windy, water-logged part of Britain again.

'For pity's sake, Customer Trago, be sensible, man: do it!' cried the voice inside his head.

He needed no prompting, he was already cantering along the track towards Launceston, faster and faster, thick mud flying high and wide about him from the hooves of his horse, spattering his face and sticking to his lips. He was *not* running out on Eber: what he was doing now was an act of pure, unadulterated kindness. Eber could take care of himself. And in more ways than one, thought Customer wryly. It would be foolish to think that Eber would forsake the cards and dice during his incarceration at Bodmin Gaol at the deputy bailiff's pleasure. Eber could easily win his freedom at a turn of the cards or a single roll of the dice. He would probably leave the town far richer than when he had entered it and thank Customer Trago for having afforded him the opportunity of leaving him to it. The blacksmith of Wynehouse Corner was a natural born winner. He did not need Customer Trago. Eber was well rid of him. Customer Trago could bring him nothing but bad luck. Or worse… An empty purse if things dragged on for too long!

An image of Lowarn Trelawney's face suddenly materialized from out of the mounting darkness. Yellow eyes taunted Customer.

It was Lowarn Trelawney who had pointed out the track to Launceston as they had ridden past it on their way to Bodmin with Eber and Rebecca's body. Lowarn had done so with a sly smile and with no apparent motive that came readily to Customer's mind now other than that Lowarn had guessed the truth about Customer Trago, that he was weak, a coward, and that he would bolt the first chance he got.

Customer drew rein sharply, giving himself no pause for thought – save to call himself every kind of fool for having played so gullibly into Lowarn Trelawney's hands – before turning round and galloping back to the highway and resuming his journey to Wynehouse Corner.

A lone horse and rider stood motionless, as if carved in black marble, at the top of Butterfly Lane. Customer neither checked nor urged his horse on. He kept his head held high and his gazed fixed on the mellow glow of the windows of the inn up ahead. He did not look at the rider as he approached him, nor as he passed him by, but from the corner of an eye, he saw the rider sweep his black, cockaded hat from his head in a mocking gesture of salutation.

There was little doubt in Customer's mind that the eyes that watched him were the yellow fox-eyes of Lowarn Trelawney, and that Lowarn had more than likely waited for many hours at that spot to see if Customer Trago would return to the Wynehouse.

Customer did not look back at the corner of Butterfly Lane until he dismounted on the forecourt of the inn. The lone rider had slipped away in the darkness.

Agnes was in the kitchen. She poured wine for Customer as he entered the room and then she began ladling a richly seasoned stew of fowl and mixed vegetables into a bowl.

He ate quickly and greedily, not realizing how hungry he was until the first mouthful of the good, hot food slipped down his throat and into his growling stomach.

Agnes let him finish his meal in peace and then, as she cleared the table and he moved up to the hearth to warm himself, she said, 'I am told that the Trelawneys have returned and that they are saying Eber will hang before this month is at its end.'

'Bold words,' said Customer.

'They say they speak with the authority of the deputy bailiff himself.'

'We shall see,' said Customer. 'The deputy bailiff will not act hastily.'

'Can us be sure of this? Us has heard it said that he—'

'We have no time to indulge ourselves in idle gossip, Agnes.' Customer spoke sharply, more an indication of how afraid he was that the idle gossip he warned her to ignore would come to pass, than a heartfelt conviction that it would prove to be baseless. He immediately took pity on the worry lines he could see engraved on Agnes's face and he cursed himself for his clumsiness. Her evident distress dictated that for once, he should put his own fears and worries to one side and continue to put on a bold front. It was a small enough thing to ask of himself that he should make every effort to ease the pain and torment that was clearly being suffered by this kind-hearted woman who had given her all to save his life. 'I have no reason to suspect that Bodmin's deputy bailiff is anything other than an honest, upright officer of the law,' he went on, 'and I do not intend to complicate matters further by listening to every unsubstantiated claim that is made against him. Be assured that Eber will get a proper hearing before a Justice of the Peace in a properly constituted court of law before any attempt is made to slip a rope round his neck. It is my task to make that hearing tell and thereby ensure that the noose is fashioned to fit the right size neck. Now, Agnes, tell me about the kittens... Did you know of the trouble between Eber and Rebecca over them?'

Chapter Twenty-seven

Agnes looked hard at Customer, puzzled by the abruptness of his question. 'The kittens? 'Tis strange that you should ask old Agnes of them, young sir, when so much else is at stake here. What part can they play in this sad affair? Old Agnes simply asked Eber to get rid of them for us; they were becoming a nuisance. Some were showing signs of the staggering sickness, and sickness spreads like wildfire among cats. No fault should attach to Eber over these poor, sickly little creatures; 'tis with old Agnes that all blame must lie for Rebecca's terrible distress about them. Eber had no idea there were so many cats out the back there. Old Agnes promised Rebecca that she could have one of brindle Bronwyn's kittens when they come in a week or two, and that it could live here in the kitchen and sit warming itself on the hearth by the cooking-fire and be fed from the pot with us. Bronwyn is not as wild as the others; her kittens will be more easily tamed to the kitchen and the hand that feeds them.'

Customer frowned thoughtfully. 'Your promise held no sway with Rebecca?'

'She was content about the kitten old Agnes said she could have, but she was still upset about those Eber had drowned. She was a bigger trial than Eber is when it comes to saving and keeping the unwanted and the sick and dying.'

'Could anyone else have known that there was bad feeling between Eber and Rebecca in regard to these kittens?'

'Eber tried to find a home for the less sick of them among the men he played cards with on Saturday night. One or two said they had need of a good mouser, but they were merely jesting because they knew Rebecca was out here in the kitchen with old Agnes, listening in to their conversation, and that finding them kind homes meant much to her. Nothing came of it. The men left and the kittens stayed. First thing next morning, Eber fetched a bucket and drowned the lot.'

Customer nodded. 'So the Trelawneys could have known something of the matter from the mealy-mouths of one or more of those men who had made cruel sport of the kittens at Rebecca's expense.' He frowned at Agnes. 'What of the stranger Pawley, Agnes? Is it possible that he knew of the trouble between Eber and Rebecca about the kittens?'

'He was not in the gaming room at all on Saturday evening, I am sure of that,' Agnes replied, 'but that is not to say he wasn't listening at a window, or on the stairs, and overheard the talk among Eber and the gamesters. Pawley is one for night prowling. Whether driven by demons to prowl the night until he tires and feels able to sleep more easily, old Agnes has no idea. She'll say this, though. There is much that goes on behind those brooding eyes of his.' She gave a knowing nod of her head. 'But what interest could this matter of the kittens and Rebecca be to him, a complete stranger? And why are the kittens so important to what has happened to Eber?'

'The kittens are only secondary to Eber's current unfortunate situation. It is Rebecca, her distress over them that is important – her running away from the Wynehouse because of what Eber did to them. The Trelawneys, for instance, will make much of this and will surely say that Rebecca was murdered by Eber as he tried to force her to return here to the inn with him. For good measure, throwing in that she was his unpaid slave – abducted by him against her will from the bosom of her loving family in the first instance, and then forced to work her tiny fingers to the bone in service to him!'

'And what part in all of this, Rebecca's distress, are you thinking the stranger Pawley might have played?'

Customer gave his head a slow shake. 'I don't know, Agnes.'

She gave him a bemused look. 'You think there might be bad blood between him and Eber and that he killed Rebecca, knowing that the Trelawneys were sure to blame Eber for her murder?'

Customer frowned. 'Eber says the man is a stranger to all of you here at the inn–'

Aye, but what of you, young sir? Agnes asked herself uneasily. *It would seem to old Agnes that there is more chance of there being bad blood between Customer Trago and this stranger than between the stranger and Eber. Old Agnes watches Pawley closely and what old Agnes sees isn't a stranger. Not to you, young sir. You may swear to Heaven above that you do not know Malachy Pawley, but Malachy Pawley knows you, or has some dark reason to know you. Old Agnes fears that the Devil himself, disguised as a holy pilgrim and dressed all in black, has followed hard on your footsteps. He crooks his finger at Customer Trago and beckons him close, but Customer Trago does not see it like old Agnes sees it and knows it for the threat of death that she fears is hanging over him.*

Customer and Agnes remained silent for some minutes, absorbed in their own anxious thoughts. And then Agnes sighed and said, 'Deep in her heart Rebecca knew that Eber was right in what he did to put an end to the suffering of those poor little creatures. She would have come back to us. There have been other times when she has run off because she was upset about something; many more times because part of her was wild, untamed, and like a creature of the meadow and the woodland, she needed to be among her own kind, free as the wind to blow and birds to fly wherever she wished.'

Agnes paused. She looked at Customer levelly for a moment or two and then, in a mildly rebuking voice, she said, 'You will forgive old Agnes for making so bold as to say this to you, young sir, but Rebecca *had* come back to us since the day of the drownings, hadn't she? Only fleetingly, I'll admit that, but old Agnes saw her with you after this – in the moonlight…out there on the forecourt shortly before the stable was mischievously put to the torch.'

Customer frowned at the memory. He knew where this was leading and it troubled him deeply.

Agnes continued, her voice now gentle and understanding: 'You mustn't blame yourself, young sir: you couldn't stop Rebecca from running off that night any more than Eber or old Agnes could when she was hurt and suffering. She needed time on her own to lick her wounds and make them better. 'Twas best what happened between you and her that night. But if it is some dark and terrible reason other than the drowning of the kittens that you seek to account for her running off from us, then old Agnes must be honest and say she would not think to look any further than her present company. She would also have to say that it is a mercy the Trelawneys know nothing of Rebecca's deep affection for you or it would be conspiracy they would be talking now – a conspiracy, they would say, between you and Eber to do away with the girl for loving you and making a nuisance of herself. It would be two necks they would hope to see cruelly stretched at the end of a hangman's rope.'

Customer looked at her despairingly. 'Where did she go after she ran off from me that night, Agnes?'

She shook her head sadly. 'Only Rebecca would know.'

'And Lowarn. He has the look in his eye of one who would make it his business to know where his sister would seek to hide herself when she had a need to heal her hurts. But how can I prove this?'

'You will find a way, young sir. Old Agnes is confident that you will not be obstructed in your search for the truth. The Trelawneys have few friends in these parts, Eber has many.'

Customer was touched by her faith in him, but human nature being what it was, that, unfortunately, would soon change with none genuinely able to lay claim to more popularity thereabouts than the Trelawneys who, as word spread, would acquire the status of saints. Customer would willingly wager his life on it. Without exception, those who had gambled at cards, or with the dice at the Wynehouse Inn on a Saturday night and had lost to Eber Pendragon, would now be only too quick to see the possibility of reclaiming their property through St Lowarn the Long Tail and his holy war against the demon gambler of Wynehouse Corner, and would rally round him to a man.

Customer sighed a little. Then, in a slow, thoughtful voice, he said, 'Tell me of the Mistress Trelawney, Agnes. I would hear more of her teeth...'

Chapter Twenty-eight

Customer retired to his bed early, but sleep eluded him. The intense emotional distress and strenuous activity of the past few days and the long hours he had spent in the saddle that day, had taken its toll on his sword wound which ached mercilessly. Finally he rose and went quietly to the room at the other end of the passage to stand at the window contemplating the calm stillness of the night.

The pain in his side disappeared while he was standing upright and he contented himself to remain where he was for the present. Going to the room at the end of the passage in the small hours of the night to stand and watch for a light at the windows of the blacksmith's cottage had become something of a ritual for him, anyway. Eber's nocturnal habit of prowling from room to room held a strange fascination for him. It seemed such a curious manner in which to while away the time, despite the perfectly satisfactory explanation given by Agnes for Eber's nightwatch.

It was ominously quiet, the more so because this was Wynehouse Corner for which the winds, both from the south-west and the north-east, seemed to have a peculiarly strong attachment. So pitch black was it outside that had Customer not known there was a cottage on the opposite side of the roadway, he would have said nothing stood between him and infinity.

Pawley had not been seen at the inn all day and that evening. That pleased Agnes, but vaguely disturbed Customer when, shortly before they exchanged goodnights, she mentioned a conversation she'd had with Pawley early that morning. Pawley had told her that he intended to ride out on his horse, but he had not mentioned having any particular destination in mind, and neither had Agnes troubled herself to note which direction he had taken when setting off. This had apparently been Pawley's habit while Customer had been occupied with Eber in Bodmin. Each time that Pawley had ridden out, the only information he had volunteered before leaving was his intention to exercise his horse. He wanted to be sure that it had recovered fully from its injury before he quit the inn and rode on to Boscastle on his holy pilgrimage.

As Pawley had failed to return to the inn on this latest occasion, Agnes seemed to think that they might finally be rid of the man. Customer hadn't wished to disillusion her, but he had his doubts. Pawley would be back, he was sure of it. He was no more a holy pilgrim than was Customer Trago, and of that Customer was equally sure.

Customer had been looking out at the night for no more than five minutes, running the happenings of the past few days methodically through his mind and thinking about Pawley, where he might be at that moment and why there had been no sighting of him since early morning, when a pale, flickering light suddenly appeared in the smith's cottage, bobbing from the tiny panes of one high window to the next.

Customer watched its progress, his heart thumping madly and his cheeks burning, first bright red with anger and then paling with fear...

Eber had returned to Wynehouse Corner. He had broken out of Bodmin Gaol, probably reduced the place to a ruin and for good measure, torn the deputy bailiff and his men to shreds and scattered their remains all around Bodmin!

There would be no saving Eber now. Word would soon reach the Trelawneys of Eber's escape, if it hadn't already. They would ride up to the inn at any moment, followed tomorrow in strength for sure by the deputy bailiff and his men, baying for blood. The lives of all at the Wynehouse were in deadly peril. The deputy bailiff would insist it was a plot and hang the lot of them – Eber first, and then jointly, side by side, his co-conspirators, old Agnes and Customer Trago. Not one of them was to be spared.

It suddenly occurred to Customer that Pawley had somehow known of this and was deliberately keeping his distance until the deed was accomplished.

Panic-stricken, his highly imaginative mind conjuring up one horrifying scene after another, each worse than the one preceding it, Customer groped his way frantically back to his room. With shaking hands, he lit a candle and then hastened down the stairs to the kitchen and felt clumsily along the wide wooden shelf just inside the doorway for the oil lamp that was kept there.

He couldn't stop his hands from shaking, his chest was so tight with fear he could scarcely breathe, but he told himself that if he were quick about it, he might just be able to get Eber out of his cottage and into safe hiding before all hell broke loose. *(Before, that is, Customer Trago found himself surrounded by the deputy bailiff and his men and arrested on a charge of conspiring to pervert the true course of justice!)*

The night was no longer still and calm. The wind from the north-east was getting up and would soon be blowing like a raging demon, battering everything that was foolhardy enough to stand in its path.

Customer ran from the inn, lamp swinging wildly, his bare feet barely touching solid ground. He stumbled across the small, unevenly cobbled rear forecourt of the smith's cottage and then fell upon its single door, banging on it with the fist of his free hand and crying out frantically for Eber to let him in.

The strengthening wind heightened the urgency of the moment, tearing at Customer's nightshirt and stinging the flesh of his face, and driving his hair wildly back from his forehead. The bitterly cold wind brought tears of protest into his eyes, blurring his vision.

His panic mounted. That rushing noise… Was that the wind ripping through the branches of the old mountain ash tree which sheltered the shippen, or was it horses' hoofbeats he could hear pounding along the highway, coming ever nearer?

He lifted the lamp high above his head and looked round fearfully over his shoulder.

Agnes watched him covertly from a high window of the inn. Something of the fear and torment showing on his ashen face in the hovering lamplight was plain to see on her own face. Her heart was heavy in her breast and she placed a hand over it and moaned. Then she turned and went to his room. The key to the wine cellar was where he had left it, tucked underneath his pillow. It took her no time at all to find it.

Chapter Twenty-nine

There was no answer from within the smith's cottage. Desperately, Customer tried again to raise some response. The door was securely locked; wouldn't budge. He held the lamp high and looked up helplessly at the black window directly above his head and then ran back across the roadway and stood at the side of the inn, scanning all three of the windows on the upper floor of the cottage that faced the Wynehouse. They, like those across the rear of the cottage, were in complete darkness.

Sweat trickled from his temples into the corners of his eyes, mingling with the tears of frustration and despair that came suddenly into them.

Was it fear that made every pore in his body leak moisture, or was it the fever back again, brought on by the emotional upheaval and exertion of the past few days?

He passed a hand quickly across his hot forehead.

Fever... He was burning up with it!

He let out a heavy sigh of relief. There was no one prowling about in Eber's cottage, he had imagined seeing a light in the windows. He had more than half-expected Eber to break out of gaol, leaving a trail of havoc in his wake, and had therefore seen not what was actually there to be seen, but what he had feverishly *thought* to see.

Shaking with both the cold and the bad fright he had given himself, Customer went back indoors. He fell trembling upon his bed. Emanuel had taught him so many things, but unfortunately, not how to be strong and brave in times of crisis, nor how to control his too vivid imagination when it ran amok.

He closed his eyes, exhaustion finally winning the day as he drifted into an uneasy slumber.

Anna-Lucrezia haunted his dreams as a spectre hovering naked in the candlelit doorway of his room. The shadowy contours of her full, soft body drifted slowly towards him.

Overcome with desire for her and wilfully betrayed by his body again, he squeezed his eyes tightly shut and then turned quickly onto his stomach and buried his face in his pillow. He cried out, 'Leave me in peace, woman: take this poor, sorely weakened body of mine, it is yours, but do not ask murder of me. Have you no mercy? Can you not see it is a sin too far for one raised as I was by pious holy brothers of our blessed Mother Church?'

The bed creaked with the spectre's weight. Customer gritted his teeth. His hands, which he had thrust beneath his pillow, clutched at the bed linen, and then suddenly releasing their grip, swept frantically across it searching for the key to the wine cellar.

His heart stopped. He was in shock, incapable of thought. He felt the hot blast of the spectre's breath on the back of his neck.

Slowly, he raised his head off his pillow and sniffed the air. *Brandy.* Just like before, that other night when his beloved had come to him like this and he had fainted away, overcome with ecstasy.

The trouble was, this was no dream. *And that other time–?*

He felt sick; he couldn't bear to think about it.

This wasn't his beloved.

This…*this was Agnes!*

Mortified, he twisted round and then sat bolt upright, like a small child terrified by demons in the night, before scrambling crab-wise across his bed, away from the bleary-eyed, drooling spectre who pursued him on all fours across the covers.

He slid clumsily off the bed and stood at the side of it, trembling, his hands crossed protectively over his genitals, his eyes widening with horror at Agnes's relentless approach.

'Stop this, mistress!' he cried. 'Go to your room this instant. I shall speak with you in the morning about this disgraceful behaviour!'

Agnes reached out playfully and grabbed a handful of his nightshirt. 'Us has got eyes, young sir. Us knows the young sir is pleased to see old Agnes and wants her as badly as old Agnes wants him.'

He glanced down at the wilting bulge in his nightshirt, smacking her hand free and then stepping back quickly out of range of her reach. 'You have been deceived by what is no more than an involuntary response of my poor, tormented body to the pitiless fever that wracked it for all those many long weeks of my pain and suffering, and which still takes a measure of pleasure in pricking and poking at it as I lay in my bed at night. 'There, *look*–' He swept a hand down the front of himself. 'I am better already.'

'Old Agnes can make you feel even better still, young sir,' she said with a wicked gleam in her eye. 'Come, give old Agnes a kiss. Don't be cruel – old Agnes cannot bear it when you are cruel to her.'

'I regret I cannot accommodate you, mistress.' A note of pleading came into Customer's voice. 'You see before you a sick man, Agnes; one whose head aches painfully with all the pressure that has been placed upon it during these past few days, and whose injured side stings and burns him cruelly.'

She started to coo at him like a dove, crawling off the bed and then beginning to stalk him stealthily round it. 'Don't be shy, young sir. Lift up your nightshirt and come to your little turtle dove, Agnes, and let her stroke and kiss the hurt better.'

He panicked, measured the distance between himself and the door and calculated his chances of getting there before she sprang upon him and dragged him with her into his bed where he had every expectation that she would tease and torment him before raping him remorselessly, irrespective of his wishes in the matter. 'No, mistress, I will neither permit you to lay a finger upon me, nor kiss me. Neither will I give *you* a kiss. You will receive nothing from me but harsh words.' He inched towards the door, shoulders hunched, his hands crossed protectively over his genitals again. 'You are drunk, completely out of your senses. Have you no shame? If you will not think of me, then think of poor Eber and what he will say when he discovers that you have been raiding his wine cellar again.'

'Us knows Eber is not coming back home to us, young sir. Eber is as good as dead, is Eber. They've got him and they mean to keep him.' Agnes's voice became wheedling. 'Old Agnes would not kill for Eber, but old Agnes would kill for just one kiss from the young sir.' She pursed her lips and made smacking kissing noises at him. 'Just a little kiss. For old Agnes who loves you.'

'*Enough*, mistress!' Customer said sternly, an eye still on the doorway. 'I will hear no more of this brandy-fuelled nonsense. Now, give me the key you stole from beneath my pillow and then return to your room and go to your bed. Sleep off your drunken stupor and then we will speak in the morning.' He took another step nearer the door.

She slumped onto the bed, pouting and scratching her groin. 'I'll go, but only if the young sir comes with me.'

'That I cannot do. I am spoken for, mistress. I cannot betray my true love's heart. We are to be wed... Soon,' he added, as if this made all the difference to whether or not he could meanwhile enjoy the sexual favours of another woman.

Agnes advanced on him again in a clumsy crawl, cooing softly and with a teasing look in her eye.

He dived for the door, lunged through it, quickly drawing it closed behind him, and then raced along the passage to the stairs. He had no idea if Agnes followed him, he simply kept running from the inn and along the highway towards the Holy Well of St James until, exhausted, he collapsed in a ditch. He had no idea what he had thought to achieve by heading in that direction. He surely hadn't had it in mind to seek sanctuary in those holy surroundings, had he? Agnes would be beyond caring, anyhow, that she had cornered him in a place of great holiness. Her juices were running swift and hot and no protestation of his, or call for mercy from the blessed St James or any Higher Authority would prevail.

Agnes did not follow him, but he heard her sometime later, out on the forecourt, baying at the moon like a raging bitch on heat.

It turned his blood to ice.

Chapter Thirty

Customer waited until a good two hours after sunrise before venturing back to the inn. Agnes was in the kitchen chopping some lamb into cutlets for a stew. She gave him a curious look as he appeared, muddied and dishevelled and still in his nightshirt, in the doorway, but she made no comment; merely nodded her head abruptly in greeting.

Chopping down hard through some thick bone, she said, 'Us had a visitor last night, young sir. Master Wine Merchant came soon after you had taken to your bed. He left for Boscastle at first light and will return in a day or two. Us told him you were in charge of things here now and that you would discuss the wine order with him when he gets back.'

Customer was momentarily speechless. Her general demeanour was that of a woman going about her normal kitchen duties with genuinely no recollection of any unseemly behaviour on her part the previous night. Nor on any other night, for that matter, which he had to admit was not entirely impossible, bearing in mind her advanced state of intoxication on the two occasions in which he had figured so prominently. It was also possible that she remembered every disgraceful moment of last night's orgiastic intemperance, and was so ashamed of herself that she had decided to brazen it out by pretending her mind was a total blank on the matter. Which was probably for the best, he decided. He must not shirk his responsibility for the part he had played in it: Eber had warned him of the consequences of allowing the key of the wine cellar to slip from his possession.

With all the appearances of being a small boy who, having been sent to bed the previous night, unfed and in disgrace, was now making his first timid appearance downstairs the following morning to test the atmosphere and see if all were forgiven, he wrapped his arms about himself and shivered a little. He watched her for a moment and then, in a small, hesitant voice, he asked, 'Are you saying the wine merchant spent the night in Eber's cottage?'

She shook her head. 'No, here at the inn. Us gave him the room at the other end of the passage.'

Customer opened his mouth to deny that the wine merchant had spent the night there and then quickly snapped it shut again. So he hadn't imagined the light hopping from one window of the smith's cottage to the next. Master Allsopp, the wine merchant, had been prowling about over there in the dead of night without Agnes's knowledge.

Doing what?

Offhand, Customer could not think of a single thing.

He frowned to himself. He hadn't taken a light with him to the room at the end of the passage last night; somebody might well have been asleep in there without his knowing it. Neither had he made a lot of noise. He had been at pains not to wake Agnes in her tiny room off the kitchen below and have her start fussing about him. The wine merchant, if he were a heavy sleeper, or drinker (more than likely!), could have slept throughout his coming and going. And there was, of course, another possibility. Who was to say that the wine merchant wasn't fully cognizant of Agnes's fondness for brandy and that he hadn't sought sanctuary from her in the smith's cottage rather than spend the night at the inn in fear and trembling of her drunken nocturnal prowling?

Customer sighed inwardly. This was the explanation for the mysterious light he had seen last night, wasn't it? Nicholas Allsopp had escaped to the cottage from Agnes's unwelcome sexual attentions, and then – like Eber, but for his own perfectly acceptable reasons – the wine merchant had wisely kept a determined night-watch until he felt reasonably sure the danger was past and it was safe for him to return to the inn.

A sudden thought occurred to Customer. 'Who holds the key to the door of Eber's cottage?'

'Eber...on a chain with his purse,' she replied, and with something Customer thought might be a faint sparkle of amusement in her eyes. 'But so far as us knows, Eber didn't trouble himself to lock up before he left here with you and the Trelawneys. Why should he? Eber trusts us.'

Not you with the key of his wine cellar, he doesn't! thought Customer uneasily. But then Eber didn't touch alcohol: there would be none in his home and so no need to secure the place against Agnes and her brandy-parched throat. The door of the smith's cottage was nevertheless locked when Customer had tried it. Eber had not gone anywhere near his cottage before they had all set off for Bodmin. He had obviously left his home securely locked up against unwanted intruders – or *"us"*, as was Agnes's wont when referring to herself (and me, thought Customer with a wince; and for all he knew, the stranger Pawley and the wine merchant, too, should he happen to call in his absence) – earlier in the day when setting out to visit his gambling acquaintance, Trenwith.

'How much did you tell the wine merchant of Eber's present troubles?'

'He and Eber are good friends–'

Customer looked at her impatiently. 'Do not be devious with me, mistress. You must answer my questions properly. Things are difficult enough as they are without my needing to seek clarification of everything you say and in so doing, waste further of the precious little time I have left to clear Eber of this false accusation that has been made against him.'

'Us hadn't finished speaking,' she said, unruffled by his sharpness with her. 'Us was about to say Master Allsopp knows all. He fears that Eber's run of luck has finally come to a sad and terrible end.'

Customer felt apprehensive. If Master Wine Merchant knew all – and had given Eber up for lost – wasn't it then equally possible that he had crossed the roadway last night to ransack his friend's cottage of anything of worth, breaking into it by some means – through a badly fitted window, perhaps – or even managing to open the lock on the door with a sharp instrument of some description and then securing it after him? He could well have been making sure he got in first, before anyone else thought of doing the same thing; and he would probably be at it again when he returned from Boscastle, collecting up the last items of value before finishing his business at Wynehouse Corner and continuing on his travels.

Well, if that were indeed his game, Master Wine Merchant was in for a little surprise on his return to the Wynehouse!

'I am going to ride over to see the Trelawneys today,' said Customer.

Agnes looked at him sharply. 'Alone?'

'And unarmed,' he said with a nod. 'You will be kind enough to take careful note of that fact when I ride out this morning and remember it afterwards should there be any questioning of you by others of the state in which I left these premises, and my intent. Should I be detained with the Trelawneys longer than I expect, please be kind enough to ask Master Allsopp to remain another night and await my return as I wish to speak with him urgently before he leaves here. If he is as good a friend of Eber as you would have me believe, there are things he can tell me of Eber's character that might prove useful to his defence against the charge the Trelawneys are bringing against him.'

'Us wishes you luck, young sir.'

'Meaning?' Customer frowned at her. 'You must be precise, Agnes: say exactly what you mean and tell me everything. Eber's life depends upon your complete and utter frankness with me in all things concerning him and his affairs. I will tell you this now in all honesty: you and I are all that Eber has got, he is totally dependant upon us to save him from the gallows, and frankly, I despair that we will be too late in our endeavours.'

She thought about this for a moment and then shrugged and went on chopping up the lamb. 'Eber does business with Master Allsopp, their dealings are satisfactory and neither has complaint against the other so far as old Agnes is aware–'

'But?' prompted Customer when she paused.

She shrugged again. 'Us would as soon trust Lowarn Trelawney as Master Wine Merchant.'

Chapter Thirty-one

Something else to worry about, thought Customer anxiously as he set out at a canter along Butterfly Lane later in the morning... Master Nicholas Allsopp and how quickly he might turn on his friend, Eber, if he thought he could gain personally by it. Agnes said Eber owed the wine merchant not a penny. But falsifying accounts and ledgers would be child's play to a dishonest man. And Master Allsopp was beginning to shape up as a truly *very* dishonest man, a man who, if the worst came to the worst, would have the necessary wherewithal, should he so choose, to add convincingly to the Trelawneys' case against Eber and who could then, all too easily, lay wrongful claim to Eber's lands and property alongside them.

There was no doubt now in Customer's mind: he had not been suffering from an overwrought imagination last night. A light *had* bobbed in the windows of Eber's cottage, and the hand that had carried that light belonged to Nicholas Allsopp. And only someone with the naivety of a child would think that his business in the smith's home had anything to do with his making a thorough search of it for some evidence that would help to clear his friend's name. The wine merchant had been up to his own good over there, not Eber's. He was most unlikely to be of any help in saving Eber's life. Would probably be just the fellow to put the final seal on his fate!

Pawley had returned to the inn sometime during the night. His horse was in the shippen when Customer set out for Butterfly Lane. Customer would have said that Pawley wasn't back when he had gone to the room at the end of the passage last night, but he might have been. It had certainly been no night for a man to be out and about on a horse: in fact, it would have been extremely dangerous, bearing in mind that the moon had showed itself only fitfully and could not have been relied upon to light one's way.

Customer pushed all thought of whether or not Pawley happened to have been on the premises and was aware of what Customer now considered to be Agnes's midnight madness. The whole shameful episode did not bear thinking about.

Customer began to take careful note of his surroundings. He had not crossed the highway to the south-west of Wynehouse Corner before this. Neither had he ventured along Butterfly Lane. He knew nothing of the terrain that could not be viewed from the window of his room at the inn.

It was wilder here than at the crossroads and yet hauntingly beautiful. Undeniably so the nearer he came to the coast itself where the gently rolling landscape gave way abruptly to more dramatic scenery. High, craggy cliffs jutted up into the sombre grey skies above and then dropped sharply away to the spumy, greyish-brown sea that thrashed itself relentlessly against them, taking one's breath with them.

Riding now along the cliffs, the raw wind cut through his cloak as if it were made of some frothy, gossamer-fine stuff, but instead of chilling him to the bone, it made him feel invigorated, ready for anything. For a few, heart-soaring minutes he was the rebel leader, Perkin Warbeck, on his triumphant ride into Bodmin during the Rising of 1497. Nothing could stop Customer Trago. He was riding to victory, an army of stout, loyal Cornishmen at his back! And then he remembered how it had been for him when he, Customer Trago of uncertain parentage, had ridden into Bodmin less than two days ago alongside his friend Eber Pendragon, a helpless but willing prisoner of the treacherous Trelawneys, and he suddenly came down to earth with a hard bump. This was no victory ride. There was no one watching his rear or his flank. Customer Trago was probably going to be lucky to leave these environs alive.

He could see below him a small, treacherously rocky cove; the sea thrashing itself hysterically into a white-flecked ferment against the jagged black and brown cliff that rose up starkly from it and then swept back inland in a wide plateau of heather and blackened gorse. All Trelawney land, open land with no trees to conceal a bowman who might think to lie in wait for a trespasser such as himself and finish him off with a single shaft.

Something to be thankful for, he supposed.

He had seen no one, not so much as a seagull on the wing, or a crow in search of twigs for the construction of its ragged nest, but the idea persisted that there were unfriendly eyes upon him everywhere and it made his flesh creep and crawl uncomfortably.

He started down a narrow, winding track into a heavily-wooded valley, concealed in which, a little beyond a pebble strewn streamlet, according to the directions Agnes had given him, he would find Samuel Trelawney's manor house. Unaccountably, Customer found himself thinking of his childhood and the boy who had spoken enticingly of a pond with strange coloured fish in it and tricked *(yes, tricked!)* him into accompanying him to see these strange creatures. The boy was older – by several years, Customer would have said – but he still could not see the boy's face. Not clearly. His only reliable memory of him was that he was tall and had a rather surly countenance beneath a shock of hair as black as his own. Customer also remembered that he had been fished out of the pond by someone. An adult, he thought – a stranger passing by who had obviously heard his cries for help when he became tangled in the thick weed festooning the pond.

A flash of annoyance went through Customer at his inability to recall the incident clearly. Where did he get this idea in his head that he had been pushed into the pond deliberately? Why was it so impossible to accept that he fell into it accidentally? The boy with him might simply have panicked when he saw him floundering in the water. Who wouldn't run away *and* make up a false story about what had happened when faced with the prospect of harsh punishment from the prior for his having taken such a young boy, a mere infant, with him from the priory without permission?

Customer sighed and pushed what little memory he had left of the incident into the back of his mind where it belonged.

Having finally come upon the streamlet Agnes had described to him, he paused to allow his horse to drink at it.

Customer dismounted and then knelt on one knee on its grassy bank. Idly, he ran his fingers through the clear, ice-cold water as it trickled over the small smooth pebbles in its path and then, cupping his hands together, he washed the fear from his face and the back of his neck which pricked and burned under the heat of the malevolent gaze he suddenly felt turned upon him.

Chapter Thirty-two

Customer dried his face on the sleeve of his jacket and then looked round over his shoulder. Lowarn Trelawney suddenly appeared before him, almost as if by magic.

'You are either a brave man or a fool, Customer Trago,' said Lowarn with a sneer. 'Or is it both?'

'I have business with your father, Lowarn Trelawney,' said Customer defensively, rising to his feet.

'None that cannot be dealt with by his eldest son here on this spot,' said Lowarn.

'Are you saying I can go no farther?'

Lowarn was on foot, standing on a slight rise. He stepped down so that he was facing Customer squarely. He stood boldly, much as he had that other morning at the Holy Well of St James, with legs wide apart and hands on hips. His voice was challenging. He was spoiling for a fight. 'I am saying that no man steps down from his horse onto Trelawney soil unbidden.'

'Do not obstruct me in this affair, Lowarn Trelawney,' Customer warned him with a scowl. 'You will please be good enough to stand aside and let me pass. It will not go well for you and your family if I am forced to report to the deputy bailiff of Bodmin that you would seek to deter me in my endeavours to clear my good friend's name and restore him to his rightful and honourable place in the community.'

Lowarn looked at him in silence for a moment before asking, 'What is your business with the Trelawneys? Tell me that and I shall decide what is to be done with you.'

'I wish merely to ask your father's permission to speak with your mother, the Mistress Trelawney.'

'And how, pray tell, will this help to clear your good friend's name?'

'I have heard only your side of things: I must hear what Mistress Trelawney has to say on this matter.'

'And if I say you shall not know what my mother would say to you of my sister's foul murder and the man responsible for it?'

'Be warned, Lowarn Trelawney.' Customer spoke a deal more bravely than he felt. 'You are tampering with the true course of justice.'

'Bold words for an unarmed man, Customer Trago,' said Lowarn. His thin lips curved into a vindictive smile. 'But in the circumstances, as it is a bold man who warns me – and who knows to what lengths a bold man will be moved if unwisely provoked by a lesser man such as myself! – I shall step meekly aside and not challenge your right to speak with my mother.'

Customer eyed him warily. 'I would prefer to follow you, sir, if you would be kind enough to lead the way to your home.'

Lowarn smiled again. 'Of course, sir. Your wish is my command. Leave the mare where she stands.' His yellow eyes flickered menacingly. 'Collect her when you leave.'

He bowed mockingly and then turned and strode away through a sparsely-wooded copse, leaving Customer to scramble after him.

Customer's progress to the Trelawneys' forbidding, Cornish stone and slate manor house was undignified; Lowarn made certain of that by his sure-footed speed of movement and Customer felt greatly disadvantaged by it. He would have preferred to ride up to their front door with some semblance of self-esteem, even if moments later, they set upon him like a pack of savage wolves and tore him limb from limb.

He followed Lowarn into the Trelawney family's private chapel which stood to one side of the manor, and scarcely had he stepped across the threshold when he but knew that he was entering upon a place of death so recent that he could all but hear the beating of angel's wings on its return flight to Heaven bearing the soul of the departed. He could smell it, a foul, unmistakable stench of sickness and festering decay, on the heavy, vaguely smoky atmosphere of the chapel in which the entire Trelawney family was assembled in hostile, brooding silence.

Customer recognized the scene which greeted him. He had intruded upon a wake, a wake for two members of the Trelawney family, mother and daughter, who lay side by side on separate biers awaiting the hour of their burial.

Both had died cruel deaths: the mother in the grip of some terrible disease which had robbed her face and the bony claws hooked into one another on her shrunken breast, of their flesh, turned her skin parchment-yellow and taut, and lowered her closed eyes into deep, black sockets.

A thin, white-faced servant girl stood alone in the shadows cast by the tall candles placed at the four corners of the biers. She was sniffling, possibly in sorrow at her mistress's death, although recalling what he had been told of the Mistress Trelawney, who had obviously been cursed with an alarmingly quick temper, Customer was more inclined to think that the girl's tears were for herself as she contemplated the burden of extra work which would accrue to her now that her mistress was dead.

Turning to Customer, Lowarn indicated to the body of his mother. 'There lies my mother, the Mistress Trelawney. Say your piece and quickly, Customer Trago: I would hear both your questions and my mother's answers to them.'

Customer dragged his eyes away from the hideous corpse of Lowarn's mother. Looking at Samuel Trelawney, he said, 'I apologize and beg your pardon, sir, for this unkind intrusion at your time of double grief. I shall trouble you no further this day. You have my deepest sympathy and sincere condolences, sir.'

'Pretty words, young sir, for one who thought to call the Trelawneys liars,' responded Samuel Trelawney, his tone aggressive but surprisingly, only mildly so.

'I shall not insult you by denying that I doubted your son, Lowarn's word about his mother's state of health, and that I compounded this injustice to him by not seeking out the truth of it from others. I have seen for myself the error of my thinking and to him, likewise, I offer my sincere apologies and condolences.'

Lowarn grinned. 'What say we teach this young whelp some pretty manners to go with his pretty words?'

To a man, the Trelawneys' eyes showed a glimmer of real interest in the suggestion. Two of Lowarn's brothers – by far the ugliest of the six of Samuel Trelawney's sons, in Customer's opinion – grinned back at him. Their father's face remained hard and unchanged.

Lowarn said, 'Say the word, Father, and we shall seize this dandified he-goat by the hocks and cast him into the heaving seas of Trelawney Cove, leaving the current take him where it will.'

Customer pictured the scene in vivid, life-size, heart-stopping detail and his blood curdled in his veins. He did not need to be told that the cove of which Lowarn spoke was the one which he, Customer, had gazed down into from the track along the cliffs. The raging, boiling sea, whipped up by a savage south-westerly wind, would dash him mercilessly against the rocks and then carry him off on the tide. The treacherous, fast-running current would then deposit him miles away, in some lonely, little visited spot. No one would know his identity, nor even as much as suspect that he had been murdered. It would be assumed that he was the victim of a shipwreck and then, having had his person callously stripped of any item of value, and with no one to speak out and declare him to be the true Christian he was, he would be buried in unhallowed ground on top of a scraggy cliff; left for storm and tempest to uncover his poor broken bones in years to come.

So great was Customer's pity for himself at this vision he had of bleached bones poking through wind and frost-blackened gorse and heather, that tears burned the backs of his eyes and he had to resist an urge to bless himself and offer up a prayer for the salvation of his dear departed soul.

'Let us be rid of this troublesome pest once and for all,' continued Lowarn. 'What say we here and now put an end to all thought of his having the treacherous blacksmith of Wynehouse Corner turned loose among us again?'

Customer looked quickly at Samuel Trelawney. 'If this truly be your fear, sir, then you could no better further your cause of seeing the blacksmith, Eber Pendragon, hang by his neck from the gallows for the murder of your daughter, Rebecca, than to allow me to return safely whence I came and continue about my business of defending him.'

Lowarn grinned. 'By Heaven, he admits it: he is all pretty looks and pretty words and naught else! Any but the blacksmith Pendragon would have my pity for having placed his life in the hands of one so quick to admit to his pathetic incompetence.'

Customer waited for the head of the family to reply. He did not like the look in Samuel Trelawney's eyes and for one interminably long minute, Customer feared that he had gone too far. Samuel Trelawney would give the order for him to be tossed from the cliffs for his impertinence.

Then Samuel Trelawney spoke. 'We shall see, Customer Trago.' He looked at Lowarn. 'See to it that Pendragon's esteemed young lawyer returns to the Wynehouse unharmed.'

Customer expected an argument from Lowarn, but Lowarn merely smiled and nodded.

Customer's heart sank. Without a doubt he was a dead man. Father had told son – in some form of coded language – to be rid of the troublesome pest somewhere along the ride back to the inn. Nothing surer.

Chapter Thirty-three

Customer followed Lowarn outside, sandwiched between four of Lowarn's brothers who fell in, unbidden, behind him.

No one spoke. At the streamlet, Customer mounted the mare and then started back along the track, with Lowarn, who remained on foot, leading Customer's horse by the halter. Lowarn's brothers rode silently behind, the last of them leading a jet-black stallion. Lowarn looked up at Customer once with flickering yellow eyes and then back at his brothers, but said not a word. Customer considered his humiliation at the hands of the Trelawneys was now complete. He felt like a small child being given his first riding lesson.

The Trelawneys accompanied him to the top of Butterfly Lane and then Lowarn let go of the halter, stepping aside while one of his brothers slapped the rump of Customer's horse with one of his gauntlets and startled it into a wild gallop. The Trelawney brothers waited until Customer reached the inn and then all but Lowarn, who had mounted the stallion they had brought with them, turned back along the lane.

This was not one of Customer Trago's finest moments, Customer admitted to himself gloomily as he dismounted on the forecourt of the inn.

Malachy Pawley, who was standing at one of the upper floor windows which overlooked the forecourt and who had followed Customer's undignified progress along the highway from Butterfly Lane in the custody of the Trelawneys, would have agreed with him wholeheartedly.

Pawley was both intrigued and puzzled by what he had witnessed. The Trelawneys obviously wanted Trago alive as much as he, Pawley, did. Now, that is. But was it for the same reason? Pawley asked himself. The Trelawneys could smite Trago down and no one in or around Wynehouse Corner would care, or so much as bother to inquire as to his disappearance. The hag-ridden old woman downstairs in the kitchen, perhaps: she would care and ask if anyone had seen him. One would have to be blind not to see how she felt about him.

The hand that took the life of that nauseatingly deformed girl Rebecca did not belong to any member of the Trelawney family, and if Trago had it in mind to find sufficient evidence to charge one of them with her murder, then he was even more dim-witted than Pawley thought.

So why were the Trelawneys allowing Trago to be such a nuisance to them? That was the question Pawley sought to answer. Was it simply that they enjoyed making sport of such a fine-looking, fancy-mannered fellow? If there were one thing Pawley had learned while passing the time in Bodmin, it was that the Trelawneys were known for not answering to any man. But for some reason they were humouring Trago and were content to lose face in everyone's eyes because of the stance he had taken against them. It had been the talk of Bodmin; the town had been buzzing with it. In no one's living memory had there been anyone who had dared to stand up to the Trelawneys.

Did they, like me, Pawley asked himself, suspect that Trago had some information from which the Trelawneys could benefit? The Trelawney family was both rich and powerful, and rich and powerful men were known for both their greed and their relentless pursuit of furthering their wealth, usually by any means. And from what Pawley had heard said of the Trelawneys, *by any means*, if not writ large on their family crest had to be a curious oversight on their part.

Should Trago not have the information he, Pawley, was inclined to think the Trelawneys sought – a secret Pawley was sure the girl, Rebecca, had been keeping from her family and would not part with under any normal circumstances – Trago would eventually stumble upon it by chance. Trago had not the wit to uncover her secret *other* than by stumbling head first over it. It could be staring him straight in the eye for days and he wouldn't see it. But see it he would...eventually, thought Pawley grimly. No one knew better than Malachy Pawley that it was an integral part of the Trago persona to have everything fall seamlessly into place for him. Maybe not at first, but certainly at last.

There was much Trago couldn't or wouldn't see. Why be so determined to clear Pendragon's name by defending him in a court of law? And what made him so sure that Eber Pendragon *hadn't* killed the girl? Why not widen the circle of his inquiries to eliminate the doubt festering in the minds of everyone else about Pendragon's innocence?

That course of action did not seem to interest Trago. On the surface of things, he seemed content to focus his attention on the Trelawneys and look no further.

Or was it simply that he was afraid to ask himself if it might have been Pendragon's hand that had snatched the girl's life from her? Or Agnes's?

Why couldn't it have been Agnes who killed the girl? What more powerful motive for murder was there than jealousy?

Pawley smiled slyly to himself. And what of the mysterious holy pilgrim who kept himself to himself, seldom leaving his room and saying little to anyone? Wasn't it equally possible that he'd had a hand somewhere in this truly tragic affair?

Customer's voice drifted up the stairs. He speaking to Agnes – in the kitchen, Pawley thought – and Pawley, placing his feet carefully on the wooden boards of the passage overhead to avoid those he knew creaked, made his way silently back to his room. He was smiling to himself because he knew that all he had to do was be patient. He could afford to wait and wait he would. What was the hurry? Another week or two would do no harm. Besides, it amused him to wait knowing that Customer Trago was a dead man walking who, when the time came, no one – not a single living soul – would lift a finger to help or save now that Eber Pendragon was not longer around to mop his brow and hold his hand.

Customer Trago was Malachy Pawley's to do with as and when he wished. Body and soul.

Chapter Thirty-four

Customer scowled at Agnes from the doorway of the kitchen. She had turned her back on him after briefly acknowledging his presence in what she considered to be her private domain. Watching her busy herself contentedly with the preparations for the midday meal, he could not help but ask himself if he had imagined how relentlessly she had pursued him for sex last night. While very much the worse for drink, of course, but that was no excuse and he felt his flesh burning brightly at the memory of every humiliating moment of it.

'I shall confess all so that you will be under no illusion about young Master Lawyer here,' he said despondently, after regaining his composure. 'Things could not look blacker for Eber. The Trelawneys hold all the cards, and they know theirs is a winning hand. I have made a serious error of judgment in going to their lair and speaking with them this day. This was as they wanted it, for Eber Pendragon's spokesman, when asked, to have to admit that they are well-behaved gentlemen, one and all. I fear Lowarn Trelawney is showing all the signs of cleverly outfoxing me. I am going to have to sharpen my wits and be quick about it.'

'Us could ask no more of you than that, young sir,' said Agnes, carefully pouring a measure or two of water from an earthenware gourd into the large, black pot that was suspended over the cooking-fire.

'Please do not be kind to me, Agnes: that only makes the humiliation I have suffered this day, all the more uncomfortable to bear. I would far rather you railed at me for my stupidity in doubting Lowarn's word about his poor mother.'

Agnes held the gourd steady for a moment as she looked round at him in surprise. 'This is why you went to see the Trelawneys?'

'It was crucial to Eber's case to prove Lowarn to be the vicious, unprincipled liar I know him for.'

Agnes's face set hard. 'Then us'll say it,' she said with a pitying shake of her head. 'You *were* stupid, young sir, for not asking old Agnes for the truth of things.'

Customer stared at her. 'You knew Lowarn was not lying when he said his mother was dying?'

Agnes looked at him crossly. 'Had it been a wicked lie, us would not have sent him to the holy well seeking Rebecca that morning. She had a right to be told that the end was near for her mother, and to choose, if she so wished, to return home with her brother and bid farewell to her. There was talk at the inn, some as said it was the terrible bowel disease that saw a finish to the Mistress Trelawney.'

Customer looked annoyed. 'But Eber said nothing of this sickness to me. Nor you when I raised the matter of her poisoned fangs.'

'You asked me to confirm all that Eber had told you of her, nothing more. And if there is one thing old Agnes has learned in this long, weary trek of hers through life,' she snapped, 'it is this: only fools volunteer more information than has been sought of them!' She glowered at him. 'You would do well to spend a little less time up there on that bed of yours daydreaming and feeling sorry for yourself, and a little more downstairs listening in to what goes on at Wynehouse Corner.'

She turned round angrily with the gourd still in her hand, banging it down so hard on the table that it shattered into three jagged shards and splashed water all down the front of her coarse linen smock.

She gazed fixedly at the broken gourd, as if in so doing, it would magically reassemble itself into one solid piece again. Then she sighed. 'Us is sorry, young sir. But old habits die hard. You speak to old Agnes first in future before you go pointing and wagging a finger at the Trelawneys and making a prize ass of yourself. It might please you not to think it, but old Agnes knows all, and sometimes even more, of what goes on hereabouts. Us knows what is true and what is false, and us sees things, things that have not yet happened, but will happen, and old Agnes cannot explain any of it. All she can say is, it frightens her and she wishes it was not so. You are too impulsive: you should be far more wary of the words you put into your mouth and where you put that well shod foot of yours.'

Customer scowled at her petulantly. He was silent for a moment or two, and then he asked, 'Has the wine merchant returned?'

She shook her head. 'Not yet. Tomorrow; the day thereafter, perhaps, if he changes his mind about returning here from Boscastle and travels on to Bodmin to see Eber first before speaking with you.'

Customer looked alarmed. 'Did he say these were his plans, to visit Eber in gaol?'

'He was definite only that his next place of call was Boscastle.'

Then let us all pray, thought Customer, *that after due consideration, greed would speed the wine merchant's feet back in this direction in preference to taking him on to Bodmin. A dishonest man, with much to gain, might whisper talk of anarchy in Eber's ear and incite him to revolt and break free of the iron bars that constrain him...*

Eber Pendragon would not sit forever, meek and mild, in that cramped gaol cell of his. If it were not in his nature to stand by and watch an injustice done to others, why should he stand by and permit an injustice to be done to himself? No, sooner or later, Eber was going to run riot. And if Customer were not mistaken, the Trelawneys were waiting patiently for this very thing to happen.

'I shall be in the smithy if you need me,' said Customer.

He made as if to turn away, but paused. He looked troubled.

He could not rid himself of the notion that came suddenly to mind that again, Lowarn Trelawney was one step ahead of him, still leading him by a halter. He had hoped to find some sign of Lowarn's presence in the smithy, left behind by him when he had gone there to tear one of the ties from Eber's leather apron for placing in his dead sister's hand as false evidence of the person who had killed her. But Customer knew he would find nothing that would incriminate Lowarn of his sister's murder, only more evidence of the guilt Lowarn and his tribe contrived to heap upon Eber's head. And if he were right in thinking this, then whatever it was that Lowarn was leading him to discover in the smithy, would have to be found and faced up to. Meanwhile, he would cling to the thought that with any sort of luck, by meekly going along with the Trelawneys' game and adhering to their rules of play, Lowarn would eventually become over-confident, a little too bold, and make a slip.

Agnes, who was busy mopping up the water from the broken gourd, abruptly stopped what she was doing and looked up at

159

Customer, returning his steady gaze. He did not like what he could see in her eyes. There was much Agnes was not telling him.

Chapter Thirty-five

This, for example...

That is was here, in the smithy, alongside the forge itself, that Rebecca was murdered.

Shocked and appalled, Customer stared at the dried bloodstains on the cobbled floor beneath his feet and then at the rust-coloured dried blood spattering the stone and cob wall behind the forge. Moving round to the other side of the forge, his breath caught at the back of his throat. Resting upright against the forge was one of Eber's tools of trade – the powerful, black cast-iron pincers he used in his daily toil. Visible strands of black hair – Rebecca's hair – were stuck to what was unmistakably dried blood on the pincers.

Unable to look at any more of it, Customer turned aside, fighting the nausea that welled up at the back of his throat and filled his mouth with bitter-tasting gall.

Agnes suddenly appeared in the wide doorway of the smithy and stood watching him. Their eyes met. He spoke angrily. 'You knew this, didn't you, mistress? You knew this was where Rebecca died and that those pincers–' he indicated to them with an angry flick of his head '–were used to strike her down and kill her.'

Agnes's beautiful blue eyes misted over. 'Please do not be angry with old Agnes, young sir,' she said. 'Us had not seen this for ourselves until this very moment. Us swears it!'

Customer's voice was cold. 'Explain yourself, mistress, and be quick about it, for I will be truthful with you and say that it is my firm belief that you knew of this all along. And please do not try my patience further by speaking another word about your mystical powers of insight. Who told you of this terrible thing?'

'No one, young sir. It was snatches of whispered talk us over-heard while fetching ale for two of the Trelawneys' servants who spent an hour or two at the Wynehouse the night you were in Bodmin with Eber. Boastful talk; said with a sly wink and a snigger. Talk, it seemed to old Agnes, that she was meant to overhear.'

Customer looked at her searchingly. She had that same lined, world-weary look she had worn on her face the morning she had come to his room anxious about Rebecca. There had been nothing false about her then, and much as he might wish it otherwise, he knew in his heart of hearts that there was nothing false about her now.

'Why did you not tell me of this before?'

'Us was afraid, afraid of what it would mean for Eber, for his defence if what Samuel Trelawney's men had spoken of was true.'

Against his will, Customer looked back at the murder scene and then, with a visible shudder, at Eber's worn leather apron, which was hanging on a nail in the wall and visibly minus one of its long ties. 'We are undone, Agnes. This is Lowarn's trump card. I can do nothing to save Eber. Lowarn has taken me by the hock and cast me into Trelawney Cove. I am a drowned man...drowned in a sea of artful cunning.'

'No!' Agnes's voice was despairing, pleading. 'There has to be something you can do to put a stop to this terrible injustice.'

Customer gave his head a slow shake. 'Not now that I have seen this. I must inform the deputy bailiff of what I have seen here this day, or Lowarn will contrive to have the deputy bailiff make me admit to him that I am privy to the true scene of the crime against his sister, and that will go even worse for Eber. All is lost, Agnes. I regret to say it, but Eber would have done well to be a little more careful in his choice of Saturday night gamesters. Some people are very bad losers... Although I am not entirely sure that this is the case here. I very much suspect that everything that has happened to Eber has gone according to Trelawney plan. Eber's mistake with them was in making them privy to his extraordinary success at the cards and dice. It is my feeling that Eber has been working all this time at the Wynehouse of a Saturday night for the Trelawneys and by default, not enlarging his purse but theirs. And now they have set their trap and are ready to pounce and seize all with the full blessing of the law. I can do no more for Eber.'

'Us must try, young sir!' Agnes frowned. She spoke harshly. 'Please...old Agnes begs you; do not give up on Eber yet. At least wait until you have spoken with the wine merchant and heard what he has to say of Eber. You said he could help you.'

Customer sighed. 'Very well, I shall speak with him, but only to please you. And I warn you now that from what you have thus far

162

told me of him, I do not hold out a lot of hope in that particular quarter.'

'You must not take any notice of old Agnes and the things she says. Us hasn't had your learning and experience of the big, wide world and all its peoples: there are things that aren't as plain to old Agnes's eye as the young sir's.' Her mouth set in a hard, uncompromising line. 'And us will be honest; us is jealous of Nicholas Allsopp. Us would have Eber think as much of old Agnes, his faithful servant all these many years, as he does of the wine merchant.'

Customer regarded her curiously. 'How much have you told the wine merchant of me?'

She gave her head a slow shake. 'Nothing,' she said, avoiding his steady gaze. 'Not a word.'

'Come now, Agnes.' He looked at her impatiently. 'He knows that I am in charge of things here. You told him this, did you not? What else does he know?'

'Only that you fell hapless victim to thieves and robbers while travelling alone on the highway and were left by them for dead, and that Eber, being Eber, took charitable pity on you and saved your life.'

'And what explanation did you give the wine merchant for my defence of Eber in this other matter of Rebecca's murder?'

'Us told him you were a young sir of good breeding and much book learning and had travelled in far off lands, and that Eber trusted you and had placed his life in your hands.'

'Did the wine merchant express no wonderment at this?'

'Eber does not think and act as other men. None knows this of him better than the wine merchant, his closest friend, and old Agnes here. What need would either one of us have to express to the other any surprise or wonderment at Eber's actions?'

'But what of my feverish night-time ramblings, Agnes?' Customer persisted, his brow knit in an earnest frown. 'How much does the wine merchant know of them?'

'He knows only what old Agnes has just told you.'

'You must never tell anyone of the things I said while I was sick with the fever, Agnes. My life could depend on it.'

'Us has always understood that, young sir,' she assured him gravely. She looked at him pityingly. Eber said the young sir lived in a dream world where the only threat to his life was his imagination and that he was more at risk of scaring himself to death with his fanciful imaginings than of finding himself impaled, as he chose to fear, on the sharp point of an assassin's sword or dagger. Indeed, Eber was quite positive that those, like Sir William Gennys at deeply troubled Launceston Priory, who might possibly remember the name Customer Trago and the boy-child who bore it, were concerned with far more weighty political matters affecting their own ambitions and personal survival than with the long lost causes that Master Trago had rightly or wrongly been led to believe were his birthright and seemed so determined to keep alive and thriving.

'Understand that I expect little from the wine merchant, and that he is our last hope in a game we had no hope ever of winning, Agnes,' Customer warned her severely.

She nodded. 'Us understands.'

'I dare not wait more than three days for the wine merchant's return, and if God grants me that time, then I must ride swiftly to Bodmin and confess what I have found here today.'

Agnes nodded again. 'Us has confidence in you, young sir.'

Chapter Thirty-six

Lowarn Trelawney was probably thinking the same thing: he, too, had confidence in Customer Trago, but for very different reasons, thought Customer wryly as he and Agnes came out of the smithy and they looked across the highway at the lone rider in the plumed black hat who watched them from a dense thicket of shrub-oak and gorse.

Customer's gaze was returned steadily by Lowarn Trelawney. The face of neither man betrayed any emotion.

Agnes looked at Customer sharply, but he indicated to her, with a slight warning shake of his head, to ignore the man who watched them.

Satisfied with what he had waited to see, and with a small smile playing about his lips, Lowarn reined in his horse and then moved off towards Butterfly Lane at a slow walk.

Customer sighed to himself. It was pointless wasting any further time in searching around for evidence of Eber's innocence. There was none to be found; the Trelawneys had made sure of that.

How would Emanuel handle this?

So often he had sat at Emanuel's feet while the elderly monk had reminisced about his old Bodmin law practice, the interesting cases he had handled. Most of the time, to Customer's present intense regret, he'd had to fight to stay awake and had only ever half-listened to what Emanuel had been telling him. Besides, this was an entirely different kettle of fish. This was cold-blooded murder, not some dry as dust civil matter.

Customer wasn't sure how he arrived at his final decision regarding how best he should approach his defence of Eber, whether it was by a determined application of his own intelligent thought, or through some pearl of wisdom left in his young mind by Emanuel, like a seed, to germinate and grow in the fullness of time.

The thing to do now, his only hope of saving Eber, was to concentrate his mind solely on proving that Eber had no reason whatsoever for killing Rebecca, and that the only people to gain by her murder were the members of her own family. What better means could they employ to seize back what was originally theirs – and a hundredfold more – than to ensure that the blacksmith of Wynehouse Corner was sentenced to death by hanging in a properly constituted court of law?

Customer felt uplifted, confident for the first time that he had finally found a way around Lowarn Trelawney, and that this new approach to saving Eber from the gallows would be suspected by no one.

Not until it was too late.

As Customer followed Agnes back across the roadway to the inn, Malachy Pawley looked down on them from the window of the room at the end of the passage.

He smiled to himself. There was the proof, he had seen it with his own eyes – a Trelawney keeping a close eye on every move Trago made. Any trace of doubt left lingering in Pawley's mind over what he had come to suspect was cast aside.

He would continue to watch and wait, though. First to see what the Trelawneys next step would be, and how much they knew. *Really* knew as opposed to merely only suspected of the secret that Pawley was now more than ever convinced the girl Rebecca had held close to her and which had led directly to her murder. Then and only then would he show his hand.

As he returned to his room, careful, as always, not to place a foot on any of the flooring boards which he knew would creak under his weight, Pawley found himself remembering an incident from his childhood, the relevance of which, in relation to Customer Trago's present circumstances, brought a faint smile to his lips.

Pawley had been taken, as a special treat, by his parents to a summer fair where he had been much fascinated by the antics of a juggler who also gave a brief performance with a narrow bodied, long-legged wooden male doll on strings. The entertainment had come to a sudden close when one of the strings the juggler would pull to make the arms, legs and feet of the doll work in a frenzy of activity, suddenly snapped. The doll fell from the juggler's hands – arms, legs and feet – in an untidy heap on the ground. This had elicited a big *aaahhh* of sympathy from the crowd gathered round the entertainer. Pawley, however, had found this tragic finale the high part of the performance and had clapped his hands in glee.

This was Customer Trago. A doll on strings that were being worked by the Trelawneys. Soon a string would break. No doubt when the Trelawneys had grown tired of making him dance to the beat of their drums. And down would go Trago...

'Aaahhh,' murmured Pawley.

Chapter Thirty-seven

''Tis simple enough in my view, Eber,' said Nicholas Allsopp. 'Trago's defence of you should be your lack of motive for killing that poor unfortunate girl.'

The wine merchant was speaking to Eber through the rusty bars of Eber's gaol cell. His eyes followed Eber as he paced the floor back and forth. 'It is your one and only hope.'

Eber nodded. 'I agree. But I have faith in the young sir: he will come round to that way of thinking eventually. I must be patient and wait until he sees that the Trelawneys have the two of us both outnumbered and outwitted in all issues save this.'

The wine merchant gave a slight start as an emaciated, elderly male face unexpectedly bobbed up out of the gloom of the cell adjoining Eber's. One wild, rheumy eye stared hard at Eber and the wine merchant through a straggly fringe of greasy white hair. The old man had lost the sight in his other eye which was opaque under upper and lower lids crusted with dried pus. A dewdrop of fresh pus had gathered in the inner corner of this eye which was obviously infected and must have been causing him great pain. He was wearing a badly soiled cloth cap with long earflaps, at the back of which several wispy strands of his hair had escaped. The earflaps were stained copiously with what appeared to be dried blood.

Gripping the bars separating him from both Eber and Nicholas Allsopp, his bony knuckles showing white, the old man whispered, 'Tonight;' and then releasing the grip of one of his hands on the bars, he placed a forefinger across his lips and then tapped one side of his nose twice and added a conspiratorial, *'Shush.'*

The wine merchant looked at Eber questioningly and then, flicking a glance at the old man, he said to Eber, 'Is our conversation wise with such wide open walls for ears, with or without covering flaps, to hear all?'

Eber stopped pacing and waved a dismissive hand. 'The ears of that one hear only the battle cry of the rebellion,' he said. 'As a young man, he fought alongside Warbeck at Exeter. Or so he claims. He is certainly old enough for it to have been true. He expects Warbeck to free us tonight and that we will then join Warbeck in a fresh rebellion.'

The wine merchant looked mildly surprised. 'No one has told the poor fellow that Warbeck is dead?'

'He is deaf. Lost most of his hearing in the battle at Exeter. A shaft in one ear, he told me, the point of a dagger in another.'

Nicholas Allsopp looked thoughtfully at the old man. 'It strikes me the fellow is insane?'

'I would think so, definitely. Little in his ramblings, which fortunately for me are infrequent, would make sense to most people.' Eber turned his attention to the old man. 'Rest!' he shouted. He clasped his hands together, prayer-fashion, and then placing them at one side of his head, momentarily closed his eyes in an attitude of going to sleep. 'Save your strength, old man, for tonight. We need your bow arm to be strong and true when we make our escape.'

The old man either understood the suggestion in Eber's pose, or gathered, with what little hearing he had left, the general gist of his advice. He let go of the bars and disappeared into the gloom, back to his pallet. Moving to one side to look at him, it appeared to Nicholas Allsopp that the man had fallen into a deep sleep the moment his head had touched the filthy straw mattress on which he was lying.

The wine merchant stepped back to Eber's cell, but took the precaution of keeping his voice low.

'What is his crime?'

'Murder. He is charged with killing one of the deputy bailiff's men. He was caught bloody-handed with the body of the dead man, stripping it of its clothing and anything of value that he could find. He protests his innocence, of course. The only escape he will make tonight is to the hangman's scaffold. I doubt that there will be a trial. The deputy bailiff is not known for troubling himself to adhere too closely to formalities if he can possibly avoid it. And he needs to be seen by the townspeople to be doing something, what with one alleged murderer already held under lock and key in his gaol and nothing much of import being done about him visibly for the moment.'

'I shall remember both of you in my prayers tonight,' promised the wine merchant in a dry voice. Then, with a frown: 'This young fellow you spoke of…Trago. He is not a true lawyer, you say?' A doubtful expression crossed Nicholas Allsopp's face. He shook his head. 'I am sorry to be the one to say this to you, Eber – your judgment has always been sound in all other matters – but here I fear you are making a terrible mistake, and with your life the price you will almost certainly have to pay for it.'

Eber concentrated his eyes on the straw-strewn floor immediately to the front of him while he considered his friend's warning, and then he continued pacing. 'The young sir will save me from the Grim Reaper's scythe as I have saved him. I have no need to empty my purse in the payment of the fancy prices a Bodmin lawyer would think to charge me for my defence.'

The wine merchant momentarily fingered the thin, jagged white scar streaking the lower right side of his face and then smoothed the short, straight hairs of his greying black beard over it. His hand fell momentarily still and then, with his thumb and forefinger, he tugged thoughtfully on the plain gold earring piercing the fleshy, pendulous lobe of his right ear, a habit of his when considering options, usually those open to himself and to his sole advantage. He was a small man, slightly-built, with a long, aquiline nose and shifty, whitish-grey eyes that narrowed as he absently contemplated Eber's broad chest. They were within a year or two of being the same age and had known one another since their early thirties when their lives had followed totally different paths from the ones they trod today. The common bond which bound them together could not properly be described as true friendship, only as that of a friendship of a kind, neither close nor distant, that went back almost a quarter of a century.

Nicholas Allsopp dressed always in black, from head to toe which, perhaps because of his slightness of stature, gave him an aura of holiness rather than an attitude of menace which came the nearer by far of the two to his true character.

'How much do you know of this saintly saviour of near-lost souls, this Customer Trago?' he inquired.

Eber stopped pacing and looked at him. 'Agnes did not tell you his history?'

'I know a little of his present history, nothing of his past. Mistress Agnes, as you well know, having little or no kind regard for me, necessitates the prising of information from her with much the same tenacity and dexterity as the pulling of an abscessed tooth from a shark's gnashing jaws, and with as much likelihood of success.'

A faint smile came into Eber's eyes, stayed a moment, and then faded. He lowered
himself wearily onto his pallet and then, after a small pause, and with a faint sigh, he said, 'His name, as you already know, is Customer Trago...'

The wine merchant's eyes narrowed further. He cut in. 'You say he is, or was, a stranger to you?' he asked in a cautious voice.

Detecting a slight hesitation preceding the wine merchant's inquiry, Eber's response had an equal measure of caution about it. 'Should I know him?'

Nicholas Allsopp contrived to look thoughtful. He needed a moment or two to think before committing himself to a reply. 'Perhaps I confuse him with the Jagos of Penzance,' he said at length. He continued to look thoughtful. 'Could Trago be a corruption of Jago, do you think?'

'This possibility has crossed my mind,' Eber admitted. 'Such things are not uncommon with family names in Cornwall.' He hesitated, picking absently at a few strands of straw that had escaped the confines of his pallet, and then, eyeing his friend shrewdly, he said, 'A wealthy, powerful family, the Jagos.'

Nicholas Allsopp made no comment. 'He has made no mention of his family connections?'

'He has spoken only of the old monk – a canon, no less – who raised him, and this while delirious with fever and all but completely out of his mind.'

The wine merchant's eyes were now mere slits in his leathery, weather-beaten face. 'What monk would this be?'

'Of the Augustinian family at Launceston Priory. Emanuel–'

The wine merchant cut him off sharply. 'And the young sir who calls himself Customer Trago... Tell me: has he wide grey eyes that silently ask questions he knows no one is ever likely to answer, jet-black hair, a pleasing countenance and a gentle, reserved manner?'

Eber looked at him sharply. 'You know him?'

Nicholas Allsopp was quiet for a moment. His right forefinger explored the scar on his face, travelling slowly up and down it. 'I shall answer that question, my friend, after I have seen and spoken with the young sir.' *And made my inquiries of him and his old tutor, Emanuel, at Launceston Priory!*

Frowning, Eber said, 'There is another matter that concerns me, though I cannot explain why other than to say that lately, as I am sure you will appreciate, I have had rather more time on my hands than usual to sit and think. Pawley – *Malachy* Pawley... Is this name familiar to you?'

The wine merchant was again thoughtful.

Eber continued, 'He – this man, Pawley – presented himself at the Wynehouse, seeking lodging, and with a sad tale of a lame horse in sore need of rest and stabling...'

'It was not true, this tale of his?'

'Let us say doubtful.'

'You feel he is up to no good?'

Eber smiled wryly. 'I see dark shadows everywhere these days, my old friend.'

'Leave this with me: I shall make inquiries,' Nicholas Allsopp promised.

'Proceed with caution...'

'You have suspicions?'

'Do not take me at my word, but my fear is that he is a spy fresh from the camp of Dr John Tregonwell. There has been talk at the Wynehouse that Tregonwell looks this way, seeking the church treasure some say we Cornish seek to deprive of their beloved Tudor King and would prefer to use to raise an army against him.' Eber hesitated, shaggy eyebrows raised expressively. 'Loose talk, no doubt, fuelled by ale and the inbred longing of all true Cornish men and women to be free of the Tudor yoke once and for all.'

The wine merchant nodded slowly. 'Then for Master Pawley's sake, let us hope that my inquiries go well for him. We Cornish have ways of dealing with Tudor spies.'

Chapter Thirty-eight

Customer considered it necessary for him to acquaint Agnes with his plans for Nicholas Allsopp on the wine merchant's return to the inn. Any objections or reservations, anything at all that she thought that Customer should know about the wine merchant that she had not previously disclosed to him, was best settled between them before he proceeded any further. In short, it was Customer's intention of catching Nicholas Allsopp in the act of pilfering from his friend's cottage when he returned to discuss the wine order with him. Agnes was not to interfere.

Customer was not entirely sure about Agnes, where her true loyalties lay. He very much feared that if she were put to the test, she would prove to be loyal to no one but herself. He understood. He had never thought hers an easy life, and if Eber's protection was snatched from her, it would almost certainly be the worse for her. She would throw in with whomsoever offered her a measure of kindness with little threat to the relatively untroubled life she lived at present.

Having since checked the door of the smith's cottage and found it to be locked, Customer suspected that there was a second key to it which Agnes was deliberately withholding from him but which the wine merchant had somehow managed to appropriate and then return to her safekeeping without her being any the wiser.

'One thing puzzles me greatly, Agnes...' Customer began carefully as his third and final day of waiting for Nicholas Allsopp to return to the inn was drawing to a close. She was deftly skinning a hare for supper and Customer's chest heaved a little as the animal's thick fur coat was ripped savagely from its body by her strong hands and she reached for a hefty chopper for the next stage of her evening meal preparations. The prospect of confronting the wine merchant was not sitting well on Customer's stomach. He had been feeling increasingly queasy with the passing of each day of waiting for Nicholas Allsopp's return.

'If my thinking is correct,' he continued, looking away as she began to quarter the hare and its blood soaked into the wooden tabletop, 'and the wine merchant has already gone through Eber's cottage once looking for anything of value, how did he get in there without benefit of a key?'

She replied without hesitation and without pausing in her work. 'Through the forge in the smithy, of course.'

Customer's eyes widened with surprise. 'There is a door leading into the cottage from somewhere inside the smithy? I did not see one.'

She was shaking her head. 'At the back of the forge there is a chimney breast of curious bulk and size, though not unusually so. Us is surprised you have not noticed it.'

'I have had matters more serious on my mind than to concern myself with the architectural features of the place,' Customer reminded her, a note of exasperation creeping into his voice. 'What of this curious, yet not unusually so, chimney breast?'

She went on with her work. 'There is a secret chamber fashioned within the thickness of its walls. Go to the back of the forge and look closely at the chimney breast and you will see a low door through which all but a small child would have to crawl on all fours. This is the way into the chamber from the smithy. Beyond this chamber is the fireplace and hearth of Eber's kitchen, above it Eber's bedroom. Us has heard it said that access can be gained to the chamber from both rooms: in Eber's bedroom by the raising of loose boards in the floor, and from an opening in the nook in his kitchen fireplace.'

'What is the purpose of this secret place?' asked Customer, amazed.

'Whether 'tis true or not old Agnes cannot say, but more than once she has heard it rumoured that the secret chamber played some important part in the Rising. Rebels hunted by the King's men made their escape from their safe place of hiding within the cottage through the secret chamber in the smithy and then slipped quietly away into the night.'

'What part did Eber play in all of this?'

'Why none, of course!' She paused, sweeping to one side the sections of the dismembered hare and looking directly at Customer as if he had gone mad. 'All of this happened long ago, a good many years before Eber came to Wynehouse Corner and the inn and the smithy.'

'And Master Wine Merchant knows of this chamber?'

'Us knows of it through common gossip: us sees no reason why it should be kept privy from him. He more than anyone us can think of would know of such a place. His long, inquisitive nose would ferret it out with no help from anyone else.'

As Customer turned to leave Agnes to her kitchen servant's duties, Malachy Pawley moved silently from the narrow, shadowy passage where he had been standing, absorbing every word of their conversation. He vanished like a sylph up the stairs as Customer came out of the kitchen and then walked through to the public room. Customer did not see him. He was deep in thought, totally engrossed with what Agnes had told him of the smithy's secret chamber.

Hastening to the window that overlooked the smithy and smith's cottage, Pawley watched Customer cross the roadway and then, much as Pawley had expected, disappear into the smithy. Pawley's gaze was intense, concentrated. Agnes's disclosure of this secret chamber within the smithy was a possibility he should have considered. Put simply, there had to be a secret hiding place in property owned and occupied by Eber Pendragon: Pawley could not think why he failed to see this before. Eber Pendragon was a rich man, a lucky man who seldom, if ever, lost at the cards and dice. Any such a man would have need of a safe place to keep and hide his wealth.

Agnes, working in the kitchen below, looked up sharply at the ceiling above her head. In his haste to reach the window at which he now stood and would remain standing, patiently waiting for Customer to reappear, Pawley had accidentally trodden on one of the creaking flooring boards he was normally at pains to avoid. His mistake did not register with him. He had more important things on his mind, like whether or not Customer Trago, either by word or deed, would disclose any of the findings that Pawley was hopeful could be made in this hitherto undisclosed chamber secreted within the walls of Eber Pendragon's smithy. *'And pray tell,'* Pawley asked himself, narrowing his eyes contemplatively, *'could there possibly be a* better *place than that for the blacksmith of Wynehouse Corner to hide his riches?'*

Agnes knew who it was up there. Pawley had not moved from his room all day and without pausing for a moment to ask herself why he should bother to stir himself now, she knew instinctively that he had overheard Customer questioning her about access to Eber's cottage other than by the accepted means of a traditional door. Why else would Pawley be standing at the window that overlooked the smithy? There was little of interest there for a holy pilgrim during the forced absence of the blacksmith whom he might wish to attend further to his horse.

She knew what it meant; what she had expected from Pawley from the moment she had first laid eyes on him.

Trouble.

Chapter Thirty-nine

Customer had no difficulty in locating the door in the chimney breast behind the forge, though having been told it was there greatly facilitated his search for it.

He did not attempt to pass through it immediately. Now that the initial shock of discovery had subsided, he wanted first to look more closely at the scene of Rebecca's murder to see if he couldn't form a clearer picture in his mind of what had taken place there when she had been killed. Piers Heard had insisted that it was impossible to say precisely when death had occurred: too much time had elapsed between that moment and his physical examination of the girl's body. Customer, however, chose to ignore Piers Heard's insistence that the time of death was uncertain. Fixed firmly in Customer's mind was a strong conviction that she had died early in the morning of the day that she had been found.

It saddened Customer to see that there was actually quite a considerable amount of dried blood to be found in the smithy. Rebecca had bled heavily from the wound to her head before expiring from it, but by far the greatest blood loss, to his surprise and puzzlement, was to be seen on the slate floor behind the forge and near the small door to the secret chamber in the chimney breast. He would have missed it completely had he not gone round the forge seeking to find the door. The wall, or chimney breast, yes, he had observed the dried blood there earlier and had assumed that blood had spurted from Rebecca's head wound and spattered the wall as she had been struck down in front of the forge where there was also a good deal of dried blood on the floor.

Customer looked quickly away from the spot and waited until the wave of nausea that washed over him had subsided.

He believed he could see now what he must have happened when Rebecca had been attacked. She knew of the secret chamber and when confronted by her killer, had been desperately trying to get down on all fours and crawl through the door to chamber and thence into Eber's cottage to summon help. He pictured her being struck from behind by her killer while down on her knees, frantically trying to escape from him. He then dragged her body away from the chimney breast and round to the front of the forge. Eber had left for the Trenwith place very early that morning, between five and six o'clock, he had said, so assuming that Rebecca knew this – and she probably did, she knew everything that went on in and around Wynehouse Corner – her cry for help would have been made either to Agnes, or not impossibly, to me, Customer reasoned. Agnes had made a point of saying that no one but Eber and the wine merchant crossed his threshold which made it doubtful that Rebecca would have been the one exception, despite Eber's strong affection for her. Rebecca would have waited until she saw Eber leave on Will before sneaking into the smithy. *But for what reason?* Customer asked himself with a puzzled frown. Was it something to do with the kittens Eber had drowned? An act of wilful spite, perhaps? Eber's cottage was Eber's private sanctuary, forbidden to all but that one notable exception, the wine merchant, and perhaps in defying Eber by sneaking in there in his absence, and in a sense defiling his own special place, she believed she would somehow redress the balance for what he had done to the kittens.

Customer followed the trail of dried blood with his eyes. It required little effort from him to visualize Lowarn Trelawney leaving his sister's bloodied body momentarily in front of the forge while he tore one of the ties from Eber's leather apron and then placed it in one of her hands, closing her fingers over it so as to give the appearance of it being held by her in a tight grip. Hence the further heavy blood loss in the one spot. There were a few spots of dried blood between the forge and the rotting wooden double-door that was never locked and gave onto the highway. Customer lost the trail immediately beyond this door, in a flash of inspiration, picking it up again several minutes later after crossing to the opposite side of the highway to the spot where Lowarn had sat upon his horse several mornings ago, keeping a watch on the smithy to see who came and went.

Customer thought back further to the morning that Rebecca had died. Lowarn had, without a shadow of doubt, carried Rebecca across the highway to his waiting horse which had then borne him and Rebecca's body to the Holy Well of St James. Dried bloodstains spotted the trunk of a shrub-oak standing in the thicket:

more dried blood, or something very similar, speckled the gorse Lowarn's horse had trampled flat beneath its hooves. Just a few droplets here and there, but as far as Customer was concerned, enough to point the finger of accusation unhesitatingly and unwaveringly at Lowarn Trelawney.

After leaving Rebecca's body at the holy well (to be discovered there by him later), Lowarn had ridden back to Wynehouse Corner and the inn to be told by Agnes that his sister was not there and where he was most likely to find her. Agnes had also told him that someone had been sent – *me*, thought Customer with a shiver of anger at Lowarn's perceived deviousness – to fetch Rebecca to her morning meal.

Customer's spirits rose. This was the indisputable proof of Lowarn's hand in his sister's murder. He killed her: nothing else made sense. Why would Eber carry Rebecca's body from the smithy across the highway like this? Wasn't it more logical to think that Eber would have gone and fetched Will to the door of the smithy and then ridden on from there with Rebecca's body to Witchypool Lane and the holy well?

Various images came up before Customer's eyes before he finally settled for the one that he considered as being the truest representation of what had taken place between brother and sister that morning...

Lowarn had ridden to Wynehouse Corner in haste and, one would imagine, in a state of some mental anguish, to summon Rebecca to their mother's deathbed. He had thought to find her at the inn, but instead chanced to see her going into the smithy. He followed her in there, leaving his horse on the other side of the highway. She had resisted his entreaties to return home with him and he had lost his temper, and with it all self-control. In a blind rage, he had placed his hands round her throat – perhaps thinking to do no more than shake some sense into her – and she, breaking free of his grasp, had run desperately to the door in the chimney breast, knowing that with his height and breadth, it would be difficult for him to follow her through it and into Eber's cottage. That had been her undoing. Further enraged by her lack of family loyalty and wrongly assuming that it was Eber Pendragon – a man the Trelawneys had good reason to loathe and despise – she was trying to reach, Lowarn had grabbed up the nearest thing to hand, the smith's pincers, and had struck out savagely, killing her.

Chapter Forty

Convinced that he had finally arrived at the truth of the matter, Customer looked about him and then, satisfied that no one was watching, he crossed quickly back to the smithy. It would not do for Lowarn Trelawney to know that he had found this evidence against him which Customer was determined the deputy bailiff should and would be advised of with all speed. Before, that is, heavy spring rains washed the shrubbery and gorse clean of its incriminating evidence. For once the strong, blustery winds of windy Wynehouse Corner could claim some justification for their existence. They had swiftly dispatched the rain clouds that had gathered threateningly in the south-west each day and had sent them scurrying farther inland to shed their load.

Elated by his discovery, Customer permitted himself a small, satisfied sigh. Lowarn had made the slip he had hoped and prayed for. Had Lowarn not been so sure of himself, had he not been so determined that everybody should know what a clever fellow he was by waiting at that spot on the other side of the highway the other morning to grin and gloat over Customer Trago's inadequacies and naivety, he would almost certainly have succeeded in pinning his sister's murder on a completely innocent man.

With Lowarn Trelawney's triumphant progress to the gallows to watch Eber hanged stayed, if not for all time, then at least until he, Customer, could turn up some further corroborative evidence of Eber's innocence, Customer concentrated his thoughts on the wine merchant and the score he felt he had to settle with him on Eber's account.

Customer pushed to the back of his mind a nagging doubt in regard to Bodmin's deputy bailiff. Now was not the moment to entertain any suspicion that the day to day happenings at isolated Wynehouse Corner were actually of no real interest to the deputy bailiff whatsoever. Nor that he would not think twice if its scantily scattered populace dealt with their problems as they saw fit – and as seemed generally to be their custom – and left him to concern himself with the far more important, inevitably political matters, that demanded his personal attention in Bodmin. The time he, Customer, had been granted to furnish the deputy bailiff with hard evidence of Eber's innocence was also time for the Trelawneys to find some means of ridding the deputy bailiff of the undoubtedly inconvenient encumbrance languishing in his gaol. Customer had to cling to the hope that again, he was allowing his too vivid imagination to run away with him, and that the deputy bailiff would honour his pledge and in the meantime guard Eber's life as he would his own.

Customer went back to the door of the secret chamber, got down on all fours and then unlatched it.

He noticed that there was very little dried blood on the door itself and assumed this to mean that Rebecca had managed to open it before she had been struck down by her brother.

Customer pushed open the door and saw that his assumption was correct. There was dried blood on the stone-flagged floor of the chamber. The pity of it was that if Eber had been in his cottage, he would have undoubtedly heard her cry for help.

Saddened by the realization that Rebecca had been but a shout from certain safety, Customer hunched his back and crawled like a tortoise, head thrust forward, through the narrow, three-foot-high doorway and into the secret chamber. He was inclined to panic in confined spaces, to imagine all sorts of alarming and usually totally improbable things happening to him while he was thus helplessly restricted in his movements, and the old familiar feeling was back with him the moment he was through the small doorway and he found that his body all but filled the chamber.

An aperture of roughly the same size as the doorway through which he had just passed, gave into the nook in the smith's kitchen fireplace exactly as described to him by Agnes. Hazy daylight filtered into the fireplace and nook from the kitchen beyond.

He measured the aperture with his eye and convinced that he would find himself stuck firmly in it, unable to move in any direction if he tried to exit from the chamber through it, he started to back up, in his mounting panic painfully striking the pointed bone on the top of his left shoulder on one of the large, square, ashlar granite blocks which formed the walls of the chamber.

Automatically, he paused to rub the sore spot and as he reached for it, his fingernails scraped along another block and dislodged it slightly from its seat with a small, scratching sound. Hastily, he pushed the block back into place and then backed out of the chamber and into the smithy.

He remained for a moment on all fours, alternatively panting heavily and coughing to the point of choking, and then, as he began to recover himself, he looked back into the chamber, his eyes scanning its left-hand wall for the loosened block.

In the gloom of the chamber, it was not immediately obvious to the eye and it took him several minutes to pinpoint it. Then, withdrawing a dagger from its sheath on the leather girdle around his waist, he placed it between his teeth and then crawled awkwardly back into the chamber, intense curiosity leaving no room in his mind for fear of anything. He seriously doubted that the block had come loose by itself. It seemed far more likely to him that someone had deliberately freed it from the mortar securing it in place in order to conceal something behind it, and he was determined to see what it was for himself.

Heavily perspiring, he skewed himself around and then worked awkwardly with the sharp point of the blade of the dagger to prise the block from the wall. He panted with exertion, several times using the back of his free hand to wipe away the perspiration stinging in the corners of his eyes. Finally, with much scraping of his elbows and cramp threatening to seize up his straining calf muscles at any moment, he managed to work the block sufficiently loose for him to lay aside the dagger and then carefully ease the block out, a little at a time, with his fingers.

Grunting, he placed the heavy block on the floor beside him and then gazed hesitantly at the gaping hole it had left in the wall. Against his will, he thought back to the hair-raising ghost stories Emanuel had relished telling him of secret wall cavities and the human corpses – grisly, wizened scraps of decayed skin and bone and mummified vitals – such cavities were intended to conceal. Then, after a further moment or two's hesitation, he reached tentatively inside the wall.

He stayed his hand, stomach muscles tensed, perspiration pricking at the nape of his neck. He had heard a slight noise behind him. Someone was in the smithy. Then Agnes's voice called out anxiously to him. As a precautionary measure, he had left her to watch the highway to the south-west for signs of the wine merchant's return and with instructions to make haste and let him know if and when she caught sight of him.

Almost thankfully, Customer withdrew his hand, calling back to her to return quickly to her duties at the inn, and that he would be with her in a moment or two.

He swiftly replaced the block in the wall and then backed clumsily out of the chamber, closing its door behind him.

He paused for a moment to gather his scattered wits. The discovery of the hidden cavity within a wall of the secret chamber connecting Eber's cottage with the smithy opened up another avenue of thought which he knew he must explore before he could honestly claim to be satisfied that he had all of his answers to the disturbing events of the past week. A hidden cavity such as the one he had just discovered might well prove to be a reason for the Trelawneys to wish urgently to repossess their former property and, at the same time, provide another, more rational explanation for Eber's habit of prowling round his cottage night after night. The wine merchant's purpose in likewise prowling the cottage late at night might also lie there.

Customer's brow knit in a tight frown. Suppose, for one moment, that Eber and his close friend, the wine merchant, knew or suspected that the Trelalwneys had murdered someone and then sealed up their victim's body somewhere in the smith's cottage, then this – a mummified corpse – could well have been what they had both sought to find in the dead of night while no one was about to witness their activities. In other words, it was proof they sought that the Trelawneys were callous murderers, hoping that this would bring an end to their reign of terror in the parish.

Fanciful thinking? Customer asked himself.

He considered the supposition carefully. Eber would know of the chamber, as did the wine merchant who, if one accepted that he had not secretly appropriated a spare key to the cottage from Agnes, had obviously used it to gain access to his friend's cottage the other night. Undoubtedly, everyone living thereabouts who was in the habit of enjoying a little gossip at the inn of a night would know of the existence of the chamber.

But only the previous owners of the smith's cottage and the smithy, the Trelawneys – and now, purely by chance, Customer

Trago! – knew of the hidden cavity within one of the walls of the secret chamber...

Customer very much doubted that Eber, with his unusually large frame, would have ever considered using the secret chamber to pass to and fro between the smithy and his cottage. He would have no valid reason for risking his becoming stuck fast in there. And the wine merchant, if Agnes was right and he had used the chamber for access to the cottage – maybe because with age, his eyesight had somewhat dimmed – had not noticed the loose block as he had passed through it and into Eber's kitchen.

It all made sense. But first Customer decided to test his theory of a murder having been committed at sometime in the past by one or more of the Trelawneys. He would put the question to Agnes, though without making any direct mention of his discovery of a loose building block within the secret chamber. For her own protection as much as anything. Lowarn Trelawney did not appear to look upon Agnes as being a threat to him, and Customer was anxious that this was how matters should remain between them.

He would not have felt quite so satisfied with his progress that morning had he but known that Malachy Pawley was still keeping a close watch from the window overlooking the smith's cottage and smithy.

As Customer started back to the inn, Pawley drew back quickly from the window and returned to his room. Pawley felt increasingly bemused by all that he had seen, but of one thing he was certain. Trago was getting close. A blind man could see that!

Pawley had to admit that he had expected more of Trago's visit to the smithy. Much more. But only if the snidely whispered conversation that he had chanced to overhear while biding his time in one of Bodmin's public houses several days ago proved to be true and was not just idle gossip.

In the room below, Agnes eyes were raised to the ceiling, listening to Pawley's movements on the floor above her head.

She continued to gaze up at the ceiling long after everything had gone quiet up there.

The decision she had been mulling over in her mind all morning as to whether or not to warn the young sir of the holy pilgrim's interest in his comings and goings was easy to make.

She lowered her eyes to her hands which were spread out before her on the kitchen table.

She would say nothing.

Us keeps our nose clean and looks after us, she told herself, and nodded her head firmly in affirmation.

Chapter Forty-one

Agnes looked at Customer apprehensively as he entered the kitchen five minutes later. 'A man in black, too small and wiry of build to be of the Trelawney tribe, rides on a pale horse in this direction,' she said.

'The wine merchant dresses in black and rides a pale horse?'

'Always; like a black, grinning, hound of death.' *At one,* she thought with a faint scowl, *with master holy pilgrim who skulks about upstairs!*

'This gossip you mentioned of a secret chamber in Eber's cottage…' Customer began. 'Has there been other gossip concerning the place? Rumours, perhaps, of what is concealed within the chamber?'

She shook her head. 'Only what us has already told you.'

'None concerning a murder that was committed there?'

Her mouth tightened into a straight, disapproving line. 'Us would ask the young sir to say what he means in plain language that all can understand. If it's another murder you're accusing Eber of…'

Customer shook his head quickly. He spoke sharply. 'Your mind moves too swiftly and in its haste, misinterprets the meaning of what I am asking you instead of it staying awhile to permit me to explain myself fully. Do not agitate yourself unnecessarily, mistress: I am thinking not of Eber, but of the previous owners of the cottage, the Trelawneys. The smith's cottage and smithy, as was the case with the inn, were originally their property, were they not?'

Her expression relaxed and she nodded her head. Then, after a small thoughtful pause, she nodded again. 'It is said of Lowarn that he was blooded as a mere boy of twelve years of age…' She hesitated; looked puzzled. 'Though us has heard no specific talk of any wickedness of his having been committed in Eber's cottage or the smithy, young sir.'

'You mean it is common knowledge, as opposed to mere Saturday night, ale-fuelled rumour, that Lowarn Trelawney has killed someone and not been called to account for his actions?'

'More than once. It is said that a girl was the first to die by his hand – when he was a mere boy of twelve tender years, as us has just told you... Master Trenwith's elder daughter, Mary. Lowarn swore she was playing at hide-and-seek with him and that she was taken by the black bog on her father's moorland which she stumbled into by accident. And now us has heard it said that Lowarn has his eye on the younger Trenwith girl – the shy, pretty one...Lucy. He moves with stealth on the girl and will have his evil way with her – old Agnes has seen it all before! – and the Trenwiths will have no say in the matter.'

She smiled sadly. 'Eber was the first in my living memory to stand up to the Trelawneys: you, young sir, are the second. Whether either one of you will live your full Biblical threescore and ten years to tell the tale is another story. The Trelawneys have lorded it over this parish for as long as us can remember. And if they have their way and Eber goes cruelly and unjustly to the gallows for Rebecca's murder and then you leave us, young sir, the Trelawneys will continue to lord it over us as lives in their parish, doing just what they want and with no one brave or foolish enough to stop them.'

'Eber will not hang for a crime he did not commit, I give you my solemn word on that, Agnes.'

She looked at him pityingly. 'Us knows you will have tried your very best, young sir.' She paused. Then, in a resigned voice, she said, 'Us wants you to understand something so there can be no mistake about it in your mind. Us wants that you should not turn upon old Agnes and say she should have said what she meant and been honest and truthful with you. No one, not even old Agnes here, will stand with you against the Trelawneys when the time comes for it, young sir, as surely it must. One day soon, when you have paid your debt as best you can to Eber, you will ride away from the Hundred of Stratton forever and leave us on our own with no one to defend us against the Trelawneys' vengeance for the part you would have us play in assisting you with Eber's defence. Us apologizes for our weakness, us wishes it could be different. But old Agnes here is only a mere servant and nowhere near as brave as she thought when this terrible thing first happened. The Trelawneys will make all of us sorry for defying them in this affair–'

Abruptly, she broke off, turning her head from Customer and holding up a forefinger in warning. She listened for a moment. 'That will be the wine merchant now. He just rode onto the forecourt. Will you see to his horse, or shall old Agnes go out to him?'

Customer hesitated and then looked at her with a frown. 'Why would Eber keep the murder of Mary Trenwith by Lowarn Trelawney to himself and not tell me anything of it?'

'Eber has his own way of doing things, surely you know this by now. Us would not question his reason for anything that he chooses not to do, and us would say to you that there is much concerning the Trelawney tribe, far more than the murder of poor Mary Trenwith all those many long years ago, that Eber could tell you if he was of a mind. Most of it gossip, nothing that anyone could, or ever would willingly stand up and say they know to be the truth as God would see it. Eber would know there is little he could tell you of that evil tribe that would be of any good use to you in your brave struggle to save him.'

Customer did not argue with her. He could only think that it must have been Divine Providence that had led to his discovery of the hidden cavity within the wall of the smithy's secret chamber which, in turn, had led to the revelation of the murder of Mary Trenwith and what could possibly prove to be the most damning character assassination of all of Lowarn Trelawney. This was if, as Customer now strongly suspected, young Mary Trenwith's pathetic remains were closeted within the wall cavity of the secret chamber, far removed from the black bog Lowarn Trelawney would have everyone believe had accidentally claimed the girl's life.

Customer nodded. 'I shall see to the wine merchant. You set out food and wine and then leave us to discuss our business. I will summon you if I need you.'

He went out onto the forecourt. Nicholas Allsopp was dismounting; had his back to him.

The wine merchant, hearing his footsteps, turned slowly to face him.

Chapter Forty-two

Customer's breath caught at the back of his throat in a distinctly sharp, clicking sound. He knew this man; knew him and feared him, though truthfully, without just cause. Looking back, it had been a small thing, but at the time it had struck terror into the heart of the seven-year-old boy whose name was Customer Trago. This black-cloaked, scar-faced man standing before him now had asked Emanuel if he would be kind enough to show him the dagger rumour had it that Emanuel kept concealed within his monk's robes. It was a magnificent weapon, pure solid silver and ornately inscribed and decorated with the finest of jewels. It had been given to Emanuel by an Arabian princeling whom he had befriended while travelling in the Holy Land. The young Customer had watched Nicholas Allsopp handle the dagger – covetously it had seemed to the boy watching him – and for one fearful, but foolish moment, Customer had thought Nicholas Allsopp meant to slay Emanuel with it.

It was too late for Customer to recover the moment; the wine merchant's shrewd eyes were full upon him. Pretence was useless.

'I know you, sir,' said Customer.

'And I you,' admitted Nicholas Allsopp, his face, apart from his coldly-calculating eyes, betraying nothing of the sudden sharp alertness of his instinctively devious mind.

'You were captain, were you not, of the soldiers garrisoned at the Benedictine Monastery at St Michael's Mount, on Henry's orders, to defend Mount's Bay against the French?'

'And you were the small, wide-eyed boy who walked silently in the lawyer Emanuel's shadow and stared hard, as you are staring now, at the pretty scar on my face.'

Pausing, Nicholas Allsopp lightly touched a forefinger to his scarred cheek and grinned. 'Answer me this: is it the grown man, Customer Trago, who now still walks in Emanuel's great shadow?'

The faintly mocking tone of the wine merchant's voice brought a frown of unease to Customer's face. This man was dangerous. He had Emanuel's word on it, though typically of Emanuel, with no

190

accompanying explanation of his own personal reason, or some other need, for issuing such an uncompromising warning about the captain of the garrison.

'It has been many years since I last saw and spoke with Emanuel,' said Customer cautiously. 'It has saddened me to learn of his recent death, and I would be obliged to you for anything you may be able to tell me of his final days.'

Nicholas Allsopp's eyes narrowed. He gave his head a slow shake. 'The town of Launceston is not on my regular wine round.' He hesitated, only slightly but enough to suggest to his listener that the next words he uttered might bear close scrutiny. 'I visit there seldom; not once this past twelve-month. I have heard nothing particular of the priory and its brethren, only generally of its squabbles which does little to encourage me to rearrange my itinerary and visit that part of the world more frequently.'

In that, if nothing else, thought Customer grimly, *they were of one mind!* He wondered if there were more that could be told; more that the wine merchant knew of Emanuel's demise but chose not to confide in him. Customer felt far from well-disposed towards Nicholas Allsopp. Still fresh in Customer's mind was the night the wine merchant had gone looking for something in Eber's cottage without, so far as Customer was aware, making some mention of it to anyone either beforehand or afterwards. Customer was quite prepared, without benefit of proof, to echo the words of Emanuel and say that Nicholas Allsopp was a dangerous man, one who would not give anything away, including any information that he might have acquired here and there while on his travels. Everything would be carefully weighed up and measured for its worth to the wine merchant before he committed himself by word of mouth.

'I am told that you and Eber Pendragon have been friends for many years,' said Customer. 'Am I to take this to mean that Eber was a soldier of the King garrisoned with you at the Mount?'

The wine merchant threw back his head and laughed until tears came into his eyes and he had to wipe them away with the back of one of his hands. His teeth were stained black with the strong red wine he drank in preference to brandy or ale, and were even more crooked and misshapen than Eber's.

'Eber Pendragon a soldier, one of the King's men?' he

191

guffawed. 'How little you know of your client, Master Lawyer!'

'Eber is a brave and true Cornishman, I know that of him,' said Customer, a shade defensively.

The wine merchant's voice hardened. 'Then you will know it for the truth when I say to you that the many long nights Eber Pendragon sat carousing with the King's men in the taverns of the town at the Mount, it was at all times as a true and brave Cornishman, with rebellion and treason always at the forefront of his mind and in his every action.'

Customer frowned. A shiver of fear went through him. What Nicholas Allsopp was really saying was that Eber Pendragon had served Cornwall as a rebel spy: still served the Cornish rebel cause, for all Customer knew. 'It would not do for the Trelawneys to learn of this and make political use of it in Bodmin.'

'Nothing I could tell you of Eber's past, good or bad, would serve either one of you in his present troubles,' said the wine merchant, his tone abrupt and final.

'It is the present that concerns me, not the past.'

'I am surprised to hear that from your lips, Customer Trago,' said Nicholas Allsopp. 'My recollection of the small boy with the wide grey eyes was that he was much concerned with the past and little interested in the present or the future.'

'Those days are behind me forever,' Customer assured him in a slightly arch voice.

'Very wise.' The wine merchant eyed him thoughtfully. 'Wiser still if you apply the same philosophy to your client's past.'

Customer looked at him. *Was this to say that Nicholas Allsopp knew of Customer Trago's past, the truth of his origins?*

Customer's mind baulked at the thought of any further inquiry of the man standing before him concerning his true parentage. Quite suddenly, and despite his still desperate yearning to learn all there was to know of his forebears, he did not wish to listen to any reference to them from this man's lips. There was a cruel twist to them, a hint of malice. If the wine merchant spoke truthfully of the Tragos – and Customer was not entirely sure that he would – it would not be to his liking.

'Have you been to Bodmin, sir, and spoken with Eber?' asked Customer.

'Two nights since,' replied the wine merchant. Then, without pausing: 'His spirits are low; this dreadful affair has all but broken him. He despairs to the point of wishing a quick end to it all, no matter how it goes for him. I fear he has grown old and tired since my last visit here to Wynehouse Corner, and indeed, I bring word to you from him concerning the inn and the smithy. If it is God's Will that he should be hanged for this terrible crime he swears by all that is sacred and holy to him, he did not commit, what was his is yours, Customer Trago, in payment of your fee and with his heartfelt thanks for your kindness and loyal support of him.'

'And if justice prevails and he does not go escorted to the gallows as the Trelawneys would have done by him, what then of my fee, Master Wine Merchant?' asked Customer in a wry voice.

Nicholas Allsopp grinned crookedly. 'That, sir, is an entirely different state of affairs. We are talking now of Eber's purse. No light matter to be dismissed in a few hasty words.'

'Regardless of how this affair goes, for good or bad, Eber owes me not a penny and I shall accept not a penny from him, neither in coin nor in land and property.'

The wine merchant considered him for a moment and then he said, 'So when you are done with your defence of the blacksmith of Wynehouse Corner, you return to your own concerns?'

'With all speed,' said Customer. He glanced back at the inn where Agnes could be seen standing at one of the open windows of the public room, watching them. 'Agnes waits. She has prepared food and wine: let us dine and then there is much I would discuss with you concerning Eber.'

Customer turned abruptly from the wine merchant and in that instant, was overtaken by such a sickening giddiness that he was forced to slow his stride for fear that he would stumble and fall to the ground.

He closed his eyes tightly and tantalizingly, Emanuel's silver dagger floated before him in the darkness. Not as he had seen it as a small boy, in the wine merchant's covetous hands, but since then, not so very long ago, flourished in front of his swiftly fading eyesight by the assassin who had attempted to kill him by first viciously thrusting a sword deep into his left side and then threatening to finish off the job with the dagger.

Customer screwed up his eyes even tighter, trying to recall the assassin's face.

It was gone. He doubted that in those dreadful moments after the sword had penetrated his side, he was capable of seeing anything of consequence aside from the swift approach of the painful death that he had every expectation would follow.

Was it Nicholas Allsopp's face he would have seen if the pain from his sword wound had not enveloped him, dimming his sight, and he had retained his senses? Was it the wine merchant who rode with that band of villains that night? *Who also, in some way, had had a hand in Emanuel's death? And finally, all these long years later, acquired that thing which Customer Trago, the small boy, had been so sure the captain of the garrison had most desired – Emanuel's exotically beautiful and undoubtedly valuable dagger?*

Customer felt the wine merchant's eyes boring into his back and with a determined effort, he fought off the giddy spell that had threatened to overwhelm him and continued on and into the inn.

He heard Emanuel's gentle voice.

Be warned, young Customer Trago, this man is dangerous.

Had the wine merchant been privy to these thoughts of Customer's he would have added an addendum.

…But not as dangerous as the blackguard who, at this very moment, looks down on us both, like a sparrow hawk eyeing its next meal.

Malachy Pawley drew back swiftly from the window overlooking the forecourt.

The man Trago had walked from the inn to greet on the forecourt was a stranger to Pawley. There was something about him, though – the manner in which he had glanced up at the high window and their eyes had met – that suggested to Pawley that while he had never set eyes on the stranger before in his life, Malachy Pawley was no stranger to him.

Pawley retreated to his room to consider this unexpected turn of events. This was a complication he had not expected to encounter. One, either way – whether the stranger knew him or, as seemed more than likely to Pawley, *of* him and his past connection with Launceston Priory – that would have to be dealt with, and swiftly.

As the wine merchant entered the inn, Nicholas Allsopp's eyes narrowed and he smiled to himself.

So that was Malachy Pawley. Who else would it be? Eber Pendragon hadn't lost his touch when it came to knowing what was true and what was false. A holy pilgrim Pawley was not! Satan's votary, more like.

Well, Malachy Pawley, we shall have a little talk, you and I. What really brought you to the Wynehouse, eh? Was it the innkeeper and his affairs, or his protégé, the young man raised from childhood at Launceston Priory and tutored by that wily old devil, Brother Emanuel?

But first things first...

Chapter Forty-three

Whether by design or because he truly suffered, as he claimed, a raw and parched throat after his long ride from Bodmin, the wine merchant drank heavily with the jugged hare that Agnes set silently before him. He was asleep in his chair before his bowl was wiped clean with the last morsel of his bread.

Customer left him to his snoring and went in search of Agnes, quietly instructing her to bring a lighted candle to the window of the room at the far end of the passage when the wine merchant finally roused himself and left the dinner table for his bed. Customer would be watching for the candlelight from Eber's cottage and he would take it as a signal to expect a visit from Nicholas Allsopp at any moment from then onwards. Should the wine merchant inquire after his whereabouts, Agnes was to say that his sword wound was sorely troubling him and that he had taken to his bed early and would speak with him about the wine order in the morning.

It was a risk, but Customer decided to take it. He entered the cottage through the secret chamber, cheering himself on with the thought that other, braver men than Customer Trago had wormed their way through the small aperture at the back of the kitchen fireplace and thence safely into the cottage, and so would he. He glanced at the loose block that sealed the cavity in the wall as he crawled past it, but left it untouched for fear that the wine merchant would be upon him sooner than expected.

A wise decision. He had scarcely reached one of the two upper rooms which faced the inn when a flickering candle-flame appeared in the window directly opposite, moved sideways twice, signalling to him, as prearranged with Agnes, that the wine merchant had either retired or was preparing to retire to his room.

This being the latter part of the month of March, it was lighter longer of an evening and as Agnes stood at the shuttered window of the wine merchant's room with the candle, Customer could make out the rounded outline of Agnes's plump shoulders and the white linen, shawl-like collar stitched onto the bodice of her dress. A second or two later, the slimmer, darker lines of Nicholas Allsopp appeared alongside her at the window. Agnes had opened wide the wooden shutters – perhaps to explain to the wine merchant her reason for standing so near to the window – and Customer watched as the wine merchant reached out and closed them again, taking the candle from her hand as he turned away and then placing it elsewhere in the room.

Customer continued to watch the shuttered window and then, something like an hour later, the candle-flame, which showed palely through the shutters, was suddenly extinguished, plunging the wine merchant's room into complete darkness.

The moon came out from behind scudding, patchy cloud, lighting up the sparsely star-speckled night sky, and as Customer waited, he saw clearly the wine merchant's black shadow flitting swiftly across the roadway from the inn and then disappearing from sight behind the smithy.

Customer turned from the window where he watched and crossed the tiny passage to the bedroom over the secret chamber, the one Agnes had said was Eber's. Within a matter of seconds, Customer heard the door of the secret chamber below being opened and then a regularly repeated, soft, swishing sound as the wine merchant crawled on his hands and knees through the chamber and then into the nook in the smith's kitchen fireplace. His boots scraped on the hearth beyond it as he got up onto his feet.

A silence lasting no more than a few seconds was followed by the sound of the wine merchant's quick, light tread on the stairs.

Customer stood behind the door, concealed in the shadows, his ears straining for sound. He gave a small start as the door opened, holding his breath as the wine merchant entered the room and then fumbled his way across the room to light a candle on the small table standing at one side of Eber's bed. Without hesitating, and with his back to Customer, Nicholas Allsopp swiftly opened the drawer in the table and took something out of it.

Customer chose this moment to step boldly forward, his hand on the sheathed dagger at his waist ready to withdraw it and defend himself if the need arose. Sensing that he was not alone in the room, the wine merchant looked slowly round at him, his face showing neither guilt nor alarm, and then calmly, he picked up the candle and turned to face Customer.

'Explain yourself, sir!' Customer demanded.

Nicholas Allsopp looked at him levelly. He held the candle high, illuminating their faces and turning their flesh dark and sallow, their eyes black. 'With pleasure,' he said. 'But first I would suggest that you consider long and carefully before unsheathing that child's plaything that rests beneath the trembling hand you hold at your waist. Do not oblige me, sir, to return with you to the inn bemoaning more than a sword wound in need of Agnes's ministrations.'

Customer hesitated and then, feeling more than just a little foolish (which seemed to be his destiny), he dropped his hand from the dagger which Eber – with a warning not too dissimilar to the one made by the wine merchant concerning it, and with a barely concealed smile – had made a gift of to him during his convalescence.

Customer covered his embarrassed blushes by speaking boldly. 'I await your answer with growing impatience, sir.'

Nicholas Allsopp walked up to him, holding out a small, tooled brown leather-bound book for Customer's inspection. 'I came for this, at Eber's request... His Holy Bible. He seeks comfort from it, but would have no one but his old and trusted friend, Nicholas Allsopp, know of this for fear his enemies would hear of it and seize upon it as a sign of weakness, or worse, an admission of guilt.'

Customer took the Bible, glanced at the gold-embossed lettering on its spine, and then, frowning up at Nicholas Allsopp, he asked, 'Am I to be considered one of Eber's enemies that you could not share this secret wish of his with me?'

'Eber would do nothing that might lead Agnes to despair and you to suppose he has no faith in you and has given up all hope of deliverance and prepares to meet his Maker. My sole reason for electing to enter his cottage by stealth in order to carry out his wishes has been to preserve in you both an optimistic frame of mind over his present unfortunate circumstances.'

Customer looked at him sceptically. 'You think almost as quickly as I do in a tight spot, Master Wine Merchant!'

A smile flickered in Nicholas Allsopp's eyes. 'Was I aware of your presence in this room before I collected Eber's Bible from the drawer in his bedside table yonder?' he asked imperturbably.

Customer made no response. 'Was there anything else Eber asked you to fetch for him while you were about it?'

'Only this, his Bible. I shall return to Bodmin with it tomorrow, and then continue on my journey south.'

'What, then, have you to say of your last visit to this cottage? Of the night you slunk from room to room with the sly stealth of a mangy, stray fox in search of food? What sought you that night on Eber Pendragon's behalf?'

'Treasured mementoes of his dearly beloved wife, Katharine, to comfort him while he awaits his fate. A lock of her golden hair; a portrait no larger than the gold locket she wore round her soft, snow-white neck; a silken kerchief embroidered by her own fair hand.'

Customer's hand was back on the hilt of his dagger, the quick flush to his face brought there by a sudden rush of anger. 'You lie, sir! My patience with you grows shorter by the minute. I demand the truth and be quick about it!'

'Then ride with me to Bodmin on the morrow and seek it from Eber Pendragon's own lips whether or not it is the truth that I speak, and welcome the company, for 'tis a long and tedious ride, as well you know.'

Customer hesitated, scowling. 'I am tempted, sir, to take you up on your offer, for I shall not pretend, I do not trust you.'

'Nor would it be meet and just that you should,' rejoined the wine merchant. He smiled crookedly. 'I shall be as honest with you, sir, as I would wish you to be with me. I took you for a fool, Customer Trago, but I see that I am in serious error and would crave your pardon.'

'Do not patronize me, sir!' snapped Customer.

'Far be it from me to make that mistake, sir.' The wine merchant paused, his lingering smile slowly fading. 'Come...' he said briskly. 'This bandying of insults between us does neither one of us any honour.'

Customer looked at him for a moment. 'You have an answer for everything, sir. I am much impressed and would beg that you should indulge me further and answer me this one last question. What is it, then, that Eber seeks in his cottage that takes him in like manner from room to room late at night by candlelight?'

The wine merchant, tugging gently on his gold earring, was

some little while in replying. 'You must ride with me to Bodmin and speak with Eber on this matter for I have sworn on oath that I will speak of it with no one but him.'

'In that case, sir, and in the swift pursuance of expediency, you must allow me to rephrase my question so that no oath made by you will be violated.' Customer paused for a moment and then he said, 'It is my belief that the persistent searches Eber carries out within the rooms of this, his home, when his day's toil at the forge is at an end, involve some past mischief of the family Trelawney. My question then is this: should I turn in some other direction for that which Eber seeks to find within the four walls of his cottage?'

Nicholas Allsopp considered for a moment. 'My answer to that is this, and you are free to interpret it howsoever you wish, Customer Trago. Eber's judgment of you as his best advocate was as sound as it has always been in other matters of serious import to him, and I no longer fear that he has injudiciously thrown away the key to his gaol cell and his life with it. And now, if you would be so kind as to excuse me, Agnes's jugged hare sits heavily on my chest and I must take to my bed to encourage it to settle more comfortably on my stomach where it belongs.'

The wine merchant was indeed a poor colour and sweating profusely; looked far from well, Customer would allow him that. But he would take no chances: he would be keeping a still night-watch, and if Nicholas Allsopp thought to trick him with his talk of suffering from indigestion and so much as poked his long nose outside his bedroom door again this night, Customer Trago would know of it.

Chapter Forty-four

Nicholas Allsopp did not stir from his room again that night and at first light, Customer rose stiffly from the chair he had placed outside the wine merchant's door and went downstairs to the kitchen where Agnes was busy preparing for the day ahead.

The wine merchant did not join them at table to break the night's fast: it was not until he was ready to leave for Bodmin that he ventured from his room.

His physical appearance had worsened since the previous night. His face, which was still inclined to look sweaty, was the colour of ash from a long dead wood fire, and as he waited for Customer to fetch his horse from the shippen and bring it round to the front of the inn, he stood with a hand clutching his cloak to his chest as if to still some terrible pain that lurked there. The wine merchant sensed that Malachy Pawley looked down on him from the window overlooking the forecourt. Glancing briefly up at him, Nicholas Allsopp intended this to suffice as a warning that before this day was out, Eber Pendragon would know that Malachy Pawley was a man not to be trifled with.

Having risen from his bed far worse than when he had taken to it, and with a gnawing pain in his chest that worsened by the minute and was making it increasingly difficult for him to breathe easily, the wine merchant had acknowledged to himself that he was in no fit state to challenge Pawley with what he had learned of him from the visit he had promised Eber he would make to Launceston Priory. Pawley's presence at the inn could well be perfectly innocent, forced upon him by the unfortunate circumstance of a lame horse in need of rest and recuperation, but if so, it was a curious coincidence and in more ways than one. As for his claim to be a holy pilgrim, it might also be doing him a serious injustice to doubt his word. Malachy Pawley was a man in sore need of making a pilgrimage to a holy place.

Nicholas Allsopp brushed aside Customer's polite inquiry regarding his health. He insisted that he had never felt better, but nevertheless requested that Customer should give him a boost up onto his horse.

No sooner had Customer cupped his hands together for the purpose than the wine merchant staggered several steps backwards with an anguished cry and then, with crumpling legs, pitched forward convulsively and already dead, fell onto the ground in a heap at Customer's feet.

Agnes came running from the doorway of the inn and together, they turned the stricken man quickly onto his back.

His eyes stared sightlessly up at them, his cruel mouth contorted in an agonized grimace.

''Tis a miracle his heart hadn't seized up on him long before this,' said Agnes with a dismissive snort.

'But he spoke last night of indigestion only,' Customer protested.

'A mistake commonly made by those too fond of their food and the tankards of strong red wine they swill with it.'

Nicholas Allsopp's saddlebag had been dragged down with him, spilling its contents – his order books and ledger, folios of other personal papers, and Eber's Bible – onto the ground.

With shaking hands, Customer gathered everything up. Turning to Agnes, he found her prising the wine merchant's earring from its lobe, and with scant regard for the fragile flesh it pierced.

He spoke to her sharply, but she merely shook her head at his rebuke. 'Better that us has it than the grave robbers disturb him at his rest, young sir.'

She deftly removed a heavy gold signet ring from the little finger of the wine merchant's right hand. Customer looked the other way, for there was much truth in what she had said. Better that the poor fellow should go to his grave as he had entered the world, with nothing anyone would wish to steal from him, and be left to sleep in peace for all eternity.

'We must inform the authorities of this,' he said. He used his best arch, would-be lawyer's voice to mask the bad shock the wine merchant's sudden death had given him.

Agnes was not fooled. She looked at him pityingly. 'What us must do, young sir, is bury him! No one will thank us for troubling them with this piddling affair. Trust that us knows what us is about. Come,' she said, her tone brisk. 'Help me get him into the shippen. I will lay him out when I have the time and then, if he's

202

not too busy with his lambing, fetch Carneworthy the carpenter, who farms up yonder by the River Ottery, and us'll bury him later. Us'll show you where. 'Tis a pity us needs to bother with the expense of a wooden box, but be certain in your mind that if we don't, the foxes'll have Master Wine Merchant up again before you can put an amen to a prayer for the dead.'

Customer stared at her. *God's teeth!* Could there be a less civilized place than this?

'You can have Master Allsopp's horse,' she went on in the same brisk, no nonsense voice.

Customer spoke tersely. 'You are very free, mistress, with the things that do not belong to you!'

''Tis the custom, young sir. Us breaks no laws. Any stranger who chances to die while travelling across land belonging to the lord of the manor must pay to him a heriot of his finest beast. Us is only doing what is right and proper.'

'I am familiar with the custom, mistress, and again I would say to you that you are too free with the things you would pay the innkeeper of the Wynehouse by way of heriot. The lord of the manor may take the deceased's finest beast, or his finest jewel, or his finest garment. Not all three, mistress!'

She smiled; removed the wine merchant's handsome woollen cloak and folded it up into a neat square, then tucked it under one of her arms and then gave it a quick pat with her free hand. 'Then us will take the other things in payment of his board and lodging and for Carneworthy's time and trouble and all shall be fair and square and us can rest easy in our beds at night with an untroubled conscience.'

Customer knew when he was beaten and gave in with a small, despairing shake of his head. The low, wispy mist that had suddenly rolled inland from the sea a short time earlier, drifted across the highway and then eddied about them, its damp, spidery fingers brushing lightly over Customer's face and neck and bringing a slight shiver to his spine. 'Today I ride over to the Trenwith place,' he said, following her indoors.

She paused and looked at him sharply. 'You would speak with Master Trenwith about Lowarn Trelawney and poor little Mary?' She was shaking her head. 'Master Trenwith will be polite and courteous – he may even go so far as to nod his head and smile every now and again so that you will be in no doubt that he is paying close attention to all that you would say to him – but he will tell you nothing for fear that the Trelawneys will kidnap his womenfolk and carry them off to their lair... Or worse, put a lighted torch to his crops and slaughter his beasts of the field.'

Customer looked at her. He spoke enigmatically. 'We shall see, Agnes. We shall see.'

Malachy Pawley was very much afraid that this would indeed be the case. Having hastened down to the public room for a clearer picture of what was taking place on the inn's forecourt and then positioning himself close to the nearest window, he had overheard the last of Customer's conversation with Agnes.

Which forced his hand.

Perhaps no bad thing, thought Pawley. He was growing tired of this game he was playing with Trago. It was time to show him that Malachy Pawley held the winning hand.

Chapter Forty-five

Agnes was right in every particular.

Jacob Trenwith, a small, round man with lively blue eyes and a ruddy complexion, was polite and courteous to his young visitor, he listened carefully to every word he said, but when Customer looked at him expectantly for a response to his request for confirmation of all that Agnes had told him of Lowarn Trelawney and the suspicious death of Trenwith's elder daughter, Mary, he merely shook his head and would say nothing.

'This, sir, will not do!' cried Customer, flushed with annoyance. 'How can it be that what I see standing before me is what I sincerely believe to be an honest and just man only to discover that this same man is unwilling even to afford me the courtesy of an explanation for his refusal to confirm the circumstances of his daughter, Mary's death at Lowarn Trelawney's hand?'

Trenwith considered for a moment and then said, 'Mary was a wilful lass, as wilful as any young maiden anxious to have her ears pinned back for her by a handsome young sir. She had been warned of the dangers in dallying with Lowarn Trelawney and of accidentally straying too near the black bog on my moorland, and that if either one of them took her–'

Customer interrupted. There was something about Trenwith's manner, a suggestion that he was choosing his words with care, which aroused Customer's curiosity. 'You are speaking, are you not, particularly of Lowarn Trelawney and the bog, and not of some third party who was with Lowarn and your daughter on the day she died?'

Trenwith carried on as if Customer had not spoken. '–She would be the worse for it. She chose neither to heed her father's words, nor the advice he gave to her that if she ever strayed into the bog, she should hold her arms out wide on its surface and not hard at her sides. Had she the wit to remember this last piece of advice from her loving father, she would have resisted the treacherous pull of the marsh-mud long enough for help to be sought.'

Customer frowned. He spoke impatiently. 'This was what

Lowarn Trelawney told you, that your daughter did not keep her arms held wide apart on the surface of the bog as she was drawn down into it, or is this what you find more expedient and comfortable to believe because it is the actions of a Trelawney that we are dealing with here? Forgive my impertinence, sir, but your daughter, Mary, was a mere child, was she not?'

'It is what I believe to be the truth: Mary panicked instead of keeping a cool Cornish head on her shoulders, and she paid for her mistake with her life,' Trenwith replied imperturbably, glancing idly at his wife, Meg, who was kneading a bread mixture on the kitchen table.

Meg Trenwith was a tall, lean woman, with hazel eyes and much grey showing in her dark hair which was wound in a tight knot at the back of her head. She kept her eyes on the mound of dough on the table beneath her strong hands, but there was a slight hardening of the lines around her mouth at Trenwith's words which inclined Customer to think that she was not fully in accord with her spouse's bland dismissal of their daughter's death. There was something missing, something they preferred not to tell him, and while he hated to admit it to himself, Customer began very seriously to doubt that Lowarn Trelawney was entirely responsible for the girl's death. Someone else was involved, Customer was more than ever sure of it. Mary Trenwith, Lowarn Trelawney and–? Two men shared the burden of guilt for Mary's death, but who was the second man?

Lucy, the Trenwiths' other daughter, stood shyly by the window, watching Customer from under her long, dark eyelashes. Her creamy pink cheeks blushed scarlet whenever he glanced at her, and she would quickly lower her head a little so that her soft, black hair would fall forward over her face and cover her confusion. She was seventeen years of age, boyishly slim, had her mother's hazel eyes, and had come late to the Trenwiths, for Mary Trenwith, if Customer's arithmetic were anywhere near the mark, would have been somewhere around thirty now had she survived Lowarn Trelawney's unwelcome attentions.

There was no doubt in Customer's mind that if Mary's looks had been anything like her sweet, fresh-faced younger sister, Lucy's, she would have been a girl for whom any young man would turn his head. It was the one and only thing Customer would not hold against Lowarn. Hadn't his own head been turned at his brief, chance encounter with the pretty, blushing young maiden he now knew to be Lucy Trenwith, outside the physician, Piers Heard's house the other day?

Meg Trenwith spoke suddenly, without looking up. 'Mary was in her fourteenth year when the Good Lord took her from us; old for her years and wise to the ways of men, and though I say it myself against my own flesh and blood, a little too eager to hear the sweet nothings they would whisper in her ear. I'll not forgive Lowarn Trelawney for his mischief that day, but it was mischief shared and I'll not shirk admitting it, nor hold him wholly to account for it, for he was the younger by a year or two and was as much led as the leader.'

There it was again. The suspicion that more than one man was involved in the death of Mary Trenwith.

Sensing that it would be useless to challenge the Trenwiths with what he suspected, and that for some reason, they would not reveal the name of the other person involved in their daughter's death, Customer decided to play along. 'I cannot believe there is a word of truth in what I am hearing,' he said. 'You know Lowarn Trelawney killed your daughter, mistress; ran her to ground in the bog like some defenceless, hunted wild animal! Have you no pity for the terror there must have been in your daughter's heart that day? Have you no wish to see justice done and Lowarn Trelawney made to pay for the terrible thing he did to an innocent young girl? Have you no thought for your other daughter towards whom, I have heard it said, Lowarn Trelawney would now seek to turn his vile attentions?'

Meg Trenwith made no response. Turning the mound of dough over, she began to pummel it afresh.

Trenwith had not invited Customer to be seated and take some refreshment. He had adopted a stance which Customer recognized. His visit was not to last long. At any moment Trenwith would make a move with some excuse for terminating their conversation and returning to the work that awaited him in his fields.

The Trenwiths were not the peasant farmers that Customer had expected to find, but more of the yeoman class, better off than most in the area and clearly accustomed to a reasonably affluent lifestyle. Their home, from the little that Customer had seen of it, had all the appearances of being comfortably furnished and was well-scrubbed and brightly polished, possibly by the neatly turned out servant girl who appeared suddenly in a doorway only to be banished whence she came by her mistress with a slight movement of her head.

Trenwith called to heel the two dogs lying under the kitchen table and they rose as one to return with him to his daily toil.

'Is no one prepared to stand with me against the Trelawneys?' demanded Customer in despair. 'Don't you see that by your silence you are co-conspirators with the Trelawneys in this miscarriage of justice that will surely come to pass if no one will speak out against them? Is this how it is to be in the Hundred of Stratton? I will be honest with you, sir: I would as soon throw myself into your black bog, arms lashed to my sides and sinking true and fast like a stone in a pond, as spend the rest of my life living in fear and trembling of the Trelawneys and crawling upon my hands and knees to them!'

Trenwith paused and looked at him for a moment. 'I should have thought it would suit your purpose, and more than handsomely, if the blacksmith of Wynehouse Corner were to go to the gallows for the murder of Rebecca Trelawney.'

Customer looked at him coldly. 'I trust my ears deceive me, sir, and I misinterpret the implication of your words!'

Trenwith shrugged. 'My meaning should be perfectly clear to you, Customer Trago, and I make no apology for it, for I repeat only what has been sworn to me as truer than any word written for God's Holy Gospel. Nicholas Allsopp, the wine merchant, rested here a full night and the better part of a morning after speaking with the blacksmith in Bodmin, and he told us plainly that all that was Eber Pendragon's at Wynehouse Corner will be yours should he be hanged for this crime of murder.'

'You forget something, sir,' said Customer coolly. 'Your best parcel of pastureland. If what you say be true, that also will then be mine should Eber Pendragon be hanged for this heinous crime he did not commit. I should therefore be obliged if you would be kind enough to point it out to me while I am here on the spot. I would also advise you to have a care, sir, for I know something of best pastureland. Having been raised within a shout of the rectory farm at Launceston where many an hour I spent during my childhood years among the bullocks, pigs, sheep and oxen, and out in the fields helping with the harvest of wheat, oats and barley, I'll not have some worthless marsh-mud passed off on me as mine to have and to hold!'

He strode past Trenwith without a glance.

The pastureland he was shown met with his expectations of what it should be, but for good measure, he warned Trenwith that he would return with Eber Pendragon, when Eber was a free man once more, and catch him out for a liar for any deceit he might attempt to practise on him this day.

'And if Eber Pendragon goes to the scaffold for the crime it is said he has committed,   what then, young sir? inquired Trenwith. 'How will things stand between us and this parcel of land that was once mine and is now Pendragon's?'

'I shall think on it,' said Customer. He hesitated deliberately and then, in a meaningful voice: 'Perhaps favourably.'

'At what price?' asked Trenwith, his eyes narrowed shrewdly.

Customer studied him for a moment. 'I have reason to believe that you know of my past association with Launceston Priory,' he said.

Trenwith's face was a mask. He gazed into the distance, as if searching for something on the horizon, and made no reply.

'I would know of Emanuel, my old tutor. The truth of how he met his end.'

'Be careful, young Customer Trago,' Trenwith warned with a faint snarl, looking back at him. 'There are some things best left unsaid and unknown. Be satisfied with what you have been told by Eber Pendragon of Emanuel's death and leave it there.'

'From what Eber has told me, I have come to believe that Emanuel's death has in some way had a deep emotional effect on your good wife.'

'Careful, sir,' Trenwith warned again. 'You tread a dangerous path and sorely try my patience.'

'I will know the truth,' said Customer. His face set stubbornly. 'I will not rest until I hear it. From your lips or elsewhere.'

'Fate will not be cheated, sir, and I will not be the one to sanction a third stab at your life.'

Customer gave him a puzzled look. 'I do not understand what you mean.'

'Think about it, Customer Trago. You who, as a child, came as close to death by drowning as is possible for any young person of tender, trusting years. You who, many years later – and now a grown man – came within a final heart flutter or two of death when set upon by a band of vagabond cutthroat killers while making your way to Launceston Priory, as was Emanuel who was likewise set upon by vagabonds while travelling equally innocently back to the selfsame priory.'

'Kindly bear with me sir, but I cannot see any direct connection between Emanuel and me and what befell us at the hands of a band of roadway ruffians. It was surely a matter of coincidence and nothing more. I was on my way to see Emanuel at the priory, to inquire after him and his health which I had reason to think was troubling him. I believe he was returning there after having been called away to mediate – I would imagine – on some family dispute which must necessarily have involved a legal matter of some description. Emanuel was a civil lawyer. He did not involve himself in petty family squabbles. Whatever took him from the priory was a matter of some serious importance that he considered only he could deal with.'

Trenwith made no comment.

Customer's exasperation with Trenwith showed on his face. He spoke impatiently. 'Forgive me if I appear to be dim-witted in my understanding of this matter, but I fail, sir, to see where your good wife fits in all of this? I do not recall seeing her among the black-bearded riders who waylaid me and left me for dead. What I do know is that Emanuel left the priory to deal with a family matter, which I have since come to suspect might directly involve Mistress Trenwith, and that in some way, she bears a certain responsibility for his death.'

There was a hard glint in Trenwith's eye. 'I see you are determined to hasten to your own death, sir. Very well, then; be it on your head, Customer Trago. I will tell you what you wish to know, and pay the price for it you surely will. You, Customer Trago, you and you alone must share, with my good wife, the burden of Brother Emanuel's death. His blood is on the hands of you both.'

Chapter Forty-six

'What I am about to tell you, Customer Trago,' Trenwith began, 'dates back many years to when you were but a mere child of no more than four or five years of age.'

Customer's heartbeat quickened. Trenwith was going to tell him the truth of his origins, who Customer Trago really was.

He was wrong.

'It is said, and this is largely true, that everybody in Cornwall is related, even if only distantly, and it so happened that around the time of which I speak, a close member of my good wife's family, a cousin, was visiting Launceston Priory. A Father Caffrey.'

Customer thought for a moment and then nodded quickly. 'I remember Father Caffrey, but only vaguely. He was not of Emanuel's family, his Holy Order – I remember that. I'm not sure, but I think he might have been a Grey Friar. He was older than Emanuel – at least, I thought he was. To a small boy, Father Caffrey looked positively ancient, well past his threescore and ten.'

Trenwith made no comment.

He went on, 'Several years prior to this, my wife's older sister, who had married well – indeed far above her station – discovered that she was barren. She desperately wanted a child to love and raise as her own, and through her sister, my wife, she learned of Father Caffrey's visit to the priory and came to know that there were occasions, certain special circumstances, where the prior would give consideration and ultimately his blessing, to an orphaned child being taken in by the brethren and raised at the priory principally under the tutelage of Emanuel.'

Customer frowned. 'Mistress Trenwith hoped that Father Caffrey, while he was visiting Launceston Priory, would recommend her sister, his cousin, to the prior as a suitable adoptive parent?' He hesitated. Then, in a puzzled voice: 'Are you saying that Mistress Trenwith knew that the prior had agreed that I should be placed in the care of Emanuel, and that she wanted Father Caffrey to urge the prior to permit her childless sister to adopt me?'

Trenwith ignored the interruption. 'It also so happened that at this time, there was an incident, a near tragedy that occurred between two orphaned boys in Emanuel's care. One was very small, only four or five years of age, the other several years older – a boy who became increasingly jealous of the affection and attention bestowed upon the other child by Emanuel, who openly favoured the younger boy.'

There was a shocked look on Customer's face. He spoke in a hushed voice. 'Say no more. I remember it well... At least, I think I do. He – the boy of whom you speak – I believe might have tried to kill me. He enticed me away from the priory on a pretext and left me to drown me in a pond.'

Trenwith continued as if Customer had not spoken. 'Emanuel could see that this older boy was a danger to the younger one and when he learned from Father Caffrey that residing in the neighbouring county of Devon, there was a good, devoutly religious childless couple who were desperately wishing to adopt a male child who would ultimately inherit their wealth and carry on the family name, he suggested to the prior that it would be in the best interests of both boys if this older boy were to be removed from the priory forthwith and placed with them.'

Customer spoke quickly. 'His name? I don't recall it.'

Trenwith declined to give it with a slow shake of his head. 'It was Emanuel's second mistake. The first in openly favouring the younger boy to the point where it could not but fail to arouse such a dangerously wicked jealousy in the older boy, the second in suggesting that boy's adoption. The boy in question should have remained at the priory under the strict discipline of the prior, for despite the love and affection that was bestowed unstintingly upon him by my wife's sister and her husband, the boy was, from the outset, sullen and wilfully unco-operative. He repeatedly stole from his new parents and compounded his thievery by placing the blame for the thefts elsewhere, on the servants. Worse still, if provoked, even as a child, he could be quite violent towards his parents. As he grew older, he fell in with a rough bunch of fellows – all of them thieves, debauchers and murderers. In short, he was a serious disappointment. In fact, the worst disappointment any loving parent or parents could be forced to endure.'

'Was Emanuel aware of this, how badly the boy had turned out?'

Again Trenwith made no reply. He went on, 'After the death of her husband, my wife's sister decided to enter a convent and devote the remainder of her life to the service of God. Her son foresaw the family wealth entering the pockets of the church and he took what he considered to be the necessary and only step he could take to ensure that this unfortunate circumstance, from his point of view, did not reach fruition. He killed his mother, this good, holy woman who had loved him wholeheartedly and consistently excused him for all of his weaknesses and failings as a human being. He murdered her in cold blood. Stabbed her in the neck as she sat quietly working at her needlework one afternoon and as she paused momentarily to look up and greet him lovingly, as was always her way with this wretchedly ungrateful son. She bled to death, choking on her own blood. And then, with his hand placed firmly on the family's Holy Bible, and a mournfully pious expression on his face, he solemnly swore that the most devoted of the family's servants had carried out this monstrous crime in a fit of anger at his mistress's decision to move into a convent and abandon him to his fate. The servant was, unfortunately, unable to defend his good name. This vile murderer of my wife's sister, quickly disposed of him – ran him through with a sword – claiming that he had caught him in the act of taking his good mother's life.'

'So this was why Emanuel was called away from the priory,' said Customer with a small frown. 'He suspected that the son was not telling the truth and he felt under an obligation to the family to see justice done.'

'Based on past experience, yes, he suspected the son. In fact, he never for one moment doubted that it was his hand that had wielded the instrument of death. It was also obvious to Emanuel that the son's desire to inherit the family fortune was the motive for the murder of this good woman. Word of her son's wholly unsatisfactory behaviour over the years had inevitably filtered back to the priory and was a particular source of great concern and unhappiness for Emanuel. He carried a heavy burden of guilt over his having been largely instrumental in securing the adoption of this boy by my wife's kin.'

'But he made amends,' said Customer with a knowing nod, 'and in the only way he could. He saw to it that the son was brought to justice and tried for murder.'

'And sentenced to death by hanging.'

'But,' said Customer in a cautious voice when Trenwith fell silent.

'Emanuel's health had been failing for some little while and it deteriorated rapidly during this period of time – while he saw to it that justice was done. It was for this reason that he chose not to stay and witness the hanging. He started back to the priory in very poor health on the day that the death sentence was due to be carried out. However, as the hangman's noose was fixed securely around the convicted man's neck and drawn taut, the rough band of fellows he had fallen in with, stormed the scene, rescuing him as he swayed on the scaffold. They cut him down and all rode away into the next county – here, into Cornwall, hot on Emanuel's heels. Emanuel was a dead man from that moment on. And because he – this treacherous man who murdered my wife's sister – had heard it rumoured that you, Customer Trago was riding back to Cornwall to see his sick old mentor, Emanuel, and say a final fond farewell to him before he died, he knew that you would not rest until you had uncovered the truth of Emanuel's death. With the hatred this thoroughly evil man had felt for Customer Trago as a child still festering deep within him, he therefore determined that he, you, would also die.'

Customer was momentarily stunned into silence. Several moments passed before he found himself able to speak. 'I thought it was Gennys who attacked me. One of his followers. I assumed that there was some long-standing dispute between Gennys and Emanuel which latterly also involved the other canons and gentry and the furious faction fight that began with the election of John Shere as the new prior at Launceston. Gennys would have learned from the prior's clerk of my intention to see Emanuel one last time before he died. More than once Emanuel had written to me of Gennys and their little liking for one another, and I thought Gennys had decided to rid himself of me before I presented myself at the priory and became a similar nuisance to him. I see now how wrong I have been in my thinking. It was this man who, as a boy, had tried to kill me and who had since grown into manhood with as much hatred, if not more, for me.'

Trenwith said simply, 'It grieves me to say this, Customer Trago, but you truly are a marked man. Your name is carved deep into this evil man's very being. He will not rest until he sees you dead and buried. In his twisted mind, he sees you as being the author of all of his misfortune in life.'

'What could he have hoped to gain that was better for him by remaining at the priory in the care of the prior?'

'He obviously feels there was something there for him. Perhaps no more than Emanuel's wholehearted approval of him.'

'I must know his name,' said Customer. He looked at Trenwith imploringly. 'You surely cannot deny me that one small charity. Knowing his name is my only chance of surviving whatever plans he may have made for me.'

Again Trenwith declined to give a name. With a slow shake of his head, he said, 'All that you seek to know of this man will be there for you to see when you look into his eyes, Customer Trago. As one day soon, you surely will.'

Chapter Forty-seven

Customer and Jacob Trenwith were standing within sight of the farmhouse. Lucy Trenwith watched them wistfully from a window in the kitchen.

'Will the blacksmith hang for Rebecca Trelawney's murder?' she asked her mother.

'As like as not,' replied Meg Trenwith. 'The Trelawneys will not be bested, and certainly not by the young whelp speaking with your father.'

'Is there nothing we can do to help the young sir to save the blacksmith?'

Lucy looked round at her mother pleadingly. Meg Trenwith felt the girl's eyes upon her, but she did not look up from her work. She had been aware of the covert glances exchanged by her daughter and their handsome young visitor and she was therefore not too surprised, nor entirely unsympathetic, when Lucy added, 'I cannot bear for him to think of us as unkind and cruel, as surely he will. Please, Mother: I know how things stand with the Trelawneys and would ask or do nothing that would bring their anger down upon Father's head, but is there not something we can say or do to make ourselves appear more pleasing in the young sir's eyes?'

Meg Trenwith dusted the flour off her hands and then joined her daughter at the window. Together, they looked out at the two men in the distance. Trenwith was walking back to the house with the dogs at his heels. Customer remained momentarily where he was and then started after Trenwith – no doubt, thought Lucy, to collect his horse and leave, possibly forever.

Meg spoke in a soft, gentle voice. 'Go, child, and tell the young sir of how kind and caring you were to the blacksmith when last he visited us, and of the two hours you spent cleaning the thick mud from his cloak and then drying it by the fire for him so that he would not catch his death of cold on his long ride home. Perhaps this will encourage the young sir to think a little more charitably of the Trenwiths.'

The girl's eyes lit up and she ran quickly from the house,

gathering her long skirts high about her knees and quickening her pace. She was fleet of foot and made little sound as abruptly she deviated sharply from the field she was crossing and made for the track that led from the farm back to the highway, her purpose being that if Customer reached his horse quicker than she expected, she would stand a better chance of intercepting him there.

Pausing at a stand of beech trees near the high hedgerow bordering the track, the sound of distant hoofbeats that had brought a small anticipatory smile to her lips, slowly faded. The horse she could hear was on the approach from the highway. This was not Customer Trago who, at any moment from now, would surely ride into view from the opposite direction. It couldn't be.

Slipping quickly behind the trunk of one of the larger trees, she waited with a pounding heart. A Trelawney, she was sure of it, and to be caught by one of them, alone, with no male protector, was an unspoken invitation to rape, or worse.

Too distant to hear any cry from her for help, two farm labourers employed by her father, were busy with the spring lambing. One of them picked up a newly-dropped lamb by its hind legs and then whipped it through the air to free its lungs of fluid and force the first breath of life into them. She thought of waving her arms frantically to try and attract the men's attention, but neither man was facing in her direction.

The horse and rider passed the trees, the rider not once looking her way, and with her heart in her mouth, Lucy backed cautiously from her place of concealment. The rider, who was not the man she had thought to see, was one she had every reason to fear a hundredfold more than any other. As he disappeared from sight, she cut back across the fields to the house, running as fast as her legs would carry her.

Her mother looked up as she burst into the kitchen.

'What is it, child?'

'Cousin Malachy,' the girl gasped. 'He is on his way here, to the house.'

Meg gazed at the mound of pastry on the board before her. She said nothing for some moments and then, looking round at her daughter, she said, in a quiet, calm voice, 'Go to your room, child, and stay there. Do not come out until either I or your father call to you that it is safe for you to do so.'

217

'But what does he want with us?' the girl whispered fearfully.

'Nothing with us, his kin, child,' her mother replied in an oddly distant voice. 'He has business this day with but one person… Our young visitor you would wish to have think well of us. Customer Trago.'

Chapter Forty-eight

Customer gathered up the reins of his horse, aware of nothing but the persistent buzz of an insect about his head which he repeatedly brushed absently away with one hand.

As he prepared to mount his horse, someone spoke, causing him to give a start and then look round quickly over his shoulder. He was looking directly into the late morning sun and momentarily blinded by its dazzling brightness, was unable to recognize the speaker.

'So, Customer Trago... I repeat: did you find your answers here?'

The speaker walked up to him casually, leading a horse.

'Pawley?' Customer squinted against the sun and then shading out its bright light with one hand held above his eyes, he asked, 'What do you want here with the Trenwiths?'

Malachy Pawley smiled faintly and as Customer waited for his reply, he saw in the intent gaze that Pawley had fixed on him, the answers Trenwith had said would be there for him to see in the eyes not only of Customer Trago's would-be assassin and Emanuel's roadside murderer, but also of those of the one responsible for the attempt made on Customer's life when a child.

'I see you remember me,' said Pawley. His tone was amused. 'Though it has taken you some while, Customer Trago. Once or twice back there at the inn at Wynehouse Corner, I thought a glimmer of recognition came into your eyes, but as you never confirmed, or so much as made it your business to ask if we had met someplace before, I assumed that I was mistaken.'

Pawley considered Customer thoughtfully for a moment or two before continuing:

'You intrigue me, Customer Trago. You have led a charmed life, right from when we were boys together at Launceston Priory. Even the halt and the lame worship at your feet. As revolting a sight, I feel bound to say, that I have ever had the great misfortune to rest my eyes upon.'

Customer looked hard at him. 'Rebecca? You dare to speak to me in this cruel fashion of that poor afflicted girl for her having demonstrated her fondness for me?'

Customer's thoughts were a confused jumble. The look on Pawley's face made him feel light-headed. '*You* killed her?' His voice conveyed his bewilderment. 'You used Rebecca to destroy Eber because he had taken me in and saved my life?'

Pawley smiled faintly. 'Perhaps I did and perhaps I didn't; that is something you will never know. If, however, I am the murderer you seek, perhaps it was not to lay the blame at Eber Pendragon's feet, but at those of the handsome young fellow whom that disgustingly repulsive creature idolized.'

Customer made no response. He realized by Pawley's tone of voice and from his general demeanour that he was under threat of death and that he was unlikely to leave the Trenwiths' farm alive that day. Twice this arrogant fellow standing before him had attempted to take his life, once by drowning in a pond when they were children and again, undoubtedly, all those painful weeks ago, as he was making his way to the priory. Customer did not expect to be able to look back on this moment and think third time lucky. Malachy Pawley meant to kill him and kill him he would. With no one at hand to aid his defence against this hate-filled spectre from his past, Divine Intervention was now Customer Trago's last and only hope.

'Have you nothing to say to me, some friendly greeting after all these years?' asked Pawley with a faint chuckle at the back of his throat.

'Did you ask the same question of Emanuel before you murdered him in cold blood?' Customer asked him in a calm voice. 'I see it written clearly in your eyes that it was by your hand that Emanuel died. And do not insult my intelligence by denying it.'

Pawley laughed softly. 'Emanuel should have contented himself with the growing of callouses on his knees as he knelt in prayer. But dear me, no. An avenging angel, that was our dear, saintly Brother Emanuel. That was why he had so many enemies among the priory's fractious brethren. He was dying, but you knew that, or suspected as much, and I simply did as much for the old fool as I would do for a wretched animal in its last painful death throes. I put him swiftly out of his misery and took this–' he unsheathed the dagger at his waist '–as payment for my services. And–' the smile on Pawley's lips was chilling as he paused momentarily to draw aside the high collar on his fine, white linen undershirt '–in reparation for this pretty necklace he made sure was fastened tightly around my neck.'

Customer felt something in his breast harden as he gazed at the knobby mottled scars that ringed Pawley's throat. The dagger he was being shown was Emanuel's and in a blinding flash, it all came back to Customer – every agonizing moment he had endured on that muddy, wind and rain-lashed road to Launceston Priory where he had set upon and then been left for dead by what he had initially thought was a band of robbers lead by Emanuel's arch enemy, Sir William Gennys.

As he had lain wounded in the fading twilight of that never to be forgotten night – dying, Customer had thought – this evil man standing before him, Malachy Pawley, had triumphantly brandished Emanuel's dagger before his eyes. Malachy Pawley had wanted him to know that he now possessed it and that there could be only one explanation for this. Emanuel, alive, would never have parted with that dagger. Emanuel, dead, had no choice.

Pawley smiled. 'I see you recognize this beautiful instrument of death and that you have finally recalled your last sighting of it. I had intended to use it to widen your mouth into a broad smile by slicing open your throat… "But why gild the lily?" I asked myself. You were dying from the thrust of my sword in your side. Or so I thought. A serious error of judgment on my part which I freely admit. It was suffice unto me that you should know, as you lay dying in that sanctified, foul-smelling Launceston mud, that Emanuel's prized possession was now mine.'

Pawley's expression hardened. 'I have a long memory, Customer Trago, and I recall, with almost unbearable clarity, that with no thought of an eight-year-old child's longing for acceptance and the smallest show of affection – and with not so much as a glance in that child's direction – that insensitive jobernowl, Emanuel, made a great show of explaining the dagger's provenance to the small boy who was openly his favourite. He even permitted you to handle it, and from that moment on, Customer Trago, I determined that one day Emanuel's beautiful dagger would be mine.'

'Have you no pity?' Customer demanded. 'Did the years that you spent at the priory leave no impression on your soul…awaken in you no sense of decency? Did the kindness that was shown to you by the entreaties I have been given to understand Emanuel made to the prior to place you in a good loving home mean nothing to you?'

'Oh, dear me, I see that that pious old fool has left his holier than thou mark on you. I wonder sometimes why I cared so deeply that I was not his favourite and that my reward for being second best was to be placed in the home of those depressingly sanctimonious Pawleys, whose only redeeming feature was their impressively large wealth. Which, as it turned out, was not to be mine, their adopted, not-so-loving only son. Thanks again,' sighed Pawley, eyeing Customer mockingly, 'to Emanuel – that holy crusader and indefatigable champion of all that was right and proper according to God and the blessed Brother Emanuel's law. It surprises me somewhat, you having this charmed existence, Customer Trago, that the Pawley pot of gold hasn't somehow fetched up in your pocket. A serious oversight on the part of the gods of good fortune, surely.' Pawley smiled sardonically. 'What *were* they thinking?'

'You will pay for your sins, Malachy Pawley,' said Customer.

'But not by your feeble hand,' responded Pawley with a scowl. 'You have idled far too long in honeyed fleshpots; gone soft, Customer Trago. You with your pretty looks may have fared well as a court jester in far off lands, but you are no match for Malachy Pawley, who–'

Pawley broke off. He could see that Customer was not listening to him. Something had caught his eye. Pawley glanced round curiously over his shoulder to see what had attracted Customer's attention.

Turning his back casually on Customer as Meg Trenwith walked up to them, Pawley said, 'What a pleasant surprise this is, Aunt Tren–'

He did not finish his greeting, sucking in his breath as Meg Trenwith plunged the carving knife she was concealing behind her back, deep into his abdomen.

Wide-eyed and staring, he clutched at his stomach as she withdrew the knife and then, falling heavily onto his knees, he doubled deeply over the terrible pain that engulfed him. Blood poured through his fingers, drenching his breeches. He gazed at his blood-soaked hands for a moment and then looked up at Meg Trenwith, the expression on his face that of utter disbelief and shock.

Customer gave a shudder and closed his eyes. When he opened them a second later, Trenwith and the farm labourers had joined them.

There was a shocked silence, an absolute stillness. It was as if no one dared so much as to breathe. Meg Trenwith's mouth was working, slowly and unemotionally. Customer watched it, fascinated, but was unable to hear what she was saying. He thought he might have heard her utter, in a breathy sigh, the name of her dead daughter, but he wasn't sure.

He lowered his gaze to Pawley, who now lay curled up in the foetal position, and he understood. Young Mary Trenwith's cousin, Malachy Pawley, was with Lowarn Trelawney the day she died. They had violated her – Customer could not find it in himself to think otherwise – and it was either while committing the foul act of rape upon her pure, virginal body, or as she had fled from them in blind terror afterwards and stumbled into the bog on her father's land, that she had met her end.

Meg Trenwith abruptly interrupted the stillness with a brief nod at her husband. She indicated to Pawley.

'Get rid of this evil, murdering swine in the black bog,' she instructed Trenwith in a cold, dispassionate voice. 'Where he belongs.'

'Have you no mercy, mistress?' cried Customer. 'Can you not see that the man still lives?'

'Then if God be for him' said Meg coldly, 'the bog will not have him. He will be cleansed of his sins and rise anew from his mud bath like the phoenix from the ashes and walk, as if on water, to safety.'

'You do not understand,' said Customer desperately. 'I need him alive.'

'It is you who do not understand, Customer Trago.' Meg Trenwith fixed him with a steely eye. '*I* need him dead.'

Chapter Forty-nine

Barbarians! Monsters! What sort of people were these? Where had all the good people of Cornwall gone?

Mounting his horse and then starting back along the track, at a slow walk, Customer found himself trying to recall the strange look on Pawley's face as they had spoken of Rebecca. It was not easy to get into the mind of someone like Pawley and know what that person was thinking, but Customer found himself wondering if Pawley had wanted him to die sure in the knowledge that he, Malachy Pawley, had murdered Rebecca.

But for what reason?

Because he wanted Customer Trago, the man he hated as much as he had hated the old Augustinian monk who'd had a hand in raising him, to believe that his motive for killing her lay in Eber Pendragon's playing the Good Samaritan and saving my life? Customer asked himself. *Had Pawley really wanted me to suffer for all eternity in the knowledge that this big-hearted man, Eber Pendragon, had hanged, not for his sins, but for whatever sins Pawley believed I had committed against him in the past?*

Surely not.

And yet what other reason could there be? There wasn't one, that was the simple answer. It had to be because Eber saved my life, Customer decided.

And yet the more he thought about it, the less sure he was that it was by Pawley's hand that Rebecca had died. Pawley was unquestionably evil and more than capable of murder, Customer had ample proof of that; but wouldn't a man like Pawley, Customer asked himself, derive a far greater, maliciously twisted pleasure from having witnessed Rebecca's murder and from knowing for sure who *had* killed her? Wouldn't a man like Pawley delight in following her killer, Lowarn Trelawney, as he carried her body to the holy well and then left it there with its incriminating evidence pointing directly at Eber Pendragon?

There was the answer.

Pawley didn't kill Rebecca. But he knew who did and had

revelled in the awesome power this had given him, thought Customer with a shudder.

The one witness who could have saved Eber from the gallows. Had Pawley lived!

Customer urged his horse into a gallop and rode on towards the highway, finding it all but impossible to put all thought of the dire consequences of Malachy Pawley's fate at the hands of the Trenwiths far from his mind.

Another nightmare, he thought, to add to those already haunting his badly fragmented sleeping hours.

For no particular reason, he glanced back along the track and saw Lucy Trenwith standing forlornly in the middle of it, watching him with her skirts held aloft. She made an enchanting picture and without thinking, he checked his horse and turned and rode slowly back to her.

She looked up at him shyly, without speaking, and after pausing for a moment, he dismounted and, again without thinking, stooped to pluck a late-flowering narcissus from some blackthorn hedging and then handed it to her.

As she took it from him, she blushed, self-consciously dropping her skirts. She looked at him searchingly. 'You are unhurt? Cousin Malachy did not harm you? I was told to remain in the house,' she went on, without awaiting Customer's response, 'but I could not let you leave without speaking to you.'

Out of breath after chasing after him, her words tumbled awkwardly from her lips, all of a rush. 'Mother wished for me to inquire after Master Pendragon's health. He was without benefit of a warm cloak in a chill wind as he walked in the fields with my father the other day and we feared he might catch cold.' She lowered her eyes from Customer's steady gaze, soft colour creeping prettily up her neck to flood her cheeks afresh. 'His cloak was much soiled and wetted from where he had paused and rested awhile at the side of the track before riding on up to meet with my father at the house.'

Customer smiled at her blushes. He thought he understood her motive in telling him all of this, the regret she shared with her mother that the head of their household had not been more courteous and helpful to him, and that they wished him to know that they were powerless in the face of the obstinacy of their lord

225

and master. 'And you did your best to clean and dry it for him?' He waited until she looked up at him. Then he said, 'I am sure the blacksmith was much obliged to you.'

'It was but a small thing...' she assured him quickly. 'And I was truly sorry not to be able to clean his cloak properly for him before he left us,' she added, the small, earnest frown creasing her brow making her look all the more enchanting in Customer's eyes. 'The blood that had mixed with the mud stains proved too stubborn for Mother and me to remove.'

Abruptly, the gentle amusement in Customer's eyes faded. 'Blood?' he asked sharply. 'What blood is this?'

'Master Pendragon came off his horse and suffered a heavy nose bleed.' She pointed along the track. 'Over there. Menfreda – the dog with one blue eye, the other brown – sprang out at him, barking like a mad thing, and Master Pendragon's horse shied, unseating him and throwing him heavily onto the ground. Menfreda means no real harm: she is young and high-spirited and not yet properly trained like her mother, Zoe. Menfreda does many wild and foolish things that make Father cross. She will learn in time, though, to be quiet and sensible like Zoe.'

The dog with one blue eye, the other brown, had similarly shot, straight and true like a shaft from a longbow, through a gap in the hedgerow as Customer had ridden up the track earlier, but he had kept his seat when his mount had reared up on its hind legs, though it had been a close thing. Both of them were taken completely unawares and he could easily have been catapulted over the low hedgerow or deposited unceremoniously in the muddied water of the shallow ditch that ran along one side of the track.

Customer stepped back from Lucy, as if to remount, and she spoke out quickly, flushing afresh at her boldness, but anxious to detain him in her company for a moment or two longer. 'My mother, Meg, asks that you should convey to Master Pendragon our kind regards. We hope he will be back among us soon.'

'I doubt that your father feels thus,' said Customer with a grim smile.

'He has no quarrel with Master Pendragon and would be the last person to wish him ill,' she assured him, a shade defensively.

'Then why does he stubbornly refuse to help me to save the blacksmith when all that he needs to do is to confirm that which old

Agnes of the Wynehouse Inn has told me is true?'

Lucy was not listening to him. She was looking past him at the black-hatted rider cantering towards them along the track.

Customer's heart gave a dull, sickening thud against his breastbone.

Was this nightmare never to end?

Chapter Fifty

The colour drained slowly from Lucy's face and without another word, she turned from Customer, hitching up her skirts again and running as fast as she could back towards the farmhouse.

Jacob Trenwith and his wife, their business at the black bog dealt with to their satisfaction, waited anxiously for her in the doorway of their home, almost as if they had preternaturally foreseen that Lowarn Trelawney and his brothers, together with the rabble who served them, would be gathering in a restless group somewhere beyond their natural range of vision and were making ready to advance on them for having permitted the Outlander, Customer Trago, to cross their threshold.

Mother and daughter went quickly inside, bolting the door behind them, and then, whistling to his two dogs to bring them to heel, Trenwith started along the track towards Customer and Lowarn Trelawney.

The farm labourers, who had returned to their lambing duties, had also seen Lowarn and his brothers and their servants riding up and they had stopped their work. Picking up the long, hefty crooks they carried about with them, they fell in alongside their master as he drew level with them.

Lowarn, circling Customer on his horse at a slow walk, laughed heartily at the sight.

'Look,' he cried. 'I do believe they come armed with their toothpicks to see us off their land.'

'Us? Or you, Lowarn Trelawney?'

'You would be no more welcome here than I am,' said Lowarn. 'Trenwith guards that girl of his as if she were made of some rare precious metal; and indeed, perhaps she is. I have not seen her at close quarters since she has blossomed into fair young maidenhood, and I think today I shall. My mood is for it.'

Looking past Lowarn, Customer could see Lowarn's five brothers, who had been joined by several of their servants, waiting restlessly on their mounts at a bend in the track.

'If your real business here with Trenwith today,' said Customer, 'is your concern that he has in some way betrayed you and your family, let me assure you that he stands solidly with you against the blacksmith of Wynehouse Corner and me. You have nothing to fear from Trenwith.'

The expression on Lowarn's face puzzled Customer. He could not define it which troubled him. Then Lowarn said, 'Neither I nor any of my family have anything to fear from Jacob Trenwith.'

'I do not doubt that,' said Customer in a dry voice. 'Trelawney swords and daggers are a deal truer and sharper than the toothpicks Trenwith and his men would carry in their defence.'

Lowarn looked at Customer thoughtfully and then he threw back his head and laughed. 'You tickle my fancy, young sir lawyer. It has been many a long day since I have had such a merry laugh. Come, sir jester, let the Trelawneys escort you safely back to your place of lodging. These wild, uncivilized tracks and roadways we law-abiding, God-fearing Cornishmen are obliged to travel, teem with murderous vagabonds who would think to rob you of your purse and your life and me of my amusement.'

'That will not be necessary, thank you, sir,' said Customer. 'I am well able to make my own safe passage back to the Wynehouse.'

'I insist upon it,' said Lowarn, grinning. 'This business intrigues me, young sir lawyer. I would see how it ends and would thank no one for denying me the pleasure.'

'I can save you the time and trouble and satisfy your curiosity here and now, if that truly be your pleasure, sir,' said Customer. 'This business ends with Lowarn Trelawney hanging on the gallows for his sister, Rebecca's foul murder.'

Trenwith and his men had come to a halt several yards back from them. Lowarn looked at them with an amused smile and then sweeping his hat from his head, he said, 'Good day to you, Trenwith. Lay down your arms and return to your toil in the fields. We came only to collect this troublesome young popi-dog here before he strays onto your land and snaps at the heels of your sheep.'

'You break your father's agreement with me, Lowarn Trelawney,' said Jacob Trenwith in a menacing growl. 'If you and your men are not off my land within the next few minutes, I shall consider all bargains between our two families broken.'

Lowarn Trelawney grinned insolently and then, making a deep flourish to Trenwith with his right arm, he turned his horse away. Customer followed him. The riders waiting at the bend in the track held back until Lowarn and Customer had ridden past them and then they fell in, grinning to a man, behind Customer.

They rode at his back in ill-concealed amused silence and in a heavy sea mist, right up and onto the forecourt of the inn. There they turned, still grinning, and then, without as much as a by-your-leave, galloped back towards Butterfly Lane.

Lowarn paused for a moment before riding off to join them. 'I bring word to you from the deputy bailiff's nephew with whom my brothers and I shared a tankard or two in Bodmin yesterday evening. He would know how goes it with you and asks that he should be remembered to you.'

'You are mistaken, sir,' replied Customer. 'I know nothing of the deputy bailiff's kin.'

'It is a lie that you have met his late sister's son – the physician, Piers Heard?' Lowarn smiled. 'Master physician has a reputation for his fondness for fine old French brandy, but this is the first I have known of his fondness for a tall story. He would have us believe that he knows you well, sir, and that he has even done you the odd favour or two in the hope of alleviating the unfortunate circumstances in which you presently find yourself.'

Customer stared at Lowarn in dismay. 'Piers Heard is the deputy bailiff's nephew?'

'Ah,' said Lowarn with a slow nod of his head. 'I see he neglected to mention his family history. Well, no harm done, I dare say.'

'Why do you tell me of this now?' demanded Customer.

Lowarn looked at him for a moment. 'I would not have you call me or any of mine a liar and a cheat, Customer Trago. I lay all my cards on the table where you can see them plainly and know what you are up against.'

'You are very sure of yourself, sir.'

Lowarn's yellow eyes glittered. 'The game is lost, Master Lawyer. Admit it and be done with this foolishness. The cards you hold are worthless. You waste everybody's time. Come, be kind and let the hangman have his reward for his patience with you.'

'Never,' said Customer.

Smiling faintly, Lowarn spurred his horse and rode off at a gallop, soon to be swallowed up by the sea mist which thickened by the minute.

Customer's eyes followed him until he and his horse had disappeared in the gloom, and then Customer turned away with a sigh.

Would that this was the last anyone was to see of Lowarn Trelawney; that the sea mist would befuddle his senses and losing all intelligence of time and place, he would gallop on madly over the cliffs and into the heaving, boiling waters of the treacherously rocky cove that bore his family name...

Chapter Fifty-one

As Customer was stabling his horse in the shippen, Agnes came up quietly behind him and spoke.

'The Trelawneys make sport of wet-nursing you, young sir.'

'I shall have the last laugh yet, Agnes.'

'Us'll see,' she said, her voice sad and resigned.

'What of the wine merchant?' he asked.

'Gone to his grave,' she replied grimly. 'Us has managed without you.'

He sighed inwardly, thankful to hear it, but nevertheless managed a small frown of rebuke. 'I need to see his place of burial so that his kin, should any come seeking his whereabouts, may know where he lies.'

'No man or woman will come seeking that one,' Agnes retorted with a disdainful sniff. 'He was born on a black, evil night of the Devil's sister and has no mortal kin.'

'They'll come,' Customer assured her. 'The wine merchant is almost certain to be a wealthy man, and make no mistake about it, mistress, wealthy men – alive or dead – attract kin to them like moths to the flame of a lighted lamp. The private papers he carried with him, which I shall examine closely tonight, will more than likely give the name of the one nearest to him.'

'Then I congratulate you, young sir, for this is indeed your lucky day. Among Master Allsopp's papers you should find an important document which sets out plainly that Eber Pendragon is sole heir to his fortune; and things being how they are for Eber at the moment–'

Customer interrupted her. 'Who told you of this?' he demanded to know.

'Eber himself. He also told old Agnes that the wine merchant was alone in the world, with neither wife nor child, brother or sister, and that he had no one but his good friend, Eber, to make sure that a Mass was said for him.'

'I shall have to check the truth of this with the wine importers he dealt with.'

'Old Agnes knows the truth of it.'

Again she was right. The document she spoke of, the last will and testament of the late wine merchant, Nicholas Allsopp, whose place of domicile was in the town of Exeter in the neighbouring county of Devon, was among his belongings. There could be no doubt: Eber Pendragon was Nicholas Allsopp's sole heir.

As if I don't have enough to worry about! thought Customer.

Placing Nicholas Allsopp's will to one side, he began an anxious search through the wine merchant's other papers for the name and address of the importers in London who supplied him so that they could be notified of his sudden demise and arrangements could be made for them to deal with any of his outstanding orders as they saw fit.

There were two relevant wine importers with whom Nicholas Allsopp did business. One in London, the other – a much smaller family concern whose name was familiar to Customer – in Exeter.

The wine merchant had a thriving business. His order books were filling up, with only three ports of call on his regular biannual round – the inn at Wynehouse Corner being one of them – awaiting an entry.

Customer turned back six months to the last wine order for the Wynehouse. It was a surprisingly large one – given that the Wynehouse attracted so little regular custom. In fact, much larger than any of the other orders that Nicholas Allsopp had taken on that particular visit to Cornwall.

Customer turned back a further six months to the visit preceding that one and found the same story. The order for the inn at Wynehouse Corner far and away exceeded all other orders taken by Nicholas Allsopp on his Cornish round.

Customer was amazed. With so little wine and brandy – and for that matter, the ale and cider brewed by local farmers – supped at the inn, the Wynehouse should be floating swiftly out to Ireland on a veritable rising sea of alcoholic beverages!

This was if Nicholas Allsopp actually filled the order.

Puzzled, Customer checked the wine merchant's ledger. The wine and brandy orders for the Wynehouse Inn – orders that Customer felt sure Agnes would confirm had never actually been delivered to the premises – had been paid in full on demand. Paid for from the purse of a man who was known to be close with money, and who would therefore insist upon full value for every penny that he was forced to spend.

Why would Eber Pendragon pay large sums of money to Nicholas Allsopp disguised as legitimate payments for wine and brandy orders for the inn at Wynehouse Corner? Come to that, how strange that so much wine and brandy, which the mostly poor of the Hundred could not afford to imbibe, was regularly ordered by Eber. Certainly not in anticipation, or hope, of an influx of travellers along the highway seeking sustenance and a night or two's rest at his inn. Could it be that Nicholas Allsopp – whom Customer knew for a fact had once served as a soldier in a regiment of the King's garrisoned at a tactically vital outpost on Henry's vulnerable southern coastline – was a turncoat, a spy for the rebel Cornish who, as everybody in the land knew, were becoming dangerously restive again? Were these unaccounted for sums of money being used by Nicholas Allsopp, at Eber's behest, to raise an army against the King here in Cornwall?

Customer's heartbeat quickened with excitement as his favourite mental picture of himself as a (maybe lesser) Plantagenet Pretender to the throne of England flashed before his eyes, only this time he was riding through Bodmin alongside Eber Pendragon at the head of a thousand-strong army of brave and true Cornishmen to the exultant cheers and loyal shouts of the townspeople who lined their triumphant route.

Why hadn't Eber confided any of this in him? Surely he would know where Customer Trago's loyalties and sympathies lay? Certainly not with any Tudor King. Customer Trago was a Cornishman first and an Englishman second and would remain so until the moment the very last breath left his body.

He rubbed his eyes wearily and returned the papers and ledger to Nicholas Allsopp's saddlebag. He had found no fault with the wine merchant's bookkeeping. It was immaculate; balanced to the last groat. Idly, Customer picked up Eber's Bible. He regretted being unable to take it to Eber, particularly now in the light of his discovery in regard to the consistent overordering of wines and brandy, as disclosed to him in the wine merchant's ledger, which continued to perplex Customer and begged a rational explanation, but he could not afford the time. There were far more pressing matters to be dealt with there at Wynehouse Corner, and so few days left before he must face the deputy bailiff with his findings.

Casually, he opened the Bible, blinking quickly in surprise at the Latin text which leapt up at him from the pages. He had seen only one such other Bible and that had belonged to Emanuel, a canon of the church.

The memory of his own bitter personal struggle to master the ancient language was tempered with his sudden recollection of the old monk sitting in a shady corner of the priory cloisters during the summer months, pretending to read from his Latin Bible when he was actually dozing in the warmth of the day. Emanuel insisted that a quiet hour of contemplative silence spent with his Bible was when he did his best thinking, and he recommended the practice to Customer, making no murmur of demur, however, when Customer, careful as ever to pick his moment, would sidle off and seek the more soul-satisfying work at the rectory farm for his daily hour of contemplation.

Smiling to himself at the memory, Customer kept turning the pages. He felt sure there must be some mistake. What use would Eber have for a Bible that only the finest scholars in the land would have the necessary knowledge and ability to read and seek comfort from? The question puzzled him. Indeed, the whole question of whether or not Eber actually *possessed* a Bible puzzled him. Very few Cornish people could read books of any description, let alone owned a book. He, Customer, was an exception, having had the good fortune to be raised in an atmosphere steeped in literature and among, for the most part, learned scholars who spent all but the hours devoted to their religious duties, in libraries filled to overflowing with ancient manuscripts and volume upon volume of weighty, leather-bound books of learning. It had not occurred to him before this to question whether or not it was true that Eber Pendragon, blacksmith, innkeeper and inveterate Saturday night gambler of Wynehouse Corner, was – according to Nicholas Allsopp – the *possessor* of a Bible.

Customer fingered his beard thoughtfully. Eber Pendragon was not the kind of man to trifle with trappings of any description. If this Latin Bible genuinely belonged to him, then he was in the habit of reading and studying it regularly. Those grubby smudges on the corners of the leaves looked suspiciously like huge thumbprints, thumbprints that, in every particular, would match those of the genial giant that was Eber Pendragon.

The answer came to Customer slowly and when he acknowledged it for the truth, it came as no real surprise to him.

Eber Pendragon was once a holy brother of the church – if Customer had to make an educated guess, a member of the Cornish Benedictine monastery granted to the Benedictine monks from Mont St Michel in France by Edward the Confessor in the eleventh century. In short, the monastery at St Michael's Mount in the south-west where Nicholas Allsopp had served as captain of the garrison. This was where he and Eber had met, what bound them so closely together.

Customer frowned, the edges of a headache beginning to spread out from his temples to meet in the middle of his brow. To the best of Customer's knowledge, the Vicar-General had not closed down the monastery at St Michael's Mount, but Emanuel's letters had nevertheless often contained some reference to the fact that everywhere in Cornwall – and the monastic house at St Michael's Mount would be no exception – monks from all of the many diverse religious families had, for some time now, been leaving their holy orders and starting either a new life for themselves, or were returning to their former lives, in the outside world. Eber Pendragon had been among them, hadn't he? There could be no other satisfactory explanation for a Latin Bible to be in his possession.

Unless, of course, the wine merchant had been lying about that and there was some other explanation for the Bible that Nicholas Allsopp had claimed was Eber's!

Chapter Fifty-two

That night Customer dreamt of Emanuel…

Emanuel sitting in the warm summer sunshine pretending to read from his Latin Bible. Emanuel on his knees humbly making his daily devotions. Emanuel hauling himself upright on unsteady legs, the knee and hip joints of which creaked and groaned and ached with every shuffling step he took. Emanuel smiling his gentle, wise smile. Emanuel frowning, scolding and cajoling him. Railing at him for not devoting his life to the pursuit of knowledge. Threatening him with damnation for his vanity and sloth while brave Cornishmen like Eber Pendragon were Cornwall's last and only hope of breaking free of the Tudor yoke once and for all…

Customer woke suddenly, tears streaming down his cheeks.

That was not Emanuel who scolded, cajoled and then threatened him for his lack of application to the problems of the moment. That, thought Customer, was his own conscience speaking to him. Furthermore, Eber Pendragon – who was, without a doubt, one of the bravest and truest of Cornishmen he had ever known – had never once shown, by word or deed, the slightest yearning to break free for all time of the grip the Tudors had on Cornwall.

Hearing Agnes moving about in the kitchen below, Customer got up and dressed slowly, feeling no enthusiasm for the day ahead, only the sick dread that now gnawed relentlessly at his vitals.

Agnes looked equally dispirited, greeting him perfunctorily as he paused to wash his hands and face in the basin of warm water she had set out for him. He made no attempt at conversation, simply gazed at the unleavened bread she had placed on a board in the middle of the table and tried to purge his mind of the images of Emanuel that remained there, and the despairing notion that he disappointed him still.

Finally he sighed and said, 'The Trelawneys do well to make sport of Customer Trago. I can make neither head nor tail of this affair, Agnes. Nor do I see any reason for supposing that I ever shall.'

'Us *is* feeling sorry for ourselves this morning,' she grunted, eyeing him disapprovingly.

He scowled at the oatmeal congealing unappetizingly in the bowl she thumped down on the table before him. 'Would you believe that anybody could be so gullible as to take a nephew of the deputy bailiff of Bodmin himself into his confidence? Do you not marvel at it? I should carry a shaking stick with tiny bells on it so that everyone will be warned and know me for the fool I am. It must have been sweet music to the Trelawneys' ears to hear that drunken knave, Piers Heard, trumpeting my foolishness throughout the taverns of Bodmin town.'

'A fool does not know himself for a fool,' said Agnes. 'How can he if he be a fool?'

He looked at her sorrowfully. 'You remind me of someone I once knew; someone very close to me, someone kind and very wise.'

'Old Agnes wise?' She shook her head. 'No, young sir. Old Agnes just speaks the truth of what is plain before her eyes to see.'

He looked at her for a moment. 'What do you really see, Agnes? If, as you say, I cannot be a fool because a fool cannot see his own folly, why can't I see a just and proper solution to this terrible dilemma of Eber's? Must he die dangling like a puppeteer's rag doll on the end of a hangman's rope because of Customer Trago's pathetic inadequacies? Dear God in Heaven, can it be merciful and just that an innocent man should have his faith in another human being so cruelly betrayed?'

'Us wouldn't know much about God in Heaven and what is merciful and just in His Eyes, young sir. Old Agnes knows only of the mercy and justice that came into her sorry life when Eber Pendragon of mortal flesh and blood down here on earth took a kindly interest in it.'

Customer hesitated and then he said, 'I made a discovery last night that has given me pause to think that Eber might have once been a saintly man of God, a holy brother of the Benedictine family at the monastery at St Michael's Mount in the deep south-west. Would you know anything of this?'

She shook her head and was silent for a moment. Then she said, 'Us is not surprised.'

'Nor I,' Customer admitted. He looked pale and tired; speaking seemed an effort for him.

Agnes looked at him curiously. 'It troubles the young sir that Eber was once a holy brother of the church?'

'Something troubles me, Agnes.' He paused and then sighed softly. 'I am searching for something I know is there but cannot find. I feel as if I am standing before a large wooden bureau, in one of the drawers of which are the answers to all of my questions, but when I open the drawers and look inside them, all are empty.'

She sighed heavily, but said nothing.

'Am I to make something of that world-weary sigh of yours, Agnes?' he asked.

'You cannot find what is not there to be found, young sir. You must turn your eyes in another direction; look elsewhere.'

He pressed his fingertips to his eyes and then rubbed them wearily. His headache lurked there still and he felt far from his normal self. He would have like nothing better than to return to his bed and draw the covers high over his head, blocking out the sights and sounds of the day and all the troubles which he sensed instinctively it was going to bring to him for his close attention.

She looked at him for a moment. 'You are tired, young sir. Worn out with worry and despair. Rest today, and then perhaps the answers you seek will come to you of their own accord on the morrow.'

He shook his head. 'I must ride today to Bodmin. I need to talk urgently with Eber about certain matters concerning himself and Nicholas Allsopp which became clear to me last evening when I went through the wine merchant's ledger and personal belongings. I fear that if my suspicions about the wine merchant and his true purpose in calling at Wynehouse Corner are correct, and this information falls into the wrong hands at the wrong time, Eber could find himself arraigned on a far more serious charge than that of the murder of a poor, wretchedly-deformed servant-girl at a place named Wynehouse Corner... A place, incidentally, that I am not entirely convinced exists other than for the amusement of the savage coastal winds that torment it.'

'You forget old Agnes hasn't had your learning, young sir. You must make yourself plain when speaking to her and not confuse her with your clever words.' Her eyes were dull, clouded with anxiety. 'Us is afraid, young sir; afraid that the meaning behind what you say of Eber and a more serious matter, is treason.'

Customer narrowed his eyes at her accusingly. 'Your tone of voice betrays you, Agnes. The charge would come as no surprise to you.'

Her mouth set hard and straight. 'The wine merchant came to the inn at Wynehouse Corner for the selling of his wines and spirits, and if you can bear to part with the key for but a tiny minute, old Agnes will show you – and anyone else who cares to come looking and asking – the wine and brandy casks stored in the dank cellar beneath your feet.'

If HE *could bear to part with the key to the cellar?* What was Agnes suggesting? That it was *he* who never missed an opportunity to sneak furtively down there with key in hand and with no other thought in mind than a sampling of the contents of the brandy casks and the inevitable wanton sexual firing of every sinew and thread in his body? Was it *he* who then stripped naked and remorselessly stalked the passages of the inn at the dead of night in search of a mate; *he* who bayed shamelessly at the moon out there on the forecourt when his lustful urges were not sated?

He shook his head. 'No, mistress. I have been down to the cellar and seen all I need to see. There are too few casks, nowhere near enough to balance the wine merchant's ledger against the payments Eber has made for his purchases from him over the years. The cellar – the inn itself! – should be stocked from floor to ceiling with wine and brandy casks.'

She looked away from him; spoke truculently. 'There are a great many down there in the cellar. Us has few customers, you know that.'

He made no response.

'Us should have buried Master Wine Merchant's things with him and then you would have thought nothing of this,' she said in a resentful voice. 'You worry too much about things that are of no concern to you, young sir.'

Bitter experience at Agnes's hands had taught him that, if nothing else, the volume of brandy stored on the premises was very much of concern to him, now and in the future, but he refrained from antagonizing her further by saying as much.

'You forget, Agnes, that I cannot begin to prepare Eber's defence without the truth, the whole truth, and nothing but the truth – everything there is to know about him and his business affairs.

This is the nub of my problem, mistress. Customer Trago knows too little of his client whereas Eber's enemies, those who would seek to destroy him, know everything and are waiting for Customer Trago with grinning faces at every corner he seeks to turn.'

She pouted a little. 'The Trelawneys have as little liking for the Tudor King and Cromwell as any of us.'

'If it suits their purposes, mistress, if it will see Eber hanged by the neck the sooner, the Trelawneys will willingly prostrate themselves before the King and then kneel at the Vicar-General's feet and kiss his ring as if he were His Holiness the Pope himself,' Customer said in a dour voice.

''Tis a sad and bitter mood you are in this morning, young sir,' she said, scowling.

He rose, pushing his untouched bowl aside. 'I am going over to the smithy before I ride to Bodmin. There is something there I must look into before I speak with Eber again and attempt to set straight these matters that trouble my digestive juices and make my stomach twist and turn uneasily beneath my belt.'

'When will you return?'

'I shall remain in Bodmin until this affair is settled one way or another.'

She looked at him with a frown and spoke querulously. 'But surely the answers you seek are here, where Rebecca was murdered!'

He shook his head. 'I have only found more questions – puzzling, worrying questions that beget more of the same because the truth is, there is only one person who can honestly answer any of them. Eber Pendragon himself.'

Her frown deepened. 'And if he chooses not to answer them: if, as you say, he was once a holy brother of the church and has taken some sacred vow of silence as us has heard some do, and cannot answer you?'

'Then he will have to face the consequences.'

She looked at him, her face suddenly pinched and grey and very old. She spoke in a voice that was raised barely above a whisper. 'Us grows suddenly chill, young sir.'

'I shall not pretend with you, mistress. I, too, grow chill...morbidly so. This affair shows signs of bringing all of us down upon our knees and praying for God's tender mercy on our poor, miserable souls!'

Chapter Fifty-three

He was desperate, beyond fear; the smithy's secret chamber represented nothing more to Customer now than a final, desperate hope that as he reached into the cavity within its wall, the skeletal remains of murdered Mary Trenwith would crumble at his touch. What other way was open to him to unmask Lowarn Trelawney for the liar and murderer he firmly believed him to be? This had to be Customer Trago's last chance of discharging his obligation to Eber Pendragon and thereby freeing himself to return, with an untroubled conscience, to the feverish pursuit of his hedonistic former life in foreign lands.

Nervously, Customer laid his dagger on top of the granite block he had removed from the wall of the chamber and then placed the flickering candle he had brought with him alongside it. He wiped his sweaty hands down the front of his leather jerkin and took a deep breath.

A strange calmness came over him as, momentarily, he experienced a warm, comforting sensation spreading across the top of his right shoulder. It was as if someone had placed a hand there to remind him that he was not alone and to encourage him to persevere in his endeavours.

He looked round quickly, almost expecting to see the spectre of Emanuel smiling down at him the way he would when his young student sat hunched miserably over some complex mathematical equation he failed to comprehend.

Nostalgic warmth seeped throughout Customer's whole being as he remembered how easily his problems had seemed to be solved with Emanuel's encouraging hand resting lightly upon his shoulder. Perhaps in spirit, Emanuel would always be standing at his side, watching over his every endeavour. It was a comforting thought.

Customer reached blindly into the cavity. His slightly trembling hand touched something hard and cold and then passed cautiously over it, exploring its dimensions.

A slow frown came to his face as his sense of touch identified the object for him – a large metal plate – without there being any real need for him to withdraw it from the cavity, as he was doing now, and look at it.

He rubbed the fine patina of dust from the plate with the sleeve of his blouse before holding it to the candlelight and examining it closely.

Solid gold!

His heart raced. He recalled seeing a similar offertory plate at Launceston Priory which, according to Emanuel, had weighed 22 ounces.

He laid the plate aside and reached into the cavity again, withdrawing first a heavy gold chain and then a solid silver chalice, a silver monstrance, a pyx of gold and finally, a small gold image.

Perspiration blurred Customer's vision as he gazed at the image. His heart kicked out wildly in his breast; blood pounded in his ears. The image was not of Christ, but of a saint, a saint with whom Customer was familiar, not because he was particularly well-instructed in such matters, but because he had seen the image before and could therefore say, without hesitation, that in his opinion, this was the original and not a replica.

If only it were!

There was more, but he had seen enough to tell him that the cavity in the wall was a treasure trove of stolen church plate.

He sank back on his heels, thinking of the nights he had looked across at Eber's cottage and watched a light flitting from window to window, and remembering Agnes's explanation for Eber's nocturnal restlessness. Was this rich cache of gold and silver the real reason why Eber roamed his cottage at night and, equally, what the wine merchant had likewise sought to find in Eber's absence?

But who had hidden this priceless treasure in the secret chamber?

Not Eber Pendragon. No way could he ever squeeze his great height and breadth into the chamber.

Was it Rebecca who had concealed it there?

Customer pondered on this for a moment.

Perhaps. But wasn't it more likely that one of her brothers had placed it there while virtually all of Wynehouse Corner – including the inn, the smithy and smith's cottage – were still in Trelawney hands? Could it be that it was their intention of leaving it concealed in the chamber until all fear of the confiscation of

Cornish church treasure had passed?

Rebecca would have known of this. Did she go to the smithy on the morning of her murder for the sole purpose of retrieving this treasure from the cavity?

What was it that Eber had said to him that long ago morning at the Holy Well of St James? That Rebecca had little hearing, spoke not a word, ever, of anything she saw... *Which was everything.*

Rebecca would also have known of the threat posed by the Vicar-General's official collector of church treasure, Dr John Tregonwell, to Cornwall's monasteries and churches. Was she afraid Tregonwell would find the hidden treasure and that Eber would be blamed for having stolen it? Or was it the treasure itself she sought to save, fearing that Tregonwell was coming and that he would confiscate it. Either way, Lowarn, who had ridden to the inn to fetch her home to see her dying mother, had obviously seen her going into the smithy and had more than likely caught her in the act of attempting to retrieve it. Her motive for protecting the treasure from the greedy, grasping hands of Tregonwell – if indeed this were her motive – would not have interested Lowarn, the more so if its theft had ultimately been for the enrichment of Trelawney pockets and in no way altruistic. Lowarn had simply struck out at his sister in a fit of uncontrollable rage and killed her.

Customer's head began to ache with the worry of it. There was only one thing of which he felt reasonably certain. There were bound to have been rumours about this rich cache of gold and silver being stolen and hidden somewhere thereabouts. No matter how careful a thief might be in carrying out his nefarious activities, there was always someone who knew or suspected something and made it his or her business to spread rumours. Unquestionably, while passing the time at the inn's gaming tables of a weekend, Eber would have been bound to hear talk of gold and silver being hidden somewhere on property once owned by the Trelawneys. As would the wine merchant during his travels throughout Cornwall while carrying out the business of selling wines and spirits.

Customer cast his eyes Heavenwards.

'What am I to do, Emanuel?' he whispered. *'If I attempt to use the theft of this sacred church treasure to unmask Lowarn Trelawney as Rebecca's murderer, the Trelawneys will simply claim that Eber was the real thief and that it was he and not*

Lowarn who murdered Rebecca while she was attempting to retrieve the gold and silver. Furthermore, I am by no means certain that I can trust the deputy bailiff with this information, anyway. How can I be sure that his political loyalties lie with Cornwall and not with a war-mongering Tudor King who would use any means, including plundering all that is holy and sacred, to fill his empty coffers?'

Customer drew in his breath in a heavy sigh. Emanuel would advise him to use prayer to find his answers, but there wasn't time for this luxury. In this, the saving of Eber and the church treasure for Cornwall, Customer knew he was entirely alone. It was a hopeless task. The Trelawneys would win, no matter which means he chose to defend Eber.

All but one of the stolen items Customer returned carefully to the cavity before replacing the block in the wall and then backing out of the chamber and into the smithy.

He stood for a moment beside the forge, putting the finishing touches to the horrifying images of the events of the morning of Rebecca's murder that filled his mind...

Lowarn Trelawney knows that his sister has gone into the smithy; he sees her entering it as he is riding over from Butterfly Lane to fetch her back home to see her dying mother for a final time. He waits for her to come out and instead, he sees Eber riding off on Will to visit Trenwith. With the blacksmith safely out of the way, Lowarn goes into the smithy, looking for his sister. He finds her on her hands and knees, preparing to enter the secret chamber at the back of the forge and he suspects that it is the church treasure she is after. Enraged, he drags her up onto her feet and then grabs her by the throat. Somehow she manages to break free of his grip, but as she turns from him, he strikes her savagely across the back of her head with the pincers he has grabbed up from the forge in an uncontrollable fit of rage...

Customer paused for a moment to consider....

Is Rebecca dead at this point or is she still alive?

Yes, she is still alive! According to Piers Heard, the blow to her head did not kill her outright...

Lowarn carries her from the smithy and then across the highway to where he has left his horse tethered in a thicket, his intention being to take her home with him. But it is too late, she dies, and there is no point now in taking her back to her family. Besides, Lowarn has all too quickly seen the possibility of laying the blame for Rebecca's murder on Eber Pendragon and thereby recovering all of the property the Trelawneys had lost to him. Lowarn cannot, however, run the risk that some might point out that a smithy was a dangerous place for a young, handicapped girl to be left all on her own, unsupervised. All too easily it could be said that she had been meddling in there without the smith's knowledge or permission while he was absent for the day visiting with Jacob Trenwith, and that she had simply met with an accident. There was also the further risk that should a deputy bailiff be summoned, he and his men might examine the scene of this alleged accident a little too closely and find the chamber and the secret it contained....

And so Lowarn takes his sister's body to a place she was known to frequent and then leaves it there with the evidence of the identity of the man he will accuse of murdering her – a leather tie torn from the apron of the blacksmith of Wynehouse Corner – clasped tightly in one of her hands.

A pitiful sight it had made, too. Customer would never forget it. Nor, he imagined, would the holy pilgrims who had found her. Further grist for the Trelawneys' mill!

And all of this time, Malachy Pawley had been standing at the window of his room at the inn, Customer guessed with a shudder. *Watching. Missing not a thing.*

And then?

Pawley had followed Lowarn, making sure that he kept well back and out of sight but never so distant as to miss seeing what Lowarn would do next. He watched Lowarn leave his sister's body at the well; saw him place the leather apron tie in her hand. Then Pawley had turned quietly away, satisfied that he had seen enough and content to wait and watch to see which way the wind would blow.

Customer felt drained, empty, and worst of all, thoroughly demoralized. To think that Pawley could have saved Eber Pendragon from the hangman's rope by simply stepping forward and speaking out about all that he had witnessed that fateful morning was more than Customer could bear. Far worse than knowing that Pawley preferred instead to savour the pathetically inept attempts that he, Customer Trago – the man he clearly loathed and despised above all men – was doing his utmost to make to save his benefactor from the gallows. Pawley had known from the outset that he would triumph, and better still – from his sickeningly perverted point of view, thought Customer dourly – that his hated rival, Customer Trago, would ultimately, and most satisfactorily from Pawley's point of view, be murdered by the Trelawneys for his trouble.

Customer gave a small, despairing sigh. For him it was a bitter-tasting irony that in the taking of Pawley's life by Meg Trenwith, the testimony Pawley could have given which, in Customer's opinion, would have successfully permanently removed Eber from the shadow of the gallows, had died with him.

Customer, having turned away with the intention of returning to the inn, suddenly stood stock-still. He sucked in his breath, trying to analyse the startling thought that had momentarily immobilized him.

What if he had it all wrong and it was the other way round and Lowarn Trelawney witnessed Malachy Pawley killing Rebecca for refusing to tell him where the church treasure was hidden?

Customer remained standing where he was for some minutes thinking this over.

While travelling about with the band of cutthroat ruffians with whom he allegedly kept company, riding roughshod over everyone who crossed their path, Pawley could well have heard stories of valuable church treasure being concealed either in the inn or in the smithy at Wynehouse Corner. Rumours of that nature spread with the rapidness of wildfire, gathering momentum with each telling.

Look round over your shoulder and Pawley would no doubt be sure to be there, standing at a window of the inn, watching, seeing everything. Including Rebecca's comings and goings.

Wouldn't it be perfectly reasonable for Pawley to suppose that there was every possibility that she would know where the treasure was hidden?

Taking things a step further, this would mean that his coming face-to-face with the man he thought he had killed weeks before, thought Customer, was pure coincidence.

He gave his head a small, resigned shake. He had to face up to reality. The end result was the same, no matter which of them, Malachy Pawley or Lowarn Trelawney, had murdered Rebecca.

An innocent man would now surely be hanged by the neck until dead.

Chapter Fifty-four

Deep in thought, Customer returned to the inn, saddled the mare and brought her round to the forecourt. Agnes came out with food and wine for his journey. Her eyes searched his face and saw a terrible change in it. Gone was the self-pity of only a short time ago: what she was seeing now was utter despair. All hope was gone: she was sure of it. There was a sickening feeling in the pit of her stomach that this was goodbye, the Wynehouse and old Agnes would never see Customer Trago again.

He mounted the mare and as she handed him the napkin-wrapped bundle of food and a wine flask, she said, 'Promise old Agnes that you will come back to the Wynehouse and not leave without saying goodbye to her.'

He didn't answer her.

'Have pity, young sir. If there is something old Agnes should know, tell her now and put her out of her misery.'

'Leave here, Agnes: run for your life, as fast as you can from this hellhole, and never look back, never come back. You still have a choice, but for me it is too late. I must fulfil my obligations as honourably and as best I know how. If I do this one thing, then I shall consider my life was not entirely in vain and be well content and ask no more.'

Agnes looked at him for a very long moment and then she nodded her head and said, 'Then us, too, is well content, young sir, and asks no more.'

She turned and walked resolutely back to the inn, disappearing indoors.

There had been little wind at Wynehouse Corner since the very early hours of the morning when, as suddenly as it had blown up into a raging, howling gale, it had faded away into an occasional, half-hearted gusty puff. Customer would not have admitted it to anybody, particularly at that moment while riding morosely away from the inn, but it was the wind that gave the crossroads its character. Without the raging tempest, the inn on the corner was an insipid thing, not worth a second glance. With it, the very mortar of the place breathed into vibrant life. Its shutters and doors rattled and creaked on their hinges and sang in joyful musical concert; its roof lifted its skirts and danced and whistled a merry tune; the smoke from the peat fire in the public room belched and hissed in accompaniment. There was nowhere quite like it!

He became aware that he was not riding alone. The Trelawneys and their servants followed in his wake soon after he passed the track that swept away from the highway towards Launceston. Samuel Trelawney rode with his sons, Customer noted. Making sure he would be in at the kill, he thought grimly.

They held back; he thought they would. The Trelawneys could afford to be patient with this tiresome young popi-dog for a few hours longer.

They rode into Bodmin in a grey, drizzling rain. Customer left the mare at a livery stable and then went off round the town in search of Piers Heard – always one long cock-stride behind him, or so Customer was repeatedly informed – from tavern to tavern.

Customer's tavern crawl was not entirely profitless, however. Much of the information he had sought from Piers Heard concerning the character of the deputy bailiff of Bodmin, had been willingly supplied to him, a little here, some more there, by the more talkative of the tavern-keepers with whom he had spoken since arriving in the town. Privately, most would have much preferred to gossip at length with him about one of the latest victims to succumb to Bodmin's virulent chest infection and be added to its grim death roll. Regrettably, a wealthy visitor to the town, a strikingly beautiful woman rumoured to be the Countess Anna-Lucrezia Ballini. But then there was no accounting for what interested some people and no one knew this better than a Bodmin tavern-keeper.

Customer had at first been deeply shocked and then genuinely saddened to learn of his former lover's death, but at the third telling, which included a passing reference to her male travelling companion, who had likewise succumbed and been laid to rest alongside her, he was shamefully admitting to himself, whilst nevertheless adopting a suitably grave countenance, his great relief at hearing it.

Finally, having been told that Piers Heard – legless through drinking brandy all day long – had been stretchered back to his home on an old door borne by two men in much the same state of intoxication, Customer abandoned his intention of approaching the physician further about the deputy bailiff.

Girding his loins, Customer presented himself before the deputy bailiff at his home first thing the following morning, rousing him from his warm bed with polite apologies for the intrusion and inconvenience, and requesting that he be permitted to speak urgently with the blacksmith of Wynehouse Corner.

The deputy bailiff received him in a long, white nightshirt and with a black, woollen shawl draped loosely over his shoulders. He reminded Customer of one of Launceston Priory's old priors – a short, fat, complacent man, more openly politically motivated than most and called not by God to holy orders but by the expectations of his wealthy kinsmen whose family motto (as translated for Customer from the Latin by Emanuel with a sly smile in his eyes) was *'To Go Forth And Prosper'*!

The deputy bailiff was of an old Cornish family, the de Disarts of Dizzard Point in North Cornwall (Dizzard Point being within a mile or two of the treacherous cove the Trelawneys called their own, and therefore something of a mortal danger in itself!), and Piers Heard was, as Lowarn Trelawney had said, his nephew on the distaff side of the family.

Deputy Bailiff de Disart's given name was Gwennol which nobody used since it was the Cornish word for the swallow, a small, graceful bird, to which the deputy bailiff, with his ungainly, portly frame bore not the slightest resemblance. The townspeople preferred "Brown Willy", a corruption of Brounwellye Hill (or "hill of swallows") near the village of St Breward and this was how he was known.

Brown Willy's sleepy, milky-blue eyes had hitherto given nothing away, but as he granted Customer's request and instructed one of his servants that Customer should be escorted forthwith to the place of Eber's confinement, Customer saw in them, more clearly than ever before, that the deputy bailiff had likewise been humouring the tiresome young whelp. Everybody but Customer Trago and old Agnes of the Wynehouse Inn believed that Eber Pendragon had murdered Rebecca Trelawney. If truth be told, even Jacob Trenwith and his wife.

The deputy bailiff sighed to himself as he shooed Customer out of his house, quickly closing the door on what was an exceptionally chilly spring morning and then climbing the stairs with pleasurable anticipation to the room and warm bed he shared with his equally generously proportioned wife, Minerva.

The bed groaned and sank beneath his weight as he clambered back into it, and his wife stirred and murmured something in her slumber which he interpreted as an inquiry regarding his early morning visitor's business with him.

'A tiresomely unimportant matter the Trelawneys were well able to handle themselves, my dearest heart,' he sighed. Then, in response to a short, nasally grunt from his wife: 'Pray God that my eyes and ears have not deceived me and this young popi that yaps and snaps at their heels has seen the error of his ways and will in future leave these uncultured bog-trotters to handle their own affairs as best they see fit.'

Minerva grunted again and, interpreting her response as an inquiry about the Trelawneys themselves, he paused and thought for a moment. 'A wild, primitive bunch,' he said at length. 'Rapists, murderers, liars and cheats. Only a fool would turn his back on that lot. But by dint of an iron fist, they keep a certain law and order in the Hundred of Stratton which leaves me free to pursue the more important issues of the moment. I cannot complain. Nor does – or should I perhaps say, dares? – anybody else. I need concern myself no further than this.'

Minerva grunted.

'Well, yes, my love,' he said. 'The young popi, like most young popis, stuck his foolish snout right in it, but I think I can safely say the habit has finally lost its appeal for him. The Trelawneys will have no further trouble from him.'

Grunt.

'Yes, I quite agree, my dearest heart... A very wise, politic move on their part. Give the rabble a leader, a handsome young white knight in shining armour, and they will rise and follow him to a man. The Hundred of Stratton has been the Trelawneys' parish since the dispersal of the Celtic tribes. Indeed, I would swear it was a Trelawney heathen barbarian who decapitated and thereby martyred St Gennys himself!'

Grunt.

'St Gennys, my love. Saint Genesius, actually...the saint they say lives to this day and walks the North Cornish cliff-tops carrying his head under his arm.'

Cough, grunt.

'It is not of Sir William Gennys, but of *Saint* Gennys that I speak, my dearest heart! Is there some trouble with your ears this morning? Eber Pendragon's head will remain where it is: the Trelawneys, as you would well know had you been paying me the courtesy of your close attention all this while, have been at pains not to make a similar martyr of that one.'

Grunt, mumble.

'With all speed. Unfortunately, there will have to be a trial first, but that will constitute but a minor delay. We will have the blacksmith of Wynehouse Corner strung up by the neck before the whitethorn wears its May blossom. The Trelawneys will have their man, the rabble their sport... And a good thing it is, too,' he added with a faint sigh after a slight pause. 'A little merrymaking will stay the restless beast that growls in their breast, if only for a short while longer.'

Minerva sat up abruptly in bed and scowled down at Brown Willy. 'Is it your ears that trouble you this morning, husband, or is it that you are not listening to me when I speak? I asked whether you thought to prod that idle girl downstair, in the ribs, and tell her to get up and about her duties in the kitchen.'

'Which idle girl?'

'The one we give bed and board to downstairs in the scullery – and, I might add, with little thanks in return for our kindness and charity.'

'Right away, my dearest heart,' said Brown Willy, throwing back the covers.

'And do not tarry, sir. I shall be counting the minutes until you return and lie again at my side!'

He sighed, though not with pleasurable anticipation at the prospect. His wife's possessiveness was sexually passive, had been for some years now, and despite his attempts (albeit less frequent of late) at rekindling the fires of their former passion. Sad and frustrating, particularly when the idle girl downstairs was so willing!

Chapter Fifty-five

Customer entered Eber's gaol cell to find Eber on his knees praying with his back turned to him. Customer was ashamed of himself for thinking it, but there was something about Eber's attitude of prayer that suggested to him that Eber had heard his approach and having recognized his step, was making the most now of every opportunity open to him to play upon his emotions.

To motivate him into greater endeavours on his behalf? Did Eber think he was not trying hard enough, that there was more he could, and should, do?

One and all, we have given up hope, even the condemned man, thought Customer despairingly.

The ominous silence of the adjoining cell betrayed the fate of its most recent, uninhibitedly loquacious elderly occupant.

While he waited for Eber to finish his prayers, he made a decision which, on reflection, proved to be disastrous for them both.

He would tell Eber of the church treasure.

Finished with his prayers, Eber rose slowly to his feet and turned to greet his visitor. His eyes searched Customer's face. 'Do not spare me, young sir. I hear it in your silence and see what you would not say to me out loud, written plainly in your eyes.' Eber sank down onto his pallet and buried his head in his hands. 'I understand…your heart is heavy. 'Tis a terrible burden you've been carrying; an awesome foe you have been left to fight alone. Place no blame on yourself in your despair for having failed in your mission.'

'There is one faint glimmer of hope, Eber,' said Customer in a cautious voice. 'One slight chance that we can turn this unjust charge against you on its head.'

Eber looked up at him. 'We are lost, young sir. Pray face it and spare us both the misery of hope that is in vain.'

'It is what is lost that may yet save you, Eber. Priceless church treasure, stolen by the Trelawneys and concealed for Heaven alone knows how long in your cottage. The smithy, actually. A secret chamber…'

The sudden sharpness that came into Eber's eyes momentarily took Customer aback although none knew better than he how attached Eber was to his purse and his commitment to its increase. It was the first indication Customer had that he had made a mistake which had the potential to cost them dear. Knowing that he had been, and theoretically still was, sitting on a priceless fortune in gold and silver would be extremely difficult for Eber to ignore and pass up.

What followed, or rather what *should* have followed and wasn't forthcoming from Eber, confirmed Customer's growing concern in taking Eber into his confidence over the treasure trove concealed on his property.

'We must not act hastily in this matter, young sir,' said Eber in a wary voice. He wagged a cautionary finger at Customer. 'Any mention by either one of us of this treasure of which you speak will surely be turned on its head by the Trelawneys and held up for all to see as further proof that the man they would see hang for murder is also a common thief.'

It was true. This was exactly what the Trelawneys would do. Eber had pinpointed the flaw in his argument, Customer saw that only too clearly. But what of the possibility of proving that the hidden treasure greatly preceded Eber's ownership of the inn at Wynehouse Corner and his occupancy of the the smith's cottage and smithy?

Customer was momentarily hesitant. He was reluctant to put into words the thought that was paramount in his mind, but he knew he must. Eber's response to it would either dismiss or confirm what was becoming a real fear in his mind.

'You ask no questions of this treasure, Eber.' The frown in Customer's voice slowly creased his forehead. 'Its size and worth would seem to be of no interest to you, and this puzzles me. I have seen it, Eber; touched and held individual pieces of it in my own two hands. Moreover, I know it was stolen from the monastery at St Michael's Mount where there surely has to be some written record kept of the date of its theft. I propose that I should leave you now and proceed swiftly to the Mount where I know I shall be remembered and welcomed as Emanuel's protégé, and there seek what information I can on its theft.'

'You have agreed this with the deputy bailiff – that you will visit the Mount on my behalf?' Eber's tone was cautious. His eyes had narrowed perceptibly.

Customer shook his head. 'No, Eber. Up until a few minutes ago, I had no intention of using my discovery of this treasure in your defence.'

'Then stay the mad rush of your thoughts a moment and hear and understand this,' said Eber. 'To do so now, to make any mention of this treasure beyond the four walls of this gaol, will surely put the rope firmly round my neck. Be advised by someone of greater years than your own who has seen the world and knows of its vile treachery and wicked ways. Speak not of this treasure to anyone, Customer Trago. Give me your solemn word that this secret shall remain between us, now and forevermore.'

Customer looked at him for a moment. There was a tightening in his chest that sent a pain through his wounded side and a shiver up his spine. He did not like what he was thinking, but the thought persisted. *Eber knew of the treasure. Knew all along of its existence in the secret chamber of the smithy.* 'Forgive me if I misinterpret your meaning, Eber.' Customer spoke in a cautious voice. 'But what is it that you are really saying to me? That to disclose the whereabouts of the stolen treasure to the deputy bailiff as proof of your integrity and the Trelawneys' avarice will see you dangling from a rope? Or is it my visit to the Mount that you fear will see a swift end to you?'

Eber gave his head a slow, mournful shake. 'Seeing that the cards I have been dealt in this sorry affair are not a winning hand, I beg that we do not prolong this thoroughly dispiriting discussion a moment longer. I sense in your words a growing desire to be free of any obligation that you feel you have to me. Go, Customer Trago; live your life, I hereby release you of the debt you feel you owe me. This one thing I ask of you – that you will carry with you the knowledge that Eber Pendragon bears you no ill will for your desire to be rid of the burden you carry on his behalf. All Eber Pendragon asks of you now is that you will never forget that you will be held in his heart with fond remembrance to the end of whatever few days remain to him on this earth.'

Customer was silent for some moments. Then he said, in a quiet voice, 'It is the Mount you fear, Eber. Because of this...'

Customer reached inside his jerkin for the gold image of St Michael secreted by him from the hidden church treasure. 'I see it in your eyes and hear it in your words.'

Eber covered up the avaricious glitter that came quickly into his eyes by lowering his head, almost as if in supplication to the revered sacred artefact that Customer held out to him. His tone became self-pitying. 'You have given up poor old Eber Pendragon for lost. That is what I hear in *your* words, young sir; what I now see in *your* eyes.'

There was a sudden heaviness in Customer's breast. 'I fear you gave yourself up for lost, Eber,' he began, pausing momentarily before continuing: 'When...' There was a tightening in Customer's throat, a slight quivering in his chin. For the moment he could say no more. Then he knew he must. What he now knew to be true – feared more than the threat posed to him by the Trelawneys – had to be said. 'When,' he went on, the unsteadiness of his voice betraying his shock and dismay, 'you raised a hand in anger against Rebecca and struck her down. But you will get a fair trial, I can promise you that.'

Eber gave a short, bitter laugh. 'At the hands of the Trelawneys and their minions? I think not, young sir.'

'No, Eber. At the hands of those who knew of Eber Pendragon's guilt but nevertheless granted his poor, gullible minion, Customer Trago, enough time to find just cause for his stepping aside, as I am about to do now, and not pleading in Eber Pendragon's defence. I will be advised by you. This sacred artefact I hold in my hand will be replaced in the secret chamber within the chimney breast of the smithy, and I give you my solemn word, I shall not speak of the stolen church treasure to a living soul. But I cannot defend you, Eber. I cannot stand before a Justice of the Peace and declare your innocence of the cruel and callous crime of murder which it grieves me to say I now believe you truly did commit, as all have said, and which, in some way I do not understand, is connected directly with the theft of the church treasure by you from the Mount. I can only stand beside you as one indebted to you for his life, helping you to come to terms with your guilt and comforting you in your last hours. I have an acquaintance in the town and I shall speak with him later this day and ask that he recommend a good and honest lawyer to represent you. I have never pretended with you, Eber. I am not a lawyer, nor shall I ever be. A good lawyer might possibly prove that there were circumstances that mitigate your crime; some justifiable explanation for the uncontrollable rages which seize you and then blind you to what is right and proper.'

Eber inclined his head a little on one side and eyed Customer thoughtfully. 'And will *that* save Eber Pendragon's neck from the hangman's noose?'

'No, Eber. You will hang for the murder of Rebecca Trelawney, and hang you should, but perhaps in the eyes of some, you will ascend the hangman's ladder as less of a monster if a good and able advocate can plead that you acted whilst in the grips of some terrible brain sickness that comes upon you unawares and renders you temporarily insane.'

Eber's face set stubbornly. 'I'll speak with no lawyer but you.'

'Then I advise you to make your peace with Almighty God for there is nothing now that I can do for you except speed you the quicker along the Heavenly path back to your Creator.' Customer paused momentarily, his face grey with worry and grief. Then, with a small frown: 'Do not force my hand in this matter, Eber. The knowledge of the whereabouts of stolen holy church treasure weighs heavily enough on my conscience as it is. Act upon the advice I have given you and permit me to instruct a lawyer to speak on your behalf.'

Eber's eyes grew frosty. 'And you, young sir; will you now kneel alongside me and make your peace with Almighty God for your hand in this affair of theft and murder? The guilt is not mine alone, Customer Trago. Think carefully before throwing me to the Trelawney wolves who wait with drooling chops to sink their foul fangs into me.'

Customer looked at him indignantly. 'Explain yourself, sir! I do not understand. I had no hand in Rebecca's murder, nor in the theft of the treasure from the Mount.'

'It might well have been Eber Pendragon's hand that held the pincers that shattered Rebecca's small, fragile skull, but you placed them there, Customer Trago. The little one would be alive today had you remained in those far off foreign lands where you belong and not come to us at Wynehouse Corner with your pretty looks and fine manners.'

Customer felt the blood drain from his face. 'You *knew* Rebecca loved me?' He paused, the bewildered look in his eyes gradually clearing as full understanding came to him. 'Of course...' He nodded his head slowly. 'Eber Pendragon – a man who never sleeps, who spends his nights prowling from room to room of his cottage in search, not as one would like to believe, of himself, but of something else – heard the commotion going on outside on the forecourt of the inn the night the stable was burnt to the ground, and he looked out and in the moonlight, saw what Agnes saw... The ardent love Rebecca carried in her heart for the poor wounded young stranger she had chanced to stumble across early one morning while making her daily devotions at the Holy Well of St James. Customer Trago.'

Customer shook his head perplexedly. 'Why was that so terrible, Eber? I cannot believe it was simply that I had usurped you in Rebecca's affections. If I am partly to blame for Rebecca's death, if I must stand alongside you and shoulder my share of the burden of guilt for her murder, then you owe me a full and proper explanation for your having taken it upon yourself to raise a hand against her so brutally and for snuffing out her life.'

Chapter Fifty-six

Eber buried his head in his hands again. He did not speak for some moments. 'The kittens Agnes would have me drown...' he began finally. 'Rebecca feared you, too, had become a nuisance to me and that I would do away with you as I had them.' He looked up at Customer, eyes wide and pleading. 'As God is my witness, young sir, I swear it! I did not mean to kill Rebecca; it was an accident. Her love for you had become a consuming passion, a raging fire within her, and she turned on me like an injured vixen protecting its young, defenceless cub, tearing the flesh from my forearms with her claws.'

Eber drew back the sleeves of his loose-sleeved blouse to expose the scratch marks on his flesh. 'Ask Trenwith, his daughter, Lucy, if it were not she who cleaned muddied blood from my cloak and then spent many hours drying it before the kitchen cooking-fire– Although I confess that I permitted the child to believe the blood came from injuries I had sustained in a fall from my horse. It is no lie that I was forced to defend myself from the wild frenzy of Rebecca's attack on my person. I held her off by the throat, but she broke free of my grasp, and then–' he held up his hands in a gesture of helplessness '–I found myself holding the pincers from my forge, spattered in her blood. I swear I had no conscious recall of any deliberate or malicious intention on my part to pick them up from the forge and use them in my defence against her.'

Customer looked at him coldly. 'I ask you again, sir, to explain yourself. Why should Rebecca fear for my poor, worthless life? I would have no doubt in my mind and a need to know exactly what threat I posed to you that she should so fear your wrath against me.'

'I saw no threat in you ever; I swear it! The little one's passion for you had driven her imagination wild; I could not reason with her. She was demented, a mad child-woman, delirious with the fever that came upon her from Cupid's dart, and raving at me with her eyes and hands as you raved at Agnes and me when you were delirious with the fever that came upon you from the sword wound in your side.'

261

Customer was silent as he thought back to that time. Then he said, 'My fever, the things I spoke of while delirious, troubled you greatly right from the beginning, Eber; that is something else I see clearly now. I would surface momentarily from the deep, black well of my delirium and see you hovering over me, gazing at me intently, and it was there in your eyes. You have never really trusted me, have you, Eber? Rebecca knew this, that I have always been a threat to you because of my old tutor, the lawyer, Emanuel, and my connections with the Augustinian Priory in Launceston where I was raised. You had reason to fear me, didn't you? Particularly if, as I suspect, you, too, were once of a monastic house which, unlike me, I believe you left under a thick, black cloud of some description. Look me in the eye, Eber, and swear to me by all that is holy and sacred that it was not you who stole the treasure from the Mount and sought to conceal it on your property. Swear to me that the nights you prowled your cottage you were not in search of the treasure which that poor, deformed child, Rebecca, who saw and knew everything that went on at Wynehouse Corner knew of and which, without your knowledge or consent, I am near certain she must have removed to what she thought was a safe hiding place from all who might come seeking it, solely to protect *you* should anyone come looking for it and accuse you of its theft. Place your hand upon your heart and swear to me that I am mistaken in my thinking.'

Eber looked up at him slowly. His face had gone slack. He closed his eyes and then lowering his head, he clasped his hands together in an attitude of prayer. 'That I cannot do, Customer Trago. But all praise to Almighty God that it was you who discovered where Rebecca had hidden the treasure. Cornwall is saved!'

There was a sick feeling in the pit of Customer's stomach. He was revolted by Eber's words. 'The church treasure is saved for Cornwall, yes, Eber, but not in the way you would have me think. It shall be returned to the monastic house at the Mount where it rightfully belongs.'

Eber's eyes snapped open. 'You amaze and confound me, sir! You call yourself a Cornishman and yet would have that lot find its way into the Tudor King's net courtesy of Tregonwell? Can it really be that it is beyond your comprehension to understand why I,

Eber Pendragon, turned thief?'

'Spare me your pathetic, altruistic whimperings, Eber: the vile pretence that supports them sickens me. You stole from the monastery at the Mount when you thought its days were numbered and that you would be wise to leave your sacred holy order while you were young and able enough to fend for yourself. You had no intention of remaining true to your vows and finding yourself reduced in your old age, to penury. You stole for Eber Pendragon, to enrich his purse, and for no other purpose.'

Eber glowered at him. 'For Cornwall, young sir. I swear it on my life. To finance a new Rising. The little one would have given it to you.'

Customer looked at him sadly. 'I think I see this now... Rebecca saw it as a means of financing Customer Trago's escape from Wynehouse Corner and your evil, avaricious clutches. I sincerely believe that she stole it from you originally, hiding it where she knew you were unlikely ever to find it, to protect you not simply from anyone who might come looking for it, but as you have inferred, from the Vicar-General Cromwell's official collector of church treasure, Tregonwell, should ever he chance to come calling at your door. Rebecca, like everyone else in Cornwall, had heard the rumours that Tregonwell was travelling in the West Country for the sole purpose of seizing from its churches and monasteries all of their valuable treasure. But all of this changed, didn't it, Eber? – when that poor, tragically cursed child arrived one morning at the Holy Well of St James and saw the answer to all her prayers in a poor, sword-wounded stranger named Customer Trago. And then, after the drowning of the kittens by you – and by now fearing as much for Customer Trago's life as she had once feared for yours – she planned on giving the stolen treasure from the Mount to the wounded young stranger she loved as soon as your back was safely turned and you were occupied with your latest acquisition at Trenwith's place.'

Customer shuddered. 'I'll say no more, Eber. The image that comes up before my eyes of that unfortunate child who, because she had so little, if any, hearing, was completely unaware of how much noise she was making below your bedroom where you were making ready to leave for your meeting with Trenwith, is too distressing to contemplate. I have bad dreams enough to last me my entire lifetime without adding further to them.'

Eber's large face had drooped with self-pity; his eyes held more of the same. 'Who betrayed me? I cannot find it in my heart to believe that it was Rebecca who led you to seek out the treasure. It had to be Nicholas Allsopp, he betrayed me as I knew he would the first opportunity that came his way, and despite what he has bled from my purse for his silence all these years since he was captain of the garrison at the Mount.'

'You betrayed yourself, Eber.' Customer's hand disappeared once more inside his jerkin and brought out Eber's Bible. 'With this, a Holy Bible written in Latin script,' he added, handing it to him. 'In his own crooked way, Nicholas Allsopp remained loyal to you and gave you full measure for every penny of blackmail you paid out to him for his silence over your theft of the Holy Mother Church's treasure. I choose to believe that he tried to conceal your Bible from me, knowing full well that had I found it, I would wonder at your possessing such a uniquely scholarly piece of work and discover who Eber Pendragon really is, or was, and what he is really all about.'

Eber stared hard at him. 'You speak of Nicholas Allsopp as if he is no longer among us.'

'His heart gave out on him after a meal too rich for his digestion. And as a kindness to you, I shall give you the comfort, even though it might well prove to be short-lived, that all of his worldly possessions are now yours.'

Eber threw back his head and started to laugh. His laughter rang throughout Bodmin gaol; was still ringing in Customer's ears long after he had turned from Eber and walked quietly away.

Chapter Fifty-seven

Customer spoke with Eber for what was to be the last time shortly before Eber was taken from Bodmin Gaol to be imprisoned in the dungeon beneath Launceston Castle where he would await his trial at the Spring Assizes. He implored Eber to place his defence in the able hands of the Bodmin lawyer Piers Heard had commended to him, but Eber would have none of it and elected to defend himself.

Fearing that the theft of church treasure from St Michael's Mount would somehow come to light, Eber entreated Customer to absent himself from the trial. The Cornish had grown heartily sick and tired of those who would meddle with their beloved Celtic saints and all things holy that they held dear to them, and this was one transgression that Eber knew they would never find it in their hearts to forgive.

In exchange for his agreeing to remain silent about the stolen church treasure, Eber made a full confession to Customer of his past which included his admitting to having once been one of eight monks living within the enclosure of the Benedictine Priory at Tywardreath. It was while he was on a visit to the Mount on a secular errand for his prior that Eber and the captain of the garrison, Nicholas Allsopp, met at a tavern in the town and between them, hatched a plot to steal the church treasure. Nicholas Allsopp had wanted no share of the treasure itself, as captain of the garrison – and bound, like everyone at the Mount, to come under some suspicion of its theft – that would have been too risky. From the beginning, blackmail had held far more allure for him.

Customer knew a little of the odd history of Tywardreath's monastic house and was therefore not too surprised by this particular revelation of Eber's. Emanuel had claimed that all who lived within the prior's enclosure, including the prior himself, were of exceedingly dubious moral character, being far too fond of carousing in tavern houses and in keeping company with loose women.

The stolen church treasure weighed heavily on Customer's mind and conscience, so much so that after swearing Piers Heard to secrecy, he took him into his confidence on the matter in the hope that the physician would suggest some means of healing the constant pain and suffering it caused him. Suffering himself from a certain amount of pain, and not just a little guilt and anxiety, caused by the tragic and totally unexpected demise of his one and only, truly wealthy patient, the beautiful Countess Anna-Lucrezia Ballini, and her male travelling companion, the only consolation Piers Heard felt moved to offer Customer was that in time, all memory of the stolen treasure would fade. In the meanwhile, Customer was advised to comfort himself with the thought that while it went against the grain, he did owe Eber Pendragon something by remaining silent about its theft.

Eber's trial before the Chief Magistrate at the Launceston Assizes lasted almost a week and was, in Customer Trago's opinion, something of a farce, with Eber using his defence of himself in the witness box as a political platform to fight like the holy terror he was to win over the people of the town to his side. Had his timing been better, things might well have gone differently for him, if only because those who supported the King and his Vicar-General would have preferred to find a means acceptable within the framework of the law of sanctioning the murder of a pathetically deformed servant girl by her master, to that of making Eber Pendragon a martyr in the eyes of the towns would-be rebels, of which there were many. It was unfortunate for Eber that while the Cornish were growing undeniably restless for another Rising against Henry, more time was needed for it to ferment and then distil into a perfect clarity within their minds. A few more years and Eber Pendragon's sorry story could easily have had an entirely different ending.

Chapter Fifty-eight

They hanged Eber Pendragon at sunrise on what promised to be a brisk, but mostly sunny day.

The townspeople of Launceston came in their hundreds to watch the spectacle, others coming from great distances beyond the town, some travelling overnight, either on foot or on horseback to be sure of a good place up at the front, and all stayed on to enjoy the fun of the fair afterwards.

It was a market day, ripe with the pungent stench of the animal pens up on the hill beyond the south gate of the old castle, that pervaded every nook and cranny of the town, and alive with the noise and bustle of man and beast as they jostled one another up and down the narrow lanes of colourful stalls and around and about the cobbled market square itself. Most of the stalls were covered. Those that were not belonged to the scoundrels such places attracted – the tricksters with their three playing-cards, or walnut shells and a pea who, with many a clever flourish of the hand, showed the gullible passerby how easy it was to find the court card from among two indifferent cards, or detect under which shell the pea was concealed, and then encouraged him to wager a bet.

These stalls, which were often little more than rickety old, worm-riddled wooden tables, were relegated to the extreme perimeter of the market place. This on the insistence of the bona fide traders who brought their wares to Launceston market regularly during the months of spring, summer and early autumn while the roadways remained passable following the long, wet and windy Cornish winter, and who had their good reputations to think about.

Among the latter, there were those who set up booths where one could stand at a high counter and sate both appetite and thirst, clothiers where one might buy a smock or tunic or some fancy hose – a pair of new boots, perhaps, if the farmer had got a good price for his stock. Others set out tables that were chock-a-block with pretty gewgaws for a wife or sweetheart – colourful satin ribbons for a young maiden's hair and combs to fix it in place. There were brightly-decorated, wooden spinning tops and dolls made of straw, some of wood and painted, for little girls. For small boys, toy swords and daggers made of wood.

From an ironmonger whose goods were stacked high on the ground all about one's feet, one could buy a new pot for the cooking-fire. On another stall a little farther down the same lane, some no less practical, bawdily-decorated earthenware pots for the bed-chamber, brooms for sweeping the floor, strong wooden pegs for the washing-line; candles of every size and hue; Breton linen and soap from Spain.

Mingling with the throngs there were the peddlers with their wares set out on wooden trays supported on long leather straps worn round their necks, pie and tart-sellers, some selling sweetmeats and tiny bundles of heather guaranteed to bring good crops and good fortune at the close of the summer ahead.

And if all of this were not enough for the eye to take in, there was the excitement of the pony traders who drove their sturdy, hardily-bred ponies at a gallop through the narrow, winding lanes of the old hillside town, kicking up such a dusty, noise commotion that one might have been given to thinking that Beelzebub himself gave chase. Not to mention the travelling entertainers – the wrestlers, for which Cornwall was famous, a juggler who did very clever things with five, gold-coloured wooden balls, and who was every bit as clever with some truly amazing conjuring tricks, and two different types of animal trainers who lived like gypsies from the moment the open country roadways became fit for travelling along, and who were constantly on the move in horse-drawn carts from one market town to the next.

All of which rounded everything off nicely so far as the people of Launceston and the town's heavy influx of visitors were concerned.

The market traders and entertainers who knew one another and who were in the habit of pausing and chatting in slack moments, could likewise find little that was wrong with the day which all remembered and spoke of nostalgically for some considerable time to come as having been one of their best for business in many a long year.

Some of the older traders when, years later they recalled the hanging of the blacksmith of Wynehouse Corner that brisk, late

April morning, likened the excitement of the day to Perkin Warbeck's triumphant ride into Bodmin during the Rebellion of 1497. Certainly, little of any real note had taken place since in Cornwall, and while talk was a fine thing, it was the doing that really got the juices flowing.

The hanging of Eber Pendragon from the gallows erected in Launceston's town square filled the desperate void admirably.

Chapter Fifty-nine

Customer did not attend the hanging; however, early on the morning of the following day, he waited on the outskirts of the town for Piers Heard to ride out and tell him that justice had been served. They had agreed to meet at a prearranged spot in a secluded thicket north of the road to Bodmin which was as near to Launceston Priory – an easy ride from that spot of only a few miles – as Customer cared to risk taking himself. Having developed a hearty respect for the vagaries of fate, he was in no mood to tempt it to take any further interest in his conduct of himself and his affairs. The priory belonged to his past and had no place in his future now that Emanuel was dead.

After a mildly frosty start, it was going to be a beautiful day, warm and sunny, with the winter landscape's blacks and browns put away and its hedgerows wearing their new spring mantles of soft yellow-greens interspersed with the first of the white blossom of the blackthorn and the pretty, slender catkins of the elder. The dawn chorus of the smaller birds, which were still in full, joyful throat, showed not a whit of respect for the grisly drama enacted the previous day on the gallows that still remained standing in Launceston's town square.

The physician eyed Customer mournfully as he rode up to him, a state of melancholy induced by the numerous stops Piers Heard had made at tavern houses along his route to their meeting place. 'It would seem that the lance held by the handsome young knight in his bright shining armour droopeth a little this sad and sorry morning,' he greeted Customer dryly.

Customer moved out of the thicket to meet him, scowling a little.

'It is done,' sighed Piers Heard in answer to the unspoken question in Customer's eyes. 'Eber Pendragon has gone back to his Maker to stand in judgment before Him, or not impossibly, straight to Hell.'

'He went quietly to his fate, or like a raging demon?' Customer inquired timorously.

'Quietly. With great, sorrowing eyes cast pityingly down on

those who stood waiting to cheer as the ladder was yanked out from beneath his feet. Had I not seen the fruits of his savage labour stretched out piteously on a bare table awaiting the indignities of my cruel probings, my heart would have bled copiously for him.'

'Say no more, sir,' said Customer, wincing a little. 'I have heard enough.'

'The Trelawneys follow in my wake,' the physician warned him. 'If you would wish to make haste and swiftly depart my company, I shall not take offence.'

'Theirs is the pleasure: far be it from me to deny them their moment of triumph,' said Customer sullenly.

'Do not whip yourself for the part you played in this affair, Customer Trago. Emanuel would be proud of you for your diligent application to the awesomely unpleasant task you set before yourself. I shall not hesitate to call upon you myself should I find the chafe of the hangman's noose looming large on my calendar in tome to come.'

The physician quickly blinked away the haunting spectre of the Countess Ballini's deathbed scene. He doubted that the part he had played in it, albeit innocently, would come to light now, but one never knew. The wealthy of this life were not so easily and quickly dispatched from memory as the poor.

'I only wish I could have done more for Eber,' confessed Customer. 'I owe him my life, a debt I can now never repay.'

'It was Rebecca Trelawney who saved your life, Customer Trago, she who fetched Eber Pendragon to your side when you lay wounded and dying. Feel sorry for yourself if it amuses you, but find some other source of misery to cheery your day for you have acquitted yourself of your debt to them both for all time. If, as is my heartfelt desire, we are to become good friends, I would hear no more of this talk of indebtedness and failure.'

Customer looked at Piers Heard scornfully. 'You say you desire to become my good friend and yet you concealed from me that your uncle is the deputy bailiff of Bodmin.'

The physician looked bemused by the accusation. His eyes widened. 'And for that very good reason! Had you but known of my unfortunate family connections, you would have turned elsewhere for help and denied me both the pleasure of your acquaintance and a personal interest in this strange affair. Uncle

Brown Willy's not a bad fellow once you get to know him. His wife, now, is another matter!'

'I have no desire to get to know either one of them, thank you, kind sir. My brief acquaintance with your esteemed uncle has more than sufficed my appetite for his company.'

Piers Heard studied him contemplatively for a moment. 'What becomes of you now, Customer Trago? Do you return to where your fancy takes you abroad, or is it here in Cornwall where you were born and bred that your destiny lies?'

'I return now to Wynehouse Corner to make my farewells to Agnes, and then I plan on journeying northwards to Carmarthen in Wales where I shall seek passage on a ship outward bound for Spain.'

'Then I wish you God speed, my friend. And if Spain it be, make sure to keep an eye out for those irritating French and the heathen cutthroat pirates I have heard tell plague our southern coastline. These are dangerous times for a sea voyage.'

'Nowhere near as dangerous as my remaining in Cornwall,' said Customer, eyeing the bunch of riders galloping furiously towards them. The more so now, he thought, should the treasure stolen from the Mount be found hidden within one of the walls of property belonging to Customer Trago. That is, if he were to lay claim to that property as was his right. Emanuel's enemies, both at Launceston Priory and at Bodmin's Franciscan Friary, were, by default, Customer Trago's enemies, too many of whom, in Cornwall's currently uncertain political climate, wouldn't hesitate to bring him down upon his knees. All the quicker should it ever become common knowledge of his claim to a family connection with the Plantagenets and the hanged rebel leader, Perkin Warbeck! This would be their opportunity; they would never get another like it. If, by some terrible trick of fate, some awful mischance, someone should discover the stolen church treasure hidden on any property owned by him, he would be charged with treason. The current provost-marshal – should he be anything like his predecessor, Sir Henry Guildford, whose word had been law and who had been said by many to have enjoyed a good hanging better than any other diversion that had been set before him – would be sent to rout him out with all possible speed, and without benefit of trial, he would be strung up... And should the provost-marshal be in a hurry for his pleasure, the nearest tree would suffice! Hanged like Perkin Warbeck and quicker than Customer Trago could draw breath enough to shout out loud, "Long Live the King"!

Piers Heard had turned his head to look at the riders. 'Ah, yes; the Trelawneys. I take your meaning.'

The Trelawneys thundered up to them, rode past without so much as any one of them troubling himself to cast a single sidelong glance in their direction, and then disappeared round a bend in the roadway.

It was quite disconcerting to be ignored by the Trelawneys in such an offhand fashion after having been paid so much unremitting close attention by them during the past few weeks. Customer had to resist an inclination to feel offended by the snub, reminding himself that good common sense should prevail, and that he should count himself lucky that so far as Customer Trago was concerned this morning, the Trelawneys had much bigger fish to fry. In any event, it was foolish to be so quick to take affront at their attitude of indifference towards him: there was time enough for them to make amends for this by lying in wait for him with swords and daggers drawn as he himself rode back to Wynehouse Corner.

'No doubt the Trelawneys' great hurry is a pressing need to stir up fresh terror and misery in the hearts of the weak and feeble,' remarked Piers Heard in a dry voice.

'I have no quarrel with them,' said Customer with a shrug. 'Nor is it my intention to tarry for long in the Hundred of Stratton to bring about any alteration in the status quo. It is their parish, and welcome to it.'

Customer reigned in his horse and turned to leave. Piers Heard raised a hand in a farewell salute. 'We will meet again, Customer Trago.'

'I should not count on it, sir,' said Customer in a grim voice. 'Not in this life!'

Chapter Sixty

Agnes said a similar thing to Customer several days later as he was preparing to ride out of her life forever, but she made a question of it. 'Us will meet again, young sir?'

He swung himself up and into his saddle and then looked down at her with a gentle smile and said, softly, 'I think not, Agnes. But I carry you and Eber Pendragon and Rebecca and the Wynehouse close to my heart and in my thoughts, and shall do so until the day I die. I honestly believe that Eber struck Rebecca down while seized by a fit of madness over which he had no conscious control, but it would be impertinent of me to say that I forgive him for what he did to her, for that is God's business not mine. The same man, however, had much kindness in him, a true zest for life, and this I shall never forget.'

'We'll never forget you, young sir, though 'tis doubtful how long old Agnes shall live to carry the memory around with her,' she said morosely. 'Lowarn Trelawney stands watch with Jacob Trenwith to see when you would leave us. The Trelawney tribe will have their feet back under the wormy tables of the old Wynehouse before the dust from your horse's hooves has had a chance to settle back on the earth from which it was raised up.'

Customer kept his eyes averted from Butterfly Lane. Today, as Agnes had said, it was Lowarn Trelawney, yesterday one of his brothers, the day before that, another of them. Customer Trago was not welcome in their parish. His presence chafed; the Trelawneys and Trenwith, who equally had a vested interest in seeing the back of Customer Trago, bade him leave and that he be quick about it.

He freed the key to the wine cellar from the thin chair he wore securing it at his waist, and then handed it down to Agnes. Small hope, he knew, but a night or two of Agnes's wild, drunken debauchery might give the Trelawneys pause for thought and make them wonder at the true worth of their hard won prize.

Agnes gripped his hand; her eyes searched his. 'You will pray for old Agnes and for the redemption of her sins?'

'Every night, and all the more fervently the farther I am from

274

her,' he promised, concealing a small smile at the hidden meaning of his words as he withdrew his hand from hers and watched her slip the key into deep folds of her bodice.

He looked at the inn, at its weather-beaten facade. He couldn't see his room from the forecourt, but recalled it with a sad smile. 'I shall miss this place: the rats which work so diligently on my door at night, that hole in the roof that widens by the day and bids the wind and rain enter and welcome, the floor upon which I must walk with reverent care lest you should suddenly find me sitting upon your lap in the kitchen below – or worse, I should find my buttocks roasting to a turn on your cooking-fire!'

He made an elaborate pretence of looking about him. 'But where, I wonder, is the plaguy wind of Wynehouse Corner this fine day? Can it be true that it has cruelly abandoned Customer Trago now that he is about to take his leave of this place forever?'

'It sorrows as old Agnes sorrows. It would not have you go from us, either.'

He smiled playfully. 'I know… It, too, waits along the highway to see me out of the Hundred of Stratton, full of tricks as ever. I am not deceived.'

'Pause a moment at the top of Highway Hill and wave a final goodbye to old Agnes,' she said. 'Us'll walk with you as far as the duck pond and us'll be watching.'

Customer kept his promise, turning and waving to the small figure standing motionless near the smooth sheet of pond water that shimmered in the bright sunlight.

Agnes did not wave back.

On his right, less than half a mile farther along the highway, was Witchypool Lane. He could not leave Wynehouse Corner without paying his final respects to the holy well, he told himself. It would not be right and proper.

He turned at length up the lane, haunted by the bittersweet memory of the morning that Eber had carried him along it, his hearty amusement at his back-passenger's sorely pricked vanity.

Pausing for a moment, Customer swore that he could hear Eber laughing still, not as he had laughed in Bodmin Gaol – there had been a touch of the madman about his humour that day – but as the gentle Cornish giant that somehow he would always be in Customer's memory.

But no, the laughter he imagined he heard was only the crows as they paused in their flight across the meadow and congregated like a row of pious, black-robed monks on the gnarled braches of the stooped old trees in the hollow. As he dismounted on the ridge above the holy well, they rose in a swishing of wings and raucous caws of annoyance at his unwelcome presence there. He stood for a moment, reflecting on his recent past and listening to the soft music of the spring water as it trickled down over the stones in the well.

He had only ever wanted one thing in his life, first as a child, then as a youth and now as a man. To know who he really was. Something that was never to be, now that he had decided to leave Cornwall and England for good.

Perhaps he had always known this; suspected as much, anyway, he thought with a sigh.

He used the granite pilgrim's step to descend into the hollow, then knelt on one knee before the holy well, bowed his head and blessed himself. He found himself gazing at his reflection in the pool of water sparkling at his bended knee and as he did so, the mists of doubt in his mind slowly lifted and cleared. Suddenly, for the first time in his life, he knew precisely who he was. He was Customer Trago, innkeeper of the old Wynehouse at Wynehouse Corner in this, the Hundred of Stratton. Turn his back on the inn, ride away from there, and he was who he was before. Nobody. A question mark floating in mid air with no hook to hang it on.

The heaviness he had carried in his breast for days began to lighten, his heartbeat quickened.

The church treasure must be returned to St Michael's Mount where it belonged and with all speed. Emanuel would want it returned; *Customer Trago* wanted it returned. There would be danger involved, but he promised himself that he would find the means to accomplish the task while still keeping his neck in its pleasant splendid shape and form.

And what of the wine merchant?

All was still loose ends there. Customer had finally convinced himself that Nicholas Allsopp was no concern of his and he had wiped his hands clean of him, leaving his belongings in Agnes's care with instructions that she was to hand them over to anyone who came making inquiries as to the whereabouts of the wine merchant. But knowing Agnes, Customer wryly accepted that she would probably purloin everything of any value, tear out the pages from the wine merchant's ledger and order books and then use them to start her cooking-fire each day, re-enlisting the aid of her accomplice in her nefarious graveyard activities, Carneworthy the carpenter, to bury the rest somewhere. Someone was bound to come looking for Nicholas Allsopp one day, and should that person find any of the wine merchant's belongings in Agnes's posses and she was forced to admit that he was dead and that she'd had a hand in burying him, she, as a mere serving-woman at a common wine and alehouse, could find herself in serious trouble. With no one to sp.eak out for her, she could all too easily find herself hauled up before a Justice of the Peace on a charge of murder and theft!

He had to go back.

Customer gave a start as he heard a soft footfall at his back. His head shot round.

Without looking at him, Lucy Trenwith knelt beside him and then, clasping her hands in front of her, she gazed solemnly into the well. Her face was a little flushed and she was out of breath, as if she had been running. She didn't speak.

'For what do you pray, mistress?' Customer inquired dryly after a moment or two. 'Or is it thanks that you give for the restoration of your father's best pastureland?'

'It is thanks I give that a father so loves his only living daughter that he will offer his best pastureland as her dowry with his unconditional blessing and goodwill to the man who will take her hand in marriage,' she replied in a soft voice.

'To Lowarn Trelawney?' Customer eyed her curiously. 'It is he, is it not, who casts a favourable eye in your direction? I fear your good father does not know Lowarn as well as I thought. Lowarn takes what he sees and wants and damns to Hades the man who would endeavour to stand in his way. It is not in his nature to wait to be offered anything he fancies, be it best pastureland or a loving father's beautiful young daughter. He will have you, mistress, whether father or daughter desire it or not.'

'You would permit this, sir?'

She turned her face full on to him, a faint blush deepening the dewy pinkness of her cheeks as she awaited his answer.

'What influence would I have in the matter?'

'My father waits at butterfly Lane. He would hear what you have to say and has promised to look favourably upon any declaration that you would wish to make that would bring honour upon his family.'

Customer gave her a startled look. 'You speak boldly for one so young!'

She lowered her gaze demurely from his. 'If there be some other, gentler way of keeping you from leaving us, sir, I will gladly follow it and forsake all boldness forth with.'

He got to his feet and then offered her his hand, raising her up so that she stood facing him.

'And what if Customer Trago chooses to ride north to Wales, heedless of the bold designs you and your father would have in arranging his future between you?'

Pausing for a moment or two to consider her reply, she said, 'Then I shall follow meekly northwards in your footsteps, as I have followed you here this morning, until I know for sure that all hope is gone.'

'Meekly, mistress? Or, as I seem to recall witnessing on a previous occasion, with your skirts held shamelessly aloft and your feet flying?'

'If it be necessary, sir.'

Was there ever a more delightful, heart-warming sight than this sweet, child-woman running after him along her father's track that day? he asked himself.

Was there ever a worse vision than the one that suddenly sprang up before his eyes, of Lowarn Trelawney and the leering, yellow fox-eyes Lowarn had turned lustfully her way that day as she had fled from him in terror?

Trenwith had lost one daughter to Lowarn Trelawney, God forbid that he should lose another.

With a mixture of hope and fear, Lucy returned the steady gaze Customer had fixed on her. She waited, her heartbeat quickening as he drew her slowly to him. Raising herself up on tiptoe, she looked up uncertainly into his face, searching his eyes. Bending his head, he kissed her warm, sweet-tasting mouth. She hesitated, momentarily unsure of her5self, and then reached up with her arms, curling them round his neck and leaning her body into his. He held her very close for several moments, conscious of his strength and her fragility and the pleasurable warmth that was coursing through his veins. Then, scooping her up into his arms, he carried her back up to the ridge to his horse, smiling contentedly to himself as she nestled her head into his shoulder.

Customer Trago was *definitely* going back. Trenwith and his wife were good, honest people and by all accounts, well-respected in the community: they would back up his claim to his right of legal ownership of the inn and the blacksmith's cottage and smithy.

But to be on the safe side, he thought with a wry smile, he would draw up some deeds and age them a little over a candle-flame the way Emanuel had shown him. Perhaps, while he was about it, he would even make out Eber's will for him.

He would think about it.

As old Agnes would say, *'Us has our own way of doing things.'*

Customer Trago was learning, catching on fast.

Emanuel would be proud of him.